PRAISE FOR
MURDER IN GRUB STREET
A *New York Times* Notable Book of the Year

"A fine tale . . . Historical fiction done this entertainingly is as close to time travel as we're likely to get." —*Newsday*

"First-rate, original, and persuasive." —*The Boston Globe*

AND THE SIR JOHN FIELDING MYSTERIES
RULES OF ENGAGEMENT

"Historical mysteries rarely offer so many depths of pleasure as this series." —*Chicago Tribune*

"Remarkable . . . Such a ripping good read that it deserves special attention." —*The New York Times*

"Triumphant." —*Publishers Weekly* (starred review)

"A marvelous parade of Georgian-era high and low characters in the London of Johnson and Boswell . . . Altogether much fun." —*The Washington Post Book World*

THE PRICE OF MURDER

"Alexander's got it all: a heroic central figure, a setting that both fascinates and appalls, and a gift for concocting plots that weave in and out of social classes." —*Booklist* (starred review)

continued . . .

JACK, KNAVE AND FOOL

"If there's truth to the raucous scenes of urban life in Bruce Alexander's atmospheric period mysteries, then London in the eighteenth century was a carnival of thieves, cutthroats, and refined folk who ate with their hands." —*The New York Times*

"A fascinating tale. Alexander does a great job of acquainting the reader with the dirty, grubby back streets of London and the high-ceilinged snobbery of the upper classes."
—*Sarasota Herald-Tribune*

PERSON OR PERSONS UNKNOWN

One of *Publishers Weekly*'s Best Books of the Year

"The Dickensian detail and characters bring life to the sordid streets and alleys around London's Covent Garden . . . Highly recommended, especially for lovers of historical mysteries who like to see another time and place blaze into life as they read." —*The Washington Post Book World*

WATERY GRAVE

"Wonderful . . . The high-minded and always astute Sir John is as companionable as ever in *Watery Grave*, and young Jeremy, wide-eyed but maturing fast, makes for a winning narrator . . . Packed with history and lore." —*The Washington Post*

"Enthralling . . . It's a joy to watch the great magistrate apply his formidable intellect to this sordid business."
—*The New York Times Book Review*

BLIND JUSTICE

"Captures with gusto the lusty spirit of the era. Sir John and young Jeremy are an irresistible team."
—*The New York Times Book Review*

Titles by Bruce Alexander

MURDER IN
GRUB STREET

BRUCE ALEXANDER

BERKLEY PRIME CRIME, NEW YORK

THE BERKLEY PUBLISHING GROUP
Published by the Penguin Group
Penguin Group (USA) Inc.
375 Hudson Street, New York, New York 10014, USA
Penguin Group (Canada), 90 Eglinton Avenue East, Suite 700, Toronto, Ontario M4P 2Y3, Canada
(a division of Pearson Penguin Canada Inc.)
Penguin Books Ltd., 80 Strand, London WC2R 0RL, England
Penguin Group Ireland, 25 St. Stephen's Green, Dublin 2, Ireland (a division of Penguin Books Ltd.)
Penguin Group (Australia), 250 Camberwell Road, Camberwell, Victoria 3124, Australia
(a division of Pearson Australia Group Pty. Ltd.)
Penguin Books India Pvt. Ltd., 11 Community Centre, Panchsheel Park, New Delhi—110 017, India
Penguin Group (NZ), 67 Apollo Drive, Rosedale, North Shore 0632, New Zealand
(a division of Pearson New Zealand Ltd.)
Penguin Books (South Africa) (Pty.) Ltd., 24 Sturdee Avenue, Rosebank, Johannesburg 2196,
South Africa

Penguin Books Ltd., Registered Offices: 80 Strand, London WC2R 0RL, England

This is a work of fiction. Names, characters, places, and incidents either are the product of the author's imagination or are used fictitiously, and any resemblance to actual persons, living or dead, business establishments, events, or locales is entirely coincidental. The publisher does not have any control over and does not assume any responsibility for author or third-party websites or their content.

PRINTING HISTORY
G.P. Putnam's Sons hardcover edition / October 1995
Berkley Prime Crime mass-market edition / November 1996
Berkley Prime Crime trade paperback edition / August 2010

Berkley Prime Crime trade paperback ISBN: 978-0-425-23560-7

The Library of Congress has catalogued the hardcover edition as follows:

Alexander, Bruce, date.
    Muder in grub street / Bruce Alexander.
        p. cm.
    ISBN 0-399-14085-9
    1. Fielding, John, Sir, 1721–1780—Fiction. 2. London (England)—History—
18th century—Fiction. 3. Judges—England—London—Fiction. 4. Blind—
England—London—Fiction. I. Title.
PS3553.O55314 M87 1995
813'.54—dc20
                                                                                    95007470

GREAT MASSACRE IN GRUB STREET

LAST NIGHT, just past the hour of twelve, loud cries and screams issued from the shop and residence of Ezekiel Crabb, bookseller and publisher in Grub Street. A group of bold fellows assembled without and, led by a constable on his rounds from Bow Street, sought entrance to the establishment.

Forcing the door, they found nothing amiss in the bookshop in front, nor the print shop in the rear, until one with a lantern put it to the floor and noted footprints thick with blood upon the floor. He called out his grisly discovery and, following the tracks back, led them upstairs to the living quarters of the Crabb family. And then what a gruesome sight was there to behold!

Ezekiel Crabb, proprietor, and his good wife were found in their beds: chopped to pieces. Blood was splashed about their bedroom most carelessly. The sheets and blankets of their bed, from which they had no opportunity to rise, were soaked in red. Mr. Crabb's arm was separated from his body. Mrs. Crabb's head was cleaved in two. A visit to the room in which their two sons had slept revealed an even more dreadful carnage. The older of the two, James by name according to one who knew him, had leapt and run from his bed, and thus was punished for his efforts to save himself with repeated blows from the murder weapon. He was found in one corner of the room, his head separated from his trunk as by an executioner's axe, his forearm similarly hacked away, and his body near split at the middle. His brother, unknown by name, died peaceably in his sleep from a single blow to the head, which left him unrecognizably wounded.

Members of the party speculated as to who might have done such horrible deeds. One who had lately returned from the North American colonies declared such slaughter could only have been accomplished by a pack of red Indians.

But hark! There were sounds from above—footfalls, creaking boards, and a long, low moan delivered in a most blood-chilling tone. Was there a survivor, or was the murderer yet about? Knowing not which was so, the band of vigilants marched slowly, though steadfastly, up the stairs to the garret room in which the apprentices made their quarters. What new horrors would they find?

The two lads, known familiarly in Grub Street as printers' devils, were indeed dead in their beds from blows to their chests and heads. But also there, lurking over them, the murder axe in hand, stood the true devil who had fiendishly dispatched the boys and the four members of the Crabb family below.

He threatened the investigators with his weapon and noised at them fearsomely in a strange tongue that none understood. Seeing that to attempt reason with one in such a state would be quite impossible, the constable, Cowley by name, stepped forward and threatened him with his pistol. Although urged by the others to shoot him where he stood, Cowley repeated his demand that he lay down his axe. At last some understanding dawned in the murderer's eyes. He dropped his weapon, and the avenging crowd surged upon him, subduing him most mercilessly, abusing him about the head until he was quite insensate.

At last they heeded Cowley's command that they desist, and the constable bore the prisoner to the Bow Street Court, where he is now in custody. He has been identified as John Clayton, a mad poet from Somersetshire. For some days past, he has been resident in the Crabb establishment, where he plotted the murders. Thus did he repay his host's hospitality.

MURDER IN GRUB STREET

ONE

*In which I but narrowly
escape an end by
murder*

In my research for materials pertinent to the murders in
Grub Street, which was indeed one of Sir John Fielding's
most infamous inquiries, I came upon the preceding document which I had kept near thirty years as a reminder of
just how this grisly matter began. Though but a broadsheet
written and printed in haste the day following for quick
sale throughout London, it gives a fair and accurate account
of how the great crime was apprehended by those who were
first upon the premises. The writer, whom I later had opportunity to meet, was not one of those present, yet he
talked at some length with three of them, including young
Constable Cowley, who was somewhat in disgrace at the
time. The information thus garnered, though colored and
flavored to the taste of buyers in the street, was quite useful
to the inquiry of Sir John Fielding, magistrate of the Bow
Street Court. He did, nevertheless, take it ill that such information was made public so soon after the event.

Yet none of this was known to me when first I became
acquainted with the Grub Street matter. I was deep in a
sleep which I had believed would be my last in the household of Sir John Fielding when I was roused from it, shaken
near awake by his housekeeper, Mrs. Gredge.

"Jeremy," said she to me, "you must rise and dress yourself quick, for Sir John wishes you to accompany him on a journey of great urgency."

"Oh, I will," said I, quite groggy with sleep, "indeed I will."

"I'll have none of that," said she. "I must see you out of your bed and in your clothes ere I leave. Boys of your age give promises in sleep they never mean to keep." She held the candle quite near my face and let its light torture my eyes open. "Awake, now!" she commanded, "and out of bed!"

"But I am not dressed," I objected modestly.

"Indeed you are not, and I mean to see you change that."

And so, having no other choice in the matter, I threw back the blankets, and did as I was bade. In truth, I wore my second-best shirt against the night chill, and so was not near as naked as I pretended to be. Mrs. Gredge threw to me my stockings and breeches, and I struggled into them, though still near half asleep. Holding her candle high, she pointed out my coat, hung on the back of my attic room's single chair, and my shoes tucked beneath. Silent and sullen, I pulled them on and stood ready at last.

She nodded, satisfied. "Come along so," said she, "and don't forget your hat."

Down the stairs then, feeling my way in the dark, for she flew before me, taking with her the scant light offered by the candle she carried. Yet once in the kitchen, I found light aplenty, as if it be lit for early evening, and there, deep in talk, were Sir John Fielding and his chief constable, Benjamin Bailey, captain of the Bow Street Runners. They took no notice of me, so urgently did they discuss. Sir John was poised in such a way as to observe my coming, yet in his blindness he saw me not.

I took a place nearby and waited quietly. Of a sudden, I was full awake. My resentment toward Mrs. Gredge for the rude awakening she had given me was vanished, now replaced by a sense of anticipation and curiosity as to the matter at hand. If leave Sir John's household I must for a life in the printing trade, I had rather it be at such a time of excitement as this might prove to be.

I considered the remarkable events that had brought me to this place. I had come to London near two months past, lately orphaned in the most lamentable circumstances by my father's death in the pillory. I had fled that foul village which had treated my father, a printer, so ill, and arrived in the great city with only a few shillings between me and destitution. On my first day there I had been gulled by an independent thief-taker, who dragged me before the nearest magistrate and falsely accused me of theft. How fortunate for me that the magistrate who heard the matter was Sir John Fielding! Though blind, he had seen through the lying deception and taken me as a ward of the court. Ere he found me a place as a printer's apprentice, however, which was his intent, he had been engaged in an inquiry into the death of Lord Goodhope, in which I proved of small assistance. I had hoped my help in that matter might sway him to keep me on in some capacity, yet it seemed this was not to be. He, brought low by the death of his wife after a lingering illness, could find no permanent place for me in his household. With the help of Dr. Samuel Johnson, he had placed me in the printer's trade.

Yet now, as I waited, I sensed something of great moment in the air. Though I might not see this inquiry through to its end, I should at least be present at its beginning. Remembering that evening, but a short time past, when we first visited the residence of Lord Goodhope and the mystery of his death began to unfold, I took heart that this night might also be one such. Little did I know the shocking revelation and attendant horror that awaited me.

And so, at a respectful distance, I made to eavesdrop a bit, catching words, names, and phrases from the conversation that continued between Sir John and Mr. Bailey. I distinctly heard the name John Clayton passed from Mr. Bailey, followed a sentence or two later by "under lock and key."

Sir John took that in, nodded, and said, "I shall talk to him, certainly."

Mr. Bailey laughed loudly and declared, "You'll not get much out of that one!"

"That's as may be, but I must try. But be on your way, Mr. Bailey. So much has so far been done wrong, you must do what you can to put it aright."

"As you say, Sir John."

"Who is on duty downstairs?"

"Mr. Baker."

"Good. Off you go then."

And with a touch of his hand to his tricorn, Mr. Bailey disappeared through the open door and thundered down the stairs.

"Mrs. Gredge," Sir John called out, "did you wake Jeremy?"

She was no longer present, gone back to bed perhaps.

"I am here, Sir John," said I.

"Ah, I had no idea. Dressed, are you? Ready to go?"

"I am, yes."

"Then we must first make a visit to the strong room to talk to one in a most unfortunate state and then be off to visit the place of his arrest."

All that sounded quite reasonable, as stated, yet what a world of pain it hid. He must have wished not to frighten me.

"Shall I put out the candles, sir?"

"Yes," said he, "do that, but leave the longest burning for our return."

I did so, and together we descended the stairs—I preceding him, and he with his hand on my shoulder. Thus came we to the ground floor, where only a few steps away lay the strong room. There Mr. Baker stood, staring with great fascination at its contents. From the angle of our approach it was at first impossible to glimpse inside, yet even then, knowing nothing of the prisoner and the cause of his imprisonment, I was quite curious, knowing not what to expect.

I confess that when I laid eyes upon the man who would come to be known to us all as John Clayton, I was somewhat disappointed. Because of the lateness of the hour, Sir

John's solemn demeanor, and Mr. Baker's keen interest, I had expected to discover a more impressive figure behind the bars. What I found, rather, was a large man dressed in a nightshirt, looking more forlorn than any I had ever before seen. He sat on a stool, his knees wide apart and his hands clasped so tight between them that they seemed together to make a single fist. His eyes were quite impossible to read, for they were shut tight. There seemed to be nothing remarkable about him at all, except the sense of desperation that his posture conveyed, and the fact that he was dressed for bed. But then I noticed that the hem of his nightshirt had been splashed with blood.

I looked to Sir John, wondering if I should tell him of that detail. Such, he had ever said, were often of the utmost importance. Yet he was off to one side now, listening close as Mr. Baker whispered in his ear.

Whatever was said, it was not much, for Sir John turned from him with a quick nod and called out to the prisoner: "You in there, identify yourself. What is your name?"

The only answer he got was a great, sad moan.

"Are you John Clayton? Is that who you are?"

At that, he who had been addressed shook his head vigorously and spoke for the first time and in a deep, heavy growl. "I am Petrus," said he. And as he did so, he seemed to take heart, opening his eyes and regarding his questioner for the first time, rising from the stool whereon he had sat, striding with apparent confidence to the bars that separated them.

"I think you are not," said Sir John. "No matter who you think you are, or say you are, I believe you are John Clayton."

"And who are you?" asked the prisoner.

"I am John Fielding, the magistrate before whom you must appear tomorrow. My advice to you, sir, is to organize yourself. Prepare to answer questions, because I have many to ask. Do you hear me?"

"I hear you."

"*Do you understand?*" Sir John put the question to him with great severity. His face was but inches from the prisoner's, separated only by the bars of the strong room. Had he sight, one would say he was staring into the man's eyes, which were both wild and vacant and most frightening to behold.

For a space of time they stood thus. At last, with no answer forthcoming, Sir John turned in my direction. "Let us be gone, Jeremy," said he. "I fear we'll find no hackney carriage at such an hour. No doubt we must make our journey by shank's mare."

As I then started to follow him to the corridor which led to the Bow Street door, Mr. Baker pulled me aside and, with a finger to his lips commanding silence, shoved a small pistol into my coat pocket. Then, with a wink and a slap on the back, he sent me on my way.

"Jeremy?"

"Coming, Sir John."

Indeed, as he had foreseen, there was no hackney waiting at the entrance, though Mr. Bailey had promised to send one to us, should he encounter it as he went ahead. Nor did we catch a glimpse of one as we went at length through the near-deserted, though not altogether quiet, streets of the city.

The reason he wished me to accompany him was made plain quite immediate. "Lad," said he to me, "you've made many a trip to Grub Street the past week or two. Can you guide me there? I know not the way."

"I'm sure I can, sir."

"In the dark of night?"

I looked down the street, which was dimly lighted by lamps. A wind had risen and taken with it the fog which so often, then as now, lay over London. The night was clear. "This way, Sir John," said I, giving him but a touch on the elbow to start him in the right direction.

Thus we went: I, moving him left or right at a crossing of the streets, giving him a word of advice when the walkway dipped, or disappeared altogether; otherwise he made his way quite by himself with the aid of his stick. We moved swiftly so, though the journey was not without incident.

I recall well that as we turned one corner, we came upon a gang of men and their drabs before a low drinking and gaming place known as the Cock of the Walk. There were murmurs among them. My right hand went down into my coat pocket wherein Mr. Baker had placed the pistol. Once, in an idle moment, he had demonstrated to me how the thing worked: pull back the hammer and pull the trigger. I had not the love of firearms that he had; I was altogether uneasy with them. Yet in such a situation, it seemed right to have one such at hand. I grasped the butt of the pistol tightly. One ball would not mean much in such a crowd. Yet the threat of the pistol might well hold them all at bay. Perhaps I should pull out the pistol and show them I was armed.

While still pondering this and about to step among them, I was quite surprised to see a way open up before us. There were greetings called to Sir John by even the roughest among them. Some knew him as "the Blind Beak," others addressed him more formally, but all seemed to know him and spoke to him with a certain respect. And so we passed through pacifically, Sir John acknowledging the greetings of those whom he recognized, giving a general hello to the rest. I walked by his side, and as I went I examined those hard faces which were turned toward him in expressions of approval, and I marveled somewhat, wondering what he had done to win it. He was not lenient, I reasoned, but he was fair. When seated upon the bench, he demanded evidence and from witnesses wanted only to know what they themselves had seen and heard and not what they had gathered secondhand. In sum, if ruffians such as these who gathered before the Cock of the Walk should come before him, they knew they had a chance to prove their innocence, or at least becloud their guilt; and this was all they hoped for. He was their man.

Moving past them, I noted that Sir John did not quicken his pace, though I myself was eager to get us away. When we were some distance away I ventured to turn back and take a look. I saw with some relief that we were not followed.

"None would dare," said Sir John.

"Sir?" said I, suspecting for a moment he had read my thoughts.

"You lagged behind a moment. I take it that like any sensible soldier you were making sure our rear was safe from attack. I commend you for that, even though there was no need. I have my eminence to protect me—sufficient is it to guard you as well, I think. Should even that fail us, there is always the pistol in your pocket—loaned to you, I believe, by Mr. Baker, was it not?"

"Yes, sir, but . . ." I hesitated, a moment dumbfounded. "How did you know?"

"Oh, he has his tricks, has Mr. Baker. He seems to believe I had need of an armed guard each time I go out after dark. Not so. Nothing of the kind. Now, if I am not mistaken, he slipped you the pistol—probably a small one— as we were leaving Bow Street. Is that correct?"

"It is, yes," said I. "But he said nothing. I said nothing."

"Your pocket spoke. You usually carry a few coins in your pocket, probably no more than a few shillings—remind me to pay you a bit for services rendered, by the by. Occasionally the coins jingle in your pocket. Yet ever since we began on our walk they have been clanging away against a larger metal object, of steel no doubt. Knowing Mr. Baker's worries about me and his love of firearms, I supposed that he must have presented you with a pistol. Though in general I do not disapprove of his precautions, I do question his wisdom in handing a loaded gun to a thirteen-year-old boy—that is your age, is it not, Jeremy?"

"Yes, Sir John."

"Mind you do not shoot yourself in the foot."

With that bit of advice he let the matter pass. We were by then hard by Grub Street, in any case, just one crossing distant. I had it in sight. In truth, I knew the way well by then, having made three or four trips there and back from Bow Street in the past week, and perhaps one in the week before. Grub Street was then, though it is somewhat less today, a place given chiefly to booksellers and publishers and the impecunious writers whom they employed. At Sir John Fielding's appeal, no less than Dr. Samuel Johnson had bruited my name about among the publishers and printers on the street as a likely lad to serve as an apprentice to one of them. Several expressed interest, and Dr. Johnson chose the one he deemed most respectable. I was sent hence with a formal letter of recommendation, and my prospective employer took time from his day to talk at length with me. He assumed I was a young protégé of Dr. Johnson's, and when he heard I was a native of Lichfield (famous as Dr. Johnson's place of origin), he took that to be the connection between us; I allowed him to do so. Quite interested was he when I told him my father had been a printer and that he had had a small shop of his own. He assumed it to have been in Lichfield; I allowed him to do so.

"And how came you to London?" asked my prospective employer, no doubt wondering why I had not formally apprenticed with my father.

"My mother died three years ago. My father passed away recently," said I, making no reference to the shameful circumstances of his death. "I am an orphan."

"Ah," said he, "of course. My condolences, young sir."

"But I can set type," said I, eager to prove myself.

"At your age?"

"Oh, indeed, sir. I've been at it since I was nine, and I truly believe I was of some help to my father during the last year or two."

He looked at me keenly; an expression between doubt and curiosity kindled in his eyes. "Would you care to demonstrate your skill?" he asked.

"I should be happy to."

And so he took me to the back shop where work proceeded apace. It was of good size, containing type stands, a press, and a small bindery. A journeyman printer worked at one stand and an older apprentice at another. Another journeyman worked at the press, and a binder pursued his labors with the aid of another apprentice of about my own age. I had never before been in a shop given to book printing and was quite taken by all the bustle inside.

The master ordered the older journeyman to step aside; a box was found for me to stand on; and I quite amazed them with my ability. The journeyman applauded me. The master named me a "prodigy." Even the apprentice was impressed, though he took pains not to show it. I lacked neither in speed nor in accuracy.

With all that, I was told my place with them was assured. I rejoiced to hear it; but then, recalling that my acceptance meant certain separation from Sir John's household, I wondered if I might not have served my cause better by appearing less able. But truth to tell, able or incompetent, separation seemed sure, and so I allowed myself to enjoy the moment and thanked them all most graciously.

And so the articles of apprenticeship were drawn up in my absence. I fetched them on the appointed day and brought them back to Sir John, as he had requested, for his perusal. I read the papers to him, and he was satisfied. But then he surprised me somewhat, asking for a quill and ink that he might sign the document. He explained then that this was quite proper, for in the absence of my deceased parents, he stood as my legal guardian for as long as I was a ward of the court. And so I did as he had directed, placed the quill in his hand and then at the proper place on the paper. He then delivered a most handsome signature, even added a flourish which surely none but he could duplicate. I had seen him do this on earlier occasions, signing documents and letters drawn up for him by Mr. Marsden, the court clerk, and I had never ceased to wonder at the remarkable skills of this blind man.

No discussion followed. He simply sent me back with the document after I had added my signature to his own. The articles of apprenticeship were accepted by my new master and signed by himself. Then it was agreed between us that I would enter his household a week hence. He apologized for the delay, saying that room would have to be found for me. This would have ended my journeys to Grub Street but for one last visit made upon his request two or three days later. It seemed the new master had been boasting up and down the street of his new apprentice, namely me, and he wished to give a demonstration of my skill to his fellow tradesmen. I was sent for by his elder apprentice, and so with Mrs. Gredge's permission, I left with him to take the walk to the shop. His name was Clarence, as I recall, and he proved quite a disagreeable young fellow. There were implications and veiled threats made along the way by him, who was four or five years my senior. What was said clear to me was that "prodigy" though I be, I would still be under his thumb, so long as he, too, was an apprentice. This was not an arrangement which pleased me much, yet I determined to make do as long as it was necessary. As for the demonstration, it went well enough: I was praised once again by my master and hailed by his competitors. I left, knowing the way well by then, though quite unsure of what would await me once I had made a new home there on Grub Street.

And Grub Street was where we then arrived, Sir John and I, at a late hour, near three in the morning, on that night which was to alter the course of my life for all time to come.

As we turned up the way, I spied a small crowd by the dim light of the lamps. They had gathered before a building of some size near halfway down the street. That place, I realized, was quite familiar to me. It had been my destination on each of my previous trips to Grub Street. That building housed the store and shop of Ezekiel Crabb, bookseller and publisher, the master to whom I had been apprenticed; it was to be my home and workplace beginning eight o'clock in the morning of that very day. Had Sir John taken it upon himself to deliver me early? That made no sense. And why this group of curious onlookers?

"Is *this* our destination, sir?" I asked. I had to know.

"Yes," said Sir John, "Ezekiel Crabb's home and place of business. A most terrible crime has been committed there."

He said not what the crime was, nor why he had not earlier told me. I had a sudden multitude of questions, yet I held my tongue, thinking it best. As we approached, I merely called his attention to the crowd at the door.

"I'm aware of them, Jeremy. Follow me through."

With that—shouting a cautionary "Make way! Make way!"—he plunged into the assembly, waving his stick before him. And as I had been bade, I went in his wake. There were no more than twelve there, but some of them of rather disreputable appearance. They parted before him in sullen obedience until we stood at the door. There, standing guard before it, was young Constable William Cowley.

. Indeed, he was the youngest of the Bow Street Runners, probably no more than eighteen years of age, and the least experienced of all, having come to that force, with Mr. Baker's sponsorship, but a month before my arrival at Bow Street. He was nonetheless large and willing and had proved himself brave on more than one occasion since his arrival.

Cowley came to an attitude of attention. "Sir John," said he, "Mr. Bailey is inside, investigating the situation. He put me here to keep out the curious."

"Would you had kept them out when you first arrived upon the scene, Constable Cowley."

"I know, sir. Mr. Bailey has reproved me sorely for my handling of the matter. And I do regret it, sir. There was mistakes of judgment on my part, perhaps, but there was bad circumstances, too."

"And what were they? Why did you not deputize some who entered with you to convey the prisoner to Bow Street so that you might stay and protect the environs of the crime?"

"Because I was afraid that once out of my sight, they would kill him. There was talk of it among them. One had gone off to get a rope."

"Then why did you not lock the place up?"

"We broke the door to make our entry, sir. It's half off its hinges now."

Sir John mused a moment. "So it was indeed locked from the inside. Is there a back door? Was it, too, locked?"

"A stout cellar door, sir, and it was also locked tight."

"Well, it does look bad for our prisoner, does it not?"

"Oh, right bad," agreed Constable Cowley, "right bad.

I caught him, sir, with the weapon in his hand.''

"Yes, well . . . we shall talk of that inside, Constable."
With that, he turned to the crowd, which had fallen back a
few paces from the door. And to them, he spoke loudly and
most solemnly: "Any of you who first made entry with
Constable Cowley are to remain here outside the house. We
shall have questions for you. The rest I order to disperse.
I am Sir John Fielding, magistrate of the Bow Street Court.
Those who fail to obey this order of mine will be subject
to arrest, fine, and imprisonment for not less than thirty
days. Think not to leave and then return, and you who
remain do not consider reentry; you have done enough
damage, as I understand it. I am leaving a guard at the door.
This young man has an evil temper, and he is armed."

It struck me of a sudden that Sir John referred to me. An
evil temper? Surely not. Yet I made a face suitable to his
description and hoped to frighten them all with it.

"Show them your pistol, Jeremy," said Sir John sotto
voce.

I pulled it from my coat pocket and exhibited it boldly.

"Loaded and primed it is," he continued, "and he is
under orders from me to shoot anyone who tries to push
past him. Is this understood?"

In response, a sullen grumble rose from the men at the
door.

"Now you have heard my instructions. Those who first
made entry are to remain. To the others of you, I now
say . . ." He paused but a moment, then shouted in a voice
of great authority: *"Be gone!"*

And indeed they went, falling back, looking over their
shoulders, retreating like a company of soldiers in sudden
disarray. There were but four left.

"Look at those who remain," said Sir John to Constable
Cowley. "Were they with you?"

Cowley went from face to face and nodded. "All who
are here, yes, Sir John. Yet one is missing. There were five
at the start."

"Did you get his name?"

"Uh . . . I took no names, sir."

"Ah, well, when Mr. Bailey questions them, perhaps he'll get the missing man's identity from his fellows."

"Yes, sir."

"And Jeremy," said he in a whisper, "that permission to shoot was given to impress them and not to be taken literally. A simple call for help will do wonders. One of us is sure to hear."

So saying, he left me there at the door, with Constable Cowley close behind. I held that ferocious face as long as I found possible, then slowly allowed it to relax into an expression of cold indifference. I looked this way and that over the heads of the four, and from time to time directly at them. The pistol I held rested in my folded arms. It seems certain, as I consider it today, that they were far more taken by it than by me, and far more deeply impressed by Sir John's air of command than by either the pistol or the lad who held it.

The four witnesses clustered together and talked among themselves in tones so low I could not hear. They did so for a goodly space of time. At one point the four erupted into a chorus of raucous laughter which, considering what they knew and had seen, was altogether inappropriate.

But of course at that point I knew not what they knew, though I had some hint, surely, of what they had seen. When Sir John spoke of "a most terrible crime," that could only be murder. But who in Ezekiel Crabb's household had been murdered? Was it the master himself? In that case, I reflected, what would that mean with regard to my articles of apprenticeship? I liked Mr. Crabb. He certainly seemed to like me. I hoped it was not him. Could it be that fellow Clarence, the elder apprentice? May God forgive me, considering my experience with Clarence and the dismal life I looked forward to with him as my submaster, I decided that if victim there must be, I hoped it would be he and no other. Beyond that, I could not think. There were others, I knew, housed in the Crabb domicile—another apprentice, sons, a wife who had been mentioned but not seen. The journeymen surely lived off the premises, as my father had in Lichfield, so that, then, was the question: Who was the victim?

It was not long before the remnant of the crowd began to taunt me.

Said one to the rest: "I'd no idea Sir John was taking apprentices for the Runners—had you, Harry?"

"None at all," said Harry. "What age would you take this one to be?"

"Near ten, I would say. Is that not what you would guess him?"

"Nay, not so old—seven or eight perhaps."

"Careful you do not anger him by putting him too young. Lads of such an age are quick to take offense at those matters. Remember Sir John's warning: He has an evil temper, Bert."

"And a pistol in his hand!"

"Strange playthings they give children in such times as these."

"Strange indeed."

And thus they continued long past the point I had grown tired of their banter, until at last they grew tired of it themselves. Or was it Mr. Bailey's predicted appearance that quietened them? I cannot rightly remember. In any case, after about half of an hour had passed, I started at a tap upon my shoulder and turned to find behind me Benjamin Bailey, who had ever a quiet tread.

"How goes it, young Jeremy?"

"Well enough," said I.

"Have these layabouts been baiting you?" He looked sharply past me at the four waiting witnesses.

"Nothing to give me pause."

"Well, p'rhaps I shall give pause to one or two of them."

He strode into their midst, grabbed one of them quite roughly, and pulled him over to the nearest streetlamp, which was some paces distant. Then, in a low, persistent, confidential tone he began to question the man, the one called Harry. They were beyond my hearing and beyond that of the waiting three, which seemed to annoy them, for after a whispered conference they began sidling over as a group toward Mr. Bailey and their fellow. Then the chief constable noted what they were up to and directed them emphatically back to their former station. Sulking, they returned and once more took up their whispering.

It was but minutes he spent with Harry. And when he had done with him, he sent him on his way.

"But that ain't fair," protested Harry loudly. "I wish to wait on my mates."

"If so, you'll do it out of my sight," said Mr. Bailey. "Now take yourself out of here, or I'll plant my boot up your arse."

Harry backed away, signaling to the others he would wait around the corner.

"You should not treat us so!" cried one of them, all indignant, to Mr. Bailey.

"By Christ, you should not!" said another.

"Was it not us who gave the alarm?" asked Bert. "Did we not enter with your young constable, knowing not what perils awaited us? Did we not help subdue the murderer?"

"*And,*" queried Mr. Bailey, striding toward them, "was it not you who went through the place and turned it topside down the moment the constable was out of the way?" He stopped, facing them down, hands on hips, arms akimbo. "What was it you was looking for? The money box?"

"Aye," said Bert, "we found it, and we turned it over to the constable when he returned."

"Caught in the act is what you were. And one of your number made off with the murder weapon. The constable gave you orders not to return inside the house, did he not?"

"We was only tryin' to be helpful."

"Come along," said Mr. Bailey to Bert. "I'll give you helpful."

And he seized upon him and walked him rudely to the place he had chosen beneath the streetlamp. There he began putting questions to him in the same subdued tone he had used before, all the more intimidating for his quiet control of it.

My attention taken, as it was, by the confrontation just

recorded, I only then became aware of the sound of horses' hooves on the cobblestones quite nearby. So near was it, in fact, that it seemed but moments before a dray wagon drawn by two horses came in sight, rolling slowly up Grub Street in our direction.

Something strange happened then. Not only had I turned to look, but so had the others, as well. The two waiting witnesses left off their whispered talk; so, too, did Mr. Bailey interrupt his earnest questioning. They all stopped to give their attention to the dray wagon which seemed to appear and disappear in a ghostly manner as it moved from streetlamp to darkness, then back into the perimeter of dim illumination provided by the next streetlamp. All simply stared, so that where loud acrimony had prevailed not long before, there was now only silence, save for the steady clip-clop of the horses and the creaking of the wagon wheels.

The two men before me shrank back, far back, to the other side of the street as the wagon pulled up before the house of Ezekiel Crabb. It was only then that I got a proper look at the mysterious arrival and his remarkable conveyance. Whatever color the wagon had once been painted, it had by then faded to a dark, dirt-streaked gray, all except for a panel in the middle of it which had been rubbed clean; thereon had been painted a skull and crossbones in white, all in stark contrast to the rest. The horses, too, were gray. Spavined and skeletal, they seemed half dead as they bowed their heads in evident exhaustion. They remained so, still as statues, for the remainder of their stay.

The driver, indifferent to them, tossed down the reins and climbed down from the wagon. He moved surely and deliberately, not a tall man but wide at the shoulders and thick at the waist. When he turned to me and started to the door, I noted his apelike bearing, how his long arms seemed to dangle and his short legs fell forward heavily with each step. He was a round-faced, ugly man, a week in need of a razor.

When he drew close, he thrust that face close to mine, smiled a carious smile and winked an eye at me—the one which was smaller than its fellow.

"Be a good lad," said he in a low, hoarse voice, "and tell them the Raker is come."

Quite overcome was I by the foul smell of him. I stepped back yet tried to maintain my stern demeanor.

Then Mr. Bailey called out to me: "Let him pass, Jeremy. Direct him to the floor above."

I stepped aside then. "You heard that?" I asked. "Up above."

"I heard," said he as he lumbered past.

I knew not what to make of him—the skull and crossbones on his dray wagon, the apparent fear he had inspired in grown men. Could he be a pirate? Of course not. There were none such in London, save perhaps for Black Jack Bilbo, and he was retired from the trade. Who then? What then? What did he mean to call himself "the Raker"? (I learned soon enough.)

Mr. Bailey proceeded quickly with his queries and was done with the talkative and facetious Bert in no time at all. He, too, was sent off and left without complaint. The remaining two also seemed eager to be away. The next witness jog-trotted from his place across the street and presented himself to Mr. Bailey without summons.

Hearing scuffling and the sound of great effort behind me, I stepped away from the door and waited but a moment before Constable Cowley and the Raker appeared with a heavy package between them. It was a corpus wrapped in a bloodstained sheet, and judging from the size and shape, it was likely Mr. Crabb himself. The two bearers made their way with some difficulty to the wagon.

"Ready?" said the Raker. "Then one . . . two . . . *three!*"

And they heaved their package up over the side and into the wagon, sheet and all. Yet as it flew through the air, the wrapping parted and revealed enough of its contents to confirm my identification.

It was so then. Ezekiel Crabb was the victim. In my mind I mourned him, for he had seemed a good man for certain sure. His liking for me would have made him a good and generous master. And as children will, who think most of themselves, I mourned my own circumstances, as well. Would I find another master as good? To whom would I now be apprenticed?

Yet the constable and the Raker returned into the house and my mind turned to the question of culpability. Who could have murdered Mr. Crabb? Could it have been that threatening fellow Clarence? Perhaps his place at the type stand was to be given me. Perhaps he had brooded upon it and struck down his master whilst he slept. No, more likely it was the madman in the strong room at Bow Street. He had been taken prisoner, after all. What could have angered him so to strike down Mr. Crabb? But of course madness required no reason.

Then there were more grunts and mutual warnings of "Mind, now" and "Have a care," coming from the room behind me. And to my surprise, the constable and the Raker emerged with another corpus. This one, too, was wrapped in a bloody sheet, yet not so well that I did not fail to notice a mass of gray hair trailing out at one end. Was this then Mrs. Crabb, whom I had not met but only heard of? Yet there was no respect given her sex. She was given the same treatment—heave-ho and into the wagon—as her husband. And once again the Raker led the way back into the house. I heard him say in that phlegmy, rattling voice, "Fat old dame, wasn't she now? I vow she was heavier than her man." He cackled at that as if he had made a great joke.

Thus had begun the parade of the dead. Wrapped in sheets and blankets they came, borne between the two and deposited in the wagon in the same primitive manner. Whether from the labor or the nature of the task, Constable Cowley perspired heavily, though the night was cool; and it may have been, as I reflect upon it, that those rivulets upon his cheeks were tears, for he had a sensitive nature and was not yet inured to such carnage.

The Raker, for his part, went at it with relish, growing ever more jolly with each load he carried, making little grisly witticisms for the benefit of none but himself. Grisliest of all was his response to a mishap there at the doorstep. Constable Cowley stumbled slightly at the exit, and from the weighted blanket popped a human arm cleft off above the elbow, bloody bone, meat, and gristle protruding from the end of it. Where did the arm land but at my feet? I jumped back in horror. But quick as a wink the Raker was there to pick it up by the hand. He supported his end easily with one hand of his own, for the man was uncommon strong, and on the way to the wagon held a conversation with the dead owner of the arm.

"Well, I'm happy to make your acquaintance, my good fellow, so I am," said he, shaking the hand of the thing in salutation, as if meeting for the first time. "How is you this fine night? Came upon you sudden like, did it? Well, that's oft the way of it—when we least expect, so they say."

Then, at the wagon, he tossed the arm upon the growing pile and with a "one-two-three" and the help of the constable sent the rest of the corpus to follow.

"Sweet Jesus' sake," said Cowley to him, near weeping with anger, "how can you carry on so?"

The Raker stood for a moment and regarded him with amused perplexity. "The dead don't care," said he at last.

Cowley pushed past him and went into the house. The Raker followed, giggling to himself.

I felt a soft grip upon my arm and found Mr. Bailey by my side. "Sorry you had to see that, Jeremy," said he.

"Would that I had not."

"I've talked to the last of that bunch who was inside the place. No need for you to remain before the door. Come inside, if you like."

"Are . . ." I hesitated. "Are there more dead within the house?"

"Yes," said he, "though none on the ground floor."

"Well and good then."

I found I had the pistol still in my hand. Indeed, when I became aware of it, it seemed quite sudden a great weight. And so I thrust it into the pocket of my coat and followed Mr. Bailey through the door.

From previous visits to the Crabb establishment I knew this to be the shop for the sale of books. Though not large, it was well stocked with those of Crabb's own publication, as well as others. At that moment it was lit by the light of a single candle. By that light I saw Sir John sitting on a chair in one corner, his hands folded upon his stick, his tricorn firm upon his head. His face wore an expressionless mask I had seen before when he was deep in thought. After some moments, however, he roused and turned in our direction.

"Is that you, Mr. Bailey?"

"Yes, sir, me and Jeremy."

"Ah yes, Jeremy. I wish I had left him abed and not tarried to talk to that poor creature back at Bow Street. Little good it did." He rose then from the chair. "Mr. Bailey, I should like you to take me to the cellar. I understand that the way is through the printing shop in back. Is that the route, Jeremy?"

"I believe so," said I.

"Why not stay here then? We'll not be long."

And thus they left me there in the dark, for Mr. Bailey had taken with them the candle that had lit the room. Yet not completely in the dark, for there were candles lit on the floor above which showed some light down where I stood; and through the shop window that looked out upon the street there came a glow from the lamp and perhaps a hint of the dawn that was to come.

As I stood waiting, two more bodies were ushered to the wagon and deposited there. With a full load, the Raker busied himself rearranging it for the journey he would make; he hauled the dead about, tossing them this way and that like so many sacks of grain, no longer mindful to keep them covered. Once he had suited himself as to their disposition, he threw a tarpaulin over them all and secured it at the four corners of the wagon. He seemed to sing some ditty or ballad to himself as he went about it. I could not catch the words to it, but they seemed to amuse him.

Sir John then returned with Mr. Bailey and, calling out, summoned Constable Cowley to him. Them he instructed to secure the building as best they could. He proposed that rope might do to tie the door. "Also," said he, "you must post a sign, warning all away on pain of fine and imprisonment. Sign my name to it, though in no wise try to copy my signature.''

"As you will, sir.''

"As I will? Yes, Mr. Bailey, I can only wish that all things were as I willed them, or as I willed them not to be. Well, no matter. Jeremy? Are you prepared to see us back the way we came?''

"I am, Sir John.''

"Would you not prefer to wait, Sir John?'' asked Mr. Bailey. "The two of us constables could accompany you back to Bow Street.''

"No,'' said he, most emphatically. "I must get this boy back to his bed, if indeed he can sleep after the horrors he has witnessed this night.'' He cocked his head more or less in my direction. "Jeremy?''

"Yes, Sir John.''

"Let us be on our way.''

I then touched him at the elbow and guided him forth from this place in which the infamous "massacre in Grub Street'' had taken place. We stepped together into the street. There I saw the Raker, who had mounted the driver's seat and was now ready to depart.

"Quite a harvest, Sir John,'' he called out. "I've not had such a haul for months or more, perhaps a year.''

"You will be paid for it, of course,'' said Sir John.

"Ah yes,'' said he, "all part of the job. Would you and the lad care to accompany me? I'm going your way.''

"No, I think we'll walk, thank you.''

And at that he laughed most heartily. "Few wish to do so,'' said the Raker. "Indeed, few do.''

And then with a whip he stirred his dead horses back to life and they started on their way. I watched them go. Sir John set off at a good pace, and I hopped along to keep up with him.

"Who is that man?'' I asked. "What does he mean calling himself 'the Raker'?''

"I know not truly who he is,'' said Sir John. "He calls himself only that—the Raker. It is a title passed down from the last century, during the plague years, when some ancestor of his went through London town collecting the plague dead. It was dangerous work, leaving all who pursued it open to infection. Somehow, his line survived, and so the ugly business passed down to him. He is employed by the city of London to collect bodies and hold them until they be claimed. If they are not, he sees to their burial in potter's graves.''

"All seem to fear him a little," I ventured.

Sir John sighed. "He enjoys his work too much. There is something unholy about the man. There are rumors about him we need not discuss."

"I understand, sir." Though in truth, I did not.

We walked along in silence until we came to the crossing where we had earlier turned up Grub Street. I guided Sir John at the corner with no more than a touch at the elbow. And thus in an easterly direction we went, picking up the pace once again.

"Uh . . . Sir John?"

"Yes, Jeremy?"

"I shall have to find a new master."

"That much is clear," I thought this perhaps his only comment upon the matter, for he had nothing more to say for a long space of time. Then at last he added: "I must think upon it. Perhaps I shall talk again with Samuel Johnson."

"As you will, Sir John."

"As I will, as I will," he mimicked me. "Indeed, all of you seem eager to give me my wish in all things. What I *wish* is that this terrible thing had not happened; I wish that what seems to be so simple were not so complicated.

"Consider this, Jeremy. We have a prisoner who was taken with the murder weapon, or at least one of them, in his hand. How was he found? By backtracking a cluster of boot prints in blood tracked down from the upper floors. Did our man in the Bow Street strong room wear boots? Indeed he did not. He was barefooted when caught and had been walked barefooted by Constable Cowley to the lockup, probably on this same route we are taking now.

"Could one man have killed so many? I doubt it. The

cries of some would have roused the rest. All were more or less murdered in their sleep. I think it unlikely that one man could have moved undetected and so quickly from one group of sleepers to the next. Yet there he was, axe in hand, a patch of vomit on the floor, looking for all the world like a murderer who had beheld his own work, and sickened at it. All agree to that. The patch of vomit is left, yet we no longer have the axe. Our constable left that—may he now have learned his lesson!—and it was no doubt taken as some sort of perverse souvenir of this awful event by one of that gang of helpers that afterwards rampaged through the Crabb house. They distributed *their* bloody footprints through every part of the building. I'll have at least one of them up for obstructing an inquiry, I promise you that. This whole affair has been handled badly from start to finish!''

I had never heard Sir John speak so angrily. He puffed from the exertion of it, though he maintained his quick step. It was all I could do to keep up with him. And perhaps I gave a bit too much attention to that and too little to what lay ahead. I recall that we had passed the Cock of the Walk and, to my relief, found no crowd at the front of it. We were entering a dark and shadowy patch of street when, of a sudden, two men jumped out before us, one of them holding a wicked-looking cutlass. I grabbed Sir John by the arm and pulled him to a halt.

"What is it?" he asked loud, turning his head this way and that.

"Robbers," said I in a whisper.

"Aye, robbers," said one of them, so close he had heard. He grinned, urging his companion forward. "Robbers we are. Come forward, Tom, and see the fish we have caught in our net. Upon my soul, 'tis a blind man and a boy. Come forward, I say."

Although Tom was more timid than his fellow, it was he who wielded the cutlass. He advanced cautiously, the point of his cutlass aimed in our near direction, wavering from one of us to the other.

"It is clear," said Sir John, quite cool to their threat, "that you know not who I am."

"Nor do we care! Give over what you got."

With that, I plunged my hand quite automatically into my pocket in search of my shillings, but it came up hard against the butt of the pistol. And quite as automatically, I pulled it from my pocket and extended it at the two of them. It took both thumbs to get the hammer back, but back it came. And then, even more difficult in those circumstances, I sought to show them that ferocious face I had put on at the door to the Crabb house.

Each took a step back in quiet respect to the small pistol. I cannot believe my face afrighted them much.

"Now, boy," said the bolder of the two, "be careful with that thing. You could hurt somebody with it."

"I am Sir John—"

"*I have an evil temper!*" I shouted at them, making my voice its deepest.

"But you have but one pistol," reasoned the more talkative. "You can only shoot at one of us." He inched a bit forward.

"At this distance I cannot miss!" There was but six feet between us. "Shall it be you who takes the shot?" I swung the pistol so that it pointed directly at the bearer of the cutlass.

"*Sir John Fielding, I say, and I am—*"

"*No!*" shouted Tom with the cutlass, and back he fell a full three paces.

"Or you?"

And I swung the pistol at the bold one. In truth, reader, I could not have missed at such range, for somehow the thing held steady in my hands, and my finger did not tremble on the trigger. Would I have pulled it? I know not, but I believe perhaps I would have.

He gave no answer but fell back with his fellow, Tom.

"Then if I may not kill either of you, I have only this to say. . . . *Be gone!*"

And so they were gone; they left, walking swiftly, arguing betwixt themselves, each accusing the other of cowardice. I watched them until they disappeared, and informed Sir John that it was safe to proceed. We went slower and with greater care than before, and I kept the pistol in my hand, guarding against their possible return.

Nothing was said between us for quite some time. At last Sir John said, "There were two of them?"

"Two of them, yes, sir."

"They must both have been new to the city, don't you think? That is, not to have recognized me—most unusual, most unusual."

TWO

*In which Sir John seeks the
counsel of Dr. Johnson and
rebuffs Eusebius*

If I often found it difficult to keep abreast of Sir John on
those frequent occasions when I accompanied him on his
walks through the streets and lanes of London town, it was
well nigh impossible for me to keep pace with Samuel
Johnson as I sought to deliver him, as directed, to the magistrate, who awaited us at a coffeehouse in the Haymarket.
Dr. Johnson led the way through the streets, I hopping
along at a jog trot beside him. As is well known, he was
quite a large man, a good six feet in height and sixteen
stone or more in weight, yet his bulk impeded him not at
all. His stout legs were no longer than one might expect
for a man of such proportions, yet he moved them with
remarkable power and swiftness for a man who was then
in his sixtieth year.

Sir John had sent me forth to Johnson's Court, letter in
hand, not much more than an hour after our arrival at Bow
Street. By then the sun had made a timid appearance and
shone forth its light irregularly betwixt banks of swift-
moving clouds. Armed with explicit directions provided by
Mr. Baker, I made my way quickly across the city through
streets that had even then begun to fill with beggars, casual
laborers, and workingmen on their way to their regular em-

ployment. It was then, as it is now, a working city, and the pulse of it had begun to beat right rapid. Strange it is to see our great place come alive. Even today it is my favorite hour in the city.

Greeted at the door I was by a female servant of Dr. Johnson's. When I presented the letter, she bade me enter and invited me to sit on a bench in the foyer whilst she presented it to her master. There I waited—and waited and waited—until at last I heard sounds of snuffling and coughing from deep somewhere within the house. Then the maid came to me and ushered me into a dining room wherein the great man sat alone, breakfasting on bread and bacon. He invited me to sit with him at table and questioned me closely on the events of the night before, or perhaps better said, somewhat earlier that very morning.

I well knew how much Dr. Johnson had learned from the letter I had delivered, for it was in my own hand. Sir John had dictated it to me in the absence of Mr. Marsden. It explained that there had been a terrible crime of murder committed in Grub Street in the home of Mr. Crabb. An individual had been apprehended by a constable at that very location and was now being held in suspect, one known to Dr. Johnson, perhaps by reputation or perhaps even personally—by name John Clayton, a poet. Sir John requested Dr. Johnson's presence at Preston's Coffee House in the Haymarket that they might discuss said Clayton, as he had proved quite reticent in answers when questions had been put to him.

Simply that and no more. For a man of Samuel Johnson's all-consuming curiosity, such a communication as the one I had delivered would merely whet his appetite to know more of the matter. Sir John had foreseen this and instructed me that I might tell all that I had seen, with the exception of his attempt to question John Clayton—nothing of the condition of the prisoner in the strong room; nothing, too, of what I might have heard from others, Constable Cowley or his witnesses, regarding Clayton's arrest; and certainly nothing of Sir John's conjectures on any of these matters.

Dr. Johnson regarded me sternly from across the table. One eye, I perceived, was near blind. The other, while none too healthy, fixed me with a solemn stare, so that I expected the worst up to the very moment he spoke.

"Have you eaten, lad? Would you care for something?"

"A cup of tea, perhaps, sir." For I had been well fed by Mrs. Gredge.

"That we can surely manage."

Then, as if summoned by the power of his thought, the maid appeared with a man-sized cup and saucer, which she placed before me. She filled it from the teapot on the table and was gone without a word. (Yet certainly not far, for she must indeed be listening at the door.)

"Now," said Dr. Johnson, "you must tell me more of this remarkable event."

"What would you know, sir?"

"Why, all of it—as much as you have to tell me. Sir John spoke in his letter of a terrible crime..."

"Yes, sir."

"Of murder."

"Yes, sir."

"Well, boy, how terrible was it? Who was it was murdered?"

"As terrible as can be conceived," said I, taking the cup to my lips and risking a sip of the strong, well-steeped tea. (I do confess, reader, that with this pause I hoped to add drama to what I had to say.) "All were murdered, sir."

"*All?*" His best eye widened in shock. "Crabb, you say, and his wife, as well?"

"And his sons," I added, "and his two apprentices. Six in all. I saw their bodies carried from the house in Grub Street."

The great man fell silent for a moment, quite overcome by the intelligence I had just supplied. Then, recovering, he asked, "You were present?"

"I accompanied Sir John to the place. There were no hackneys on the street at the hour we set out. He needed my help because of his...." I hesitated. "Because of his affliction."

"Yes, yes, of course. So you were there indeed. Tell me what you saw and heard."

And that I did, editing my report along the lines that Sir John had urged. Even so, I included details aplenty to fascinate and revolt Dr. Johnson. I did not spare him the tale of the Raker's arrival, nor his grisly jokes, nor indeed his quite outrageous play with the severed member. Through it all, he listened attentively, yet he was neither so fascinated nor so revolted that he ceased to eat through my long recitation. Indeed, he ate a great, huge breakfast of bread, butter, and near a whole flitch of bacon. His servant made trips to and fro, replenishing his plate. He chewed with such fervor and intensity that perspiration stood out on his brow.

We two finished, by happenstance, at about the same moment—I with my story and he with his eating. He pushed back from the table and trumpeted forth a grand belch. Then he regarded me once again with another steady gaze, though one which seemed in some sense less severe than earlier.

"Well told," said he. "But what can you tell me now of John Clayton?"

"Who is that, sir?" I asked, all innocent.

"Why, he is the prisoner. It was he who was taken at the Crabb house, was it not? Sir John mentioned him specifically in his letter."

"Did he, sir? That's as may be, but there was none taken whilst I was there. I do allow, however, that I heard the name mentioned in Bow Street before being sent along here with the letter."

"Then you can tell me nothing of him and his present state?"

Thankful that he had phrased the question so (for I had no wish to lie to such an august personage), I answered the question truthfully thus: "I regret that I am unable to shed any light upon that matter."

(I reasoned that Sir John's instructions had rendered me unable to do so, and that indeed I did regret it, for were my tongue not tied by my promise, I could have given Dr. Johnson a description of sullen Petrus in his cell clothed only in a bloodstained nightshirt which would indeed have astonished him. If such play with words seems specious and jesuitical, dear reader, it is nevertheless a habit of thought which comes natural to lawyers and lawyers-to-be.)

"Well, then . . ." said he, and making a bellows of his mouth, let forth a great puff of air which seemed nearly to empty his lungs. Then, with a nimbleness that surprised me, he jumped to his feet. "Let us be off to our meeting." He seemed quite eager to go. I followed him out into the hall and to the street door. There he grabbed up his tricorn and stick and made ready to leave. Yet he turned to me then and asked with something like a smile, "Why does Sir John wish to meet in an obscure coffeehouse and not in his chambers?"

"Upon that I could only speculate, sir."

"Proceed then: speculate."

Though Sir John had not covered this in his instructions to me, I could well suppose the true reason: The way to his chambers led past the strong room where the prisoner was housed. He had no wish that Dr. Johnson see the man in such a state. It would not do to tell this, and so I was forced to improvise.

"It could be," said I, "that he wishes the meeting to be of an informal sort, to put you at your ease. What is said in his chambers is often taken down by the clerk in deposition. This makes some shy to speak."

"I? Shy? Hmmnph! It could be, too," said Samuel Johnson, "that he wishes no one at Bow Street to know that he seeks my advice!" With that he laughed a great, conceited laugh, threw open the door, and plunged out into the courtyard.

I pulled the door shut after me and ran to catch him up.

And I continued to run, it seemed, through the length of our long journey by foot. Yet if he was a fleet and energetic walker, he was also a silent one. We were nearly to the Haymarket before he ventured his first words to me. They came in a grumble tossed over his shoulder in my direction.

"I suppose," said he, "that I shall have to find you a new position as apprentice."

"It would seem so," said I, hopping up beside him, awaiting further words on this subject. But none came. He simply set his face in an attitude of thought and pressed on through the growing crowd of pedestrians. After a few paces together, I fell inevitably behind.

But once more he spoke out before we reached our destination: "When were you to begin with Mr. Crabb?" he called out.

"That would have been today, sir," said I, once more running up to him.

"Fortunate for you that it was not yesterday, eh? There would have been seven victims then. Had you thought of that?"

"It has been pointed out to me," said I, most politely.

"Hmm. Yes . . . well . . . indeed." He stopped suddenly and whirled about, looking this way and that, thus causing some confusion amongst those around him. We had come to the Haymarket. "Now, boy, tell me," said he, "where is this place we are to meet?"

I knew it well, for I had drunk coffee there myself, having been introduced to the practice but a few short weeks before at Lloyd's.

"This way," said I, and for once took the lead, crossing the cobblestoned way with him impatient at my heels. We entered and were immediately assailed by the wondrous aroma of the brew; quite welcome after our long immersion in the foul smells of the streets.

Looking about, I spied Sir John alone at a corner table and beckoned Dr. Johnson to follow. The place was not near as crowded as it would be. The table given us would do well for the sort of quiet tête-à-tête which the magistrate wished. Yet Dr. Johnson was unaccustomed to quiet; and if noise were in short supply, he could provide it in plenty. He barked out a greeting in a voice loud enough to frighten off a footpad.

Heads turned. The nearest serving girl, pot in hand,

stopped sudden as a shying horse, slopping coffee on a floor often slopped before.

"Dr. Johnson, though I may be blind, I am not deaf," said Sir John, with a smile meant to soften the sharpness of his words. "But do please sit down, so that we may discuss this matter I mentioned in my letter."

"Has you baffled, has it? You wish my counsel in it?"

"Your counsel is always welcome. Yet what is most needed is your knowledge." Sir John raised his hand then in hope of being seen by the serving girl. "Let us have coffee first to sharpen our minds."

She was there in a trice, setting two cups and pouring three. I grabbed mine up at once, sipping it hot, sore in need of the stimulation it would give. My day had begun much too early.

"My knowledge, you say, sir?"

"Yes, your knowledge of this man, John Clayton. I sought you out since you seem to know, or know of, nearly every literary man in London."

"That may be, sir, yet your man Clayton has happened merely to be *in* London. He is not *of* it—if you will honor my distinction."

"Certainly," said Sir John. "Nevertheless you do know him?"

"After a fashion," said Dr. Johnson. "We met but a scant twelvemonth past upon the occasion of his first book's publication. A collection of verse it was. And Mr. Crabb invited me, among others, to his bookshop to meet this remarkable discovery of his."

"Remarkable, you say. In what way? You said it as if there were something quite unique about him."

"Indeed there seemed to be," said Dr. Johnson. "Crabb presented him as a 'peasant poet.' " At that point he broke off, screwing his powerful features into a great frown. "And now poor Crabb is dead, murdered. Is it so?"

"No question of it."

"The lad gave me quite a graphic account—*six* victims, dear God!" He shook his head solemnly. "Ezekiel Crabb could be quite a contentious man, but he had standards. He published only what he deemed of value. He certainly made the reputation, if not the fortune, of John Clayton. As I say, he presented the fellow as a 'peasant poet.' And it is true that Clayton had a distinct rural background—a farm laborer from some benighted parish in Somersetshire. Can you imagine it? He's had little formal education, yet there is no doubt, sir, that he has a poetic genius of sorts.''

"Of sorts?''

"Well, yes. His verse is not altogether to my liking. He glories in nature, yet glories in it for nature's own sake. I should say that there is no better writer of descriptive verse in England today, if one is to judge from that first book of his—yet it is *merely* descriptive. He does not go beyond that to philosophy, and much less to wisdom. The poet's duty is to draw lessons from nature, and not simply to portray it. That, however, may be too much to ask of a peasant poet, or perhaps in particular of a peasant poet's first collection of verses.''

"I see,'' said Sir John. "Yet you would say that John Clayton is possessed of a true poetic talent?''

"Oh, without doubt, sir. I have brought with me a copy of that first book of his, by name *The Countryman's Calendar and Other Verses.''* Thus saying, he dove deep into the voluminous pocket of his coat and pulled from it a small volume that fit easily into his large hand. "One may open this book to any page and find phrases of particular charm, some quite brilliant. But here, let me demonstrate.''

Dr. Johnson brought it within inches of his poor eyes, shuffled a leaf or two, and stopped. "This will do,'' said he. "It is a section of the longer poem which provides title to the rest. This one is given as 'February.' ''

And then he read, his loud voice filling the listening room: " 'When winter heaves a sigh and makes to go / From country lands and fields all ripe with snow : . . ' ''

He lowered the book then and looked from Sir John to me. Conversation resumed around us. "Such words as these,'' said he, " 'fields all ripe with snow,' may make no literal sense—snow does not grow from the earth; it is not a crop—yet they present a firm and definite picture to the mind. Clayton's verse is full of arresting figures in this mode. He is, truly enough, a poet. Perhaps he will develop so as to give such phrases greater meaning.''

Sir John lowered his head and leaned across the table toward his partner in conversation. "My inquiries of this man," said he, "have brought back to me the suggestion that he may also be a *mad* poet. Do you know anything of this?"

Dr. Johnson's attitude changed quite abruptly. I noted him straighten and stiffen in his chair. He said nothing for a moment, and when at last he did speak, it was in a quiet, somewhat guarded manner: "Sir, why do you ask me that?"

(His sensitivity regarding this matter may be explained by rumors bruited since his death, that he was at this very time himself experiencing bouts of severe melancholia and had fears for his sanity.)

"Because," said Sir John, "as I have said, you have special knowledge of these men and their humors. Take no offense, Dr. Johnson, but was it not Plato who said that all poets were mad and should therefore be banished?"

"He meant that, sir, in a hypothetical sense: be banished, that is, from an ideal republic. Besides, Plato was half a poet himself and guilty of vagaries of overstatement."

"That is as it may be, but what of this man Clayton?"

Both men had of a sudden become a bit tetchy.

"Well, what of him?" demanded Dr. Johnson. "The man is a bumpkin, sir—he talks as a bumpkin, mispronouncing some words, and he moves about as one. He is shy, well-meaning, respectful, yet as tall as I and quite strong from years of labor in the field. He is, in short, a peasant, quite unexceptional in all ways but one, and that is, he is also a poet—which makes him something of a freak. It was as a freak he was presented to us by Crabb, and thus his book was sold and sold remarkably well. I have heard that there is a second on the way. It is quite difficult to see how such a man, which is to say the man I met briefly, could be held in suspect for a crime such as has been described to me. And as for madness, I . . . well, indeed, I . . ."

At this point, Dr. Johnson's vociferous response sputtered in anticlimax. Sir John did not prompt nor question; he simply waited until that great master of words had found the proper ones with which to continue, and eventually he did:

"Indeed, I did hear something at a dinner some months ago from a Somerset gentleman of no special consequence. Having nothing in common with the man, I made a remark on the sudden success of John Clayton and his descriptions of the beauty of his native place. The man responded in rather mean fashion, saying that as far as he knew, Clayton was not much respected there, that he had a reputation as a toper thereabouts, and other such irrelevant slander. But then, sir, he capped his recital by telling me that he had heard that a few years past, long before the 'peasant poet' had even begun to achieve some degree of renown, he had been confined for a period of weeks in the shire's mad hospital. Quite frankly, I did not credit the report. I considered it false and malicious gossip, inspired by the envy of the gentry for the sudden fame of one of a much lower station. I have never repeated it until now, and I give it no more credit at this moment than I did at the time I first heard it. But since you asked, sir, I suppose I was bound to tell."

Dr. Johnson's stentorian voice had declined through this to a mere whisper. The honor of the man, for which he was so justly famed, shone through to me in these scruples of his as never before.

"Thank you," said Sir John, "and be assured that I will keep your reservations as to the source of this information firmly in mind as I weigh it. I have but one question more for you, and it is this: You said that Ezekiel Crabb had made John Clayton's reputation, if not his fortune. What did you mean by that, sir?"

"Not to speak ill of the dead, Sir John, but it is general knowledge that Ezekiel Crabb was rather parsimonious in his relations with authors, among the stingiest of all his competitors and colleagues in the book trade. He justified it to others by boasting that he published books of quality that others would not risk to issue. By and large, this was no doubt true, but the man had a talent for commerce, rightly enough, and there were times he paid low out of habit, knowing full well he would likely make a considerable profit. John Clayton's *Countryman's Calendar* presents just such an instance. I have heard it reliably reported that he purchased all rights to the book for twenty-five guineas. Crabb must have made near a hundred times that in pure profit, for the book sold in the thousands.''

''Was Clayton resentful of this?''

''Sir, to my mind he should have been, but he was not. He seemed at the time of our meeting, and later by report, to be quite humbly grateful that Crabb had put him before the public. Perhaps he had arranged a more profitable contract for his second book. Indeed, I hope he did.''

''Well, I thank you, Dr. Johnson, you have been most helpful,'' said Sir John most mildly.

''Am I dismissed then, sir?'' said the Great Cham, taken somewhat aback. ''Where is the quid pro quo, the tit for tat? I came in answer to your summons to this lowly place in the hope—nay, the expectation—of learning more of this lamentable matter. I have given all and gotten precious little in return. I would know the circumstances of the crime, the evidence against poor Clayton. I count this unfair!''

''Well, fair or not,'' answered the magistrate, ''this case is before the court and cannot be discussed. You have my invitation, however, to visit us at Bow Street in three hours' time. There and then, I believe, your questions will be answered and your curiosity satisfied.''

Rising to his feet then, he bade me show him the way out. I was up and at his elbow when Sir John stopped quite suddenly and, with a sly smile, put a request to Samuel Johnson: ''I wonder, sir, if you would consent to lend me that book of Clayton's from which you read. Its contents may be material to the case. It will be returned when these matters are disposed of, I promise.''

Dr. Johnson sputtered and fumed, yet in the end he gave

it up. Ne'er was a book lent with such ill grace—or so it seemed to me.

Although Sir John Fielding conducted the proceedings of the Bow Street Court with reasonable dignity and certain respect for both the letter and spirit of the law, he was nevertheless no more nor less than a magistrate. As such, his direct power was limited to the judgment of minor offenses and settlement of modest civil suits and disputes. His greater power was indirect: On him fell the duty to weigh evidence and testimony in capital crimes (of which then there was even a greater number than today), and if sufficient and impressive, to bind the prisoner before him for trial before the King's Bench at Old Bailey. And greatest of all, though the least commonly understood and appreciated, was his power to conduct inquiries that might lead to indictment.

The principal matter before the Bow Street Court on that day was, quite naturally, the terrible massacre in Grub Street. Even before it had been properly reported, it was the subject of much talk in the street. I well remember that on our walk from Preston's, Sir John was detained by a few of the gentry who wished to know details of the matter. No matter how outlandish or how pertinent their questions, he forestalled discussion with a mild phrase or two. "All in due time," he might say; or, "My court is ever open to the public," et cetera. To those who simply yelled out to him as he passed by, "What about Grub Street?" or, "How many killed?" or some such, he gave no true answer, but simply a curt shake of his head or a disapproving wave of his hand. He was, I could see, quite troubled by those rude intrusions; such was the price he paid for the "eminence" of which he himself had boasted.

As we walked in from the street, our way took us within sight of the prisoner, John Clayton—or Petrus, as he would be called. He was attempting to dress himself in breeches and stockings, and so on (clothes more fitting for an appearance in court than a bloodstained nightshirt). Sir John seemed to have no interest. He had tried to persuade the prisoner to talk to him at least once since our return from Grub Street—all to no avail. It was evident that he felt that further efforts of this sort would be useless, at least for the present.

Once settled in his chambers, he sent me off to fetch Mr. Bailey, and I found, not to my surprise, that the prisoner had completed his dressing, and now sat sulking in worn and ill-matched garb. Sir John put me to work with the copy of *The Countryman's Calendar* borrowed from Samuel Johnson. His instructions I thought curious: "Search it for opinions, Jeremy—opinions of any sort. We must try to get some notion of how this fellow's mind works in its more reasonable phases." And so, sitting on the bench before Sir John's door, I began rummaging through the book, looking for I knew not quite what. There was, in a sense, a superabundance of opinions—on the blue of a rare cloudless summer sky, the nesting of birds in an autumn rain, and the midnight conversations of nightingales. In short, the poems written by Clayton were much as Dr. Johnson had said: descriptive rather than philosophic, yet filled with verbal felicities of the most arresting sort. I read, rummaged, and ransacked—Mr. Marsden came and went; young Constable Cowley made an appearance—yet when Sir John called me in and asked what I had discovered, I was able to offer precious little.

"He does not seem to like doctors," said I, "and he loathes confinement."

"Well, in those," said Sir John, "he is joined by the entire population. Yet I suppose it does give some slight support to the tale told Johnson by the gentleman from Somerset." Then, pulling a face: "Bah! An altogether bad business, this. The man is incompetent."

Such was the magistrate's frame of mind as he made to begin that day's proceedings. The crowd that had gathered there was quite the largest I had seen up to that time in the Bow Street Court. It was loud and a bit unruly, as interest ran high in the matter. Among the usual assemblage of layabouts and dregs from Covent Garden were others—distinguished gentlemen and their ladies; others in printing

and publishing, such as Mr. Boyer and his young partner
Mr. Nicholson, Mr. Davies, and Mr. Evans; and finally,
front and center, Dr. Samuel Johnson.

It soon became evident that Sir John meant not to conduct this in the usual way, but rather as a further inquiry
into the case, a sort of hearing in open court. The prisoner
was not called forward to face his accusers but brought in
unbound to sit between Mr. Bailey and Constable Cowley;
Clayton behaved quite reasonably, taking interest in the
proceedings, and giving close attention to what was said.
He appeared ready at last to respond.

Sir John first called Constable Cowley to give his account of the events of the previous night. Since by now,
reader, you are familiar with them, there is no need to repeat here what he said. He did make it clear, however, that
"an individual" was discovered in the attic room occupied
by the two apprentices, deceased, and that "said individual
held in his hand an axe which was thought to be the murder
weapon."

At this point, Sir John interjected a question: "Is this
weapon now in our possession?"

"No, sir, it ain't. Its whereabouts is unknown. Whilst I
conducted the individual to Bow Street for questioning, I
left orders with the group of five men who entered the
premises with me to remain outside and keep it safe till my
return. When I came back, all was inside except one, and
he was missing."

"As was the axe?"

"Yes, sir."

"Do you know the name of the missing man?"

"No, sir, I do not."

"One more thing," said Sir John. "You made it clear
that it was necessary to break down the door to Grub Street
in order to gain entry. Was there another door to the establishment?"

"There was, sir—a rear door in the cellar."

"Was it locked or unlocked?"

"Locked, sir, by key. There was no drawbolt on it."

"Very good, Constable Cowley. Will you now, finally,

point out the individual whom you conducted to Bow Street
for examination and safekeeping?''

The young constable did as told, indicating John Clayton,
alias Petrus.

''Mr. Marsden,'' said the magistrate to his clerk, ''will
you make note of that, please?''

Then he dismissed Cowley, who returned to his place
next the man he had pointed to, and called to witness one
Albert Burnley, a name unknown to me. Yet when he
stepped forward, I recognized him as the ''Bert'' who, with
his companion Harry, had made such sport of me the night
before.

All that Burnley could add to the tale told by the constable was something by way of a preface in which he
described the screams from the Crabb house heard by him
and others, and then the rush to find a constable with whom
they might enter the place.

But early in his recital, at about this point, Sir John interrupted Burnley: ''Would you describe the screams?''

''Describe them?'' echoed the man. ''They was horrible,
they was—a jumble of screams from folk bein' murdered.''

''And how long would you say they did last?''

Burnley screwed up his face for a moment in concentration. Then at last he said, ''Not long.''

''Make an estimate for me,'' said Sir John. ''Would you
say the screams continued during the time it would take a
man to count slowly to a hundred? Two hundred? Three
hundred?''

''I can't be sure,'' said Burnley. ''I never had occasion
to count so high.'' The room, which had been quite silent
up to that moment, exploded into sudden laughter at that.
Burnley looked around, greatly annoyed at his audience.
Then, once Sir John had shouted them down and beaten
his gavel for silence, Burnley said with some show of dignity: ''I would say, sir, that it wasn't near so long as that—
more like a count of fifty and maybe less.''

''Very good. Now, I should like you to tell me the length
of time that elapsed between the time that you first heard
the screams and the time you and the other men, along with

Constable Cowley, managed to beat down the door and gain admittance to the place.''

"You mean, counting like?"

"Yes, Mr. Burnley—counting."

He thought about that a moment or two. "Oh, that would be a high number, it would—fetching the constable, and so on, upwards to a count of three hundred and maybe more. We was not eager to go inside without a proper armed man in our number."

"All right then, continue with your story."

And that he did, sketching in a few grisly details left out before and bringing sighs and shudders from his listeners. He took heart from this and gave a great deal of drama to his account of their meeting with Clayton in the attic room with the dead apprentices. In doing so, he made the mistake of referring to him as "the murderer."

Sir John slammed down his hand sharply on the table before him. "That will do, Mr. Burnley."

"Sir?"

"You will leave the judging to the judges. The man in question has not been tried, has not even been properly charged. His guilt in this matter has yet to be determined."

"But he was standin' right there with his axe in his hand!"

"That will *do!*"

A great hubbub followed this exchange. The riffraff seemed to side with Burnley, for no better reason but that he seemed to be one of them. It took far too long to bring them back to order. Yet at last this was accomplished when Mr. Bailey grabbed up a loud individual sitting nearby and marched him to the door and out of it. The ease with which he accomplished this quietened them all.

At last Sir John resumed, diverting Burnley from further discussion of what he might or might not have seen in that upper room and directing him to account for the disobedience of Constable Cowley's orders.

"Orders, sir?"

"Indeed. His orders that you and the others in your party remain without the premises."

"Well, as it happened, sir, we got to talking, us fellows did, and we thought we might be of service to you and the constables if we was to go in and look about the place for evidence, as you might say."

"And whose idea was this?"

"I couldn't rightly say, sir."

"Was it yours?"

"Oh no, sir. I'm sure it was not mine."

"Just a follower, are you? A tool in the hands of your fellows?"

"As you say, sir."

"Mr. Burnley, were you and the others not searching for the cashbox? Did you consider that material evidence?"

"Uh . . . yes, sir, we did. We reckoned that such a considerable crime as this could only be done for a great sum of money. And if we could find where this . . . uh . . . 'said person' had hid it, we would have helped you establish the reason for the crime. Is that clear, sir?"

"Go on."

"So we looked right hard for it, sir."

"And you found it. Tell us where."

"Well, it was in poor Mr. Crabb's office, it was—in his desk."

"Under lock and key?"

"Well, it was necessary to force the drawer to get it open."

Some snickers were heard from the crowd. Burnley turned and looked indignantly right and left in search of their source. But he was soon called back to his duty by the magistrate.

"And what," asked Sir John, "was used to force the drawer?"

"Uh . . . well . . . an axe, sir."

"Was it the same axe that Constable Cowley took from the individual he has identified for us?"

"It *might* have been at that, sir."

"And if it was, then one of your number went up to the attic to get it from where it had been left."

"True, sir. Aye, it must have been so."

"Who was that man? Who was it disappeared with what appears to have been the murder weapon the moment that the constable returned and surprised you as you carried away the cashbox?"

"We did no such thing! We handed it to the constable the moment we spied him. We was being helpful."

"Albert Burnley, let me tell you something. All in the world that will prevent me from charging you with hindering the investigation of a crime—and attempted robbery, as well—is to hear from you the name of him who disappeared with that axe."

"But I—"

"And I must hear it this moment without further palaver or equivocation."

Burnley was for a long moment struck dumb. His position was indeed not one he relished: to snitch was one thing—all of his class had done it one time or more—but to snitch in open court before a crowd of his fellows was quite another. He looked around him in a distinct state of unease. What was he to say?

"Might I ask something first, Sir John?" he asked at last, quite hopefully.

"You may ask. I cannot give guaranty of my answer."

"What will happen to this hustler who napped the axe?"

The magistrate nodded thoughtfully. "A fair question," said he. "Let us say, nothing—*if* said weapon be surrendered before this day be done."

At that, Burnley brightened. He looked around him, nodding hopefully this way and that as if seeking permission to speak from the onlookers.

"Then," said he, "I seems to remember his name is Rum Ben Tobin."

"And his place of residence?"

"I . . . uh . . . well, sir, of that I'm not quite sure."

"Let me, then, dismiss you not only as a witness but from this very courtroom. Go and find Ben Tobin and inform him of the terms I offer. For while we may not know his place, we know yours, Albert Burnley. And while I intend to honor my bargain with you, if your friend Tobin does not advantage himself of my terms, then it may go ill for you if and when you should appear before me here again. Is this clear?"

"Oh yes, sir."

"Good, then be off on your search."

Burnley lost not a moment but made straight for the door. There he was joined by one whom I then recognized as Harry, his companion of the night before. A ripple of laughter followed them as the two exited hastily.

"Mr. Marsden," said Sir John, "I have not been given the name of the next witness but merely his position. Will you summon him properly?"

With a nod, the clerk rose and consulted the topmost of a sheaf of papers in his hand. "Will Isham Henry please step forward?"

The man who obeyed that summons was quite unknown to me. Tall, dark of hair and complexion, he wore a somber, dour mien. He took his place before Sir John, but neglected to remove his hat. I thought this somewhat disrespectful, but the magistrate, of course, took no notice, and his clerk, though frowning his disapproval, said nothing.

"Your name, sir?" asked Sir John.

"As was announced," said the witness in a deep voice that seemed to suit the rest of him quite well.

"Repeat it, please, for the court record, and state your position."

"I be Isham Henry, and I be a journeyman printer in the employ of Ezekiel Crabb. Or so I was until what was happened last night."

He had a strange manner of speech, slightly archaic, and in a mode that indicated his origins as somewhat northerly. I could not call him direct to mind from my earlier visits to the Crabb establishment. He was not, in any case, the typesetter whose place I had temporarily taken.

"Your address, sir?"

"I have a room in Half Moon Passage."

"You, I take it then, lived apart from your place of employment."

He let forth a deep dark laugh at that, that had the odd

sound of a rumble. "Aye, oh indeed, else I would be dead before you now."

"We would not have that, would we?" said Sir John. "I am told that you came forth wishing to give witness here, but that you are only this day returned to London from a visit to your home in—where was it?"

"Nigh on Nottingham," said he. "I come here, for I knowed there was bad blood between this man John Clayton and Mr. Crabb."

"Is this man Clayton known to you by sight?"

"He is."

"Point him out to Mr. Marsden."

Isham Henry did so, plainly indicating the man seated between Constable Cowley and Chief Constable Bailey. Mr. Marsden took note of it and indicated to Sir John he had done so.

"Now then, what makes you so certain that there was, as you say, 'bad blood' between Mr. Clayton and Mr. Crabb?"

"Everybody knowed it."

"Who is everybody?"

"All who worked for Crabb, or in some wise had to do with the publication of that first book of Clayton's."

"And that includes yourself?"

"Ain't that what I'm sayin'? This Clayton fella grew quite fierce when it was revealed to him the great number of his books was sold, and him receiving just a pittance for to publish it. Threatened Mr. Crabb, he did."

"You heard him do this?"

"Well, I . . ." Isham Henry hesitated.

"With your own ears?"

"It was well discussed amongst us all."

"But you yourself, I take it, were not direct witness to any threat, nor to any rancorous conversations between the two?"

Mr. Henry made no answer to that.

"I shall assume that your silence is intended as a negative response." Sir John waited, but nothing further was forthcoming. "I had been made aware of the great discrepancy between Mr. Clayton's meager reward for writing the book and Mr. Crabb's considerable profit in publishing it, and indeed, as you suggest, there may have been bad blood between them because of this matter. But what you offer, Mr. Henry, is mere hearsay, and as such is not acceptable in this court. I thank you for giving forth that the man in question is John Clayton, which is indeed more than I could get from him. Nevertheless, I fear that we must disregard all else that you have had to say about him.''

Sir John paused, and in that brief space a grumble began from the assembled court crowd.

"You are dismissed, sir.''

Isham Henry looked right and left, as though not quite able to comprehend what had transpired between them. The grumble grew louder as he at last turned and retired to a place kept for him at the rear of the room. Things could have got quite out of hand had not Sir John then shouted out louder still the name that all had waited to hear:

"I call John Clayton to witness.''

There was no immediate response to the summons. All had grown silent of a sudden in expectation of a first long look at him who was even at that moment advertised in the streets as the murderer of the entire Crabb household. He seemed reluctant to display himself. At last, however, he was pulled to his feet and marched forward between Constables Bailey and Cowley to stand before Sir John.

"You delay, sir,'' said the magistrate in a voice most calm. "Let me assure you, however, I call you as a witness and not as a man accused. I wish to know from you what you remember of the events of the night just past.''

"Not meaning the slightest disrespect,'' said Mr. Clayton, "but my hesitation was due to the fact that I was not called in a proper manner.''

His demeanor was altogether altered from the brute nature he had displayed but hours before. From where I sat I could see his face in profile. He was alert, near too alert if that be possible. Which is to say, his face, fine-featured and handsome, seemed unnaturally flushed and keen with nervous excitement. I noticed that his hand, dangling from a coat sleeve far too short, twitched in a motion in which the thumb seemed continually to be counting the four fingers as if to be sure he had them all. Yet his voice remained calm.

"Oh?" said Sir John. "How then? Would you prefer to be summoned as Petrus? You gave that name last night, did you not?"

"What's in a name?" said he, flapping his arms of a sudden in a great shrug of his wide shoulders. "A rose by any other name would smell as sweet."

"Or a knave as foolish," said the magistrate in a tone more severe. "I charge you, sir, give a name to yourself. Are you John Clayton?"

"I am not. I am properly addressed as Eusebius."

"Last night you were Petrus, and now you are Eusebius. What other surprises have you?"

"I have no surprises. I have only sweet reason at my command, and I shall use it, with your kind permission, in defense of John Clayton, for though you say you call him as a witness, I feel around me great anger and a thirst for blood, his blood. But let us not speak of that! No! Too much of that, sir, too much of what is pumped by the heart into the arteries and through the veins—too much of that which leaked and spurted last night!"

An uneasy titter ran through the courtroom crowd. It seemed they were not so much amused by this man Clayton as they were embarrassed in his behalf.

"Whether you are Eusebius, or Clayton, or that rude fellow Petrus, you must tell me of *last night,* and you must tell me now." Having spoken, Sir John set his jaw and waited. I had never before seen him thus in court: his face quite a mask of cold resolve.

Clayton then began a-pacing before he spoke a word; back and forth he went before the judge's bench. The two constables, who had returned to their places, exchanged glances, no doubt wondering if they should allow this impropriety to continue. But at last the witness did speak, and as he did so, he began flailing his arms about in a most impassioned manner.

"There are things," said he, "that must *not* be remembered. Who are we, after all, to enter the past? It is another country. They do things different there! They speak another language. They would communicate as we do, but can only talk in dreams. What are your dreams, sir? Are they of blood? Of hanged men? Do they speak to you so, as—"

"Silence!" Sir John gaveled him down with the great wood mallet he kept at the ready. "If you keep bladdering on so, I shall hold you in contempt of my court."

"And well you might, sir, for indeed I hold this court in contempt. It is neither a court of reason, nor a proper court of lords and ladies, nor could one, for all that, court a maiden here. What good is such a court? I ask. Who could but hold it in contempt?"

"Mr. Clayton," said Sir John, "I believe you are mad."

"The name is Eusebius, if I may remind you, sir, though indeed I speak for him you mentioned. Mad, you say? That is your belief. You are entitled to it, but why should it count for more than mine? I believe John Clayton to be sane—as sane as any man ere I knew."

"Prove it then!" cried Sir John harshly. The room had gone most deathly silent but for his voice. "Multiple murder has been committed in a house not far from here. You were the sole survivor. How came you to survive? It has been given that you were found with the murder weapon in your hand. How came you by it? Did you murder those six in their beds? If not, deny it. Tell your story, man."

"Sir, since you perversely insist upon addressing me as if I were John Clayton, I shall speak for him, if I be allowed. John Clayton is a gentle soul. He has his faults like any other, yet I have known him to weep at the murder of birds by hunters in the field. Such a man as he could never commit the horrible crime you describe. You have my word upon it."

"And you, Eusebius, could you do such deeds?"

A laugh escaped the witness then, one doubtless inspired by anxiety, yet full-throated, almost merry in manner. "I, sir?" said he, having at last calmed himself. "Oh, indeed not. Eusebius speaks with the voice of pure reason. The taking of another's life is the most unreasonable of acts. Therefore, it is proven: Eusebius is incapable of it. That, sir, is a syllogism—a *proof* of reason! *Quod erat demonstrandum.*"

"Indeed," said Sir John, "and what about the fellow I met last night—Petrus by name?"

At that, the man who called himself Eusebius stood quite still, frozen as it were in an attitude of deep consideration. "Petrus I know not so well," said he. "In truth, he troubles me. He obeys not the rule of reason but that of the passions only. He lacks John Clayton's sweet nature, though I cannot believe he would behave in so violent a manner, unless . . ."

"Yes? Continue. Unless . . . ?"

"Unless he was greatly provoked."

"In what way?"

"I cannot say. He has never been thus provoked."

"But am I to believe then that you know nothing of the activities of your friend Petrus during the night just past?"

"He is *not* my friend!" This objection he made most strenuously. And then in a manner that seemed timorous by comparison to the bold way he had spouted his idiocies and impertinences, he added this: "No, sir, I regret to say I know nothing of Petrus and his doings."

Sir John nodded and gave thought to his next words. I noted then, as I had not before, that drops of perspiration stood out on his florid face. With the crowd of people inside that big room, it had become a bit close; yet he had not exerted himself physically, and so I could only suppose that it was the strain of this moment that had brought him to this condition.

"Mr. Clayton, Eusebius, or however you wish to call yourself," said he, "I have borne with you long enough. Since you are unable to answer the questions put to you by me and you give every symptom of madness, as I understand them, I have no choice but to remand you to the Hospital of St. Mary of Bethlehem until—"

A sudden murmur arose from those around me—whisperings of "Bedlam . . . Bedlam!" I had heard of *that* place.

Sir John slammed down his open palm and called for silence. *"Until,"* he then repeated, "when, and if you are capable of responding reasonably. And if, sir, you are shamming, then a stay in that godforsaken place will persuade you, as nothing else can, to cooperate in this inquiry."

There was a terrible to-do among the spectators following Sir John's pronouncement. They had come, the gentry no less than those of the lower orders, to see the "mad poet" sped on his way to the gallows. And they had then been disappointed. It took the exertions of Constable Cowley to clear the courtroom.

As Sir John disappeared into his chambers, followed (as was usual) by Mr. Marsden, I chanced to cross the path of Dr. Samuel Johnson. The lexicographer was making his way toward the door, one of the last to leave because one of the first to arrive.

"Well, boy," said he to me, "what did you think of that?"

"In truth, sir, I know not what to think," said I.

"Your master was very brave to conduct this matter as he did. He will receive censure for it, no doubt, most especially for his decision not to bind that poor fellow for trial, but he did right. Indeed, he did right. That man Clayton is quite mad."

"I have never seen such," said I.

"Nor have I." He moved away. "Good day to you, and give my commendation to Sir John."

Thus he departed, leaving me to dawdle. There was no call for me to report to the magistrate's chambers, no need for me to search out Mr. Marsden to volunteer my services, since he had taken counsel with Sir John and would not be found at his usual desk in the space beyond the strong room. There was but one place for me to go, and that was up the stairs to present myself for duty to Mrs. Gredge. There might still, at this late hour, be pots to wash. There would surely be floors to scrub—though I hoped not to be assigned the stairs, a remarkable hard task even for one with the energy of a thirteen-year-old boy.

And so up I went, dragging a bit for want of sleep, I opened the door to the kitchen and called out in a quiet voice, announcing my presence. Receiving no answer, I assumed she must be off to do her buying for dinner. I sat down at the rough old kitchen table to wait for her return—and promptly fell deep into the arms of Morpheus.

My dreams were troubled and, in the way of dreams, utterly confounding. I cannot, at this distance in time, give a true summary of them, but I do recall that the setting was, for the most part, the village print shop in which my poor, dead father labored so hard to make a success of his cautious venture into commerce. He was there, of course, overseeing my efforts at typesetting, yet so also was Sir John in the rarest sort of guise—or how can that be put more clear?—in a sort of metamorphosis. In one instance, I looked up from the type stand, and there was Sir John, looking with sober approval upon my work. But then he did what I had never seen him do: he reached under his tricorn and untied the black ribbon which covered his blind eyes. As the mask fell, his face became my father's. While this seemed curious, it was not frightening. Yet I was frightened by what followed: The Raker appeared and, with another whose back was always to me, began hauling, one after another, a parade of the dead from the upstairs living quarters I had shared with my father. It was just as he had done in the Crabb house, though he made no jests and gave no leering smiles; and the unwrapped dead were not the same. The body of my mother and little brother, who perished of typhus in Lichfield, were first. They were followed by the wasted corpus of Lady Fielding, who had died of a tumor but weeks before. As she passed, I felt Sir John at my side and looked up to find him with his proper face, silk band in place and copious tears flowing from beneath it. Finally, carried between the Raker and his unknown helper, came the body of my father. His face was, as I had last seen it, half covered with ordure from his pelting in the stocks; yet it was he, unmistakably, and he was unmistakably dead. As he passed, I looked up at Sir John as he looked down at me, and then he placed his hand upon my shoulder. Strangely then, he began to shake it most briskly.

And I came reluctantly awake, with the hand of Mrs. Gredge on my shoulder where I had dreamed Sir John's to be. I was greatly relieved to be returned to the land of the living. So relieved, in fact, that I minded not Mrs. Gredge's screeching exhortation to be up and about and help her in the preparation of dinner. There were potatoes aplenty for me to peel and carrots to chop, as Sir John liked them.

As it happened, Mrs. Gredge herself had been asleep most of the afternoon. She made no secret of it, complaining to me of the weariness she had felt of late. In truth the woman, who was then near seventy years of age, had quite exhausted herself in caring for Lady Fielding during the latter's debilitating and protracted illness. I wonder, looking back, how she had managed it, along with her regular duties as housekeeper and cook.

"I shall be sorry to see you go," said she to me. (Yet she said it in such a grudging manner that I near doubted her words.)

"I fear I have not been as much help to you as I might."

"More than you know," said she. "These old bones don't move around as they once did. Once down on the floor for a fair scrub, I doubt at times I shall ever be able to rise again. If for no more than that, I shall miss you, Jeremy. You're a good scrubber."

I thanked her kindly, then called her attention to the fact that my departure had been somewhat delayed by the death of Ezekiel Crabb. I knew full well that the good woman paid no attention whatever to what went on in the court below, and even less to talk circulated on the streets of the city outside.

"Yes," said she. "Sir John told me of the death of him you had apprenticed to. Pity, I suppose."

And that was all she had to say about that.

The preparation of dinner proceeded apace. Sir John arrived and chose to take his meal with us, as had lately become his custom. He had little to say during the meal;

none of it pertained to the events of the afternoon or the night before. Upon finishing, he congratulated Mrs. Gredge on her preparation of the chop he had just downed right quickly. Then he rose and announced he was early for bed that night and made his way toward the steps to the upper floors. Yet he lingered there, as if struck by a thought.

"Jeremy," said he, "I have something to discuss with you."

"Yes, Sir John," said I, jumping to my feet, ready to follow.

"Yet let it wait a bit. Wash up for Mrs. Gredge. Do what she needs of you, then come to me in my study."

"As you will, sir."

With that, he left us, and I began clearing the table, eager to be done with my tasks so that I might get on to my appointment with Sir John.

"Mind now," spoke Mrs. Gredge from her place at the table, "not so fast. I'll not have none of those dishes broke."

With her cautions, water to heat, and pans to wash, it was near half an hour before I was excused to climb the stairs to the smallish room that served Sir John for a study. The door was open, but the room was unlit. He sat in the dark, as he always did when alone, for what should it matter to a blind man whether it be dark or light?

I knocked lightly upon the door.

"Jeremy? Come in, boy, come in."

I entered, and without much difficulty found the chair set opposite him, with his desk the barrier between us.

"Would you like some light? There is a candle by you, I believe."

"No, sir. I'm quite all right."

"What did you draw from that grotesque display in the courtroom today?"

"I was shocked," said I, "for I have never seen a man in such a state."

"I should never have let him go on so long," said he. "But I thought perhaps in this new guise he would have something to say—anything!—in his own defense."

"Dr. Johnson spoke to me as he left," said I. "He said that you were brave to conduct the matter as you did and could only have sent John Clayton away. He asked me to give to you his commendation."

"He did, did he? Well, I shall remember that when the stones and arrows begin to fly my way. My threats did, in any case, force the delivery of the murder weapon. Albert Burnley brought it in shortly before I left my chambers. He also delivered the apologies of Rum Ben Tobin for the trouble he had caused."

Sir John spoke not a word then for quite some time. I could just make out his form from the dim light that entered through the window. Yet it was his form only that I saw, for the features of his face and their expression were quite hidden from me.

"It was not, however, to discuss this afternoon's proceedings that I called you here, Jeremy," said he at last. "You may have expected something to be discussed in that meeting this morning which was not discussed."

"The meeting with Dr. Johnson? Well . . ."

"Not more than two weeks ago, when we talked about your future, you expressed the strong desire to remain here in my household. Do you still feel so?"

"Oh yes, sir, I *do!*" All my heart was in that answer.

"Two weeks ago, it seemed to me that the right path— the only path—for you to follow was the one you had started on before you came to London. It seemed to me that you were made for the printing trade, for publishing—and what brighter future could a boy with your intelligence and skill with words hope for? I only wanted what was best for you. Please believe that, Jeremy. But it was, perhaps, presumptuous of me to take it upon myself to decide the future of another. That was brought to me in the events of last night. There was, first of all, the awful probability that had you left us for your apprenticeship even a day earlier, you would have been counted the seventh victim in that great killing that took place in the Crabb house. I am not, by even a generous standard, a religious man, but when an omen is given to me I am humble enough to accept it as such.

"Having accepted it," he continued, "I began to reconsider. Among the matters that pertained in this reconsideration was your great help in the Goodhope inquiry: You did everything I asked and then exceeded that. You learned quickly. You showed bravery when the situation demanded it. And indeed you showed courage again last night in driving away those two footpads with your pistol, when I, in my vanity, thought us immune from attack. All this I took into consideration, as I did also your good nature, your helpfulness to Mrs. Gredge, and the way you quite won the heart of my poor, dear Kitty when she was with us. It was against her wishes, I confess, that I sent you off to apprentice yourself to Mr. Crabb. You see the extreme limits of my presumption?

"And so," he concluded, "when I talked with Dr. Johnson today, there seemed no need to ask his aid in finding you another place in the printing trade before I had discussed this with you. And since you still desire to stay, I should be delighted to have you."

I was quite overcome. I managed to stutter out my thanks and started to give assurances of loyalty and my desire to please him in every way. Yet in the dimness of that room, I saw him raise his hand and wave me to silence.

"Consider my invitation and your acceptance as a bond between us. There are no conditions and no period of trial. You are from this day forth a permanent member of my household. You will continue to help Mrs. Gredge. She has grown older of a sudden and needs aid in all manner of ways. At her best she can be difficult. Continue to show forbearance with her. There will also be duties you will perform for me. I have no idea what they will be. They will vary from day to day, perhaps from moment to moment. I invite you to ask questions of me, even challenge me privately when you feel I am seriously in the wrong. Though you are ignorant of much in the way of the world, you have a good mind. I want you to use it."

Having said all this, he lapsed into a silence so long that

I thought he might have drifted off to sleep where he sat. But then, as I rose quietly from my chair, he spoke up again: "We must get you some new clothes. Mrs. Gredge tells me those you wear have grown shabby."

THREE

*In which I take my place in
Sir John's household and
rescue a lady in distress*

The days passed. Spring had blossomed forth in its full glory—even in London, in which flowers bloom in dirt patches and back gardens, and the trees leaf forth for the most part only in those parks and lanes which are habituated by the gentry. It was spring everywhere. I felt it in my life. It was as though it had begun again. Imagine, reader, a boy such as myself—orphaned, virtually penniless, come to London bare of expectations with only his hopes to buoy him—such a boy thrust before a magistrate, falsely accused, rescued by the keen judgment of that great magistrate and now installed as a member of his household! For the first time in weeks I felt that I had a future. Though I could not foresee what precisely it might be, the rest of my life seemed now to open up before me like some great adventure on which I was now about to begin.

In truth, however, life continued for me at Number 4 Bow Street about as I had known it in the past few weeks. I ran errands at the bidding of Sir John, for the most part of an inconsequential nature. Mrs. Gredge continued to avail herself of my talents as a "good scrubber," and more and more she made use of me to do her buying at the greengrocers and butchers of Covent Garden nearby. I was, in fact, on just such an expedition when a chance meeting occurred that foreshadowed another, more momentous one days later.

Where but at the butcher stall of Mr. Tolliver, to which I was introduced by Katherine Durham, should I happen to spy her? I had met the good Widow Durham through Sir John, who had seen her son into the Navy; grateful to him was she for that and continually inquired after him at our meetings while buying in Covent Garden. She was then engaged in pleasant conversation with the proprietor himself, having made a purchase, and seemed about to leave. I held back, not wishing to interrupt; then she made to go and in turn spied me.

"Jeremy!" cried she. "How well met! I had only moments past heard from Mr. Tolliver that you have become his regular customer. How long has it been since I brought you here?"

"Oh," said I, "three weeks—a month, perhaps. Much has happened since then."

"I note that for one you've acquired a new coat—and that shirt also appears to be new. You look most handsome."

I swelled a bit at her praise even as I thanked her. "I've been given a few new things by Sir John, as befits my new state, Mrs. Durham."

"And what is that, Jeremy?"

"He has accepted me as a member of his household." I meant to make it sound solemn and important, for such it was to me, yet it so excited me to announce it to one outside my immediate ken that I fair blurted it out.

"How wonderful—and how fitting," said she, "but—" And here she frowned quite prettily. "Do I not recall that you were set for the printing trade?"

"Indeed I was. In fact, apprenticeship papers had been signed with Mr. Ezekiel Crabb."

Her hand went to her mouth in a gesture of shock. She spoke not a word for a moment. Then: "Good God! That horror in Grub Street—thank the Almighty you were saved from it."

"But narrowly," said I. This, reader, you know to be true enough, yet I confess I put a bit of drama into those two words, rolling my eyes heavenward and punctuating them with a sigh. I wished to be pitied. Thus in so short a time had I begun to lose my earnest innocence.

A sudden tumult of shouting broke out some distance away. We two turned to find its cause and saw a group of men and a few women, most of them dressed in black and deep gray, calling out in unison to the crowd passing through Covent Garden. Though loudly they shouted, their manner of speech was indistinct and some of the Garden crowd called back just as loud, so that it was near impossible to know just what was being shouted. Yet there was such enthusiasm in their manner, such strength of purpose in their voices, that it seemed certain to me that their message, whatever it be, was of a religious nature.

"Who are those people who make so great a din?" I asked Mrs. Durham. "I have seen them before, I believe, though at a distance and not near so many."

"I fear," said she, "that a plague of preachers has descended upon us. They seem to be here in this corner of the Garden every day at this time—oh, I have seen them other places, as well."

"Are they Methodist?"

"Oh no, no, nothing so conventional. It is as though they came to us from the last century—Ranters, Levelers, all certain that the time of Apocalypse was upon us. They call themselves the Brethren of the Spirit. They have lately arrived here from somewhere."

"The Midlands?"

"No, the North American colonies, I believe."

"And they have come to preach?"

"Clearly," said she, "in order to save Londoners from perdition. No doubt we are all in need of salvation, Jeremy, I most of all, yet what they preach is so, well . . ." She paused, unable for a moment to continue. "To give them credit, though, they have opened a shelter to house and feed the most wretched of the poor. They do good works. And that, to me, is the test."

She addressed me as she would an adult, and I liked her for it. Yet, as sometimes happens between adults, our exchange seemed to hang at that point, as she stared distractedly at the dark-garbed group and the unruly audience they had attracted.

Raising my voice above the continuing din, I endeavored to get us unstuck: "I noted you present at Lady Fielding's funeral."

"What? Oh . . . yes, of course. I could not but share in the dear man's sorrow. I sent a note of sympathy to Sir John."

"He received so many. We work together, answering them all."

"Yes, well, I understand. But Jeremy, I must away. Remember me to him, if you will."

"Goodbye, then."

She moved away with a quick smile. Yet as I watched her go, she threw a hard glance at those who had interrupted us, gave a shake of her handsome head, and then hurried on.

I stepped up to Mr. Tolliver's stall, but then found I must needs consult the list Mrs. Gredge had dictated, to be reminded what it was I had come to buy there.

Whilst out and about, doing errands for Sir John, I became involved in another portentous event, which gave me a shock and near took my life. It made plain to me that London was a dangerous place in ways I had never supposed.

As I mentioned in passing to the Widow Katherine Durham, Sir John had made it his task to respond to each and every message of condolence sent to him upon the death of his wife. In this considerable work, I served both as amanuensis and messenger. He took an hour or so each morning, yet in that time he would manage to dictate no more than four, since in each he tried to make some personal reference to the message received, or to his relationship to the addressee. It took some thought on his part and often a bit of ingenuity. His prodigious memory served him well.

As for myself, I took down his halting words and was usually left with a sheet replete with blottings-out and emendations, and so it was then my duty to make decent copies of that day's production and present them to him for his scrawled signature. Then came delivery, which I liked much better. My journeys here and there with these letters of response took me all over London. They added greatly to my knowledge of the streets, alleys, and lanes of the great city. I soon began to put together a sort of map in my head, taking shortcuts when it suited me but sometimes returning by the longest route, so that I might take in all that was to be seen along the way.

And there was much there to catch the roving eye of a boy of thirteen. I discovered, for instance, that our particular part of Westminster, namely the parish of Covent Garden, was filled to bursting with single women seeking accompaniment. Just where it was they wished to be taken was then something of a mystery to me, though when they addressed me direct, "bed" was often mentioned. Since these walks of mine took place in the daytime, it seemed to me passing strange that what these women and girls offered, and sought to be paid for, were naps in the daytime. Yet here I play the fool somewhat, for I confess that I had come to understand, even in my imperfect way, what it was went on between men and women, and that whatever that something was, it took place between the covers. I was, in short, not so naive that it did not thrill me a bit in some mysterious way to be solicited by these women, though in truth I never sought them out.

I well recall the surprise that awaited me when I delivered the missive Sir John had addressed to Peg Button, prostitute and probable pickpocket. She had written Sir John as a child might, in big block letters, regretting, as she put it, that "his wyf dide and lef him." She went on to say that she "knowd abt dine cause it took her ma a teribl long time to get it don." To this, Sir John had replied, in part, "Indeed the worst of Lady Fielding's departure was its length. Neither I nor she would have had her suffering protracted so, life in pain being not at all precious. You,

having watched your mother so long in mortal illness, will
know how helpless I felt, though my dear wife's pain was
eased toward the end by means of physic." And so on—a
right honest reply, his was, from one sufferer to another.

When I sought to convey it to the address from whence
her message had come, I found that Mistress Button had,
in a manner of speaking, gone up in the world. She certainly would have reckoned her new station at Mrs. Gould's
infamous bagnio in the Little Piazza an ascent from her
previous life on the streets. I was admitted by a woman of
color in servant's dress, yet large as any man. In fact, when
she spoke to me, inquiring of my business there, I was not
altogether sure she was *not* a man, so deep was her voice.
The name of Sir John Fielding admitted me at once, and
once inside, I had but to display the letter to Peg Button to
have her brought down from one of the upstairs rooms to
the parlor. There she greeted me and asked me to read the
letter aloud to her. "I ain't never got one before," said she
with innocent pride to her sisters in the parlor, all of whom
were dressed, as she, in shifts and less. And so, to this
troupe of lounging odalisques I gave forth the contents,
which I knew well myself—so well, in fact, that at each
full stop I was able to look up from the text and survey the
room, then return to my place without confusion. It was,
all in all, an impressive reading. They applauded their appreciation at the conclusion. I bowed and handed the letter
to Mistress Button. Though they begged me to stay for
refreshment and conversation, I reluctantly declined, saying
truthfully that I had other letters to deliver.

None of the others was delivered to quite such colorful
circumstances. Some, in fact, were brought to places of
commerce and to grand houses of the gentry and aristoc-
racy. Mr. Alfred Humber received his where, it seemed, he
was always to be found: at Lloyd's Coffee House. There
he treated me to a cup of his favorite brew, for I could not
refuse it. To the East India Company I journeyed to deliver
two of Sir John's messages of thanks: to Sir Percival
Peeper, who gave me a shilling for my trouble; and to his
young lieutenant, Mr. Roger Redding, who had assisted at

the inquiry into the Goodhope affair (a penny from him). In short, I saw London, high and low, nor did I ever see it so high or so low as I did on that fateful day to which I earlier referred.

It was a windy day, threatening rain. There had been a run of proper March weather in that first week of May, uncommon but not unknown. For two days previous, great dark clouds had been scudding in swiftly from the east, bringing rain squalls. As messenger for Sir John, I had been caught and drenched in my new suit of clothes early on my rounds, so that I had no choice but to return to Bow Street and don the old duds I had worn on my flight to London. I later had reason to be glad I had worn them—though not at first, for my next delivery took me to the residence of William Murray, Earl of Mansfield, Lord Chief Justice of the King's Bench.

It was by no means a long hike to his considerable abode, for it was in Bloomsbury Square, just beyond Covent Garden. The wind was at my back for the distance, and a great wind it was, propelling me forward nearly at a run. From time to time I glanced ruefully at the sky, for I had no wish to be drenched again. Yet though there were clouds, and they moved as swiftly as before, they were white and billowing as full as sails on a three-master.

With all this, it took me no time to arrive at Bloomsbury Square and not much more than that to find the proper house. It took me much longer, however, to get inside—in fact, I never did so. I rang the doorbell with one hand and held my tricorn hard on my head with the other. The door was opened by a man in butler's livery. He was larger in every way than Lord Goodhope's Potter; it would be quite impossible to imagine such a man as he listening at the keyhole.

"Yes, boy," said he, "what is it?"

"I have a letter for Lord Mansfield."

"Give it me. I shall see he gets it."

It seemed to me then that butlers, ushers, and others of their kind all over the realm must regard themselves as the last line of defense for their masters against the world outside. I determined to make an attempt to breach the ramparts.

"The letter is from Sir John Fielding. It is of a personal nature."

"Oh?"

"He prefers me to lay the letter in the hands of him to whom it is addressed." I fair shouted this out, for the wind swept hard across the unsheltered porch.

"No doubt," said he, "yet here we have a problem, for Lord Mansfield is not at the moment present. Now, you have your choice of waiting on the porch where you stand and handing it to him upon his arrival, or leaving it with me. You may, however, have a long wait, since I have no idea when he will return, and the wind may make you most uncomfortable. It might also rain again."

"There is a bench behind you in the vestibule. Why could I not wait there?"

He looked me up and down in a manner most skeptical. "Because, boy," said he at last, "you are far too ragged to be admitted here."

I seethed, seeking within me the wit to puncture his self-assurance; yet I found nothing there sufficient to the task.

"I shall wait for him here," said I.

"As you like."

And with that, he shut the door upon me.

I cannot say exactly how long I waited; mere minutes it was. I put my back to the wind and held my place against the iron rail, my collar up and my shoulders raised. I shivered and shuddered there, until at last I admitted to myself the futility of my gesture. Having thus made the admission, I did the reasonable thing and rang the doorbell once more.

The butler reappeared in a moment. He could not have been far away.

"Yes, boy?"

Making no further argument, I dug the letter to Lord Mansfield out of my pocket and handed it over. He took it with a curt nod and set about to close the door as I backed down the stairs.

"I have better clothes than these!" I yelled rudely at him, determined to have the last word.

Yet it was his to have. "Good," said he. "Wear them, and we shall then see." And then he shut the door with a sharp bang.

I left in such a state of agitation that I gave little thought to where I was headed. I simply held down my hat, clenched the collar of my coat, and hurried onward into the wind—until I realized my lack of proper direction. I sought the shelter of an arched doorway and pulled out the day's last letter and studied the uncertain address noted upon it, together with Mr. Marsden's equally uncertain directions. With a sigh, I stepped forth back into the wind and began the journey, which took me to the other side of Covent Garden and into another world entirely.

It was a curiosity to me when first I came to London, and still is such today, how near the grand residences of the rich stand to the most squalid dwellings of the poor. There is untold wealth cheek by jowl with miserable poverty: no wonder the policing of these parishes proved so difficult even then for Benjamin Bailey's men, the local constables, and the watchmen. Footpads and burglars could do their dirty work under the cover of night, often no more than a street or two away, then quickly disappear into the warrens and dark alleys they called home.

Thus it was that it took me no great while to move from Bloomsbury Square to an area near Chandos and Bedford streets commonly called a "rookery," where all manner of queer birds flocked. Mr. Marsden had noted on the envelope that I was to look in "the Caribbees," which was how this district was called. To this he appended a bit of advice borrowed from the Bible: "Seek and ye shall find." Nothing very helpful there.

She whom I sought I remembered well from my first day in London when, gulled by an independent thief-taker, I stood accused of theft before one then unknown to me, Sir John Fielding. Having been discharged by him and remanded to the custody of the court, I had then waited as the magistrate heard his last case of the day. It involved a

debt owed by Moll Caulfield, a pushcart vendor, to her
greengrocer supplier, a debt settled by Sir John himself. I
had seen the woman a couple of times afterwards in Covent
Garden, as she returned from her rounds, a somewhat dole-
ful woman, not elderly but seeming so. I recall her being
addressed as "Widow Caulfield," though she made no
mention of her state in her letter to Sir John; hers was brief,
simple, and quite touching: "I seen the grief writ on yr
face, and it right pained me to see a good man like yrself
brought so low. Take heart in the words of Our Savior: 'To
day shalt thou be with me in paradise.' So spake He to
Lady Fielding, and so shall He speak one day to you. You
shall join her there, rest assured." In his response, Sir John
joined in her confident expectations for Lady Fielding's salvation, thanked her for her hopes for his own, and blessed
her for her concern and kindness.

This was the Moll Caulfield I searched for once I arrived
at the crossing of Chandos and Bedford streets. I asked after
her, shouting my questions against the wind, to all who
seemed local to the area. Some knew her as "the pushcart
woman," others were ignorant, and the most were quite
indifferent. It grew late in the afternoon, and Mrs. Gredge
would want me home for my usual dinnertime duties. I
wondered would I ever find the Widow Caulfield that
windy day. But just then it was that I found one who knew
her and knew well where she lived.

The person in question was one like Moll Caulfield herself, a pushcart vendor. Having sold out her wares, she was
plodding home when I detained her and asked the question
I had put to so many others.

"Aye," said the old dame. "I knows her. We're chums,
we are."

"And do you know, then, where it is she makes her
home?"

"Home, is it? Well, I know where the poor dear keeps
her cart and has her pallet, but 'home' is too grand a name
for it—for mine as well, for all that. But come along now,
I'll show you."

And show me she did, while telling me all the while of

their friendship, their reading of Scripture together of a Sunday, with a few hints, as well, of their separate struggles to survive. We kept our heads close together as we talked so as to be heard above the rushing of the wind. In no time, it seemed, we came to St. Martin's Lane. She took me a bit down that infamous way in which no less than Benjamin Bailey himself had recently been wounded in a late-night affray. We stopped before an imposing edifice—imposing yet rickety.

"She lives in there, she does," said she.

It was an ancient, wooden court building, built along the lines of a galleried inn of the kind seen in larger towns all along the highways of England. From the look of it, this one was built well back in the last century, or perhaps in the one before it. There were three floors to the place—but no, four, if one counted the gables looking out through the roof, each one an attic room. Looking around me, I estimated there must be a hundred people living here—or more like twice that number.

"But where?" I asked Moll Caulfield's friend. "Where is she here?"

"All right, my lad," said she. "You turn to right as you go inside the gate, and you goes up the first stairs you come to—up to the first floor above the ground floor. Moll pulls her cart up those stairs every day but Sunday. Then you go to the third door, right near the corner it is, and then you give a good, stout knock upon it, for that be Moll's door. Only mind me in this," said she, suddenly grown most serious. "Mind you do not stay long, for it will soon grow dark, and it will not do to have you here after dark."

"You have my thanks," said I. "I could not have found this place without you."

"Just tell old Moll that Dotty set you right," she shouted back at me.

"I shall!"

And with that, I left her, waving my goodbye and turning through a wide space where once a gate must have hung.

The stairs she described stood half exposed to the gusty wind. I looked around me ere I started up them, and found that all manner of debris from the old building had blown down from the floors above and piled in the courtyard—shingles, shutters, broken glass, whole sections of railing. As I observed, a chimney pot and a great armful of shingles came sailing past me and crashed quite near me. With that, I sought the shelter of the stairs.

Yet found no shelter there, for open as they were to the wind, the stairs swayed dangerously beneath my feet as I climbed. Buffeted by the wind, I near lost my balance at one point, grabbed for the railing—and found it missing, grabbed again and saved myself with a piece of it that had not broken free. Thus I made it to Moll's floor—yet again found no ease there, for the balcony down which I made my way shook near as bad. In truth, reader, the whole building shook. I saw it move quite visibly, the very walls giving out and in with the great gusts of the wind, like the irregular breathing of some huge animal.

I reached Moll Caulfield's door in something of a panic, experiencing those symptoms of dread which all feel when put in fear for their lives. My direst dread was confirmed when I saw residents on this floor and below throw open their doors and flee. One pushed past me as I banged hard upon the Caulfield door, calling her name. I banged again, and at last it came open. The poor woman stood transfixed with terror, eyes wide, head turning this way and that.

"Moll Caulfield," cried I at her, "you must come away. This place may collapse!"

I grabbed at her wrist and made to pull her through the door. Yet she resisted. At the same time, I was given a bump as two more tenants pushed past me for the stairs.

"But I cannot go without my cart!"

I saw it just behind her. Perhaps she was making to leave with it when I came knocking on her door.

"Go!" said I. "I shall take the cart."

Only with that promise did she allow herself to be pulled over the threshold. I reached in and grabbed it and followed her down the balcony way, which seemed then to be shaking even more fearsomely than before. A window burst, scattering shards of glass before us, thus making the way even more treacherous than before.

And so we reached the stairs, where I was faced with a problem I could not have anticipated. I had been pulling the cart, which was light enough and moved well on its wooden wheels. Yet it seemed dangerous to try the stairs in this way; I feared I might lose control of the thing. At the top of the stairs, she looked back at me, as if asking for instruction. I signaled her to proceed as I began to turn the cart about. She went on bravely enough, and I followed with her halfway down, pushing the cart before me. The stairs yawed left and right. I could but barely keep my own balance; managing the cart made it near impossible. Then, as I saw Moll Caulfield reach the ground, I was bumped from behind and pushed aside by a large woman near crazed by fear, who ran before me. I teetered dangerously. I hung on to what was left of the railing with one hand and to the cart with the other. Almost slowly then, whatever rotten and flimsy foundation it was that held the stairs gave way completely, and I saw the stairs before me begin to crumble forward. I lost my footing as the step disappeared from beneath my foot, lost my hold upon the cart, and as if in a dream sailed out and down ten feet or more to the courtyard below.

Had it been paved, I might not have landed so well. Had I been the age I am now, I might have broken a bone or two. Yet as it was, I came through the fall right enough, yet Moll Caulfield's cart did not fare so well. While I went out and away from the stairs, the cart went under. Planks, rails, deals, and boards fell on top of it. And as I recovered myself, picking myself up from where I had fallen, I saw poor Moll frantically throwing off debris from the fallen staircase that she might recover her means of livelihood. I went to her, thinking to help, then happened to look up and saw that the balcony above her was swaying in the same dangerous way that the stairs had. I reached for her.

"Moll! Come away!"

But she shook me off. "I cannot! My cart!"

And with that, she uncovered it, and we both saw that it

had been quite destroyed by the burden of wood that had landed atop it. She rose to her full stature, which was somewhat less than mine, and cast me the most baleful look e'er I had seen on a human face before.

Then I took her by the hand firmly and pulled her away, and not a moment too soon, for a moment later a great piece of the balcony came tumbling down where she had stood. But that was just the beginning. Large parts of the roof followed—a whole chimney, a gable. It looked to me as if the whole structure was in danger of collapse.

"We must away from here!" I shouted at her.

She, having lost her cart, was quite submissive. I led her toward the gateway as fast as she would go, as section after section of the old building began to tumble down. As I looked back last, having pushed her through the old gate hole where she joined others, I saw a great piece of her floor give way, and with it the little place where she made her modest home. But she was there behind me as well, looking over my shoulder. She saw it all.

"Oh," said she, "what shall I do? What shall I do?"

And still the old structure tumbled. We watched, now a great group of us, as the wind wreaked further havoc, separating timber from timber, nails from wood, and down, down it went into the courtyard.

At last there seemed to come an end to it. Men behind me surged forward. I was carried along with them. They began digging through the wreckage. Was it for bodies we were searching? Survivors? I listened for moans or cries for help but heard nothing. Then I saw that it was goods they were after—pots, pans, bedding, clothes, whatever might be salable. There were a few women joining in the search, as well. Yet it was the men who pushed and scrambled, as still debris dislodged by the wind rained down from above. They were as coastal wreckers pillaging a ship caught on a reef. Each had begun his pile of salvage. Disagreements erupted as to what belonged to whom. I was pushed aside not once but twice.

"Go away, boy," one said to me. "This is man's work."

And so I decided that indeed I would go away and see

what I could do to help poor Moll Caulfield. I found her where I had left her, though now great tears streamed down her cheeks. It was not the wind that had set them flowing.

"It seems," said I to her, "that there is little to be done, little to be saved."

"Aye," said she. " 'Tis no longer even safe to go in there." Then she turned to me and, as if wondering for the first time, asked, "Who are you that came to fetch me from my place when it was about to tumble down?" She brushed away her tears with her sleeve and sniffed a good, loud sniff.

I took but a moment to explain that I had come from Sir John Fielding with a letter in response to her message of condolence. I produced it from my pocket, surprised that, though wrinkled and besmirched, it had not been lost in all that had transpired. She took it from me and held it absently, not bothering to inspect its contents. I told her I had been directed to her dwelling by her friend Dotty.

"Ah yes, Dotty," said she. "We read Scripture together. She's a good old girl."

"I . . . I'm sorry I lost your cart."

"Oh, I do not blame you. You did what you could. I saw. But . . ." And here she hesitated most pitiably. "But what am I to do? I have no cart, no place to sleep, nothing. What *am* I to do?"

"Could you stay with Dotty?"

"She has her daughter's child with her. There is bare enough room for the two of them."

"But . . ." Then, rather than argue with her, I gave some thought to it and remembered something that Katherine Durham had told me a few days past. And of a sudden, my mind was made up.

"Is there anything you can claim as your own in there?" I asked.

"I would be afraid to try."

"Then come with me, Moll Caulfield, and we shall see what can be done."

We set off together toward Covent Garden. The wind, having done its worst, began to abate somewhat. By the time we reached the wide piazza, it blew only half as strong as before. Yet it now grew dark; the buyers were few, and the hucksters and merchants were closing their stalls. I knew it had grown late, far later than my expected time of arrival at Number 4 Bow Street. Yet I was determined to do what I could for this woman who had just lost everything she had.

I saw the group I sought at the far end of the Garden and together we walked to them. Dark-garbed as before and easily recognized, yet no longer engaging in their somewhat eerie practice of preaching in chorus, they now lifted their voices in song, singing together a hymn which was quite unfamiliar to me. At this late date, though I was to hear it sung again, I can recall but a bare few lines of it:

> *Brethren of the Spirit, we*
> *Shall bring to all Good News*
> *And prophesy what sure must be:*
> *The conversion of the Jews.*

It seemed to me then, and has ever after, a strange concern for Christians. Yet little I thought of it at that moment, for my mind was concentrated upon the problem at hand.

I waited respectfully until they finished, with the pathetic Moll at my side. Around us were just a few stragglers from the stalls, idlers, and skeptics who came, paused, and went, taking what was offered so earnestly by the six men in black and the two women in gray as mere entertainment.

At last the singers concluded their song and made ready to leave. I tugged the sleeve of him who was nearest me. He withdrew his arm so hasty that one might have thought I had done him injury.

Yet certain of my mission, I said what I intended: "Sir, are you the leader? And if not, could you direct me to him?"

He stammered something and seemed for some reason quite unable to speak. I had spoken up loud and clear. The others had heard. All eyes, it seemed to me, went to one man, the most arresting among them. Though smaller in stature than all but the women, his face was handsome in an ascetic manner. His eyes, a clear, near-colorless blue, seemed almost to shine, even in the fading light. He stepped forward and looked me up and down.

"We have no leader," said he to me. "We are all brethren, equal in the sight of the Lord."

"But perhaps you can speak for the rest," I suggested.

The hint of a smile flickered on his face. "Perhaps I can," said he.

In brief, I explained what had happened—the collapse of the building, Moll Caulfield's escape, the loss of her pushcart and all else that she possessed.

Having listened, he turned to Moll. "Is all this true?" he asked her.

"Aye," she said, "all of it, except he left out that it was him who took me from that place and made a brave try to save my cart. Took a nasty fall for it, he did."

Then he turned to me: "And what business had you there? Did you, too, live in that den of thieves and cutthroats upon which the Lord hath made his judgment? Oh, we heard the great crash as it came down and saw the rush of the crowd to get there, and we rejoiced, reckoning it an answer to our prayers that the Lord might aid us in the great cleansing of this foul city of London. Yea, but only the beginning of our mighty work. Are you, too, a thief?"

"No, sir, I am *not*," said I, all indignant. "Nor is Moll Caulfield. I had come to deliver a letter to her."

"Yet she lived with thieves."

"And the Lord spared her. She is a good Christian."

"You argue well," said he. "Yet why do you come to us?"

"I had heard that you people in black kept a shelter for the very poor. Moll can work again as soon as she has a new cart. I had thought you might give her shelter till then. But evidently, sir, I thought wrong. Come along, Moll," said I, taking her hand. "Let us look elsewhere."

"Nay, go not so swift," said he. "It is true we have such a place, and we should be happy to give food and a roof to your Moll whilst she may need it."

"And where is this place?" I asked, made bold by my success.

"Why do you ask?"

"So that I might visit her."

He hesitated a moment. "Oh, Half Moon Passage," said he at last. "You have but to ask there, for it is well known. But let me put a question to you, young man. You said you had come to deliver a letter to her. Who was the sender of that letter?"

Though it was none of his affair, pride made me answer: "It was from Sir John Fielding, magistrate of the Bow Street Court." Then I added, all puffed as a pouter pigeon, "I am a member of his household."

"Ah," said he, "and why did you not offer her John Fielding's hospitality? Charity begins at home."

I had a ready answer to that, for I had thought it through on the walk with Moll to Covent Garden. "I could not offer what was not mine to give," said I. "I am a member of the household and not its head. But if you prefer, I shall take her to him."

"Nay, nay, again well argued. These are unusual circumstances. I wished only to understand them better." And then to Moll Caulfield: "Are you ready, then? For we are set to leave."

"As ready as I shall be," said she.

They organized themselves, and I detained Moll a moment. "Are you content with this? Something will be done for you, I'm sure."

She sighed. "At the moment I am a pauper, and paupers ain't meant to be choosers."

With that, she joined the procession, taking a place with the gray-clad women, who trailed a few feet behind the men in black as they set off toward Half Moon Passage. Just as she disappeared into the dark, she turned to give me a wave of her hand and called out something which was lost in the wind; it was, doubtless, her thanks.

Now even the twilight had faded. I fair ran for Bow Street, hoping that my tale would suffice, yet sure I had done the right thing.

• • •

Sir John seemed satisfied that indeed I had done so. Though Mrs. Gredge made a great to-do, squawking and screeching and scolding from the moment I stepped inside the door, he quietened her with a sharp word and listened judiciously, hand to chin, as I told him in detail of all that had happened from the moment I left the residence of Lord Mansfield. I did not dramatize, for there was no need, the events themselves being so grand that they needed no heightening. Even Mrs. Gredge was caught up in my account.

When he had heard me through, he considered for a moment and asked, "These people . . . these Brethren . . . they seemed like decent folk to you?"

"In general, yes," said I, "but a little strange."

"Oh? In what way?"

"Well, the one who spoke for them seemed to take great delight in the collapse of that old building, believing all who lived there to be thieves. I had to convince him that Moll Caulfield was not one of them."

"He was right enough. The place does have a bad reputation. Or it did. What was his name, him who spoke for the rest?"

I was struck quite dumb for a moment, for I had not bothered to learn it. Though ashamed and embarrassed at my omission, I had no choice but to confess it: "I . . . I failed to get his name, Sir John. I'm sorry."

"Details, Jeremy, details—don't neglect them."

"I did learn the place they reside and maintain the shelter for the poor, however. It is on Half Moon Passage."

"Half Moon, is it?" He gave a grunt and considered for a moment. "Well, drop by there in a day or two and see how Moll is getting on. We should be able to raise a little money to help her. Assure her of that. Also, give me some estimation of the place they keep. I know not why the city of London cannot take better care of its indigent. Why must the greater part of such work be left to these half-mad zealots who are so sure of God's will in all things? I have heard something of this new bunch. They have decided to save all London, but have set up particular to preach in Covent

Garden, the Haymarket, and in various locations in East London. They are an odd sect, I am told—fond of speaking in chorus."

"It does indeed have a strange effect," said I.

"No doubt," said he. "Ah, well, they should do to keep poor Moll together for as many days as it takes to get her back on her feet. The old girl wishes to work, which is more than can be said for most of the layabouts, beggars, and thieves in Westminster."

With that, he turned and climbed up the stairs to his study, which I had come to think of as more in the nature of his thinking room.

Mrs. Gredge fed me well that night. Though the meat was cold, as were the vegetables, she produced a bit of bread, and for a sweet poured it all over with bee's honey.

And so to the next day, which went at first as many had of late—letters taken in dictation, fair copies made and signed, and then delivered. Since the weather was not near as bad—only one brief shower, which I managed to avoid, and little wind to speak of—I hastened through those of my tasks with time to spare. Having hoped to spend the time saved in attendance at the Bow Street Court, as was my wont, I was somewhat disappointed to hear from Mrs. Gredge that a letter awaited Sir John at the coach post bureau. I was to claim it and bring it to him forthwith.

I set out, knowing the way, for I had already fetched letters from there, sent to him by his sister in Bath. I chose the common route, cutting diagonally across Covent Garden, mixing through the crowd yet moving purposefully along, for I was not one to dawdle on such an errand.

Thus was I perhaps not paying sufficient attention as I passed near the corner of the Garden which the Brethren of the Spirit had made their own, for though I was quite near, I did not even look their way until the commotion began. There was sudden laughter and a few cries of indignation from their spectators and a repeated unison chant from the Brethren: *"Jezebel! Jezebel! Jezebel!"* I pushed through the bystanders and beheld a woman being most fearfully abused by them. She was not one of their number but far more gaudily dressed—but fashionably so. Her back was to me, as I saw them push her between them to and fro to the rhythm of their chant—"*Jezebel! Jezebel!*" And then the poor woman fell and tried to scramble away, much to the amusement of the crowd, and I saw she was none other than Katherine Durham.

As the men in black bent to pummel her, I dove to help the poor woman to her feet. I interposed my thin body between them and her, and in the course of that, took a few cuffs on my back—though nothing of great moment. But then, suddenly, they stopped, and I heard a great shuffling retreat behind me. Heaving the Widow Durham up, I found she could bare stand on her left foot. I managed to look about then, and saw that the Brethren had been driven back by a large and powerful man in a bloody apron who bran-dished a meat cleaver. It was our butcher, Mr. Tolliver. He had rescued us both.

Tears coursed down her cheeks, spoiling her rouge. Her hair was in a tumble. Her dress was muddied, and in one place ripped. She seemed quite beside herself, yet she rec-ognized me.

"Oh, Jeremy," said she, "thank you."

"It is us both who should thank Mr. Tolliver."

I pointed. She looked and nodded as he came back to us.

"Ah, Katherine," said he, "how be ye?"

"I will survive, Mr. Tolliver. We are in your debt."

"He's a good lad, he is, how he jumped in to help."

Though I was not indifferent to his praise, I was at that moment scanning that black-clad group, looking for the man to whom I had talked the day before. I found him absent. In some vague way, I found that reassuring. Surely he would not be responsible for such behavior. Yet I was quite taken aback to see Moll Caulfield among the women dressed in gray. She looked wide-eyed, near as frighted as I had seen her in the door of her little room, when our eyes met. She pointed to herself, then shook her head vigorously, signaling to me that she had had no part in what had hap-pened. I nodded my understanding.

"Jeremy," said Mr. Tolliver, "can you get Mrs. Durham home? I cannot leave my stall."

"I shall have to lean on you," said she to me, "for I fear my ankle is quite destroyed."

"I should be happy to help," said I.

And so we started forth. The mob, seeing that their entertainment was done, had drifted away. The Brethren, too, had organized themselves for an early departure. Saying our grateful goodbye to Mr. Tolliver, Katherine Durham and I set out in the direction of Berry Lane, as she advised me.

She leaned heavily upon me. I circled her shoulder with my arm. Together, as some three-legged beast, we made our way slowly but steadily up King Street toward Bedford. We attracted a bit of attention. Though I paid no mind to the gawkers, they seemed to worry her a bit.

"I'm distressed that you should have witnessed that," said she, "but glad you came along."

"And Mr. Tolliver."

"Indeed Mr. Tolliver."

We limped along together for a bit in silence.

Then, thinking to explain my tardy effort to help, I said to her, "I did not arrive until just when they knocked you down."

"Then you were not there when I fell to shouting at them? Oh, I attacked them proper, asked them who they were to judge, demanded to know what a poor woman was to do when she had no trade, no means. Do they think we would choose this?"

Though I did not fully understand, her anger stirred me greatly. I wished that I had had Mr. Tolliver's meat cleaver with which to threaten them. I wished that I had hit back. Most of all, I wished I had not entrusted Moll Caulfield to their care.

Thus we came to her little place on Berry Lane, not far from Benjamin Bailey's residence with the Widow Plunkett. Along the way, Mrs. Durham gave it as her opinion that her ankle was not broken but merely sprained. She swore that it was beginning to loosen up a bit, though I do not think she could have managed the ascent of the stairs without my help. Yet manage it she did, and stood on one foot to unlock her door, as well.

Making to leave, I told her, "I shall see Sir John knows of this."

"Do you think it wise?" said she. "I would not have him know I had been made such a public spectacle."

"Well, perhaps not." How was I, a boy of thirteen, to comprehend such matters?

"I shall leave it in your hands." She hesitated but a moment. "Goodbye, Jeremy. I am more in your debt than you shall ever know." And then she hobbled inside. I eased the door shut after her and hurried off to the coach post bureau.

Though put off my course somewhat by my trip to Berry Lane, I found my way right enough, collected the letter to Sir John, and made it back to Bow Street in good time. The court session was done. I found Mr. Marsden, the clerk, at his desk, writing up the day's record, and I inquired of him after the magistrate.

"He's gone out, he has," said Mr. Marsden.

"Did he give some idea of when he might return?"

"None. He went to keep an appointment with that man Johnson, who's such a great talker. So there's no telling." He noticed the letter in my hand. "You've something for him?"

"A letter."

"Best take it upstairs," said he. "He has nothing to come back to here. I'll be gone myself as soon as the constables arrive."

And so, somewhat disappointed, I trudged up the stairs to Mrs. Gredge, let myself in quietly and listened. I determined rightly that she had taken herself into her room for a "lay-down," as she called the naps she seemed to need these days.

There was nothing in the kitchen for me to attend to, so I sat down at the table to thrash out a problem. It was, of course, the question of whether or not I should inform Sir John of the ugly incident involving the Brethren of the Spirit, as they called themselves, in Covent Garden. It was plain that Katherine Durham was sore embarrassed by it, and her feelings mattered mightily to me. Yet there was more to consider here, for I had entrusted Moll Caulfield to the care of these people. She seemed frightened and shocked at what had been done by them to Mrs. Durham. It seemed evident I had made a considerable error. I hoped to make it right, and so there seemed nothing to do but make a full revelation.

It was not long after I had come to that decision that I heard Sir John upon the stairs. His heavy step was unmistakable. I was already on my feet, preparing my speech, when he entered.

"Jeremy?"

"Yes, Sir John?"

"Mr. Marsden said you had a letter for me."

"I do, yes, but—"

"Read it me."

"Well, all right . . ."

"It's not from my sister, I take it," said he, as I broke open the seal.

"No, from a place I've not heard of in Somersetshire."

"Ah, good. Proceed."

That I did, beginning with the rather flowery salutation and a first paragraph which spoke of the honor felt by the writer at receiving a communication from so distinguished a personage as Sir John Fielding.

But then he interrupted: "You may skip all that. Get to the meat of the thing."

"As you say, Sir John." I skipped down to the next paragraph and began to read aloud: " 'In answer to your query regarding John Clayton. It is true that he was a patient in our hospital for a short time three years past. The circumstances were these: He had fallen into an altercation at a tavern with no less than three men, and in defending himself against them was said to have behaved as "a madman," claiming to be another and not John Clayton. In any case, he defended himself so well that he fought off the three and did great bodily harm to one. The constable who was summoned was able to subdue him only with a stout blow to his head with a club. Because the tavernkeeper gave it out that John Clayton was not at fault in the beginning of this affray, but was rather set upon by the three, the magistrate was unwilling to punish Mr. Clayton, bodily harm or no. But because an attitude of "madness" was mentioned, and confirmed by the tavernkeeper, Mr. Clayton was entrusted to our care to determine if he truly was mad, and if so, in what way.

" 'As it happened, it was necessary to keep him no more than two weeks to make what I felt was a complete observation and determination. From the beginning he seemed quite reasonable, even docile, and exhibited a natural curiosity in the care and treatment of other patients and an interest in his own case. He was alert, helpful, and of good temper. I at last came to the only possible conclusion: that if he seemed irrational during the altercation at the tavern, it was the result of strong drink. If he had behaved as one "mad," it may have been a matter of intimidation by the constable. When I communicated all this to the local magistrate, he instructed me to release John Clayton. Since the altercation at the tavern was not of his starting, he pressed no charges, but directed only that he was to contribute one quarter to the repair of damages done to the tavern.

" 'I have had occasion to meet John Clayton on two or three occasions, though not in a professional manner, since his stay in our hospital here. While I was quite happy at his literary success, I cannot say that I was surprised. He showed me samples of his work while he was with us, and I recognized then that he was possessed of a true poetical talent.

" 'I am naturally distressed to hear of his involvement in the way that you described in such an appalling crime, and doubly distressed that he was unable to speak in his own defense. Give him another chance, I pray, and I'm sure he will do better. Alas, the Hospital of St. Mary of Bethlehem has a bad reputation. There are so many there that they cannot be attended to. I put my faith in your goodwill in this matter and in your excellent reputation to see justice done. Secure in them, I remain your humble and obedient servant, James Andrews, Doctor of Physick, OX.' ''

Upon my completion of the reading, Sir John, who had remained standing throughout, gave a sharp bang of his stick upon the floor, and a vigorous nod of his head.

"A good letter," said he. "Jeremy, would you not say that one was a good letter?"

"Oh, indeed I would, sir."

"Does it not seem that the doctor and the magistrate exhibited remarkable good sense?"

"Oh yes, sir, I would say so."

"Well, keep that close to you, and we shall use it to draft some documents tomorrow. I shall be glad to be quit for a day with this business of thanking people."

And with that, he began to make his way to the stairs, quite pleased with himself of a sudden. I felt I had to stop him before he ascended the stairs and disappeared for an hour or two.

"Sir John?"

"Yes, Jeremy? What is it?"

Then did I deliver the speech I had prepared, describing the attack of the Brethren upon Katherine Durham, making little of my part in her rescue, but presenting also a picture of Moll Caulfield and her shock at these events, and her wish to dissociate herself from them.

He listened soberly; then, with a much darker expression, he said to me: "Damn, I do wish Mr. Donnelly were still with us. I have so little use for other doctors and surgeons that I can recommend none. Get a name from Mr. Bailey. He is downstairs. Then run to the one he sends you to and have him go forthwith to Mrs. Durham. Tell him I shall pay. You say she is now at home?"

"Yes, I helped her there to Berry Lane."

"Good boy. I'll *not* have this sort of disturbance under our noses. That fellow you talked to yesterday, the one without a name, was he present during the attack?"

"No, Sir John. I give him credit that they may have acted more sensibly had he been there."

"Yes . . . well, perhaps. In any case, I see a busy day for

us tomorrow. We shall pay an overdue visit to Mrs. Durham, and then look in on Moll Caulfield to see how she is getting on. But for the moment, go, Jeremy, while there is still light, and send that surgeon on his way.''

FOUR

*In which I make a friend
and Sir John is visited by
the Lord Chief Justice*

Thus came I to be seated upon the steps next morning at
Number 3 Berry Lane. They led upward to the abode of
the Widow Katherine Durham, wherein Sir John Fielding
sat in earnest conversation with the householder. While
from above their voices mingled in manner generally grave,
there were nevertheless moments of levity in which I heard
her voice rise in dignified laughter and his join in, rumbling
in amusement. They were, in short, talking as friends, and
though I sat too low on the steps to divine the precise nature
of their discussion, its tenor and length were such that I
was greatly pleased by it. And why not? It is always pleas-
ing when those one holds in high regard share happily, each
in the other's company.

We had come, Sir John and I, not much past nine that
morning in order to confirm the state of her health following the visit to her by one Amos Carr, a surgeon of former
military practice. He had been recommended by Mr. Bailey
as "a good man for bones," and so indeed he proved to
be. After making his call, he came to make his report at
Number 4 Bow Street and, not incidentally, to collect his
fee. Met by Sir John's sharp questioning, he indignantly
declared himself to be good enough at his trade to tell a

sprain from a break. As for treatment, he had done no more than was required: he had applied a poultice and wrapped the ankle and expected her to be walking without difficulty in two or three days.

It seemed the next morning that his optimistic prognosis would prove accurate. When I advanced up the stairway and knocked upon her door, she answered in good time and seemed much improved since last I had seen her. The blush of well-being was in her cheeks, and her spirits were altogether better.

"Why, Jeremy," said she, "what a good surprise this is. And how good of Sir John to send that Mr. Carr to me to look after my poor ankle. It is ever so much better."

"That was what we hoped, Mrs. Durham."

"You say 'we'?"

"Yes, ma'am. Sir John sent me in advance to inquire if he might pay a visit to discuss the details of your injury— that is, the attack upon your person."

"Oh, *certainly*. I should be happy to welcome him under any circumstances—even these. When will he arrive?"

"Uh, well . . . indeed he is here." I gestured below. "He awaits your welcome at the bottom of the stairs."

Her eyes widened at that. She, who had been standing in such a way as to favor her hurt foot, leaning against the doorpost, shot out suddenly and glimpsed him below. Then, just as quickly, she pulled back, a look of great consternation upon her face.

"Goodness, Jeremy, he is here *now!* What shall I do? I am not properly dressed. My rooms, such as they are, are not cleaned for such an occasion."

Then quietly, in a whisper, I pointed out to her the obvious. "Mrs. Durham, it matters naught to him. Remember his affliction."

"But of course," said she, a look of generous sympathy replacing the anxiety that had been written there but a moment before. "Please tell Sir John that he is most welcome. Let him come ahead. Perhaps you might show him inside."

And so I retreated down the steps, offered him my arm, which he refused, yet accompanied him up the stairway, if only to say, when we reached the top, "To the right—just here."

But there was Mrs. Durham to guide him, her hand at his elbow, her voice at his ear. If he could not see the smile upon her face, he could not mistake the pleasure in her voice as, hobbling, she brought him to a comfortable chair and sat him down in it.

"Ah, thank you, Kate. Very good of you to see me," said he.

"None of that. Very good of you to come."

Thus they argued over who had conferred upon the other the greater favor, as I backed toward the door. Mrs. Durham separated herself from the disputation long enough to charge me to leave the door open.

"I'll not have him compromised," said she. "Oh, and Jeremy?"

"Yes, ma'am?"

"Guard the stairs. Let us have no interruptions."

And so I took my position quite near the bottom, content to watch the parade of passersby there on Berry Lane (a motley lot) and listen to the harmonious buzz of talk from the rooms above. Thus was I occupied for near an hour.

As I observed, I was in turn observed by the crowd. And what did they see in me? A boy moderately well dressed in his newest duds, chin in hands, daydreaming through this morning hour. A number who passed my way gave back my gawk. None stopped—yet one did return. He walked up to me, and said: "Hey, good me chum, would yez want to buy a wipe?"

He was a most peculiar-looking little fellow. Judging by his size, he seemed a good year or two younger than myself, yet he spoke with a voice more like a man's than my own. He wore a capacious coat, with sleeves rolled, from which protruded his thin arms and soiled hands, one of which clutched a worn and dirty kerchief. The hat he had on covered near half his head; had he not addressed me direct, I would have sworn he could not see me, so low was that oversized tricorn balanced on the bridge of his nose. I was so fascinated by the picture he presented that I fear I failed to respond.

"I'll let yez have it for a bobstick, though as any could see, it's worth a ned."

Still I could not answer. What was this queer talk of his? "Silk it is."

"You mean that handkerchief?" I managed at last. "You're selling it? Is that it?"

"Ain't that what I said? Don't you jaw the cant?"

I ignored his arrogant rejoinder, but pointed to the rag in his hand. "It's not silk," said I. Any fool could see that.

" 'Tis silk."

" 'Tisn't."

" 'Tis. Give it a dabble, and you'd see."

" 'Tisn't."

He was beginning to annoy me, and I him. He took a step toward me, and I rose from the step whereon I sat. My firm attitude seemed to discourage him, for he stood a moment, head tilted back, regarding me rather more in curiosity than in hostility. The moment of tension between us had passed. He pocketed the kerchief.

"You're a queer one," said he then. "There's a rum blowen dorses above. You her Tom slavey?"

Though I understood little of that, I thought I grasped enough to respond to his question. "I am no one's slavey," said I proudly (knowing, however, that Mrs. Gredge might consider me hers).

"That bein' so, you'll not mind if I climb to her door and give her a glim of me wares."

"She would not want your handkerchief."

He sighed loudly, as if to signal his exasperation. "I got fams to show, and a tick."

Then, as if to prove his boast, he dug deeper into his pocket and came up with two rings that appeared, unmistakably, to be of gold. He thrust them toward me for my inspection, and from the other pocket of his coat, he drew a watch, which he dangled before me. With this display, he made clear to me his occupation and his purposes. A dirty rag of a kerchief might be found in the street. But such as these could only have come into his possession by illegal means.

"You, young sir, are a thief," said I to him, "and you'd best be on your way ere I take you off to Bow Street."

He took a step back, dropped rings and watch in his pockets, and smiled a crooked little smile at my threat.

"You keep a dubber mum," said he, which I understood as a threat. "You'll do nicks to me, for I see no Beak-runners by your side, nor barking irons in your daddles."

Believing I half understood him, and considering his puny size, I made to intimidate him further. Had I not, after all, frightened footpads away from Sir John but a few nights past?

So, boldly, I descended a step or two, and looking down upon him still, I declared, "I myself would take you there."

Nothing passed between us for a long moment or two. Then, of a sudden, and quite without warning, he hurled himself bodily at me, throwing me back upon the steps. I fought back at him. We rolled down the two or three remaining stairs onto the street, flailing and banging at each other, clasping and grabbing in our fury. While I tried to wrestle him, there was no name for what he did to me, hitting and kicking like some lesser devil, poking his dirty little fingers at my eyes—I later found he'd given me a sound bite on my shoulder.

Though I had no way of knowing, we gathered a crowd around us as we twisted and rolled so savagely in the streets. No doubt we offered them amusement and they wished us to continue, for none made a move to separate us and end the fray. Who knows how long we continued thus? Far too long to suit me, for, reader, I confess that had our fight continued very much longer this young wildcat bred in the streets would have whipped me soundly.

Yet I was saved from such disgrace when we two were abruptly pulled apart—he by Mrs. Durham, and I by Sir John. To my humiliation, I was given a sharp blow on the buttocks by Sir John and a sound shaking, as well.

"You should know better, boy," said he, greatly vexed.

"Fighting in the streets like some wild urchin. Your father taught you different, did he not?"

"Y-y-yes, sir," said I, stammering in excitement.

A general grumble of disappointment went through the crowd that surrounded us, as our combat was concluded. I saw that Mrs. Durham was sore tested to keep her hold on my young opponent as he thrashed and twisted about in her hands. Yet she held on, until he came sudden stock-still when he peered across at me and recognized the personage in whose tight grip I was fixed.

"Gawd!" he exclaimed, " 'tis the Beak himself! I must hop the twig, or I'm sure a goner!"

Then he gave a great wrench of his frail body and broke free from Mrs. Durham. Scooping up his too large hat from the street where it had fallen, he ran pell-mell through an opening in the crowd that had of a sudden parted for him.

There was laughter at that, and our audience, satisfied then that the show was ended, began to disperse. Mrs. Durham came to us, wringing her hands.

"Ah, Sir John," said she, "I fear he escaped me."

"It's of no matter," said he. "We have the true villain here."

"Oh, surely not," said she, with a most sympathetic look to me. "If we but hear the circumstances . . ."

"He was a thief!" I cried. "He—"

"Silence, young man. If he was as you say, then he was a boy of low situation. And you, being better educated and in superior circumstances, should have known better than to tussle with him. You bear the greater responsibility. And in the streets! Really, Jeremy, you shame me."

I could make no reply to that. I said nothing. At last he released his grip on my collar, and I made to brush my clothes clean of the dust and dirt that had attached to them as we had rolled about. Mrs. Durham gave me a rueful smile.

"Perhaps, Sir John," said she, "I might take Jeremy upstairs and clean him off a bit."

"No, Kate, I must be off. Had I not enjoyed our talk and your company so long this might not have happened. Yet we shall talk again on this matter before us, and I shall look to the practical aspect of it. As for Jeremy, let him now wear his dirt as his mark of disgrace. Come along, boy.''

Oh, indeed I came. Not a word from me. Scampering over to the stairs, I retrieved my own hat and received a whispered goodbye from Mrs. Durham. Then I set off at a jog trot to catch Sir John up.

I seemed never quite to accomplish that. He went at a fierce pace, which he could only have done knowing the streets and lanes around Covent Garden as well as he did. Yet I followed behind as loyally as any whipped dog might. Nothing was said to me the entire length of the foot journey, except near the end, when Sir John called back over his shoulder, ''We should just have entered Half Moon Passage. Is that correct?''

How was I to know? I grabbed at the first passing stranger and asked the name of this narrow way between Maiden Lane and the Strand. He confirmed it as Half Moon Passage. I then ran full ahead to Sir John, for he had not slackened his speed in the slightest, and reported to him what I had learned.

''I know not how the numbers run hereabouts,'' said he. ''We seek Number seven, I believe.''

This was spoken in a tone somewhat less severe than before. Thinking I might win back his favor with a quick reply, I raced ahead in search of a proper address, but I returned to him, disappointed, to report that we had passed it by.

''Yet where would it be?''

''Just at the corner of Chandos Street, I believe, sir.''

''Truly so? That space was occupied by a fair place for eating and drinking known as the Key. Yet I allow I have not been by this way for more than a twelvemonth, nor in the establishment for far longer. Is it a building of wood, somewhat ramshackled?''

''More than somewhat.''

''And is there no hanging sign in the shape of a key?''

''None.''

''Ah well, things change, I suppose. Let us try it.''

And so we marched back down Half Moon Passage to the corner. Coming to the door, I noted a number 7 of goodly proportions painted upon it and informed Sir John of this. Yet there was nothing without to indicate who dwelt within. I guided him with a light touch to the door. He found it with his stick and rapped stoutly upon it. There came no answer, and so he beat ever more stoutly. Then some noise was heard from beyond. We waited until at last the door came open, and a man dressed in black like all his fellows appeared before us. In truth, except for the man I spoke to in the Garden who had agreed to take in poor Moll Caulfield, I had difficulty in telling one from the rest.

"Praise the Lord," said he. "How may I help you?"

"A pious greeting," said Sir John. "I commend it. You may help me by conveying me to your leader. I am John Fielding, magistrate of the Bow Street Court, and I am come to make inquiries into your sect."

"We are no sect," said the man in black, "but a brotherhood. And as a brotherhood, we have no leader. We are all equal in the sight of the Lord. We are the Brethren of the Spirit." He recited it as if by rote.

"If that be so, then you will do as well as the next. Therefore, I charge you to invite us in, show us your shelter and meetinghouse, and introduce us to all who are here."

He who had greeted us at the door was clearly disconcerted by Sir John's insistence. He turned away from the door, looking this way and that and mostly behind, as if the answer to his problem lay elsewhere.

"If you do not do so," resumed Sir John, "I shall return with my constables, break down your door, if need be, and carry out the inspection I propose by force. I advise you to admit us at once."

Reluctantly, the doorman stepped back and made space for us to enter. As we did, we found ourselves in a short hall. At the end of it stood the short man with the ascetic face and clear blue eyes with whom I had spoken. He stood exposed in light which slanted down from an upper window. He, like them all, was dressed in black and wore a round hat upon his head.

Sir John was immediately aware of his presence. "Who is there?" he called out.

"It is I, Brother Abraham."

"You, at least, have a name. Perhaps you would serve as our guide here."

"Perhaps I might." Said with a smile that to me seemed somewhat insolent.

"This is no social call, but an official visit."

"We recognize no authority but the Lord's."

"Whilst you are here in the City of Westminster, you had best recognize mine."

"Render unto Caesar that which is Caesar's?"

"Precisely."

"Then you are welcome, Sir John Fielding. I shall show you about and answer your questions. Yet I fear you will be disappointed, for not many of our number are here just now. All are out in diverse parts of the city preaching the Word of God."

"I shall contain my disappointment if you yourself prove forthcoming."

"Then this way, please"—he glanced at me for the first time, giving me a sign of recognition—"both of you."

As he led us off, the nameless doorman vanished behind some heavy curtains just past the entrance. I wondered what lay behind them.

Brother Abraham led us into a large room, in which rough-hewn benches were laid out in rows toward a front which was dominated by a large, high pulpit of good construction. Doors led off to the right, but the front, the wide area behind the pulpit, was curtained off in black. Our guide had walked somewhat deeper into the room. As he looked about it, taking obvious pride, I whispered a brief description of what I saw to Sir John.

"This is our meetinghouse," said Brother Abraham. "We hold services here, morning and evening. They are simple. We sing hymns. Scripture is read. Some words are spoken, and together we pray."

"Words are spoken? There is a pulpit, is there not? Who leads these services?"

"We take turns, as the Spirit of the Lord inspires us. We are all equal in the sight of the Lord."

"So I was informed by your brother at the door." Sir John turned his head as if giving the place an inspection. "I know this room," said he. "I know this building. It was until not so long ago an eating place called the Key. It was known for its spacious eating area. More than a hundred at a time could be seated in this room."

"Our congregation is not near so large, but it grows."

"How came you by this building?"

"It stood vacant when we arrived in London. It was said to be unsafe, but we put our trust in the Lord, and we got it for a good price. We have carpenters in our number. Gradually, some repairs have been made."

"And when was it you came here?"

"Just three months past."

"From whence? What part of England? I find it difficult to place your region by your manner of speech. It is a talent of mine, and I find myself confounded by your style."

Brother Abraham smiled that same smile once again. Was it truly insolence? There could be no doubt that the man maintained an air of superiority that contradicted the claim of the equality of all which he bruited.

"From no part of England," said he.

"Then where, sir?"

"From a New Jerusalem of our own creation deep in the forests of a valley called Monongahela. We resisted the French and fought off the Indians. Monongahela is ours alone. The name has a magic sound to it, would you not say so?"

"I seem to recall it from reports on our late war with France. You have come then from our American colonies?"

"We have our own colony there. As I said, we recognize no authority but the Lord's."

"Ah yes, well, we shall leave that for the moment. You have come on a religious mission to London then?"

"To preach the Gospel and convert the populace."

"Admirable. How many are you?"

"There were but thirteen of us made the voyage to this Sodom. Yet we have increased our number since coming; and have opened our doors in charity to a great many more. Some of these will be added to our number. Others come and go." He turned his gaze direct upon me. "Like your Moll Caulfield. She will leave us soon." This last was said in a most dismissive manner.

I could not but retort: "She is a pious woman."

Sir John touched my arm to restrain further comment from me. "May we speak with her alone?"

"No." It was said in the manner of a refusal, but then he added: "She is off with others on a preaching mission to Shoreditch."

"Ah, so far. Perhaps another time then."

"As you say, perhaps."

Sir John seemed about to reply sharply to that, then let the moment pass. "You have more to show us, I believe," said he.

Thus Brother Abraham was made to show us all. There was a large kitchen off the meeting room. Below that was a cellar divided into a room for eating and two for sleeping—bare pallets upon the floor, no more. These, he explained, were the dormitories kept for the men and women off the streets. "Though perhaps not comfortable," said he, "they are clean. And we all eat the same food. We make no distinctions."

"There are floors above, are there not?"

Brother Abraham sighed. "Yes," said he, "I believe they were kept for bawdy purposes."

"The place had no such reputation—a small hostelry, an inn, rather. There are many brothels in Covent Garden and not so many inns."

"I'll not dispute the matter with you."

"Good. Show me the rooms, if you please."

They were shown to us. Although small, the quarters on the upper floors were far more comfortable than the dormitories below the stairs. Each was furnished with a rough-made bed and a chair and a Bible. I described them to Sir John—all quite neat and clean.

"These, I take it," said Sir John, "are the sleeping quarters of the Brethren?"

"They are, yes. Surely you do not wish me to open each and every door."

"There are many, I take it, and all alike?"

"Yes, many."

"Then that should not be necessary. Show us only your own."

He seemed to have some difficulty with Sir John's request. He stood awkwardly for a moment, thinking one thing and then another. At last, he nodded and led us down to the end of the hall to a door like the rest. When it was opened, however, it revealed quarters quite different. Though not grand, it was better equipped than the rest. There was, in addition to the rudimentary bed and chair, a second chair more comfortable, a writing table with a double candleholder, and above it a shelf, spilling over with books. Atop the writing desk was a large sphere of a kind I had never then seen before, but now know to be an astrolabe.

I began, in a whisper, to describe all this to Sir John. But he stilled me with a touch on my arm. Then he himself ventured forth into the room, touching each item I have noted here lightly with his stick. He paused, particularly curious at the astrolabe, attempting, by the touch of his very hand, to discern its nature. Then, satisfied, he turned and walked out into the hall, where Brother Abraham awaited him, no smile but a scowl upon his face.

"Thank you," said Sir John.

"Will that be all?"

"Not quite, but you may take us to the door."

We followed him to the short hall wherein we had entered. Just there, Sir John pulled aside the curtains with his stick, behind which the doorman had disappeared. Nothing much was there—a space that was more than an alcove and less than a room. There was a chair and a table there—but no doorman. Again, Sir John sensed this.

"Where is the fellow who let us in?" he asked.

"Gone on an errand, no doubt," said Brother Abraham. "Each of us has his particular duties here."

"Oh? And what are yours?"

"Mine are like unto all the rest, except . . ."

"Yes, except what?"

"You will recall," said Brother Abraham, "that I said that we have carpenters in our number. As they work with wood and tools, I work with pen. I write."

"And what do you write?"

"What the Lord commands me to—hymns, sermons, commentaries. I am but his tool. He speaks through me."

Sir John considered this for a long moment, then nodded. Of a sudden, he banged his stick sharp upon the floor, commanding attention.

"Brother Abraham," said he in a tone quite severe, "I have had a report of an incident in Covent Garden of late yesterday afternoon. A woman was badly handled by members of the Brethren, and bodily injury was inflicted upon her. What do you know of this?"

"I was not present."

"That I have heard."

"But as I understand, she was a common strumpet, and they sought to denounce her as such. They became carried away somewhat, but she, it was, who tripped herself. Whatever bodily injury was done, she caused herself."

Sir John had a firm grip on my arm, thus warning me against speaking out.

"That woman is as nimble-footed as any can be. I have discussed this matter with her, and she declines to lodge a formal complaint. That is her choice. Yet a surgeon was called, and for his treatment of her took a fee of half a guinea. That sum will be paid to the Bow Street Court as a fine for this disturbance. Since you are all equal, it matters not who pays it. See only that it is paid."

Sir John nodded at me, and I opened the door.

"See, too, that such a disturbance never again occurs. Let us be good neighbors here in Covent Garden."

With that, he walked through the door, and I shut it behind us, catching only a glimpse of the angry face Brother Abraham set against us at our leaving.

Though Sir John was quite as silent during our walk from Half Moon Passage to Bow Street as before, I felt it was no mere sulk. My offense in Berry Lane seemed forgotten as we ambled along together at a more reasonable pace. I considered making an apology, but the time seemed not propitious. Clearly, he had deeper things on his mind.

When we arrived, he sent me up to Mrs. Gredge, as I had expected, and went off to discuss the day's docket with Mr. Marsden. Mrs. Gredge greeted me with screeches of dismay at my appearance, again as I had expected, and declared I looked as bad that morning as when she first laid eyes upon me, fresh off the road to London. In truth, I was not near so dirty, yet into the bath I went, a fair cold one it was, too, for she wasted no pity on me. It was then that I discovered the bite upon my shoulder. My adversary had not broken the skin, yet left proper welts there. Afterwards, Mrs. Gredge treated it with brandy and warned me against playing with such rough boys.

"We were not playing," said I to her. "We were fighting."

"Tish-tosh," said she. "For boys such as yourself, that is a form of play. Remember that I have had three of my own."

Though softened somewhat, she was not so sympathetic that she excused me from my household duties. These, which included a bit of scrubbing up and a buying trip to Covent Garden, were accomplished in good order. Though Mrs. Gredge put no meat on her list, I stopped at Mr. Tolliver's stall in the Garden to tell him of Mrs. Durham's improved condition. He, in turn, called my attention to the absence of the black-clothed troupe that had so abused her.

"Perhaps we frightened them off, eh lad?" He bellowed a great laugh at that and bade me wish her a quick recovery for him.

Thus I returned with ample time to hear an hour of the proceedings of Sir John's court. I never missed a chance to attend. I confess that like so many of the layabouts and drabs who attended, I was often entertained by what came to pass there in the courtroom. Sir John Fielding had a way of dealing in short fashion with petty pretensions and deceptions that left all but the pretenders and deceivers quite amused. Yet in ways of which I was not then fully aware, these sessions, at which were paraded all the miseries, foibles, and sins of humankind, provided an education that a bookish thirteen-year-old such as myself might only otherwise have obtained at great risk to his character. I was given a window through which I might view it all, protected as it were by a stout pane of glass. And lest from my observations I draw conclusions too dark regarding human nature, I had before me in Sir John an exemplar of those qualities most worthy of emulation. He was the chief actor in these dramas—no mere protagonist but rather, to me, the hero.

I slipped into a seat along the last bench quite in the rear of the room, as Sir John summed up a civil case that had been brought before him. The complainant and the defendant stood with some distance between them, as if separated by keen animosity. Looks passed between them, yet neither dared mutter a word whilst the magistrate spoke.

"And so I am to understand, Mr. Cotter," said he, "that having heard from the defendant that the house he had rented from you was unsafe, you gave false assurances that all would be put right, and the house would be made safe for habitation. When repairs were not made, as promised, Mr. Lilly withheld rent for two months running. Now you come asking that the court force him to pay those two months' rent *after* said house had collapsed in the windstorm of two days past. Is this correct?"

"Well," said the more richly dressed of the two men, "not altogether, m'Lord. I would not say I made false assurances to this man here."

"What would you say then?"

"The intention was there. I had not found the proper carpenter to do the work, was all."

"That was all, was it? And in the meantime, you judged the house safe for habitation?"

"They inhabited it. I mean to say, if they lived in it, they should pay the rent, ain't that so?"

"Mr. Lilly, tell me," said Sir John, inclining his head in the direction of the defendant, "when and why did you judge the house unsafe?"

Although he responded quickly to Sir John's question, the defendant seemed to address the complainant. "There was another day of just such strong winds last March," said he. "The house rocked and creaked something fierce. We feared then it would come down on top of us so. And when the blowing was done, you could tell, just looking, that there was danger of collapse."

"I recall the March day whereof you speak. Mr. Cotter, was the condition of the house just so evident?"

"It leaned a bit," said he grudgingly.

"Why then, Mr. Lilly, did you not simply move out of the house if you judged it unsafe?"

"Because, sir, I had signed a lease in January, and this . . . person would hold me to it, no matter what. He threatened me with the law then, just as he does here and now. We are weavers, sir, and our livelihood depends on having a place large enough for our loom. We had to keep working, in spite of the poor condition of the house. I saw no help for it but to withhold the rent. I had the money laid aside and would have paid him, had he braced the house proper. He railed and raved, yet in the end, he made a promise which he never kept."

"Is this a fair account, Mr. Cotter?" demanded Sir John.

The complainant said nothing.

"Mr. Cotter?"

"He signed a lease, m'Lord, and a lease is a contract. It is no crime to hold a man to a contract."

"Do not lecture me on the law, sir. I know it far better than you." Then to the defendant: "Mr. Lilly, you said you had the rent money laid aside. Do you still have that amount?"

Mr. Lilly sighed. "No, sir, I do not—not in whole. My

wife's leg was broke in moving our two children out of the house. The doorpost fell upon her. I paid a surgeon to have it set and bound.''

"And what of your loom?"

"It was crushed in the collapse. It is quite beyond repair."

Sir John leaned forward toward the complainant. "Well, Mr. Cotter, what say you to this problem? Mr. Lilly has confessed that he no longer has the entire amount you seek from him, nor has he the means of earning it, for his loom was lost when the house came down. What solution do you see for it?''

"That is not *my* problem, is it? Let him borrow the sum, say I. And if none will lend it, then into debtor's prison with him."

Sir John sat silent for a considerable time, as if considering the matter. Those who crowded the courtroom were also silent, awaiting the outcome.

"No," said he at last. "I believe I have a better answer. First of all, I deny your petition for the sum of two months' rent in arrears to be paid by Mr. Lilly. He is forgiven the debt by the court. Secondly, I must say that in the years I have sat on this bench, I have never heard a suit so unfair brought before me. You, Mr. Cotter, have shown contempt for this court in bringing said suit, and in recognition of this, I fine you for contempt of court, the exact sum of which will be the price of a new loom to be provided Mr. Lilly and his family."

As Sir John banged out his judgment on the table before him, Cotter raised his voice in disjointed phrases of protest. There were many "but"s, a declaration that the judgment was "unfair," and a howl of "outrage."

"I warn you, Mr. Cotter, if you do not silence yourself, I will fine you further and further again, until you find *yourself* in Newgate. *Is this clear?*''

Cotter fell silent and nodded. Lilly wept for relief and gladness. Sir John instructed Mr. Marsden to fix the sum of a loom from Mr. Lilly and collect it from Mr. Cotter.

He waited as this was done, and then he bade Mr. Marsden call the last case of the day.

"John Bilbo," Mr. Marsden sang out, "accused of grievous assault on a city street on yesterevening; taken into custody by Constable Cowley on his first round of the evening; released on his own recognizance; please come forth."

There was a great stir among us watchers to hear the name of one so famous called in open court. Black Jack Bilbo, as he was better known to one and all, was proprietor of what was then London's best-known and best-attended gambling club. He was, withal, a plain man, a blunt man, one who had no more respect for the lords and gentlemen who patronized his establishment than he did for those he employed. Sir John had introduced me to him in the course of his investigation of what came to be known as the Goodhope affair. He confessed to me at the time that in spite of the dark rumors regarding Mr. Bilbo's past—said to have been a pirate, no less—he liked the man well and held him in high regard. For my part, I was quite in awe of him.

He looked the part of a pirate done up in his plundered best as he strode in through the door to the street and took his place before Sir John. Black-bearded, swarthy of complexion, he removed his tricorn and displayed to the court no periwig but a head of dark hair, cut short, bushy in some parts, thinning in others, with a short braid in back. He stood erect before the bench, not a tall man but thick of body. He was, with the possible exception of Benjamin Bailey, chief constable of the Bow Street Runners, quite the most capable-looking of any I had seen in London.

"John Bilbo? It is you before me?"

"It is, Sir John."

"How plead you to this charge of grievous assault?"

"I plead guilty, sir," said he, then added, "with just cause."

"Guilty with just cause. Is that it? Well, I can see we shall have a bit of unraveling to do before this skein is laid out proper before us. It would seem that the first we must hear from is the arresting officer. Is Constable Cowley present?''

"Here, Sir John." Young Cowley stood and took his place beside Black Jack Bilbo. He looked much better than he had when last I saw him, carrying bodies forth with the Raker from the publishing establishment of Ezekiel Crabb. Alert, modest, ready to give his report, he seemed properly professional in his demeanor.

"Then give us your account, Constable."

"I shall, Sir John," said he, "and I can be brief. Whilst making my first tour of the streets surroundin' Covent Garden, around the hour of eight in the evening, I chanced to spy a commotion of considerable proportions on Maiden Lane. In spite of the crowd that had gathered, it being near a streetlamp, I could tell there was much happening within the crowd. There was arms flailing, a head bobbing, and great cries of excitement from the crowd. And so I hastened me there and pushed hard through them that was assembled, identifying myself as a constable. Once through them all, I saw this man, John Bilbo, crouched over a man in the gutter, striking him with his fist. Another man lay senseless beside this fellow, half in the gutter and half out. The two was dressed as in some uniform, or some manner of preacher's garb, all in black they was. Anyways, I gave this man, John Bilbo, a stout rap upon the shoulder and told him to cease what he was doin'. He turned to me and looked near to attackin' me, as well—the blood was in his eye, so to speak. But then he must've noted my red waistcoat, or the crest on my club, for he said, after gettin' his breath, 'Are you a Beak-runner?' and I said I was, and that was that."

"He gave you no trouble then?" asked Sir John.

"None at all," said Constable Cowley.

"What of the victims?"

"Well, they posed a problem, they did, for we could not leave them where they lay. Nor could I give them my full attention—not if I was to bring this here gentleman into custody in a proper way. In the end, though, he took care of the matter."

"And how did he do that?"

"Called for water, he did. He pitched a pail of it into the face of each one. That roused them proper. And though they was much the worse for his assault upon them, I took their names and charged them to appear at the Bow Street Court this day."

"And are they here now? Let them come forward."

There was a pause of some moments as Constable Cowley looked about the courtroom, yet in a manner, so to speak, of confirming what he had already concluded.

"No, sir," said he at last, "they are not. They were right strange about all that. Though they heard me through, they made no promise to appear. In truth, one said to me that they did not accept the authority of your court."

At that, Sir John heaved a sigh audible even to the back row where I sat. "And what were their names?"

"Brother Isaac and Brother James. That's all the names they would give, Sir John."

"And the address they supplied was on Half Moon Passage, was it not?"

"How did you know, sir?"

"Second sight—you may be sure of it. No, I make light, and I should not, Constable. Members of this religious community have lately made themselves known to me in diverse ways. I simply assumed. Thank you, Mr. Cowley. You conducted yourself well, both at the time of the arrest and here in the courtroom. You may go or stay, as is your will."

The young constable then retired to the seat he had left on the front bench, leaving Black Jack Bilbo alone before the magistrate. Sir John leaned forward and folded his hands before him. Had he sight, one might swear he was staring at him through the band of black silk that covered his eyes.

"Mr. Bilbo," said he then, "you have heard Constable Cowley's report. Do you wish to take exception to it in any regard?"

"No, sir, I do not. It was a good report, fair and right."

"You do not contest that you set upon these men most cruelly and knocked each of them senseless?"

"No, sir, I do not."

"Well, then, what have you to say in your own behalf?"

Until that moment, Black Jack Bilbo had stood quite still before the bench in a posture almost military. His hands were clasped behind his back, and his legs were set wide. But as he began to tell his tale, he began to rock and shift, and his hands soon shaped into fists. It was as if he were, in nerve, sinew, and muscle, repeating the action even as he described it.

"Well, sir," said he, "it was in this way it happened. I was walking down Maiden Lane on my way to the theater in Covent Garden to attend a play of no particular consequence. It was my intention to join a party of gentlemen and their ladies and convey them afterwards to my gaming establishment—visitors they were, from Holland."

"You were on foot. Do you often go thus?"

"I do. I sit on my arse far too much during the day and night, and so I must take the chance to stretch my legs when I can."

"And do you go armed?"

"Almost never. I would fear the consequences for any who opposed me. I've had no trouble on the streets until now. I would wish nothing more serious than what befell me last evening."

"Very good," said Sir John, "proceed."

"Well, as I say, I was walking down Maiden Lane when I was set upon by these two in black."

"Set upon? In what way?"

"Well, that was it, Sir John. What they did, they started preaching at me in a most peculiar way. Oh, I have been preached at often enough in my time, and in my own way I try to heed the Word, if you get my meaning. I run fair tables. I'm known for a good touch when a man or woman is down. Beyond that, well, I hope to make my peace before my time runs out. I've a thing or two on my conscience we need not go into here."

"No, we need not."

"But these two, they're walking beside me, step for step, and telling me that I and all my people must accept Christ as the Messiah ere the great time come. They are shouting at me in this manner, you see, and I was much annoyed, so I quickened my pace, and then they began jog-trotting beside me, crying, 'Jew, Jew, you must listen. You must convert to prepare the way!' Well, in truth, Sir John, I am often taken for a Jew, and I would as soon be taken for one as any other. It is the beard which I wear, and which I shall always wear. I know Jews to be good gamblers and sensible men—which is more than I can say for those two. What they done was very foolish indeed.''

At this point, reader, Mr. Bilbo's body was quivering so with the recalled action of the moment he described that I thought he might show as well as tell what came to pass. His arms were now at his sides, his elbows bent, his fists making little circles in the air. He took a deep breath before he continued as follows:

''Well, in order to detain me that they might preach the harder at me, one of them grasped me by the shoulder and dug in his heels. And the other—the *other*, he grabbed my beard and *pulled it.*''

The courtroom crowd, which had been in an attitude of silent attention throughout this recital, exploded into a commotion of comment, so that Sir John was obliged to hammer them into silence. For his part, he then leaned forward even further, apparently eager to hear the end of the tale.

''Proceed,'' said Sir John.

''There is not much more to tell. For to touch my beard in such a way, to''—and here Mr. Bilbo hesitated, as if to put such a deed in words were too much for him—''to *pull* it, is an offense I cannot and will not abide. I struck out at them, and I struck out often: I have no true sense of what then happened, nor how long it happened, for I was in a fighting rage until your young constable gave me a tap and told me to quit. Only then did I come to myself. Quite right was he to stop me.'' Then he added darkly: ''Quite right was I, too, not to have a sword by my side.''

A tremor seemed to pass through the courtroom, a collective sigh, more or less. Sir John leaned back at last and put together his fingers, left upon right, one upon one.

"And so you plead guilty with just cause, John Bilbo.
Have you any witnesses to corroborate your account? Anyone who saw the"—and here he hesitated, as well—"offense to your person?"

"No, I do not," said Mr. Bilbo, "but you have my word
I have given a true account."

"Let me assure you, John Bilbo, I value your word
highly," said Sir John. Then, addressing the court: "If we
have an absence of witnesses, we also have an absence of
victims. In this situation, seeing that Mr. Bilbo's story of
the incident in no way conflicts with that of the constable,
seeing, as well, that he offered no resistance and even aided
in the revival of the victims, I am willing to accept Mr.
Bilbo's account and take it, too, that he had sufficient provocation to deal punishment of some sort to those who had
offended him. Whether or not the extent of the punishment
he dealt was just is another matter, however.

"I like it not that Mr. Bilbo was singled out, detained,
and given offense because he was thought to be a Jew.
Whether he is or is not is not pertinent in this matter. Were
Brother Isaac and Brother James here before me now, I
would give them stern warning against ever repeating such
actions in the streets of London. As it is, for their failure
to appear when charged by Constable Cowley to do so, I
hold them in contempt of court and bid them appear before
me, or face a term in prison as a consequence.

"With all this so, such fighting in the streets cannot be
tolerated by this court or any other. John Bilbo, you are a
grown man and should know better than to behave as you
did. Punishment of some sort is in order. Let it be a fine.
You said, as I recall, that you are good for a touch for those
who are down. I know of a particularly needy case—a good
woman who lost her roof and her livelihood in the high
wind that also left Mr. Lilly ruined. Let it be understood
that your fine will go to put her back on her feet."

"I would welcome the chance," declared Mr. Bilbo.

"It will not go cheap. Let us say, oh, five guineas."

"Let us say ten, and it will be done."

"Your generosity is admirable, Mr. Bilbo, but I hope

never to meet you again—in my court, that is.''

"Nor more than I, Sir John."

I wondered, as I filed out with the rest, if any but me knew that it was Moll Caulfield for whom Black Jack Bilbo's fine was intended. I wondered, too, if knowing the circumstances, any but me would have seen a parallel between his case and my own. What was it Sir John had said? "Fighting in the streets cannot be tolerated by this court or any other." I feared that punishment of some sort awaited me. If his hot anger toward me had cooled somewhat, I believed that this meant only that he now had time to calculate in leisure what form that punishment might take.

My fear was made most real when Mr. Marsden stopped me as I passed by his alcove and informed me that Sir John wished to see me in his chamber. Knowing what awaited and liking it not, I nevertheless went as directed, knocked upon Sir John's door, and announced myself.

I entered and was told to sit.

"Jeremy," said he, "we have something to settle between us."

"Yes, sir."

"You disappointed me greatly this morning, rolling about in the streets as you were. I'm afraid some punishment must be doled out."

"Yes, sir. I'm sorry, sir. But, sir?"

"What is it, Jeremy?"

"I could not but notice certain similarities between Mr. Bilbo's case and my own."

"I suppose, to stretch a point, there were a few. But I would remind you that he was punished with a fine."

"I have money," I said, "a few shillings. You may have them."

"Damn! I must look into giving you some sort of regular amount." He shook his head, annoyed at himself. "No, Jeremy," he said then, "I do not wish to take your money from you. I wish only to make an impression upon you so that you will not shame me in the street again. If that takes corporal punishment, then so be it. I'll have Constable

Cowley administer it—or Mr. Bailey, if need be." This was a problem he clearly wished to be quit of.

"Sir John?"

He sighed. "Yes, Jeremy?"

"Wouldn't you say that in one way, chiefly, Mr. Bilbo's case differed from my own?"

Again he sighed. "And what way was that, boy?"

"You allowed Mr. Bilbo to give his own account of the matter."

"So I did, so I did. All right, Jeremy, you have me. Let me hear your story."

So saying, he leaned back and listened as I gave a full and true account of what it was transpired upon the steps of Number 3 Berry Lane that morning. I yielded not to the temptation to improve myself in the telling; and while I could not quote the rude boy who had used such strange talk in hawking his stolen goods, I could and did make the point that they were doubtless stolen. When I called him a thief and threatened to convey him to Bow Street, it was then *he* attacked *me*. I had done naught but defend myself, I assured Sir John.

"You have no witnesses to speak in your behalf?" said he, stating the obvious.

"No, sir, none, but you have my word that it was so."

"I accept it. But just as you have no witnesses now, you had no witnesses then to prove the boy a thief. In all probability he had picked some pockets to gather his booty. Though the rings—well, they could have been slipped from the fingers of some bawd in a drunken doze. But you did not see these acts of theft, nor could you produce others who had seen them. Had you succeeded in getting him to Bow Street, and had he appeared before me, he would have sworn he had found these valuables in the street. Unlikely as this might have seemed to me, I would have released him, for in English law we must assume innocence unless guilt can be proven. So you see, Jeremy, how useless it would have been for you to have brought in your captive? You see that, don't you?"

"I do, Sir John, but—"

"And another thing, my lad—by what authority were you to have arrested this young pickpocket? You are no constable. You have no warrant. Surely you yourself suffered enough at the hands of an independent thief-taker not to wish that profession for yourself."

That last was a painful reminder of how I, new to London, received my introduction to Covent Garden's criminal society and came before the Bow Street Court. Though much good had come of it, the incident was one I would put from my mind. I attempted to frame some sort of reply, yet I found it difficult, for the plain truth was that I, a thirteen-year-old boy, had no given authority.

My attempt to devise a response was also made difficult by a commotion of shouting that arose of a sudden beyond the door.

"Jeremy," said Sir John, "go see what that is about, will you?"

I arose from the chair and started for the door, yet it flew open ere I reached it, and Mr. Marsden pushed his head through.

"Sir John, I wish to announce the—"

"Oh, enough of that, enough of that!"

This from a large man, richly though not gaudily dressed, who bustled past the clerk, pushing him aside in his passage, and made straight for Sir John. Though I had never seen him before, he bore unmistakably the air of authority. He came in, waving pages of what proved to be a pamphlet, and threw it down upon the table before Sir John.

"Have you seen this?" shouted the visitor.

Sir John, who liked not to be caught in company without his periwig upon his head, struggled to replace it.

"My Lord," said he, "I . . . I . . . well, what is it you refer to?"

"Well, I know you haven't *seen* it. Even I couldn't see a thing through that black band you wear about your eyes."

(William Murray, Earl of Mansfield, may have been Lord Chief Justice of the King's Bench, and for his time a good judge, but it will be understood from this rude remark that like many men content in their power, he lacked much in common courtesy and even more in human consideration.)

At last, satisfied he had his periwig on aright, Sir John answered with greater composure: "If you will but seat yourself, my Lord, I shall be happy to discuss with you whatever it is you have put before me."

"It is an annoyance," said the Lord Chief Justice, "near a provocation. In short, sir, it is a pamphlet, one that is now being hawked and sold all over the streets of the city. Its title is given as 'A Call for Justice for the Victims of Grub Street.' And though its anonymous author is presumptuous enough in his text to tell us our duties, I grant that he has done no more than to say in print what others have spoken in the streets."

"I take it," said Sir John, "that it treats the murder of Ezekiel Crabb and his household."

"Indeed it does! Just listen to what is written in this damnable thing." He shuffled through its pages until he found a proper passage. He cleared his throat and began: " 'While the entire Crabb family and the two luckless apprentices who dwelt with them now molder in their graves, the villain who was captured at the scene, bloody axe in hand, goes untried, uncondemned, and unhanged. He has been tucked away in Bedlam by the magistrate of the Bow Street Court, safe from justice, safe from the hangman.' "

"Why, that is monstrous," said Sir John. "It presumes his guilt. Any who might happen to read it would be prejudiced against him instantly."

"But more! Give an ear: 'Perhaps in committing the man with the bloody axe to a hospital rather than to Newgate for trial, Sir John Fielding was acting upon orders from the King's Bench. Grub Street, its printers, its publishers, and its poor scribblers, have long been a trammel to licentious authority in this Kingdom. Ezekiel Crabb himself published many works extolling the Rights of Man, such as—' Oh, never mind all that. But here, listen how it ends: 'Let the Crabb family be avenged. Try John Clayton for their murder *now!*' What think you of that, John Fielding?"

"Well, it's . . . It's . . ."

"It's seditious, that's what it is," the Lord Chief Justice

blustered on, "seditious of the King's justice. And it is plain falsehood to suggest you sent this fellow Clayton off to Bedlam on my orders. You know very well I sent you a note in which I disapproved of your decision. But if this pamphlet, such as it is, were all we had to contend with, I would not trouble you with it. I'd simply search out the author and throw him into Newgate."

"What more then, my Lord?"

"An influential Whig lord has given me his opinion that the man should be tried, no matter his condition. They are talking of it in the House of Commons. I understand that one, an old ally of Wilkes, has threatened to bring a question to the floor."

"What then do you propose?" asked Sir John.

"That we put this Clayton on trial in Old Bailey."

"But you cannot try a man for murder who is in no condition to answer for his crime. If you had seen John Clayton during his appearance here at Bow Street, there would not have been the slightest doubt in your mind that he should be carted off to Bedlam."

"Did he rave? Murderers are often known to resort to dramatics to avoid the hangman."

"He did *not* rave. He talked nonsense. He even earnestly denied that he was John Clayton."

"It could have been to deceive," the Lord Chief Justice insisted.

"Further, three years past he was confined for a time in a mad hospital in Somersetshire. I have a letter to that effect from the doctor in charge."

"All this matters, of course, but the only proper answer is that we must hold a hearing to determine whether or not he is capable of standing trial."

"*We* should do this? Two men of the law?"

"Well," said Lord Mansfield with a shrug, "it is a legal matter, is it not?"

"Not wholly, no. I believe we should receive advice from those who are familiar with such matters—from doctors."

"Mad doctors?"

"That is the popular name for them, yes."

"Well, they have them in good supply at Bedlam, I suppose. Let us hold the hearing there."

"When?"

"Well, I think it important to attend to this as soon as possible. Why not tomorrow then?"

"Saturday? Well and good. And at what hour? Morning is best for me."

"For me, as well. We shall meet before the gate at Bedlam then at half past nine, agreed?"

"Agreed, my Lord."

FIVE

*In which we visit Bedlam
and learn of a most
distressing development*

Not even Newgate, which I had lately visited with Sir John, had presented so forbidding a picture to me as that gray, grim-structure at which our hackney carriage pulled up outside Bishopsgate. An old building of stone, centuries old, it was not overly large, yet with the high barred fence and ill-kept grounds that surrounded it, the place had the look of an ancient fortress. What windows I saw had stout bars upon them, as well.

As I climbed down and surveyed the drear aspect of the scene before me, Sir John paid the driver and bade him wait for us.

"I should prefer not to," said the hackney driver.

"What do you mean?" said Sir John crossly.

"I mean I like this place so little that I would sooner give up the waiting time and the fare back to Bow Street than stay here," said he. "There is too much misery inside that place. I may sound foolish to say so, but I fear that to remain here I would risk infection by it."

"Go then," said Sir John. "I'll not order you to stay, though by rights I could. This is official business."

"I hadn't supposed you came here for pleasure—though some do."

"Be not impertinent. Just be on your way."

At that, the driver turned his team of two about and left us standing by the side of the road in front of the gate. It was a chill morning for May. The weather had mixed fair days with foul so thoroughly and in such confusion these last weeks that one knew not what to expect. Dark clouds rolled low over the building before us, moving swiftly west to east. There was a gatekeeper nearby who stood watching us expectantly; no other was to be seen before the structure. Yet on either side of its portals stood two guardians in stone, powerful figures in the Greek mode, pathetic rather than heroic: one wore an angry grimace and held his arms in a threatening way; the other seemed downcast, quite overcome with sorrow. They seemed to have been added as a later inspiration and fitted not so well with the square look of the rest.

"There you have it, Jeremy," said Sir John, with a wave of his stick, "The Hospital of St. Mary of Bethlehem, which is known universally by its corrupted name, Bedlam. What is your impression of it?"

"Not a good one, I fear, sir. It is an old and ugly building."

"Far uglier inside than out, and you may take that as gospel."

"There are two figures, one on each side of the door. What do they represent?"

"Well," said he, "while I have never actually *seen* them—"

"Forgive me for asking," said I in a great rush of embarrassment. "I meant no—"

"Nonsense. Think nothing of it. I merely intended to say that I'm told they represent Mania and Melancholy. I should expect you would easily be able to tell them apart."

"Oh yes," said I.

"I suppose they are meant as some generalized portrayal of those inside—maniacs and melancholics. I wonder which outnumbers the other," he ruminated aloud. "Melancholics, surely—oh, most certainly melancholics, considering the state of our world."

To that I had no reply.

Even as we spoke, we had been passed by a number of conveyances. As each approached, Sir John gave it a moment's attention until it passed us by. At last one did slow and stop just shy of where we stood. The horses stepped restlessly just ten paces away from us. Great, huge things, they seemed. They made me uneasy.

"That surely is not a coach-and-four," said Sir John.

"No, a hackney carriage quite like the one we came in."

"I thought so. Lord Mansfield has a coach-and-four. After all, the Lord Chief Justice of the King's Bench deserves nothing less." This was said quietly, in a tone of jesting irony.

From the hackney four people descended—two young blades and their women. Even to my young eye they appeared to have caroused the night through. Their countenances, no less than their modish clothes, had a worn and wasted look to them. They wobbled when they walked. They talked in a kind of dazed style of purposeful merriment, assuring one another as they went what fun awaited them inside Bedlam.

"Some of them perform," instructed one blade, "do tricks upon demand."

"What kind of tricks, Harry?" asked his mistress.

"Quite naughty."

There were forced giggles from the women and a guffaw from the other male in the group.

They ignored us completely, but went straight as their weak legs would carry them to the gate and rattled for the gatekeeper to admit them. He opened without comment, accepting the coin that was pressed into his hand by him who was called Harry. Again, he gave us a curious stare before resuming his chosen place to one side of the gate.

Then, with a great rush and flourish, the coach-and-four arrived. It was all I could do to move Sir John out of the way ere we be trampled by the matched team of four white beasts which pranced down upon us. The driver reined them in at the last moment, and the footman beside him bellowed, "Open wide the gates for Lord Mansfield!"

The gateman hopped to, pushing the barred gates far back on their hinges to admit the oversized conveyance. Then in 'it went, all in a rush, and up to the portals of Bedlam.

"Oh, damn," said Sir John, "now we must foot it in and play welcomers to his Lordship. Come along, Jeremy. Point me in the right direction."

He waved aside the gateman, who tipped his hat in salute as we walked on.

"I recall he said distinctly '*before* the gate.' Is that not as you remember it?"

"Exactly so, Sir John," said I.

"Ah, well."

Lord Mansfield had, by the time of our arrival, moved his considerable bulk out of the coach with the aid of his footman. He moved about in an impatient manner, looking in every direction, it seemed, but ours.

"A good morning to you, my Lord," said Sir John.

The Lord Chief Justice gave a glance at the sky. "Not so good as it might be. Sorry to be late—the press of office, you know." Then, in a gesture meant no doubt to establish his leadership in this matter, he clapped his hands together. "Well and good, eh? Let us get this done as quickly as is possible. We both have other things awaiting our attention, do we not?"

"Indeed. They have been forewarned here of our coming, have they not?"

"Of course. I sent word by messenger."

"And a doctor will be present?"

"Yes, damn it! All the niceties have been nicely arranged."

"Then by all means, let us proceed."

"Henry!" Lord Mansfield called out, and he gestured at the grand, arched doorway. The footman, who had been waiting a discreet distance at attention, sprang up the few stairs and to the great portal, whereon he banged with a knocker in the shape of a human hand. The portal swung wide, and as the footman conversed with someone inside, I became aware of a great hum of noise within.

The footman beckoned us with a "m'Lord," and we three started forward. At that moment I happened to glance upward into the face of Melancholia. Though eyes in stone seldom seem to express much, those downcast orbs of his showed forth a look of misery so deep that it seemed to pierce my very soul. In spite of myself I gave a shudder and moved on, managing to keep step with the rest.

The man who met us at the door identified himself as Dr. Dillingham. He was quick to fawn over Lord Mansfield, civil to Sir John, and gave me not the slightest notice. Once we were inside, the hum of noise rose to a low roar. Since I was last in his line of followers, I caught none of Dr. Dillingham's words as he led us to another large door of strong, thick oak. The doorman had left his post at the main portal and hastened ahead to open the inner oaken door for us. With that, the low roar intensified to a dreadful cacophony. The noise was nevertheless human, the sound of many human voices raised to a din of frightening proportions. Up a short corridor, which brought us three steps higher than where we began—then a turn to the right, and we were suddenly in the midst of the tumult. No, not among the inmates, quite; a long row of iron bars like unto that at Newgate saved us from such an ordeal. But the inmates circulated freely, each trying to outshout the other, it seemed. They yelled. They danced. There was a fiddler in their midst, sawing noisily away at a tuneless tune.

It was, at first impression, quite like Newgate. The smell of urine and ordure was heavy in the air, as it had been in that awful prison. Yet Bedlam seemed in some ways worse, and in some ways better. One or two were chained to the wall—I had not seen that at Newgate. But this place was much lighter—all of Newgate seemed a dark dungeon— and there were small individual cells, each against the wall, doors opened, some of them occupied at that moment and some not.

There was great contrast amongst the inmates, as well. They fascinated me. I had to spur myself on and keep up with our group as it stepped at a lively pace along the walk that ran the length of this extended common room. Given

time, I would have dawdled and studied each one, diag-
nosing them after my own fashion, attempting to divine
from each the secret of his malady. Even so, with my
glances and quick looks, I discerned that all manner were
mixed together—the feebleminded with the mad, the melancholics removed from the rest, slumped and indifferent
along the wall. For the most part, the maniacs paid little
attention to us, so taken were they with their own merriment. Those who noticed jeered or shouted obscenities.
One showed his bare rump to us as we passed.

Another—well, near the end of our long walk we passed
the mixed quartet that had preceded us into the building. I
was close enough to hear the leader, who was called Harry,
point through the bars with his stick and remark, "But look
at the fellow. He is a veritable Priapus. See for yourself,
Betty—Georgina, look!" I looked, too, whereat he pointed,
and colored red for shame at my sex.

Oh, it was a show we were given, in truth, but a show
most sane men or women would have paid dearly to avoid.
Yet again I confess there was indeed something about this
poor, misbegotten mass of humanity that fascinated me. I
wanted no "tricks," as Harry's crowd had come to see; I
wanted only to study the inmates at greater length in order
to understand them better. (Thus was kindled in me my
keen interest in those matters and later, those cases in which
questions of madness or sanity were to be settled by law.*)

Our astonishing passage come at last to an end, we were
shown down three stairs and into a room of modest size. It
was sparsely furnished—a table and some chairs—and the
only evidence of decoration to be seen was the addition of
a colorful woven rug of no particular pattern and a few
rather bizarre pictures hung upon the wall. This room, I
assumed, was used for the visitation of relatives and friends
to the inmates of the hospital. I guided Sir John discreetly
to a chair behind the table and sat him down in it, taking
a place behind him. Lord Mansfield sat heavily in a chair

---

*I modestly call the reader's attention to my little book, *De Jure et De-
mentia;* only the title is in Latin.

beside him, emitting a grunt of exertion as he did so.

"Well, Sir John," said he, "if your man Clayton was among those poor wretches I just viewed, then you'll have no argument from me."

"Though I could not see them, I heard aplenty. Madness does have a frightful sound, does it not?"

"Indeed so, an unholy din it was."

"I think you will agree that I showed no leniency to John Clayton by placing him here until such time as he could answer as a rational man."

Lord Mansfield hesitated, then: "Reluctantly, yes."

The door to the room opened. Dr. Dillingham entered, followed by a tall man whom I recognized as John Clayton, though he had previously claimed two other names, and last of all by a warder, who closed the door behind him and waited there.

Dr. Dillingham stood by his patient and addressed the following remarks to the seated judges: "I wish to say only that Mr. Clayton has been made to understand the nature of this inquiry and has agreed to cooperate with it fully. I shall take my seat with you now, but be assured that I stand prepared to answer any and all questions you may have and to offer my opinion, should it be solicited."

He then did as he said he would do: circled the table and took the empty chair beside Sir John.

Whilst the doctor spoke, my eyes were fixed upon John Clayton. I noted a number of things about him. First of all, he held in his hand a sheet of foolscap which I discerned had been written upon. Secondly, I noted the condition of his person: he was surely as well groomed as his circumstances permitted; his collar and cuffs were a bit begrimed, his cheeks were in need of a razor, yet his hair was combed and his hands and face were clean; I had seen many a man on the streets of London in less respectable condition. Lastly, and most striking of all, were his eyes, for from them shone unmistakable and bright the clear light of reason.

"Your name, sir," asked Sir John in a tone most severe.

"John Francis Clayton."

"And not Eusebius? For it was as him you presented yourself to me at our last meeting."

"No, sir, not Eusebius."

"And what has happened to him?"

"With all due respect, that is difficult to explain."

"With all due respect to you, sir," said Sir John, "it is incumbent upon you to try."

At that, John Clayton began a story that had us three visitors to Bedlam quite agog. As the telling progressed, Sir John and Lord Mansfield sat forward in their chairs, amazed at what they heard. Only Dr. Dillingham, I noted midway, seemed to take it all in good stead, leaning back, nodding, unsurprised, as if he had heard it all before; and perhaps, I reflected then, he had.

"You see before you," said Mr. Clayton, "one in whose body three natures reside. Eusebius you have met, but there is another named Petrus who—"

"Him I have met also," interrupted Sir John.

"Ah yes, that would have been at the time of my arrest. So you know them all. I first learned of them when I was but a schoolboy, in or about my thirteenth year. My parents, though mere country laborers, wanted me to have all the schooling I might take. I had done well up to that time, but because of my size and adolescent awkwardness, I attracted the attention of older bullies in the school. They threatened me. Then their threats were made real one day just after school, and Petrus made his first appearance. I did not summon him. In fact, I myself knew nothing of his actions, for what specifically had happened was blotted from my memory. But it seemed that I had battered both boys senseless and broken the arm of one. My classmates who had witnessed the affray told me that during the course of it I called myself Petrus and would not listen to the bullies' pleas for mercy. There was a great to-do about this, as indeed there should have been. The family of one of them, him whose arm I broke, wished to see me tried for assault and put in prison. Yet because of my young years, the local magistrate let it pass as a childish broil. He did, however, require my parents to pay for the treatment of the broken arm by a surgeon.''

"That seems only just," put in Sir John.

"Perhaps, but the cost of that broken arm near broke my poor parents.''

"What of Eusebius? When did he first appear?''

"Not long afterwards. The incident with Petrus disturbed me greatly, particularly my inability to remember what had transpired. I avoided contact with my fellows, afraid that a simple disagreement might bring forth this monstrous double, who would then wreak havoc upon some innocent. Occupied with such thoughts, fearing the worst, I neglected my studies. And one day, called upon by the schoolmaster to answer a question to which I knew not the answer, I stood up, hemmed and hawed a bit, and then suffered a similar absence of consciousness. When I came to myself again, I heard the laughter of my classmates and realized that the schoolmaster was pushing me bodily back down into my seat. Confused and abashed, I sat quiet in my seat until the end of the schoolday, wondering what I had done. It was only then that I learned that rather than admit my ignorance of the question's proper answer, I had rambled and spouted upon the subject in a most peculiar manner, as if I had great wisdom and the schoolmaster had none. He tried to silence me. I would not be silenced. I went on talking nonsense for minutes, all in the name of Eusebius, until the schoolmaster took action and pushed me back into my seat. Luckily, Petrus did not take offense at the laying of hands upon me and make his appearance.''

Lord Mansfield spoke up for the first time. "And how often were you visited by these two . . ." He hesitated, then submitted to the term Clayton had used: "These two *natures?*''

"Not often, sir.''

"I am properly addressed as 'my Lord.' ''

"Then, not often, m'Lord. Because of this incident and because of the other, I found myself unwelcome at school and soon left. Though still a boy, I was man-sized and could do a man's work. Earning money of my own, contributing to the family economy, I began eventually to think myself quite independent, drinking beer and spirits. There were a few embroilments at which Petrus made an appearance over the years; one of them brought me to a small hospital such as this one in my native shire.''

"I know of that incident," said Sir John. "I received a letter from a Dr. James Andrews describing it and your stay in his hospital.''

"A good man," said Mr. Clayton. "I fear I held back a little of my personal history from him. I made no mention of Petrus. In a way, all this had a beneficial effect upon me, for as I troubled over this odd aspect of my life, I was driven inward, and inside myself I found poetry. As a schoolboy, I had a love of words and made a few childish attempts at verse. But working in the fields as I grew up, I found lines, whole stanzas welling up within me. I could hardly wait until work was done so that I might get home and write down what had come to me, perhaps continue it, should my inspiration drive me on. When I—''

"Well and good, well and good," broke in Lord Mansfield, "but what of this other presence—what name has he?''

"Eusebius, m'Lord. He also has made appearances, and somewhat more frequent. When John Clayton stands mute before authority, Eusebius speaks for him. He prattles on, often making no sense, perhaps usually so, but sometimes he convinces. There was the time before our local magistrate that he argued me into Dr. Andrews's hospital for study. That was not me but Eusebius. I found myself on the hospital roll as Eusebius Clayton. I explained that away by claiming Eusebius as my middle name. Then not long ago, when I was in negotiation with Mr. Crabb, Eusebius intervened and, I fear, made a fool of me. Mr. Crabb immediately perceived what was amiss, did not challenge Eusebius, but waited until I had come to myself again and calmed down. I confessed then this difficulty of mine, and he accepted it.''

"Did you tell him also of Petrus?" put in Sir John.

"No, sir, I did not.''

"And why not?"

Mr. Clayton did not answer readily, but after some consideration, he said, "Because I did not wish to frighten him."

"I see. Tell me now what happened when you appeared before me at the Bow Street Court."

"I came to myself in that room for prisoners to the side of the court."

"The strong room."

"Is that what it is called? In any case, there I sat in a bloodied nightshirt. The clothes that had been fetched from Crabb's were there for me to put on. I sat, as I say, for near an hour trying to remember what had happened. There were memories, awful pictures in my mind, but they came to me in a great confusion. Had I imagined these things? That seemed unlikely, for here was my bloody nightshirt to prove that they were real. Reluctantly I dressed, still trying to remember, still trying to put in some order these impressions and pictures. When I was taken into the courtroom and was sat before you, I left myself completely and Eusebius came in my stead. No doubt with disastrous results."

"If all this be so," said Sir John, "how is it you can speak now to us so convincingly and reasonably?"

"Well taken," said the Lord Chief Justice, "indeed, indeed. How comes it so then, sir?" He ended with a laugh, as if to say he had caught him out.

"Because, sir and m'Lord, in the days I have been here at Bethlehem Hospital, I have had time to concentrate upon this matter. In truth, I've thought of nothing else. I have ordered my memories, focused my impressions, and now I believe I can give an account—though not a full one—of my experience there at Crabb's on the night in question. In fact, I was so sure of it that I began a letter to you, Sir John Fielding, asking if I might impart this to you. Dr. Dillingham was kind enough to provide me with paper, pen, and ink. I failed to complete the letter because Dr. Dillingham informed me last night of this interview. Anything I could say in the letter, I could say to you in my person.

To put it briefly, I am well prepared. When my mind is ordered, and I am well prepared, there is no need for Eusebius to intrude. I am capable of handling my own affairs. Here is the letter.''

With that, John Clayton stepped forward and placed the sheet of foolscap on the table. Lord Mansfield then grabbed up the letter, which of course was addressed to Sir John, pulled out a pair of spectacles from his waistcoat, and began reading it with great concentration.

Sir John, aware of what had happened, turned to Dr. Dillingham to his left and said in a quiet tone, somewhat above a whisper, "What say you to this, Doctor? *Three* natures in a single body? I myself have never heard of such a thing.''

Lord Mansfield looked up from the letter. "Indeed!'' said he. "It all sounds quite like the story of a cock and a bull to me.''

"No, no, let me assure you," said Dr. Dillingham, "such cases are not so rare as you might suppose. I have seen a number of them in my years here at Bethlehem Hospital. And while cure seems impossible . . .''

"Impossible?''

"Well, of course, it's very difficult to determine, for once a man has returned to his true nature, he seems altogether ordinary, as does Mr. Clayton now. He may remain ordinary, or in a given set of circumstances may allow the return of another, more riotous self, one who may cause problems.''

By this time, Lord Mansfield had lost interest in the discussion and returned to the letter. John Clayton, for his part, was much interested in it. He strained forward, favoring an ear in the direction of the magistrate and the doctor.

"In your opinion, Dr. Dillingham,'' asked Sir John, "would you say that John Clayton is a sane man, one capable of standing trial?''

"Oh, indeed I would, but I cannot say the same for Petrus, or that other fellow—what was the name?—ah yes, Eusebius. I have met neither. The question is, of course, whether John Clayton can be tried for the crimes of Petrus.''

"Indeed, that is the question, is it not? Were we to—''

Lord Mansfield jumped to his feet, tucked away his spectacles, and grabbed up his hat.

"Let us be off, Sir John,'' said he. "Our business here is done.''

Sir John turned this way and that in confusion. "What is it? What do you mean?''

"Why, it is all here, put plain in this letter of his. Have your boy read it you. Mr. Clayton says as clear as can be that he wishes to be tried for the murders in the Crabb household. That was the purpose of this inquiry. If he wishes to be tried, we must certainly oblige him.''

"Is this true?'' Sir John asked of John Clayton. "You wish to be put before the King's Bench at Old Bailey?''

"Oh yes, sir,'' said he, with great certainty.

"But why, man? The question of responsibility, I would say, is still quite open to doubt.''

"Because I am sure of my innocence.''

When we emerged from the Hospital of St. Mary of Bethlehem, a steady rain was falling. The driver and the footman held the team and looked mightily unhappy as the rain dripped down from the short brims of their round hats. The footman gave up the traces and rushed to open the coach door for Lord Mansfield. For his part, Lord Mansfield splashed to the door as best he could; then with the assistance of the footman, he managed to climb up inside.

As he leaned out to say his goodbye, his glance took in the road beyond the gate. There was, of course, no hackney carriage in sight.

"Come along, Sir John,'' he called. "I'll not have you tromping about in this rain looking for a hackney. The boy can ride up top.''

"I prefer to have him ride with us,'' Sir John called back, holding his ground.

"Nonsense. He is your servant, is he not?''

"No, indeed. He is a member of my household, a ward of the court."

"Oh, bother such nonsense. Come along—come along, both of you."

With that, he threw wide the coach door, and the two of us jog-trotted down the steps, through the puddles, and up to the conveyance. The footman aided Sir John inside, but when it came my turn, he helped me only so far, then gave me a shove that sent me sprawling into the interior of the coach."

"Untangle your feet, boy," said Lord Mansfield. "Be more careful."

"Yes, m'Lord."

"Here, Jeremy, beside me."

As I took my place next to Sir John, I looked out the coach window through the streaking rain, and caught the smirk of the footman just as he turned away. Then, only moments later, we were under way—out the gate and onto the highroad.

We rocked along, Sir John and Lord Mansfield keeping their silence for a spell as I brooded upon the tale I had heard from John Clayton. It had not escaped me that his difficulties with Petrus and Eusebius had begun when he was thirteen—my age precisely. Had the fates some such nasty surprise awaiting me? I sincerely hoped they did not.

Upon consideration, I decided I had not much to fear. For if ever I had needed a Petrus to aid me, it would have been in that rough encounter the day before with the putative pickpocket. More likely, judging from the way he had fought beyond his size and strength, he had a Petrus within him. And then I reflected upon the story told by Black Jack Bilbo in Sir John's court. He had readily admitted that he had no memory of his assault upon Brother Isaac and Brother James from the time his beard was pulled to the moment Constable Cowley tapped him on the shoulder. He had no idea of the length of time that had passed; it was sufficient, in any case, for a crowd to have gathered. What was it he had said at the end of his account?—that he was glad he had had no sword or pistol with him. The implication, of course, was that he might have slain them both. Mr. Bilbo had described his state as a "fighting rage." Was that not perhaps a visitation by his Petrus?

I felt no better for my ruminations. But the thought of Mr. Bilbo and his strange encounter with the Brethren of the Spirit had pulled up a memory, a detail that I determined to impart to Sir John at my earliest opportunity.

Yet not here and now. The silence between him and Lord Mansfield invited no interruption. We passed by St. Giles Cripplegate and quite near Grub Street. I noted that the rain had diminished somewhat. Even so, I was well satisfied to have made this journey warm and dry within the coach, rather than cold and wet atop it. So I was not a servant but a member of Sir John's household. I wondered at the distinction.

"Sir John," spoke up the Lord Chief Justice, "why not just send this fellow Clayton up to us at Old Bailey? You've given him one day at Bow Street. Shouldn't that suffice?"

"He was not competent on that day," said Sir John firmly. "You heard his explanation just as I did."

"You mean Eusebius and all that nonsense? It made quite a good story—I own I was fascinated as he told it—but really, what can all that mean in a court of law? The law gives no recognition to such a circumstance. One man, one nature—that is how the law sees it."

"Then perhaps the law should be changed."

Lord Mansfield laughed indulgently at that.

"Besides," said Sir John, "Mr. Clayton clearly had something, perhaps some several things, to communicate to us. Our departure was premature in my opinion. I think he should be listened to as any witness would be. He has not been convicted, not even formally charged as yet. So far as I am concerned, he is a witness. As the only survivor of that dreadful massacre, he may indeed be our best witness."

"Ah, Sir John, it was ever thus with you, was it not? You see labyrinthical difficulties when the facts provide a straight path. Just send him to us."

Sir John's response was a grunt, nothing more nor less.

They rode along in silence once again for a certain space of time. We were now quite near Covent Garden. I glimpsed St. Paul's rising above the lesser structures nearby. Somehow I had been made uncomfortable by these long pauses between them. I decided I would be glad when this drive was done.

Yet the silence was broken once again, this time by Sir John.

"My Lord Chief Justice," said he, "you will soon receive from me a begging letter."

"Oh? What will it be this time? A few more constables for your force of Runners?"

"No, though they would be most useful on the streets of Westminster and in the City. Please bear that in mind when next it comes up."

Lord Mansfield sighed. "I shall. What then do you now have in mind?"

"A charitable enterprise."

"Oh, another one, eh? Something on the order of that fund to send young criminals out to sea, as you promoted a few years past?"

"Something like that, yes."

"Well, that won you a knighthood, did it not?"

"I had thought my service as a magistrate had brought me that."

"And your Runners. Don't forget your Runners. They have made you famous. I've heard grumbles that indeed they have made you *too* famous. But what is it this time?"

"I am preparing a subscription for a house for penitent prostitutes. I am particularly interested in getting young girls off the street."

"A house for young bawds, is it? Well, you'll fill that up fast enough."

"My wish is that they be taught trades and skills, then go out into the world and support themselves."

"Not likely." Lord Mansfield laughed. "Indeed not likely. They choose the life because they like it, nine times out of ten."

"Let us help the tenth," said Sir John.

Again a sigh. "Why not? How much did I give to your subscription for boy criminals? Is the one who sits beside you now one of them, by the by?"

"Emphatically *not*," said Sir John.

Inwardly I thanked him for that.

"How much then?"

"A hundred pounds?"

"Surely not so much. Why not, oh, fifty?"

"Something between. I'm sure we'll work it out."

"Will my contribution bring me John Clayton a bit faster?"

"Not one minute."

"I thought not."

The coach had come to a stop. The rain had ended. We were at Bow Street. I threw open the door and hopped down to the street, wanting no assistance from the footman.

Some time before leaving for Bedlam, Sir John had made a particular request of Benjamin Bailey, captain of the Bow Street Runners. Though he had worked the long night through, he had been asked to end his watch with a visit to the Brethren of the Spirit at their meeting hall and shelter in Half Moon Passage. There he was to present the contempt-of-court citation to Brothers Isaac and James, then collect Moll Caulfield and send her on to Bow Street to receive the ten guineas appropriated in her behalf from Black Jack Bilbo.

Sir John had expected to see her at Bow Street before our departure. Thus it was that immediately upon our return he went searching for her. He sought out Mr. Marsden and inquired after her.

"I have seen nor hide nor hair of her," said the court clerk.

"That seems passing strange," said the magistrate.

"Mr. Bailey is here, however."

"The poor fellow must be exhausted. It is nigh on noon."

"So he seemed. I gave him my alcove that he might nap there."

And there we found him, seated at Mr. Marsden's desk, sleeping deeply.

"Shake him awake, Jeremy. He would not have returned had he not something to impart."

It was not easy. So deep was his slumber that it took many shakes and gentle pummelings to bring him out of it. When at last he sat erect in Mr. Marsden's chair, alternately squinting and opening his eyes, Sir John judged him fit to be addressed.

"Mr. Bailey," said he, "your return here tells me you have something to report. Gather your wits and give it me."

With his eyes fully open, he took a couple of deep breaths and rose to his feet, stretching his mighty frame to his full height, moving this way and that.

"Indeed I do, Sir John," said he in a sort of gasp. "It's, as you might suppose, about my visit to that queer lot on Half Moon. They've taken over the Key, have they not? Place should've been torn down long ago, I vow."

"Yes, yes, Mr. Bailey, but go on, please."

"Yes, sir, sorry, sir," He continued, now speaking in more orderly fashion: "I banged on their door, demanding entry, showing them the contempt citations Mr. Marsden had writ out, insisting that I serve it to Brother Isaac and Brother James personal. They was ill, says him I spoke to. And I've no doubt of that, having heard from Constable Cowley what old Black Jack done to them. But I insisted, as I said to you, and they conveyed me upstairs to the old hostelry rooms, where I presented them one each to the brothers in question. They was in poor shape, no question, but on the mend, as you might say, and I informed them of the consequences if they failed to report today to the Bow Street Court. They agreed to be here, reluctantly like."

"Tell me, Mr. Bailey," put in Sir John, "on what floor were these two men recuperating?"

"At the top, sir."

"We were not brought up there," said Sir John, half to himself, half to me. "But go on, Mr. Bailey."

"That done, I announced to them that I had also been charged to take Moll Caulfield off their hands and send her to Bow Street. This, for some reason, caused a great to-do amongst them, and they went off and fetched another of their number from morning devotions. Though they claim to have no leader, this one they fetched is, in my opinion, in charge."

"And his name was Brother Abraham."

"Exactly so, sir. So I put it to this Brother Abraham that I wanted old Moll—and since I was growing tired of their company, I put it to him as a demand, so I did. But he says to me as easy as you please that she ain't there no more, that she left of her own will the night before. I insisted to be shown where she slept, and I was taken to the cellar and shown an empty pallet. It could have been that of any of the poor souls I glimpsed at their devotions. When I asked why she had left, he said quite simple, 'She liked not our company.' Well, in all truth, I liked not his, for something there was that annoyed me, whether his certain manner, or his telling of the circumstances of her departure, I cannot say."

"What were the circumstances?"

"He—this Brother Abraham—said that she was a contentious woman and had disrupted the harmony of their group. 'Well, then,' says I, 'you expelled her.' 'No,' says he, 'we gave her a choice. She could go or stay, as she chose, but if she stayed she would have to hold her tongue and talk no more heresy.' And so, he said, she chose to go—quite indignant, she was."

"Did he say what manner of heresy she espoused that had offended them so?"

"No, he did not, nor did I ask him, for I have little understanding of these points of doctrine over which the preachers broil so."

"And for which wars have been fought."

"As you say, Sir John."

"So the result is that Moll Caulfield is no longer with them. Since . . . when?"

"About nine o'clock yesterday eve."

"Well, we shall tell the Runners to be alert for her in their rounds tonight. Go home, Mr. Bailey, you must sleep. It was good of you to stay to make your report in person."

Mr. Bailey began his departure, then turned back, putting a troubled face to us.

"There's no doubt old Moll is a willful woman, as you might say," said he, "and could cause a bit of trouble when she put her mind to it, but it don't seem right the way she was treated by them. I mean, after all, this bunch in the old Key, they're supposed to be Christian, ain't they?"

With that, he started, as if struck of a sudden by a thought: "Oh, and another thing, sir. These brothers, them I talked to anyways, they ain't true-born Englishmen. They're all from the American colonies. I'd know that queer manner of speech anywheres."

"So Brother Abraham informed me," said Sir John. "He named a place with a fantastical name, Monongahela."

"Monongahela, is it? Near Fort Pitt, as I recall it. Let me think on that a bit."

"Nay, dream upon it. Go now. Sleep. You've done well."

With that, Mr. Bailey made his departure and left Sir John stroking his chin, deep in thought—and me beside him, trying to read those thoughts. I waited until the magistrate himself had given up his pondering and made to depart Mr. Marsden's alcove bureau. Only then did I speak up.

"Sir John?"

"Yes, Jeremy?"

"I should like to go out and search for Moll Caulfield."

"Well . . ."

"You've only two men on duty now—the keeper of the strong room and the day-runner. She should be sought— and the sooner the better, or so it seems to me. And besides . . ."

"Yes, boy, what is it?"

"I feel responsible for her situation. If I had not led her to those brothers, she might—"

"She might be precisely where she is today," Sir John

interrupted me, "out on the street. Mr. Bailey was correct in saying that Moll Caulfield is a rather willful woman. She has had her share of scrapes before. She herself must be held partly responsible."

"But, sir," said I, "she may not be in the streets. She has a friend, an old party named Dotty—though I know not her surname—who guided me to her that day of the windstorm when her place collapsed. Moll might be with her."

"Well and good," said he. "Look for her then, and if you do not find Dotty, take a good close look in the Garden, corner to corner. You may find Moll about, reduced to begging."

"That I shall do. Thank you, Sir John."

"And by the by, I should judge it a favor if, in your searches, you looked in on Mrs. Durham to see how she is getting on. You might tell her, too, that I floated her plan to Lord Mansfield and got a good response."

SIX

*In which I meet my
former adversary, and
Moses Martinez presents himself*

If Moll Caulfield seemed to have disappeared, so also had her chum Dotty. I looked high and low for both of them in the streets surrounding Covent Garden, then went beyond, continuing to look and ask for them both—all to no avail. In my wanderings, I passed three women pushing vegetable carts, each one a piece from the other. To each I made inquiries first about Moll and then about Dotty. All said they knew them. None said they had seen either of them on that day.

When I had come full circle around the Garden, I found myself only a few streets from Mrs. Durham's quarters at Number 3 Berry Lane. And so, remembering Sir John's request, I sought to honor it and made direct for that address. Arriving, I climbed those stairs which had been the scene of my disgrace the day before (wondering what punishment Sir John had in store for me, hoping he might forget the matter altogether); then I knocked upon her door. She, calling through it, asked me to identify myself. When I did so, she threw open the door and greeted me most happily.

"Jeremy, this is indeed a pleasure," said she. Then, lowering her voice, not daring to look, she asked, "Does Sir John wait below?"

"Oh no," said I. "He's having his court at this hour."

"Of course," said she, obviously disappointed yet doing her best to disguise it. "Right stupid of me not to realize it. But do come in, won't you? Give me all the news you have."

"I do have a bit," said I, as she showed me inside to a chair. "But first, I was instructed by Sir John to inquire after your condition."

(I had noticed in her short passage from door to couch that she hobbled still.)

"I do well enough," said she. "I fear I rushed things a bit today, going off to do my buying in the Garden. I returned with my ankle a bit worse than when I left. I must own, too, that trying to hold that young wildcat with whom you fought yesterday put some strain on it. Whatever was the cause of that?—that is, if you don't mind telling?"

And indeed I told her, giving her also Sir John's objections to my actions, admitting their wisdom. She listened to my tale, nodding, encouraging me to continue. It was only when I had concluded with my description of my interview in the magistrate's chambers that she ventured to speak.

"He *is* wise, you know, as few men are and few women. I wonder that he has not been raised to a higher court. Perhaps they value him more for his Bow Street Runners than for his work day to day handling that mob of thieves and pickpockets who come before him." She paused then, hesitating, as if assessing what might be told and what might not. Then she said to me: "He showed great wisdom with me."

"And how was that, Mrs. Durham?" Clearly, she wished to be asked.

She proceeded carefully: "I put before him an idea of mine, a modest notion, really. And he, being the man that he is, listened charitably, saw the sense of it, and made of it a practical plan—on the spot, so to say. He took it all with the utmost seriousness."

"Ah well," said I, "then the news I have for you should please you."

"Quick then, give it me!"

"Sir John asked me to tell you"—and I paused, seeking to quote him exact—"'that he had floated your plan to Lord Mansfield and got a good response."

"But, Jeremy, that is truly wonderful, the best news you could have brought!" She clapped her hands at that. "Imagine, Lord Mansfield! Why, he is an earl, if I'm not mistook. I wonder what was said between them."

"Perhaps I might be of some help there," said I, puffing a bit.

"Were you present? Oh, Jeremy, tell me."

Swearing her to secrecy, I imparted what had passed between the two in the coach on the drive back from Bedlam—the begging letter, the subscription, the negotiations, all of it, except the specific nature of the charity. Mrs. Durham was much impressed.

"A hundred pounds?" said she in a voice expressing amazement. "Truly, he asked for so much from one man alone?"

"Lord Mansfield offered fifty."

"That is a great sum."

"Sir John suggested they would settle eventually for a figure somewhere between."

"Oh, Jeremy, this is indeed thrilling. You've made me so happy."

"But please," said I, "no mention of this to Sir John. I doubt he would like me repeating his conversations with the Lord High Judge."

"On that you have my word," said she.

"Only that he floated the plan, and it got a good reception."

"Agreed."

With that, I rose to take my leave, aware that I had already spent far more time with her than I had intended. Though I urged her to keep her seat on the couch, she followed me up, and with a sore step showed me to the door.

"I hope your foot mends soon," said I. "Perhaps I could do your buying for you, if you wrote me a list."

"Perhaps you could—on Monday. I enjoy your visits, in any case, Jeremy. As for my foot mending, I have no wish to return to my daily life. I have a bit of money put aside. I shall use that and hope for the best."

And so we said our goodbyes, and I swiftly departed for Covent Garden, where Sir John had advised me I might find Moll Caulfield a-begging. As I made my way through the crowded streets to the even more crowded piazza, my mind turned back to my visit with Mrs. Durham and to my pleasure in her company. I wondered at that and reassured myself that she, as Mr. Donnelly, the surgeon who had been most helpful to Sir John in the Goodhope inquiry, spoke to me simply as a person—not as a child. With the death of my mother, my brother, and late of my father, I had quite had my fill of childhood and wished to be a man. Sir John spoke to me as both child and man, which was probably more fitting, for I seemed to act often as both, faltering toward manhood and falling back toward childishness. This was indeed a difficult time for me, as I believe it is for all boys, and I found the generous attention of such as Mrs. Durham most encouraging.

I had a stratagem in mind for Covent Garden. While keeping on the watch for Moll, I would circulate through it entire and ask each and every greengrocer if he knew Dotty, perchance served as her supplier. And should I find the proper man, I would sure find her, for a supplier must know where his pushcart sellers reside. It may not have been a very grand plan, as I was well aware, but at least it offered an alternative to a face-by-face search through that great crowd which seemed always to inhabit the place.

I found out early in my attempt to canvass the greengrocers that these gentlemen and their female assistants are far more helpful when you appear to them a potential buyer than when you attempt to solicit information from them. Had I worn the red waistcoat and carried the club of a Bow Street Runner, they would have been helpful enough, you may be sure. But appearing as I was, a mere boy asking questions, most I approached were indifferent to me at best and some were downright rude.

"Never heard of her." This was the response most frequently heard.

Some simply waved me off and turned away. I kept mental note of these and vowed never to return to them again as a buyer.

I had become quite discouraged toward the end of my circuit and knew I must soon make just such a corner-to-corner search of the great square as Sir John had described. It was then, just as I approached the last greengrocer but one there in the Garden, that I felt a tap upon my shoulder, looked round me quickly, and, to my dismay, saw there none other than my opponent from yestermorn. There was no mistaking him, decked out as he was in his oversized coat and tricorn. I knew not whether to pounce upon him, to get back my own from the day before; or to turn and bolt from him, quite literally putting temptation behind me. Thus riven by contrary impulses, I stood frozen before him.

"Now, don't you dast lay your daddles on me," said he, as I stood in this state, "and don't tip a mizzle. I've something for the Beak."

That damnable queer talk again! All I gained from what he had said was that he had something for Sir John. Yet he talked in a placating manner and seemed to have peaceable intentions.

"The Beak," he insisted, "he's the cove of your ken, ain't he?"

"I . . . I don't understand."

"You know nicks of flash, ain't it? Can't patter the gammon? Well, chum, I'll put it real plain." Then slowly, as if speaking to a child or some dim-witted foreigner, he proceeded: "I"—pointing to himself—"have a letter"—producing it from his voluminous pocket—"for your master, Sir John whatsisname."

"Fielding."

"So it is," he agreed.

I reached for the letter, yet right quick he pulled it out

of reach and behind his back; then he danced nimbly a step or two backward.

"Give it me," said I, "so I may deliver it."

"Nah, nah, nah, I ain't daft. I can deliver it me own self."

"Then why do you trouble me? Why not simply take it to Bow Street?"

He hesitated, then said with reluctance, "I could do with a bit of help from you."

"Oh? How is that, pray?"

"See, I'm a known prig, a proper scamp—a thief to you, chum," said he proudly. "You was right when you put the name to me and we had our tussle—and a rum tussle it was, to my mind. I've won many a race from a constable, made them eat the dust from my hockey-dockeys. But many's the one got a good look at me, too. I fear if I show me face at Number four, then I'm quick bound for Newgate. But that's where you play a part."

"What sort of part?" I was most skeptical.

"A rum one, to be sure. I ain't askin' nothin' queer of you. Just you come along, see, and tell them this is like in war with a white flag."

"A surrender?"

"Nah, nah, Jimmie Bunkins gives up to no man."

"A truce?"

"You got it, chum—a truce—that be the word. Like time taken out from the usual, ain't it?"

"I suppose so, yes. But I still don't understand why you don't just give me the letter and let me deliver it."

"Clink, chum, clink. It may be worth a ned or a bob— who knows? It all adds up." He immediately saw the incomprehension writ plain upon my face, for he then translated his cant to plain English: "I hopes to get a re-ward. See, this letter must be pretty important, for the party what gave it to me did so real secret like. Only it was seen by the folk she was with, and one of them gave me chase, and a proper chase it was, near ran me down, but I got free, and I been walkin' about ever since, tryin' to work it out how I might get it to the Beak without risk to myself. Then

I spies you here in the Garden, and I sees the way of it. Maybe pick up a bit of clink in the bargain.''

My mind had raced as I heard this. ''Who was that gave you the letter?''

''It was a rum old blowen I knowed for a while named Moll.''

''Moll Caulfield?''

''That's the one. Many's the time I was without a fadge, and she gave me to eat from what was left over in her cart. How she got in with that bunch in black I cannot figger.''

''When was this?''

''Last darkey—last *night* to you, chum—but early, not long after I heard six struck on the clock.''

Realizing the importance of this, I determined there and then to suspend my search. ''Come along,'' said I to him. ''It will be done as you like. Though I cannot ensure that you will be able to put it in Sir John's hands, we shall make the effort.''

He hung back a bit distrustfully. ''You'll make the truce?''

''You may depend upon it.''

With this final assurance, he was at last satisfied. We set off together for Number 4 Bow Street, which in truth was but a short distance from where we had held our parley. Along the way I asked him if his name was truly Jimmie Bunkins. (It seemed to me a rather strange sort, even comical—though I dared not tell him that.)

He was immediately on his guard. ''Who told you that?''

''You did,'' said I. ''You declared that Jimmie Bunkins would never surrender. I took it that you were referring to yourself.''

''You talk queer,'' said he. '' 'I took it you was referring to yourself.' '' He made a jeering imitation of my speech, which annoyed me somewhat. ''You talk like you was studyin' to be a milord or some such. Why can't you learn proper London speech? Why can't you talk flash? Gammon? Cant?''

''I don't choose to,'' said I.

'' 'I don't choose to.' '' He echoed me again, annoying

me further. "Listen, chum, what you need is a rum teacher."

"And I suppose that would be you."

"It might be. You treat me proper, and I'll treat you proper."

What could he mean?

There would be no chance to find out, for we had arrived at the Bow Street Court. I opened the door on the right, which led down a long hall which passed the courtroom and the strong room and eventually ended at Sir John's chambers. I gestured Jimmie Bunkins inside. He held his ground.

"You go ahead," said he. "Do it like you said, white flag like."

"A truce?"

He nodded, suddenly shy and uncertain.

"Oh, come along," said I, just as suddenly impatient. "There are but two Runners inside, no more. If they take an interest in you, I shall tell them you have a letter for Sir John and are not to be bothered."

"And they will listen?"

I thought about that a moment. "Yes," I said, "they will."

"You lead."

He followed. We went past the courtroom on the left, where, as I had expected, matters were long concluded for the day. Then we walked by the empty strong room, saw no Runners, and met Mr. Marsden in his alcove. I greeted him and asked if Sir John was available in his chambers. He allowed that he was, looked curiously at Jimmie Bunkins, then returned to his court records. We continued on our way.

"He didn't say nicks about me," whispered Bunkins.

"Perhaps you're not as famous as you think," said I.

"But he wasn't no Beak-runner."

"No," said I, "he is the court clerk. The Runners are no doubt off conveying the prisoners to jail."

"Crikey!" said Bunkins, and gave a shake of revulsion.

I knocked upon Sir John's door, identified myself, and

was invited to enter. Both I and Bunkins went inside—he most careful, looking this way and that, altogether uneasy. He removed his tricorn, exposing his mop of untidy hair.

"You have someone with you, Jeremy. Is it Moll Caulfield?"

"No, Sir John, it is one named Jimmie Bunkins, who was given a letter by her for you yesterevening not long after six."

"Well, then, let him come forward and give it me."

Bunkins did so, quaking at every step. He laid it, wrinkled and folded as it was, upon the table just at Sir John's fingertips, then stepped quickly back.

"Have you read it, Mr. Bunkins?"

"No . . ." He tested his voice. It was much too weak, and so he tried again. "No, sir, I got no letters."

"I see. Perhaps then you could tell me just how this letter fell into your hands."

And that he did, in about the same words he had used before, describing the event and his relation to Moll Caulfield, though in a tone not near so bold as he had when relating it to me. Indeed, Jimmie Bunkins seemed quite in awe of Sir John Fielding, as well he might have been, judging his situation. Sir John listened with interest, nodding, encouraging him to continue. When at last Bunkins had done, there was silence between them for a spell.

Then Sir John asked: "Master Bunkins, would you say that Moll Caulfield was being held against her will?"

"A prisoner like? That I cannot say for sure, sir. All as I saw was that she went in line with the rest and was most careful to put the letter in my hand without nobody seein'— all folded up, it was."

"But she was seen?"

"Yes, sir, and I got chased. I distanced them like they was constables. I know the streets."

"How, if you have no letters, did you know that what she gave you was intended for me? Did she dare speak to you?"

"No, sir, but she made the sign."

"The sign?"

"Like this, sir. Oh, but you can't see, can you, sir?"

"No, but describe it, please. I'm interested."

"Well, you put your finger so, and make a kind of bird's beak of your nose. See, old Moll, she wasn't no thief herself, but she knew the flash and all the signs of the street. That one's your sign, or the sign for one of your Beakrunners—same thing. Maybe I shouldn't tell you, but that's the way of it."

"You did not then go to a Runner?"

"Uh, no, sir, I keeps my distance from such."

"But you approached Jeremy."

"Uh, yes, sir. Him and me, we had a tussle, but he seemed a right rum joe."

"Then I thank you for coming forward, with Jeremy, and delivering the letter. Perhaps you hoped for some reward?"

"Well, I . . ."

"All I can offer you is this. You have given a strong hint that you are a thief. Jeremy suspected you, and that, I believe, was what occasioned your fray. Let me ask you this: Have you parents? Father or mother?"

"No, sir."

"No trade, no other means of earning your bread?"

"No, sir."

"Then I strongly advise you to give up thieving, but I realize this may be difficult in your situation. So what I can offer is this. When you appear before me as magistrate, as you surely will if you persist, I shall take this service you have performed in consideration in judging you. Does that satisfy you in the way of reward?"

Bunkins nodded vigorously. "Oh yes, sir, it does right rum."

"Agreed, then. Jeremy? Will you show Master Bunkins out, and return so that we may examine the contents of Moll Caulfield's letter?"

"Yes, Sir John," said I.

With that, I touched my young companion on the arm, for he had continued to stare dumbly at the magistrate. The spell thus broken, he consented to go. We were as far as the door when Sir John called after us.

"Master Bunkins," said he, "one thing more I would say to you. I have the means of sending boys in your state to sea—either in His Majesty's Navy or the merchant navy. Had you ever considered such a life?"

"No, sir, I ain't."

"Well, give it some thought. Please do. If you wish to discuss it more with me, you have but to seek out Jeremy."

"Thank you, sir."

"Thank you, Master Bunkins."

And so we left together. Jimmie Bunkins said not a word to me until we reached the door to the street. I opened it, and he stepped out absently, as if thinking of other things— as indeed at that moment he must have been.

Then, of a sudden, he burst out: "What a rum cove he is! I ain't never met such a joe, and I don't never hope to. I could be sent to crap by such as him and thank him for it."

He grabbed my hand and pumped it hard. "Keep your glims open. I'll be seeing you soon, old chum. 'Twas a good meeting."

He ran from Number 4 Bow Street, showing me a bit of the fleetness with which he had kept clear of the law up to that moment. I wished him well but feared that it was, as Sir John said, only a matter of time until he fell afoul of it. That, however, was not the immediate problem. I hurried back to Sir John's chambers that the matter at hand might then be treated.

"Ah, Jeremy," said he, "come in, come in. Read this thing to me, please."

Moll Caulfield's letter was something of a disappointment. It gave no specific information regarding the Brethren of the Spirit, nor did it give any hint of where she might have taken herself. It read as follows: "Sir John: Things is not right here with these folk. I would tell you more if you could get me away.—Moll C."

"Well, it is not much, is it?" said Sir John. "It does indicate, however, that she felt herself near a prisoner with them." He paused a moment, then added, "I take it you had no success in your search for her."

"No, sir."

"Nor for her friend, Dotty?"

"No, sir. I was working my way through Covent Garden in my search when Jimmie Bunkins found me. I thought it best to bring him right to you."

"You did well. An interesting boy. There are scores like him in Westminster alone—orphaned, penniless, without a trade. They can do nothing but steal. Amusing what he told about the sign Moll gave him—the sign for me and the Runners. Had you heard of that?"

"Nothing, sir."

"I hope we can persuade him to leave the streets."

He fell then into one of his long, musing silences. I knew enough not to trouble him during them. He simply thought what had to be thought during such times and often emerged from these deep waters at a point much distant from where he dove in. Many minutes passed.

"If it were not sacrilegious to say," he declared, "I would call a damnation upon this ranting sect, these Brethren of the Spirit. They are disruptive; they are disturbers of the fragile peace we maintain here at Bow Street. I like them not, and least of all do I like that Brother Abraham."

"There is something I would tell you about them, Sir John."

"Oh? What is that?"

"I was minded of it in listening to Mr. Bilbo's account of his meeting with the two of the sect in Maiden Lane."

"Ah yes, perhaps I shouldn't have fined him. I could have thus shown my displeasure at the way those two troubled him, thinking him a Jew. At least I fined Brother Isaac and Brother James equally today for their contempt of my court. But I go on. What was it came to you during the Bilbo matter?"

"It was this, sir: On that unhappy occasion when I delivered Moll Caulfield up to the Brethren of the Spirit, there in the Garden, I heard them sing one of their hymns, which was unlike any other I had ever heard. It seemed to prophesy the conversion of the Jews. And that, it was, was most on the minds of those two in Maiden Lane. There is a Jewish church there, you may remember.''

"But of course there is! That had slipped my mind completely. They cause so little trouble that they skip my notice. Strange Dutch Jews they are, who I'm told grow beards like Bilbo's and dress as black as the Brethren of the Spirit. Isaac and James may have thought old Black Jack was going into or coming out of the synagogue.''

That was a term unfamiliar to me. It had a strange, foreign sound. "A synagogue, sir? Is that a Jewish church?''

"That is what they call it, yes.''

"I know little of Jews," said I, "though my father spoke well of them—Spinoza and Maimonides, in particular. His favorite, Voltaire, spoke against them, but he said that he provided an instance to prove that one should never take a philosopher whole, but in pieces.''

"I wish I had known your father," said Sir John. "He seems to have given you naught but wisdom.''

"I never knew a Jew," said I.

"They are like all men," said he, "most good, sóme bad. I have had a few of the bad before me in court. One was hanged, and justly so, for he had committed murder. But the rest go unnoticed, for they incur no blame upon them.''

He paused, thought but a moment, then returned to the subject: "This business of the conversion of the Jews was a matter much discussed, and was expected by some, in the last century. An age that could manage the execution of a king expected great wonders and portents to come of it. Since the preachers preached that Christ's second coming could only happen with the conversion of the Jews, and a certain mathematical hocus-pocus had been done to prove that the second coming was near at hand, it was supposed that the Jews would do their part and become Christian, and Christ would descend from heaven and set foot first in England—there was never any doubt that London would be his New Jerusalem. Yet why he should ever wish to appear in such squalid surroundings as these, I cannot suppose. In any case, this worldwide conversion of Christ's own people was supposed to begin sometime in the middle of the last century. Though I cannot recall the precise date, the date was most precise. I do, however, recall that the process was to be complete by 1699, making the way clear for the second coming, I suppose in 1700—these biblical literalists are all very fond of such round numbers.

"Well, the Jews did not cooperate. They stuck to their Old Testament and conducted themselves as they had for the last four thousand years, give or take. This was of no great moment in England, for these precise calculations and prophecies were the concern of preachers and theologians only. And a good thing that was, too, for had they excited the populace to their expectations, there might have been reprisals against the Jews as are seen in those benighted, so-called Christian nations in the east of Europe. We'll have none of that here, I pray."

He had ended at that point. And so I spoke up as follows: "But now come these Brethren of the Spirit. This seems to be part of their plan, does it not?"

"Who knows what mischief they are up to? Damnation! They—"

A stout knock sounded upon Sir John's door.

"Attend to that, will you, Jeremy?"

I went to the door, opened it, and found two men there—Mr. Marsden, whom I knew quite well, and another whom I'd never before seen. The second man, who wore a short, neat-trimmed beard and a good suit of clothes, hung back most polite, yet showed an urgency in his manner that he could bare restrain.

"Mr. Moses Martinez wishes to speak with Sir John," said Mr. Marsden.

"Who is there, Jeremy?"

"Mr. Moses Martinez, sir."

"Well, show him in, show him in."

Mr. Marsden and I stepped aside, and the guest whisked past us and up to Sir John. He shook the hand that was extended to him. Although new to my sight, I knew him by his good reputation. It was he who had set Lady Goodhope's financial affairs in order. I recalled that in commending him, Sir John had described him as "a Jew and an honest man." So now, it seemed, I looked upon my first Jew. In truth, I was somewhat disappointed. Except for the beard, which was not the fashion, he looked as other men, though better-dressed.

Mr. Marsden had disappeared. Quite curious as to the nature of this visit, I eased the door shut and remained. I had not, after all, been asked to go.

"Sir John, I would not trouble you so," said Mr. Martinez, "but I have just been made aware of a distressing matter that I feel must be brought to your attention."

He spoke as other men, too.

"Sit down then, sir, and tell me," said Sir John. "Unburden your legs and your heart."

Mr. Martinez took the chair, yet he was in such an agitated state that he held back a moment to calm himself. Then he began: "You are aware of the synagogue on Maiden Lane?"

"Indeed. I've just been reminded of it."

"They are good people there. They may appear a bit odd to their neighbors for their dress and the length of their beards, but they keep to themselves and cause no trouble to anyone."

"Dutch Jews, are they not?"

"So they are called, though in truth they are from the Ukraine and Poland, where they were much oppressed and suffered greatly. By the distinction we accept, they are Ashkenazi Jews."

"And you are . . ."

"Sephardic."

"Would this be like unto Catholic and Protestant?"

"No, Sir John. There is no real dispute between us. We are simply Jews of differing histories. No need to go into those histories now."

"As you say, Mr. Martinez." He waved him to continue.

"But at this synagogue on Maiden Lane, yesterevening, the Sabbath services were interrupted by a group of men in a most threatening manner. These men were well known to the congregation, for most had been accosted on the street by them in a rude manner and preached at most aggressively.''

"The Brethren of the Spirit," put in Sir John.

"Ah! You know them.''

"All too well, Mr. Martinez, all to well. But tell me, do, what have they now done to disturb the peace and anger me further?''

"As I say, sir, they interrupted the Sabbath services, blocked the exits, and forced the congregation to listen to a . . . well, a sermon by one of their number.''

"Brother Abraham, I'll wager.''

"That may be. I was not present.''

"How came you to hear of this, then?''

"One who was present reported it to me. He is a man, however, whom I know, and I trust his account.''

"Did he say how they blocked the exits? Were these men armed?''

"He did not say.''

"Did he give some idea of the content of this sermon that was preached to this captive congregation?''

"That he did, yes. He said it was a most impassioned and angry bid—nay, demand—for the conversion of the congregation to the Christian faith.''

"To preach thus is no crime, of course," said Sir John. "Yet if coercion was used upon the congregation to force their attention . . .''

"Exactly," said Mr. Martinez, "or the exits blocked to prevent their departure . . . ?''

"Yes, and then there is the matter of trespass. Surely these Ranters were not invited in.''

"Certainly not.''

"I should like to know more of this. We may have a whole list of charges to lodge against them.''

"Sir John, I should *like* you to know more of this," said Mr. Martinez, with a great smile. "Perhaps you might go to the synagogue a little later, and hear all this for yourself.''

"Why not now? I am quite willing to go this moment.''

To demonstrate this, Sir John rose to his feet and began

searching the surface of the table for his tricorn and stick.

Mr. Martinez rose less certainly. "This may not be the most opportune moment," said he.

"Oh? How is that?"

"Until the sun goes down, it is still the Sabbath. The rabbi will be conducting services until then."

"The rabbi? He is the priest? The preacher?"

"On the order of a preacher, I would say."

"And it is to him I should speak?"

"Just so, Sir John. Let me call for you just before sundown. I would deem it an honor to accompany you, and I think I may be of some help to you."

"I think, sir, that you can provide a great deal of help, and I shall be glad for all you give."

As good as his word, Moses Martinez called for Sir John at some time about half past six. When we two emerged from Number 4 Bow Street, he was there standing at the door to his closed carriage, ready to play footman to the magistrate. If he was surprised at seeing me beside him, he gave no sign of it. Sir John had extended an invitation to me on the spur of the moment, saying this was sure to be an educational experience for both of us. And indeed it proved to be so.

"I was so taken by your report," said he to Mr. Martinez, "that I failed to introduce you to my young assistant, Jeremy Proctor. Let me present him to you now."

I shook hands solemnly with the bearded gentleman and noted that he seemed to make a favorable assessment of me as he murmured his pleasure at making my acquaintance.

Then into the carriage—I first, then Sir John with a hand up, and Mr. Martinez last of all. With three across, it was a bit tight, but we had only a short distance to go.

Sir John remarked upon that: "We could have walked, you know."

"Perhaps so," said Mr. Martinez, "yet even with your Runners, the streets are dangerous—perhaps even for you, certainly for me."

We rode along without further conversation between them until the carriage turned up Maiden Lane. As it did so, Mr. Martinez spoke up, engaging both Sir John and myself with certain words of explanation.

"Have you ever before been to a synagogue, Sir John?"

"In truth, I have not."

"Nor you, young Jeremy?"

"No, sir."

"Then I should probably say that the one we are about to visit is in no wise typical. Were you to visit my Sephardic temple, you would find it not greatly different from your own church services. Prayers are said and sung in Hebrew, which you, Jeremy, would no doubt find a strange-sounding language, but much of the service, perhaps most of it, is conducted in English. And the conduct of the congregation is, as you might expect, dignified and quiet.

"Things are much different at the synagogue, Beth El, which we are about to visit."

"Because they are of that other persuasion, the Ash . . . ?"

"The Ashkenazi—yes, partly. Because they are newcomers to this country they hold their services in Hebrew and Yudish, which is the language of the Jews of eastern Europe. But this particular congregation is of a movement among the Ashkenazim called the Hasidim."

(So many *strange* words, thought I.)

"Their behavior is thought scandalous by many. They are said to be rowdy. They sing, they even dance, and they rely greatly upon the wisdom of their rabbi, Gershon, who is at heart not so much a preacher, but a storyteller."

"And it is with him we shall speak?" asked Sir John.

"Yes, indeed," said Mr. Martinez.

"In plain English, or must you translate?"

"Oh, he speaks English very well, one of many languages he has mastered. I find him a remarkable man. As I say, these Hasidic Jews have scandalized many, yet I have had many conversations with him and each time have come away well nourished. I think you will like him."

"That concerns me less than the question of whether he will make a good and willing witness."

"As you say, Sir John."

Only moments later, the carriage reined up at the synagogue on Maiden Lane. Mr. Martinez hopped out and, giving firm instructions to his driver to wait, helped Sir John down; he also offered a hand to me, yet I refused it, being of an age to require little assistance and want none of it.

I had recognized the small house on Maiden Lane as a synagogue because of the six-pointed star in the window, which my father had told me was the symbol of the Jews as the crucifix was the symbol of the Christians, and for the strange writing above the entrance in those curious vertical letters that puzzled me so. Other than to note its location here in the area of Covent Garden, I had not given it much thought. It served me only as a reminder of what a great and worldly place London was—and is still today.

Mr. Martinez knocked upon the door, and though he received no response, we heard the muffled sounds of a commotion beyond. With a shrug, he tried the door, and it opened to his touch.

"Well," said Sir John, "we know how the Brethren of the Spirit accomplished their entrance."

Mr. Martinez shrugged. "It is, after all, a house of worship. One cannot lock it to the worshipers."

"True enough."

"If you will but follow me."

With that, he led the way—I in the rear—down a short hall and on to a large meeting room.

"It seems," said Sir John over the increasing din, "that we interrupt the service."

"They go on and on. They would keep Rabbi Gershon all night if he let them—and at times indeed he does."

Upon reaching the meeting room, I stood quite overwhelmed by what I saw and heard. If this was a house of worship it was unlike any I had seen before, and the worshipers quite the most unrestrained. The room was simple enough. There were chairs, most of them pushed aside, and an elevated platform at the far end of the room upon which stood a curtained closet of small dimensions. All this I saw but with some difficulty, standing on tiptoe, looking this way and that, for the members of the congregation—all of them men—were on their feet, raising their voices in the most terrific hubbub, all of it in a language of a rough and guttural sound that hit hard upon the ears. They seemed to be arguing amongst themselves, paying little attention to the small, bearded man who stood in robes upon the platform. Once or twice a phrase was tossed at him, yet he simply smiled and spoke something in return.

Signaling us to wait, Mr. Martinez made his careful way forward to the platform and spoke to the little man in robes, who nodded and looked our way. Then he shouted out something to the contentious multitude—which was really not such a multitude but only about twenty or twenty-five—and they gave him their attention immediately. Then, slowly and rhythmically, he began clapping. And the rough, bearded men, some of them in boots and none in fancy clothes, began to raise their voices in a strange song. Some were caught unawares by the music, joining in late, so that the song, whatever it was, seemed to swell with each measure. Was this a hymn? No, the sound of it was happier than any I had ever heard in high church or low. It was sung to a heavy rhythm, so that soon the beat kept by the rabbi as he clapped his hands was picked up by the men, stamping their feet. As they stamped, they whirled in place, snapping their fingers in unison as I had once seen Gypsies do. Soon, singing, they were also dancing. It was quite the most remarkable thing ever I had seen—grown men dancing and singing, not in a show for the entertainment of some audience, but rather for the pure exuberant joy of it.

Was this not what Mr. Martinez had said they might do? Indeed, but it was one thing to be told and quite another to see it done. I glanced over at Sir John that I might see how this strange behavior affected him. He, it seemed, wore a fixed, puzzled smile upon his face, as if not quite sure that he could accept the evidence his ears provided.

Then, sudden as it had all begun, it ended. The rabbi left off his clapping. All fell silent and faced him. Raising his arm, extending his hand, he pronounced what seemed to be a blessing upon them in that same thick and throaty tongue which the others had spoken amongst themselves. Mr. Martinez then appeared, assuring us that it would be but a moment now, and they would all be gone but for the rabbi. They were milling now, preparing to depart. Then, from above, I heard similar sounds. I turned and looked up behind me and realized that there were women up there behind a latticework. Their voices sounded. I heard their feet upon stairs, and then they came, one and two at a time, to join their men, and departed together with them.

Soon the hall was empty. The rabbi stepped down from the platform and came over to where the three of us stood. Mr. Martinez presented him to Sir John as Rabbi Gershon of Kishinev, and the two men shook hands. The rabbi gestured to the empty chairs that had been pushed over to one side. I touched Sir John at the elbow and moved him over in that direction.

"Is your congregation always so demonstrative?" he asked as he eased down into the chair I had set behind him.

"Always," said the rabbi.

"They sang as lustily as drunken men."

"Drunk with the love of the Almighty."

"And if my ears did not deceive me, they danced, as well. I've been to sea. Sailors dance just so in celebration."

"As King David danced in celebration before the Ark of the Covenant. There is no sin in joy."

"Simply a question of what it is that inspires that joy."

"What is base or evil cannot inspire true joy."

"Nor will it be celebrated by righteous men."

"I see there is good ground between us," said the rabbi, with a shy smile. "Let us explore it together."

The two men leaned forward in their chairs, each toward the other. I noted that Mr. Martinez remained standing, as I had—he to one side of the rabbi. He watched both in a manner of expectation.

"Tell me of the visit made to you last night," said Sir John.

The other man shrugged. "There is not much to tell,"

said he. "It's true, we had some visitors. We did not invite them in, but it's not unknown that some enter from the street out of curiosity. We allow them, of course. This is the house of him who created us all. What would we be if we barred some of his people? Most who come are Jews. Moishe Martinez has been here often. Our visitors last evening were not Jews."

"How many were there?"

"Not so many. Four or five—five, I believe."

"Your congregation could easily have overpowered them—that is, if your visitors were not armed. Were they armed?"

"Not with sword or pistol, no."

"Which implies they were otherwise equipped."

"Four of the five carried stout clubs."

"And the fifth?"

"He had come to preach to us."

"Ah, Brother Abraham, I'll hazard."

"He gave it as his name, yes. He thought it gave him a certain claim upon our attention, as if he were our new patriarch."

"I daresay you did not accept his claim?"

"No, but we have had experience of such men before in other lands. If they wish to talk, then we listen, always respectfully. That is the counsel I gave the congregation—to be respectful."

"You gave this counsel to them in your own language, the one which I heard tonight?"

"Yes, it was odd, but this man who calls himself Abraham seemed not to realize that many there would not understand if he spoke in English to them. And so he asked that I translate his words so they might be better understood by all. This fellow, this Abraham, he was not so worldly, but he was not so stupid, either. He knew his Torah, and he quoted well, but with the prophets, he was not so good. Them he quoted to his own purposes, and I translated with commentary—a word of caution here, a wink there; they understood."

"And what was the purpose of his preaching?" asked
Sir John.

"One known to all Jews—to Moishe Martinez just as to
me. His people heard it in Spain from the Franciscans two
centuries ago, and I—"

The rabbi broke off of a sudden thought but a moment,
then smiled and said, "Let me tell you a story."

"I understand," said Sir John, "that you are a good storyteller."

"I try, for all important truths are in stories. This one is
not so new, in fact very old, for I have borrowed it from
an old book called the Haggadah. But I shall alter it to
better answer your question on the purpose of the preaching."

"Proceed," said Sir John, and therewith settled back in
his chair.

"Once," said the rabbi, "there was a kingdom ruled by
a very just king who wished his subjects not only to pros-
per, but above all to be just and generous to one another.
In this kingdom there were two farmers, landowners both,
who lived one beside the other. One, the older of the two,
had many sons who helped him work his land, but one left
to seek his fortune in the city and another to follow a life
on the sea. This left him with a piece of good land and no
one to work it. But the older farmer had other sons and
more land and was still prosperous, so he decided to sell
that particular piece to the younger farmer next to him. That
he did, for a good and fair price. Both landowners were
happy with the bargain they had struck.

"But while digging a well on the piece of land he had
just acquired, the second farmer found deep in the earth a
coffer filled with gold coins—a buried treasure. He knew
from the age of the chest and the coins that they were
ancient and could not possibly have been buried by the man
from whom he bought the land. Nevertheless, the second
farmer went to the first and said, 'Take this coffer filled
with gold coins, for I found it buried on the land which I
bought from you.' Now, we must stop and ask why the
second farmer would do such a thing? He had a plan. His

intention was that the just king who encouraged good works among his subjects should hear of his generosity and hold him in special favor, probably reward him with greater pieces of land, perhaps elevate him to the nobility.

"The seller of the land objected, however. 'This treasure you have found is not mine,' said he. 'I did not bury it. I sold you the piece of land and got a fair price. What you found upon it is yours.'

" 'No!' said the buyer sharply, for he was growing angry. 'You must take the treasure, for I bought only the land. What was on it, or in it, is yours.'

" 'Your generosity is great, but I cannot accept,' said the seller.

"Feeling great anger now, for his plan to win the king's favor was about to fail, the second farmer said, 'You must accept the treasure I offer you, or I shall kill you.' "

With that, the rabbi sat back with a smile, signaling the end of his story. Sir John waited, and waited a bit more, quite expectantly.

"Well, get on with it, man," said he, somewhat in exasperation. "What is the end of your story?"

Rabbi Gershon shrugged, raising both palms upward. "Who knows?" said he.

"Well, did the buyer force the seller to take the treasure with his threat? Did the buyer kill the seller?"

"All this happened a very long time ago, so we can be sure that the seller of the land is dead. When he died and what were the circumstances, I cannot say. All men die— though that, in itself, is no matter for mourning. For him who dies it may be a matter for rejoicing. Who can tell?"

"Hmmph."

Sir John let out just such a grunt and folded his fingers across his belly. He sat thus, uttering not a word for a considerable space of time.

Then at last he said, "Rabbi Gershon, was any threat made against you or your congregation?"

"Let me give it exact as I remember it. This man who calls himself Abraham opened his arms and declared that he greeted us all as brothers. If we were to accept the one you call Jesus as the Messiah, all the riches of heaven would be ours. How he knew this I cannot say. He asked all who would do so to come forward. I repeated his invitation in our tongue. When none came, he became angry and said, 'The Roman Church knew how to deal with such as you—by fire and sword.' "

"That was how he put it? The Roman Church knew how?"

"That was what he said."

"Well, that much is historical fact."

"Indeed," said the rabbi.

"But the threat is implied," put in Moses Martinez.

"Yet not stated," said Sir John with a sigh. Then, summing up: "Trespass seems out of the question, since you welcome visitors from outside and have had them before. What about assault? Was any man hit by those who carried clubs?"

"No."

"Was any handled roughly who tried to leave?"

"No. I instructed the members of my congregation to hold their places."

"It seems then that all I can charge them with is the intrusion itself. All you need do is swear to the circumstances, and I shall fine them to the maximum for disturbing the peace."

"Much as I would like to," said Rabbi Gershon, "I will not do that."

"But why not? We cannot allow such an outrage to go unnoticed. If we do nothing, then it could well happen again—and again and again. You cannot want that, sir."

"No, I do not, but even less do I wish to call attention to ourselves. We have known such events before—in the Ukraine, in Poland, even in Holland. It always seems best to choose the quieter course."

"But you must understand, Rabbi Gershon," said Mr. Martinez, "that this is England. The law is with you. Sir John Fielding wants to help you and your people."

"Where I grew up," said the rabbi, "there was a great forest, and for a while there were wolves in the forest. They

made themselves known every night, howling to one another, howling at the moon. Then one year, the nobles of
the district organized a great hunting party, one that lasted
a week or more. All the wolves in the forest were killed.
No more howling was heard from that time on. Now, there
were foxes in that forest, too. The fox is a very shy animal,
very quiet indeed. And there are foxes in that forest still
today.''

SEVEN

*In which John Clayton has
his say, and Jimmie Bunkins
takes me on a journey*

Sir John Fielding allowed himself no day of complete rest
of a Sunday. He could not, for the harvest of villains and
malefactors was always greatest on a Saturday night. These
felonies he would tend to, lest the strong room become too
crowded, yet he heard no civil cases on Sundays, nor low
misdemeanors. This made, generally, for a more leisurely
day. He would rise late, for church attendance was not his
habit, eat well, hear such cases as were necessary, then be
on his way for the rest of the day and evening. Mr. Alfred
Humber, whom I had met at Lloyd's Coffee House, had
become his frequent companion on these weekly rambles
about the town. He was a bachelor and Sir John, of course,
a recent widower, but both men were of an age and dignity
that their nights out consisted of no more than a bit of
pleasant strolling while still it was light, a good dinner at
some eating place, and a bit of drinking afterwards. I believe that Mr. Humber's intent was to ease Sir John's be-
reavement. Thus in the past few weeks a pattern had been
established, a pattern which would be broken on this Sunday whose action I am about to describe.

I was first surprised by his relatively early appearance.
Though not yet fully dressed, he was well on his way. As

I sat sipping my tea, finishing my bread and dripping, he emerged from his bedroom in breeches and shirt, asked Mrs. Gredge for a dish of tea, and me he asked to shave him. This was a duty I had taken over from Mrs. Gredge, her failing eyesight putting him somewhat at risk. Though I was a couple of years away from shaving myself, I had watched my father at it many a time and had a fair notion of how it was done. I had become better at it in the past days, and he now seemed quite satisfied with the work I performed for him three or four times a week.

And so, as Mrs. Gredge heated water for the shaving pan, I finished my breakfast and laid out the shaving gear. How I loved to strop that razor!

"Shave me close, Jeremy," said he to me. "It might be well to do the job twice."

I did as he wished, taking care, drawing no blood; and after I had finished, he tested his cheeks with his fingertips and nodded his approval.

"I shall be needing you today, Jeremy. Dress well and wash. Be ready in an hour."

I was. Yet it was still at the midpoint of the morning when we two descended to the ground floor. Sir John there asked after the number of prisoners in the strong room, which was not great, and the circumstances of their arrests. Satisfied, he led me to his chambers and inside.

"Leave the door wide," said he, "for we shall be having company. Come to think of it, we may need some chairs. Three more are expected."

"Then we shall need three more chairs," said I.

"Attend to it, please."

His manner that morning was most direct, almost brusque. He wasted few words. I took this not as a sign of his displeasure, for I had done naught to displease him, but rather that he was preoccupied by his consideration of matters that lay ahead. I made no question as I brought in the chairs. I kept my silence as I settled into one of them and waited. After a bit, he spoke.

"There was no report of Moll Caulfield," said he. "The Runners were instructed to look sharp for her—she is known by sight to many—and to ask after her, as well."

"Then she seems to have vanished."

"I like it not."

"Perhaps her friend Dotty could—"

"Perhaps."

Silence again. Then:

"If only she had said something of substance in that note she passed to that urchin boy you brought here."

"Yes, sir."

"By the by, he *was* the same with whom you fought, was he not?"

"Yes, sir," said I, wishing the matter had been forgotten and fearing the worst.

"Well," said he, "since you have made your peace with him and he with you, it would be superfluous to punish you."

Feeling great relief at that, I was about to thank him when he pressed on:

"*However*, remember my words to you regarding the event. Remember, in particular, what I said to you at the time: You, being better-educated and better-situated, bore the greater blame in the matter. A boy such as Bunkins knows nothing but the law of the streets."

"He seems to have some good qualities, though."

"Bunkins may be salvageable. Let us hope so."

"Yes, sir. Thank you, Sir John."

He grunted in response.

Then from the far end of the long hall came the sound of the door to the street opening and closing. Firm footsteps followed.

"It would seem," said he, "that one of our party has arrived. There will be an interrogation. As it proceeds, I wish you to witness both what is said and how it is said. You have a good eye. Report to me afterwards any signs of visible stress or strong reaction to my questions. You have done it before. You know the sort of thing I seek."

The footsteps grew close. Half expecting to see Brother Abraham appear, I was somewhat surprised when Dr. Samuel Johnson appeared.

"Since the door is open," said he, "I take it I am free to enter."

"You are indeed," said Sir John. "Come ahead, Dr. Johnson."

Come ahead he did, moving his great bulk swiftly across the intervening space, grasping Sir John's extended hand. He acknowledged my presence with a nod of his head and took a seat at a far remove from me. Was Samuel Johnson to be interrogated? That seemed unlikely. Of what crime or misdemeanor could a distinguished personage such as he be guilty? Of what could he even be suspected? Still, I listened with care and watched his face as the two men began to talk, though it soon seemed to me that their talk was of such a casual nature that it could have no investigatory purpose. It was of a literary nature. Sir John mentioned to him that he and I had been reading in our evenings, and that we both took a good deal of pleasure in it (which was quite true).

"And what have you been reading?" asked Dr. Johnson.

"Shakespeare, for the most part. We are near through his *Dream of a Midsummer-Night.*"

"A pleasant work, certainly, full of fairies, rude mechanicals, and the like. No doubt the boy finds it pleasurable. You cannot do wrong reading Shakespeare."

"You say that in such a way as to belittle the play."

"Well, the great power of the man lies in his tragedies and some of the histories."

"No question of that, yet there are times when amusement satisfies better than tales of murder and revenge, no matter how powerful they be."

"No doubt," said Dr. Johnson, somewhat patronizing.

"Perhaps you might recommend something of recent publication. I confess I know nothing of what is now being written."

"Well, if it is amusement you seek, then perhaps *Tristram Shandy* would suit you. The final volume was published just last year. The author died, I believe, just two months past."

"A man named Sterne, was it not? He had a bad reputation—immoral. To tell the truth, when the first volumes of the book appeared some years ago, my late wife, Kitty, read them to me, and I thought them too fantastical, downright silly. No," said Sir John, as if settling the matter, "if we're to read a romance, it will be *Tom Jones*. I should like to hear it again—it will be my third time through, and Jeremy has never had the pleasure of it. You may not credit this, Dr. Johnson, but his father kept it from him, thinking it an immoral book. Can you ever suppose that my good brother would ever write an immoral book? Who could think such a thing—much less say it?"

"Must we go down that road once again?" asked Dr. Johnson with a great show of exasperation. "I never *said* his was an immoral book; at least I did not say so in print, which is the matter at hand."

"And what about that issue of your paper, *The Rambler?*"

"That was years ago, and I did not mention the book by name. And, sir, what I think it to be is my own affair."

"Well, I think it to be the best romance ever written."

"Each is entitled to his opinion. I myself think *Amelia* is a better book."

I had the notion, as I listened, that they might go on so for an hour or more, at which time Dr. Johnson would leave in a great huff. Yet just at that moment, the door to the street slammed shut and footsteps sounded again in the hall. This quietened them both.

"Let me ask you," said Sir John in a more temperate tone, "have you ever been to Bedlam?"

"I visited Kit Smart there a time or two. The place is pure hell. If a sane man were confined, he would soon be driven mad there."

"My thought precisely. That is why I have had our peasant poet removed to the Fleet Prison. I asked you here, Dr. Johnson, that you might question him where you see fit and afterwards comment upon his sanity, his ability to stand trial."

"The man I saw in your courtroom was in no wise able, sir."

"I agree. Yet I encountered a much different man when I visited Bedlam with the Lord Chief Justice. Be aware that John Clayton has asked to stand trial. But hush. He comes now."

John Clayton appeared in the open door. His hands were manacled, but he had been spared the indignity of leg irons. He was invited forward by Sir John and followed in by Mr. Fuller of the day watch, who was armed with a brace of pistols.

"Sit yourself down here before me, Mr. Clayton," said Sir John. "You are acquainted with Dr. Johnson, I believe. The young man is Jeremy Proctor, who serves as my assistant. You may remember him from our interview yester-morning."

John Clayton bowed solemnly to me; then he turned to the distinguished personage at his right.

"Dr. Johnson," said he, "I had not expected to meet you here. I own I am abashed for you to see me in these circumstances."

So saying, he raised his manacled hands in demonstration.

"Sir, put it from your mind. I have been in circumstances near as low myself," said Dr. Johnson. "I am come only to assist. You have my sympathy."

"Please take your seat," said Sir John in a manner somewhat more stern.

Mr. Clayton did immediately as directed. His keeper, Mr. Fuller, had meanwhile pulled his chair back near the door, which he now closed. Thus could he better watch his prisoner and bar his way should he try to escape.

"Now, John Clayton, our interview of the day past was cut somewhat short by Lord Mansfield when he discovered that it was your wish to be put on trial so that you might prove your innocence. How do you propose to do that?"

"Why, sir, by giving an account of what I remember of that night."

"It seemed to me," said Sir John, "that you were ready to do so then. Is that true?"

"Yes, sir, indeed it is."

"That being the case, I thought it best to remove you from the Hospital of St. Mary of Bethlehem and install you in the Fleet Prison so that I might have easier access. While the Fleet cannot be pleasant, I trust it is at least an improvement on your earlier accommodations?"

"Yes, sir."

"Good. Then I charge you to forget the barred cage to which you must return and the chains that bind your wrists. Speak as a witness and not as one accused. That is how I shall hear you. Give me your account of the events of that terrible night."

"Well, sir," said the witness, "I was asleep in the cellar when—"

"I must interrupt you," said Sir John. "We need not rush through this. In point of fact, we ought not. It would be best for my purposes if you were to answer this: How came you to be there?"

"I had come," said Mr. Clayton, "to see my second book through the press. It was thought that if I were to be present, reading proofs and making corrections as the type was set, the cost of printing could be kept low, and there would be no delays as were caused in the past with my first book."

"Your new book was also a volume of poetry?" asked Dr. Johnson.

"Yes, sir, it was. I was hoping to make such a great success with this book that I might never have to return to Somersetshire. I hoped to make a living by writing poetry."

"Vain hope, sir," declared Dr. Johnson sternly. "To make a living on poetry is like trying to live on air. I well remember that I, too, came to London with just such a hope more years ago than I care to remember. I was then forced to put in a long apprenticeship as a Grub Street hack. What would I not write about if given a fee? Knowledge played no part in it, and less did art. I caution you, sir, Grub Street is not the answer."

"I note that, Dr. Johnson," said Sir John, "as I'm sure Mr. Clayton does. But shall we get on with this? Mr. Clayton, I was counseled earlier by Dr. Johnson that although

Ezekiel Crabb was all in favor of publishing books that added to the store of art and the intellect, he was less inclined to pay a fair price for them.''

"He was cheap," said Dr. Johnson, "no other word for it.''

"As you say," said Sir John, "but you, Mr. Clayton, went with him again. Was there some degree of acrimony in your negotiations on this second book?"

"There was, yes."

"And Eusebius appeared as your negotiator?"

"Yes, sir."

"And what effect had that?"

"Not a very good one, I fear, though in the end I was satisfied with the bargain we struck."

"Which was?" asked Dr. Johnson.

"A royalty on each copy sold."

"Would there have been any lump sum advanced?"—again, Dr. Johnson.

"A very modest one. It was because it was such a small sum that I agreed to stay in his cellar and eat with his apprentices."

"When did this arrangement begin?" asked Sir John.

"The day before the night in question."

"So you had had one night in the cellar previous to that one?"

"Yes, sir."

"And there was nothing that happened on that first night of an unusual nature."

"Nothing at all, no. I slept very well that night."

"But you did not on the second night?"

"In a way, I believe I slept all too well."

"That, I fear, is unclear. Explain, please."

"Well, perhaps if I described my sleeping arrangements in the cellar?"

"Proceed."

"I had been given a cot in a corner. Some efforts had been made for me since it was expected that I would be there the better part of a week. Boxes of books had been piled high around the cot and some space had been left, so that I had a bit of privacy to myself, something like a room. Although one to pinch a penny, Mr. Crabb could be quite considerate in such ways.''

"Well and good—so you were tucked away out of sight.''

"Exactly so. As I say, I had slept well the night before and was deep in sleep on the night in question, still tired from my tramp to London. But some hours after falling asleep, I found myself half roused by noises in the cellar. It seemed that there were men there, a gang of them—four or five at least, probably more. Yet they were there only briefly before they must have made their way up the stairs. Supposing I had dreamed their presence, I turned over and went back to sleep; indeed I had barely left that state.''

"Can you say what sound they made that stirred you?'' asked Sir John.

"No, I cannot, sir. It seemed that I was simply and of a sudden aware of their presence—yet only dimly, dream like.''

"I accept what you say, yet if indeed they were there, they must have forced the cellar door. You would have heard that, surely.''

"Surely," agreed Mr. Clayton, "unless they had a key.''

"That seems unlikely," said Sir John. "But obviously you were roused from your sleep— unless you took to sleepwalking that night.''

"In a sense that *is* what I did, though not until later. It could only have been minutes before they began their butchery, and I was made fully awake by the cries and screams of their victims. I wish to say at this point, sir, that these screams came all in a chorus, as if at some arranged signal the killing was begun. I think this of great importance.''

"Let me judge what is of importance and what is not.''

"As you say, but . . . well, I sprang from my cot in terror and started to rush up the stairs. Then I heard this gang of murderers descending from the floors above. I heard them talking amongst themselves. Luckily, my feet were bare, or I might have been heard at that moment. Fearing for my life, for those cries I had heard were unmistakably mortal, I hid myself in a closet at the rear, in the print shop.''

"And so you got no clear look at them, I suppose.''

"No, sir, I did not. But I was aware that when they came to the first floor, they remained some minutes to search for something.''

"How do you know that?''

"Because there was a good deal of walking about, and there were calls back and forth.''

"Of what nature? What was said?''

"It was all through the door and indistinct, but I heard one say, 'It is not here.' And another in response, 'It must be.' Whatever they sought must have been found, for they left soon thereafter.''

"You heard them go? What exit did they take?''

"Once more through the cellar. I heard them descend the stairs and waited until I was sure they had gone. Only then did I venture forth. Memory begins to fade at this point. I remember climbing the stairs. I remember looking upon the bodies of Ezekiel Crabb and his wife, horribly bloodied and hacked in their bed. And that, I fear, is all I remember.''

Sir John, who had been sitting forward through this recital, leaned back at this point and considered for a moment. I had noted that Dr. Johnson had, throughout the interrogation, watched Mr. Clayton with growing fascination. At the end of it, his face bore an expression of shock and consternation.

Then said Sir John: "How do you, Mr. Clayton, account for your time between the moment you looked upon the dead bodies of Mr. and Mrs. Crabb and your discovery by Constable Cowley and his party?''

"I can only guess, sir, but I understand that I identified myself to you and to others as Petrus. As Petrus, I must have made a tour of the upper rooms, visiting each floor, for I was found in the topmost.''

"Found there with a bloody axe in your hand. How came you by that axe, Mr. Clayton?''

"That I cannot say, Sir John. I can only suppose that it had been left there by one of the murder gang.''

"Which seems unlikely, does it not?"

"Let us leave it then that I cannot say."

"Yes, let us leave it at that. Just one more question have I for you. Are you acquainted with a man named Isham Henry?"

Mr. Clayton thought a bit; then: "I believe he was one of the two journeymen employed by Mr. Crabb. He was not about the day previous to the murders."

"No, according to him, he was returning from Nottingham, as I recall. Eusebius, I take it, did not inform you, but Mr. Henry appeared as a witness against you during the aborted proceedings following the crimes. What he gave was hearsay, and therefore not admissible, but he did declare that you felt great hostility toward Mr. Crabb after the publication of your first book, that you felt cheated by him when you learned the great number of copies it had sold and the consequent profit he had made at your expense. He said that you threatened Mr. Crabb. How much of this was true?"

"Some of it," said Mr. Clayton. "Most of it."

"Oh? Then tell me of this, sir."

"Indeed, I did feel badly treated by Mr. Crabb. If I could not say he had cheated me—and that I could not say—he had, I felt, taken advantage of me in my ignorance. However, I did, as I say, reach an agreement on my second book. By then, I would say that we had reached a settlement of our differences. I told you earlier of the arrangement."

"Yes, yes, but what of the threat? Did you, in fact, threaten him?"

"Yes, sir, I did."

"And in what way?"

"I threatened to go to another publisher for my second book."

At that, Dr. Johnson let out a great guffaw. "That brought him to heel, did it?"

"We reached an agreement."

"With the help of Eusebius?" put in Sir John.

"In spite of Eusebius," said Mr. Clayton.

"Very well, very well. Dr. Johnson, do you have any questions?"

"Sir, I do have one. Mr. Clayton thought it of great importance that the screams of the dying on that terrible night came, as I believe he put it, 'in a chorus.' I, for one, would like to know why he thought this of such moment."

"All right," said Sir John, with a sigh, "answer Dr. Johnson's question, Mr. Clayton."

"With pleasure, sir. I thought it important because, having given great thought to it in Bedlam, I had decided that the murder of six people in their beds could only have been accomplished by more than one man—at the very least, three. The fact that I heard those horrible screams, which echo in my ears to this moment, for a comparatively brief period and coming from every floor of the house indicates that the butchery was done simultaneous."

"There," said Dr. Johnson to Sir John, "does that not make good sense? Is that not well reasoned? I congratulate you, Mr. Clayton."

Sir John rose from his chair.

"And I," said he, "dismiss you, Mr. Clayton. Constable Fuller, you may return the prisoner to the Fleet Prison."

Mr. Fuller jumped to the command, and in no time at all, John Clayton had been ushered from the room. He threw a troubled look back at Sir John as he went, no doubt puzzled at his swift dismissal. I, too, wondered at it.

The prisoner and his keeper were scarce through the door when Dr. Johnson jumped to his feet and brought his stick down sharp upon the floor.

"Why did you do that, Sir John?" he asked, his face all red with anger.

"Because," said the magistrate, "I feared that the next thing I might hear from you would be a demand for his release."

"Why not?" thundered the lexicographer. "He is obviously telling the truth."

"It is not near so obvious as you believe."

"His point about the number of men necessary to kill

six people in their beds is perfectly well argued. His logic is unassailable.''

''Yes,'' said Sir John, ''and if you'll recall, that lout Burnley, who testified before Eusebius made a shambles of the proceeding, gave witness that agrees precisely with Clayton's version. What was it Albert Burnley said? 'A jumble of screams from folk being murdered'—very colorful language, that—and it lasted less than a minute.''

Dr. Johnson looked blankly at Sir John. ''I do not understand, sir,'' said he. ''You seem to be agreeing with me.''

''Of course I am agreeing with you, you pompous, conceited old bear! I, too, believe he is telling the truth in the way, and to the extent, that he remembers it. But if you think that what we have just heard from him will be sufficient to win him a not-guilty verdict at Old Bailey, then you are a bigger fool than that fellow Boswell who seems to hang upon your every word. And further, if you think his logic is unassailable, then just wait until Lord Mansfield begins to assail it. No, Dr. Johnson, before John Clayton goes to trial, he must be made to account for his presence on the scene with *the murder weapon* in his hand. That, and only that, is what Lord Mansfield will tell the jury is significant in the matter.''

''But it *could* have been left behind.''

''All things are possible, yet that is not probable.''

Dr. Johnson sank back into his chair, lost for a moment in thought.

''No,'' said he. ''I suppose not. But, sir, tell me, what was this talk of 'Petrus'? I remember the name being passed between you two in the courtroom, as well. Who or what is 'Petrus'?''

''In a way,'' said Sir John, ''it is of little importance who or what he is, but briefly, let me explain. John Clayton claims—and for what it matters, I believe him—that three natures reside in his single body. They are, first of all, his own; secondly, that of Eusebius, who prattles intellectual nonsense when challenged by authority; and lastly, of Petrus, who acts for Clayton in the face of violence. Eusebius you saw in the courtroom; you will recall that he insisted that it was he who was speaking in John Clayton's behalf. Petrus I met when Clayton was brought in by Constable Cowley—right nasty and brutish he was, let me assure you. Such wonders of the soul are, I admit, new to me, but Dr. Dillingham of Bedlam assured us that such cases are known, though of course not common."

"But how can you say this is not important?" blustered Dr. Johnson. "It is obviously of the utmost importance. It explains everything—or a great deal, at any rate."

"I say it is unimportant because Lord Mansfield will say it is so. In trial, he will hold it immaterial. In fact, in private conversation he has already given that as his opinion."

"Then what can be done for the poor fellow?"

"What can be done will be done, I assure you," said Sir John. "But let him not be given false hopes. Clayton has already betrayed himself as greatly naive in thinking that all he need do to establish his innocence is tell his story. *He* knows he is innocent, yet it is quite another thing to convince a judge and a jury of that. If I was a bit harsh with him, it was because I want him to keep thinking, trying to remember details that may help us catch those he calls 'the murder gang.' Something said, something . . . *anything.*"

"But could you not on your own authority discharge him? You could say that you have heard his account and believe him innocent of all wrongdoing."

"The man who was apprehended at the scene with the murder weapon in his hand? You have seen the broadsheet? The pamphlet against him? What would then be the uproar among your colleagues on Grub Street? But uproar or no, my belief or no, there is still inarguable cause to bind him over for trial. Besides, he has *asked* to be tried—in writing."

Dr. Johnson sat glum and discouraged. I saw him then, as I had seen him before, as the good man he was. Bluff, gruff, and probably pompous, but a good man, withal.

"May I convey this to him?" he asked.

"You intend to visit him in Fleet Prison?"

"Yes, poor fellow."

"You may tell him some but not all. Stress the importance of thinking further on it, of remembering details, even the slightest sort, that might help us. But do *not* tell him that I accept his story. Make me the ogre, if you like, but present me as one who must be convinced."

Dr. Johnson rose and made himself ready to go.

"All right then," said he, "it will be so. I shall go this very afternoon. Thank you, Sir John. Though you have insulted me and made me feel a nitwit, you have given me a right strong taste of the law's harsh reality."

"You have my sincerest apology, sir. I was carried away somewhat. Goodbye, then. There are matters I must attend to before the court begins."

With his goodbye, Dr. Samuel Johnson then departed. Sir John called me over to him. As he stood there, he betrayed a certain nervousness in his demeanor, fidgeting with his tricorn, turning it this way and that. This surprised me. He was usually the very picture of composure.

"Jeremy," said he, "I have an errand for you. But first I must ask you, what impression did Mr. Clayton's account make upon you?"

"A powerful one," said I. "Truly, I was quite astonished."

"And convinced?"

"Yes, sir. He did not claim too much."

"A good point indeed. And what, if anything, did his face betray?"

"Not as much as I might have expected, sir, considering the weight of the tale he told. He was direct and cool, for the most part, as if recounting what he had worked through carefully in his mind."

"As he no doubt had."

"Yes, sir. Only once did he show powerful emotion, and that was when he described climbing the stairs and looking upon the dead bodies of Ezekiel Crabb and his wife."

"Odd. I detected nothing then in his voice. What did he show you?"

"He wept. As he spoke in a peculiarly calm tone, tears

ran down his cheeks. Not many, but I did indeed see them.''

With that, Sir John nodded, indicating that I had given him as much as he needed. Then said he to me: "Jeremy, I have a message of a personal nature that I should like you to deliver to Katherine Durham.''

Though there was no need to do so, I ran the distance to Berry Lane. It was not a great distance, nor did I run it at full speed. Yet to be the bearer of such a message as I had to deliver, from one great friend to another, filled me with such exuberance that mere walking simply would not do. As I loped along across Covent Garden, dodging among the worshipers exiting St. Paul's, I felt the sun of early summer upon me as a source of fuel to my young body. I sensed the health and vigor of adolescence broiling within me.

Thus came this healthy young colt in no time at all to Number 3 Berry Lane. I was up the stairs in a trice, banging loudly on the door of the Widow Durham. I felt suddenly chagrined, realizing how rude my knock would seem. And so I knocked again, quieter and in a manner I deemed more respectful.

The door opened, and there she stood, looking for a brief moment slightly disconcerted as she recognized me hopping eagerly upon her doorstep.

"Oh," said she, "Jeremy, how good of you to come by.'' Yet she seemed a bit uncertain of that.

"I have a message from Sir John," said I.

"Well, then," said she, "deliver it me, by all means.''

"He asks, if your ankle be up to it, would you accompany him on a ride through the town, a dinner at a respectable dining place, and afterwards to a bit of musical entertainment at the Crown and Anchor Tavern in the Strand. He wishes me to assure you that although it is indeed a tavern and usually frequented by men, on musical nights such as this one sponsored by the . . .'' And here, reader, I hesitated, for the word was long and unfamiliar to me. "By the An-ac-re-on-tic Society, it is widely attended by ladies of good character accompanied by gentlemen. The entertainment tonight is something by Handel with interludes by a small orchestra.''

Because of the rigor with which I had exercised myself in reaching her quarters, and because of the length of the message, I ended my recitation somewhat out of breath. She noted this and smiled sympathetically.

"Have you run so far to tell me this?'' she asked.

"I ran, yes, but it was no more than my good spirits bade me do it.''

"Well, you may run or walk, as you choose, with my response,'' said she, "but tell Sir John that I accept his invitation most happily, and that I shall look forward to seeing him—at what hour?''

"Oh yes, I omitted that, did I not? At five o'clock, if that will be suitable.''

"That will be most suitable.''

"Thank you, then, Mrs. Durham. I shall tell him.''

I backed off with a wave, and she bade me goodbye. Leaving, I heard the door close after me. And then, to my great surprise, I caught the muffled sound of voices behind the door. I would not, could not, go back to eavesdrop, so of course I continued down the stairs, yet I was seized with great curiosity to know who was there with her. For one of the voices, deep and rumbling, had been distinctly masculine.

And so, reader, I did something which it now shames me to admit. I found a secluded doorway, deeply recessed, from which I had a view of the stairs leading to Mrs. Durham's quarters but could not, I was sure, be seen. I determined to keep to this post until her visitor appeared.

I had not long to wait. It was but a few minutes when I heard a door close loudly, and then a moment or two after that, Mr. Tolliver, the butcher, stepped down the last few stairs, turned, and started down Berry Lane in the direction away from me. I was of course surprised to see him. Yet upon a moment's reflection I understood that there was no reason for me to be surprised. He, after all, was a friend to her. Had he not rescued Mrs. Durham—indeed, rescued me, as well—from that squad in black who had caused her injury and such keen embarrassment? Certainly he had. It was only natural that he should call upon her to inquire after her recovery, and proper that he make his call on a Sunday morning. Yes, I was greatly relieved to see that Mr. Tolliver was her visitor.

Why then did I further shame myself by following him? I cannot say, but in doing so I saw what puzzled me somewhat. Though I had seen his face only briefly before he turned and started away, Mr. Tolliver did seem to wear a right solemn expression. Yet as I trailed behind him, I seemed to read his face without so much as glimpsing it. Never did a man display so plain with his body what was inside him. He shuffled along, head hung low, the very picture of discouragement and low spirits. I wanted to run forward and comfort him, to thank him for his quick action there in Covent Garden a few days past. Yet I did not. I did nothing at all but turn off at the first corner and leave him, for I feared that I might be seen.

I walked back to Bow Street, all in turmoil, once again by this mighty matter that lay between men and women. For indeed I sensed that it was this that lay at the heart of it all, responsible no less for Sir John's uneasiness of the morning than for Mr. Tolliver's evident sadness. I was much confused and wanting counsel.

I was told, upon my return, that Sir John's court was in session, and for the first time in my memory forwent the opportunity to attend the session. Instead, I fetched down the book from above that I had been reading at the time, and returned to sit on the plain bench outside Sir John's chambers and wait for him there. I read desultorily as my thoughts returned again and again to my discovery and the question of what it might mean. All this did, however, lead me to a reasonable resolve, one which now seems to me to have been remarkably mature for one so young: I determined to say nothing of this to Sir John.

Eventually he came. I greeted him and informed him of Katherine Durham's answer to his invitation. He, it seemed, was immediately elated by her acceptance.

" 'Happily,' did she say? She accepts 'happily.' Well, I doubt not I can show her a pleasant evening. What say you to that, Jeremy?"

I did not say what I thought, which was that I wished that I, too, could be invited to accompany them. What I did say was that I was sure they would both enjoy themselves mightily.

"Indeed, oh indeed, but now, Jeremy, I shall be going to meet Mr. Humber at the London Coffee House on Ludgate Hill to inform him of my change of plans. I had put him on notice. This should not come as a complete surprise to him."

"I'm sure he will understand, Sir John."

"Oh, he more than most. Do tell Mrs. Gredge that I'll be dining out, will you?"

"Oh, certainly, Sir John."

"And I'll not be needing you the rest of the day. Go, boy, enjoy yourself. Here," said he, digging deep into his pocket, "take a shilling—nay, have two or three. You've gone too long unpaid."

He extended his hand to me, palm full of coins. We argued briefly. He insisted I take three shillings at least, which I did with thanks. "Will you be satisfied with a shilling a week? Nay, you deserve more. I must talk this over with Mr. Humber."

So saying, he popped his tricorn on his head and set off for the street door. "Don't wait up for me," he called.

I wandered about the streets for more than an hour, pitying myself greatly that I had been left out of Sir John's plans. Somehow, even after I delivered the invitation to Mrs. Durham, I had supposed that at the last minute he would realize his omission—or say to me, "But of course you were meant to come, too, Jeremy. Did you not realize?"

Yet, as I have reported, he said no such thing, and so I was forced to wander alone, wallowing a bit in my disappointment. For the first time since I had come to London I felt myself in the grip of loneliness. I felt myself truly orphaned.

I returned through Covent Garden, which seemed to bustle with activity and rough entertainment at any time—even, indeed, quite late on a Sunday afternoon. A troupe of jugglers and acrobats had taken a place at the exact center of the piazza, where the pillar then stood. I lingered for a while, amazed at their skills, wondering at the years it must have taken to perfect them. Yet not so many, surely, for here was a boy no older than I, keeping no less than four balls in the air at a time. And over there a girl even younger—pretty and dark-haired—climbing to the top of a pile of men and boys to stand precariously, her feet planted on the shoulders of the two boys. Then at once the entire arrangement came down, as all its human elements dove and rolled about the pallets that were set beneath them. She dove the furthest, rolled skirts atumble with the boys—her brothers? I applauded with the rest of the crowd that had gathered around. Feeling rich with the shillings Sir John had forced upon me, I tossed one to her. She looked at me, picked it up, kissed the coin, and called out what I took to be her thanks in a language I knew not. Then she turned from me and busied herself picking up the rest of the coins that had landed near her.

I was quite thrilled by the jugglers and the acrobats—by her, in particular—but felt drawn back at that moment to Bow Street. Though it was not yet near the dinner hour, I thought it time to return. Perhaps I could see her again next Sunday. Perhaps I would somehow get to know her, and she would teach me her strange language. Perhaps . . . My young brain raced with the rich possibilities of life.

As I entered through the door that led to the rear at Number 4, I noted that Constable Fuller, seated a good distance down the hall, looked my way and bestirred himself from his chair. He walked toward me, frowning, as if annoyed at me. Yet I had done him no harm, as I knew, so I simply smiled an innocent smile and greeted him by name.

"You should not associate with his like," said he.

"Beg pardon, Constable? With whose like?"

"The one what's waitin' for you down yonder. I've had

my troubles with that one, no doubt about it. We all have. Leave him be.''

Then, a bit late, I realized that it must be Jimmie Bunkins, boldly come to visit me at Bow Street. Had he been made so daring by his meeting with Sir John Fielding?

He was there, seated uncomfortably on a bench by the strong room. He rose, looking right and left; then staring over my shoulder at Constable Fuller, he whispered, ''I been waitin' on you—a long time.''

''I was in the Garden,'' said I, ''watching acrobats.''

''Ain't that a rum way to spend your day.'' Then he added, ''Just like I figured, the hornies here don't like me.''

''The hornies?''

''The constables, chum. That one's been glimmin' me right queer.'' At last he turned his gaze from Mr. Fuller and looked me full in the eye. ''We must hop the twig, chum. There be something I wish to show yez.''

''Is it important?''

''Would I stick my head in here if it warn't?''

''How long will we be?''

''Not long. How do I know? As long as you wish it to be.''

I thought a moment. I trusted him, no doubt of that; neither was there doubt that he had run some risk in coming here. Indeed, he must hold it important that I accompany him.

''All right,'' said I to him, ''but let's be quick.''

''As you wish, chum.''

And with that, he led me off down the hall, past Constable Fuller, whom he chose to ignore completely.

''Sir John will hear of this,'' the constable called after me.

''He has confidence in me,'' said I. ''This is, I believe, an important matter.''

''If we catch you thievin', you'll be treated the same as any other.''

''Agreed,'' said I.

Constable Amos Fuller was not my favorite of the Bow Street Runners.

Once on the street, he set off at a jog trot, and I alongside him. He took me through the crowded streets by the shortest route to the Thames—catching a bit of the Strand to Fleet Street, past the Cheshire Cheese, then down from Fleet Street to the riverbank. It was difficult to talk while keeping such a pace, and besides, for once, Jimmie Bunkins showed no inclination to jaw.

On we went, along a pathway at the water's edge, where there were warehouses, fishermen's shacks, and strange houselike vessels floating in the water. At last we reached our destination. I had not known there was such a place along the river, nor would I have expected it. It looked quite like a small farm. There was much empty ground around the place, though nothing grew there; it was as if those who might have been closer neighbors had forgone the opportunity—or have I supposed this in hindsight? We crossed this uncultivated field and made for what might have been a small farmhouse. Behind it was an outbuilding that could have been a barn, though it was not entirely that. And then in a pen adjoining that outbuilding I saw first one horse and then a second. Two horses, then, both of which looked ill unto death—gray, sickly, spavined; each moved with a slow, swaying motion, as if each step might be his last. I recognized those horses. Having done so, I stopped abruptly as Jimmie Bunkins went on ahead. Then he, realizing he was alone, stopped and walked back to me.

"Come on," said he, "this be the place."

"The Raker is here."

"Right, chum, and we must now go to meet the gent hisself."

"No, Jimmie Bunkins, I saw far too much of the man the night of those terrible murders in Grub Street."

"Ah," said he, "you was there, was you? Well, to tell the truth, I ain't too fond of the cull meself. Right queer he is. But we wants somethin' from him, so it be best if we treats him with respec'."

"Well . . ."

"Come on now, show some sand. Shove your trunk."

I consented and started off with Bunkins at a walk. I

suspected and feared what the Raker might have to show us there. The Thames flowed darkly at our right. The lowering sun threw long shadows toward us. I swore to myself I would not be in this place after dark.

As we came close, I caught at last the awful smell of the place. I believe there is something deep-seated in all humans which makes that smell particularly repellent to them. It is the smell of that which awaits us all—death and decay.

I forced myself to move ahead, however, with Bunkins to the door of the place, on which he knocked. We waited but a moment until the door creaked open. There stood not the Raker but a woman in a dirty gown near as ugly as he. And ugly in the same way, for one eye, the right, was distinctly smaller than the left.

"Hullo?" said she in a manner most suspicious. Then, fixing Bunkins with her queer gaze, she gave a little smile, relaxing somewhat. "Ah, you be the boy come by before. Want another look at the ladies, do ye? I see ye brought a friend along. It'll cost you another shilling, though." She turned to me. "And a shilling for you, too."

Reluctantly, I dug into my pocket and handed over the two shillings remaining of the three Sir John had given me.

"The mister is in back," said she. "You knows the way now. Just tell him you paid, and I passed you."

She gave a nod then and shut the door in our faces. We started round the house.

"Ain't she a queer 'un!" said Jimmie Bunkins. "A proper old witch."

"And with his same misshapen face," I whispered.

"She's the cove's sister, or so I hear tell. She talked on and on when I come before about how none come by but for to claim their kin and she's so lonely and all. Only then would she let me on to the back. She gave me pan bread to eat, and I was that hungry I ate it. But I would never take meat from her, no matter how hungry!"

It took a moment for me to grasp the significance of that. When at last I did, my eyes widened. "You don't mean . . . ?"

"There's talk," said he.

We had reached the wooden fence which held in the sickly horses.

"Up and over," said Bunkins, scrambling.

"It's Moll Caulfield inside, is it not?"

"Come along," said he.

I climbed the fence, which was so rickety I feared it might collapse upon me.

"Mind the horse apples," said he.

I followed, picking a careful way behind him. The stink of the place was now quite remarkable. Bunkins whipped out the kerchief he had tried to sell me and covered his nose with it. I wished for a moment I had bought it from him.

Then into the building, part barn and part charnel house. The Raker was there, pitching hay for the horses. Along the two walls were the bodies of the dead, each covered with what looked to be a piece of sailcloth. They were not a great number—a dozen on one side and half that number on the other. Bare feet protruded from the sailcloth. There were two great piles of clothing, men's and women's; the men's was much the taller of the two.

The Raker planted his pitchfork, then walked heavily toward us.

"So," said he to Jimmie Bunkins, "you've come back with a chum, have ye? Why not, says I, why not?"

Then he stared at me, looked me up and down, as I stood uneasily, fighting my impulse to bolt.

"I knows ye, do I not? Aye, you were at the printer's door, keepin' watch for the Beak. Warn't that a haul! Six, if I recalls aright." He stood, fists on hips, considering. "Be ye here for curiosity—there's some comes so—or be ye here for the Beak?"

"For Sir John," said I forthrightly.

"In that case," said he, digging into his pocket, "I'd best return your price of admission." He hauled out a handful of coins and offered me a shilling.

"I paid for two."

"Ah well, here you are."

I took the two coins without another word.

Then to Jimmie Bunkins: "The old party you seek is just there"—pointing—"second from the end."

He turned away, wheezing or laughing (who could tell which?), and went back to his work. Bunkins gave me a nudge.

"Come on," said he, "you must glim her for yourself."

He led the way to the covered lump that the Raker had designated, pulled back the top of her sailcloth shroud, and exposed the face of poor Moll Caulfield. Bare recognizable it was, all collapsed and drawn so in death. I felt tears well within me but fought them back, wishing in no wise to appear weak.

"Raker," I called to him, "when was this woman brought in?"

Once more he planted his pitchfork and tramped over to stand beside us.

"Two nights past," said he. "She's due to go under tomorrow."

"And where was she found?"

"In an alley somewheres round Covent Garden."

"Half Moon Passage?"

"No, 'twas nowhere near there. 'Must to Hart Street it was. I've it in me book. I keeps good records. Have to."

"Who summoned you?"

"The keeper of a gin shop in the alley, said the presence of her corpus was bad for business, though he swore he'd given her naught to drink."

"And what was the cause of death?"

"Who's to say? Sickness, chill, old age. She ain't no child."

He bent over and pulled the covering from her complete.

"You can see," said the Raker. "There ain't a mark on her body. I saw no need to alert the Beak."

In spite of myself, I stared. Hers was the first naked female form that ever I had seen. Poor Moll awoke no lust in me, nor would she in any male. I gestured for him to return it.

Then said I to him, with all the spurious authority I could muster, "She must in no wise be buried in a potter's grave.

There is money aplenty to bury her well. The body will be claimed at some time tomorrow. Keep the body in the coolest place you have. Is all this understood?''

"Aye," said the Raker. "Mind, there was no marks upon her, no wounds, so I saw no need to call the Beak-runners."

"I understand," said I. "Sir John will be told, just as you told me. Mr. Bunkins," said I then, "let us return to Bow Street."

And together we left, without a look behind us. Once over the fence, we picked up our pace yet kept a dignified step well past the house.

"Crikey," said Jimmie Bunkins. "You are a right hard cove."

EIGHT

*In which a great fire is fought
and a report is made to
Sir John*

I returned to Number 4 Bow Street bursting to tell of the discovery, yet reluctant to inform Constable Fuller. His low opinion of Jimmie Bunkins and his evident distrust of me had, I confess, turned me against him somewhat. Gladly would I have confided in Mr. Benjamin Bailey, but I knew this day, Sunday, to be his day of deserved rest. I determined to make my report to Sir John and to none other.

When I parted company with Bunkins at the door, knowing well I had dinner waiting for me above, I offered him my penultimate shilling so that he might go and eat his fill. He took it gladly and gave me the wink.

"This be my re-ward, is it?"

"By no means," said I. "If it were in my power to give one, I should be far more generous. It is in recompense. You must have paid that terrible woman a shilling on your first visit, so I repay you."

"Done right fair," said he. "What will the Beak do now?"

"That I could not hazard."

"Will he arrest those buggers in black?"

"He will if he has proof against them."

"Proof?" cried he. "There's your proof back at the Raker's. She was frighted of them out of her wits, she was.''

"Sir John will do what is right," said I firmly.

"He better," said Bunkins. "There's them who liked the old blowen and would take proper re-venge."

Without another word, he turned and darted from the door, leaving me to stare after him wondering what rough justice he lay in his fantasy for the Brethren of the Spirit.

Then went I inside and up the stairs to listen to Mrs. Gredge's scolding for my tardy appearance at dinner. Yet she scolded neither so long nor so hard as she might have, for I was back not much past the appointed hour, and in truth not late at all: she was still stirring the stew that would serve as our meal, and confessed that it would be a bit before it was cooked proper. That bit was near an hour, yet following my visit to the Raker, having seen what I had seen and smelled what I had smelled, I was in no rush to eat.

Even when I sat down to table I dawdled over my food. I managed a good chunk of bread smeared with butter well enough, got down a potato or two, and a carrot. But the meat, all brown but for the fat and floating in gravy, was quite beyond my powers of consumption.

"You're not eating," said Mrs. Gredge in a manner most accusing.

"Not hungry," said I.

"Well, we'll just see about that."

So saying, she snatched up my plate and scraped the leavings into the stewpot.

"It's not like you at all," said she, clapping a hand to my forehead. "You're not ill, no fever to the touch. You must have filled yourself with sweets and such out in the Garden. What you did not eat today you can have tomorrow. Now get on with the washing up."

I jumped to the task, eager to make amends for the perceived insult to her culinary skills. As I worked, she pouted. As she pouted, she ate, sullenly eager to prove to me that I had done a terrible injustice to the great feast she had put before me. (This, no doubt, was true.) She even returned to the pot for a modest second helping, perhaps seeking out the very pieces I had rejected. She ate her fill, and then some, and ended by belching a mighty belch just to prove a point.

"I've never done a better stew," she declared.

I said nothing in reply, but seeking her permission with my glance, took her plate, knife, and fork, and washed them clean with the rest. When all was done to her satisfaction, I excused myself and went up to my garret room and fetched down the book of my choice. I returned with it to the table and began to read. Mrs. Gredge cautioned me against it.

"You'll do your eyes no good reading so half the night, as you do," said she.

"My eyes are fine, ma'am," said I, quite mild.

"Keep it up, you'll be as blind as Sir John."

"I read that someday I might have his knowledge and wisdom."

"Ha! Little chance of that."

"As you say, Mrs. Gredge."

I bent my gaze back to the page. Then, out of curiosity, I raised my eyes, ever so slight, and studied her in secret. Old she was and growing older by the day. Her own eyesight was failing. She managed the stairs with greater difficulty than when I had arrived only some weeks before. Yet she cooked well still and oversaw my labors with stern exactitude. Her attitude to me had changed. While in the beginning she met me with disapproval and showed me only grudging tolerance at best, now that I regularly did the buying for her and a hundred other odd chores as she required them, she accepted me as a household necessity; sometimes even with signs of affection. I wondered at her age but only in later years had the courage to ask it. Further, I wondered at her length of service with Sir John. That much courage I had at least.

"Pardon, ma'am," said I to her, "but if you don't mind my question, when did you start with Sir John?"

"I do not mind," said she, "for it has been a happy time for me here, all in all. But the truth of it is, I cannot rightly reckon the years, for I have lost count. It was, in any case, direct after they moved here from where they was situated in the Strand. That was a time of great turmoil, when his brother made off to Portugal, where he died, and Sir John took over from him here. Mr. Saunders Welch was also a magistrate, and had grand expectations of claiming this house and court as his own. But brother Henry would have none of it. He installed Sir John and dear Kitty, God rest her soul, in these upper floors, and then sailed off to his death. Mr. Saunders Welch, you may know, went off to Long Acre and opened a magistrate's court of his own.''

"Where he lives well on fines, and traffics with independent thief-takers," I put in.

"That's as they say."

"All this happened in 1754, or that was what I heard from Mr. Bailey—just one year before my birth.''

"Was it really so long ago? It could be indeed. But those was happy days, truly they were. Sir John and Lady Kitty had not been married so long, and both wished to make the most of this new life, and so they hired me, thinking I might do as cook for their meals when they had special dinners, like. Oh, and they had them, and didn't I cook for them then! My own youngest—he was yet a bit older than you are now—he would take off from his duties as a cabinet-maker's apprentice, with his master's permission, of course, and he would serve, all donned in proper dress. There was people who would come, grand people, and they would talk, and laugh, and drink, until all hours of the night.''

She stopped of a sudden with a great sigh. "But all that stopped when Lady Kitty got her wasting sickness some years back. It came upon her gradual. It wasn't near as bad in the beginning as it was at the end—what you saw, Jeremy. That was the worst. That was the worst that could be. What was it that Irish doctor said was the cause of it?''

"A tumor," said I.

"Ah yes, just so. He was wiser than the rest and not near as puffed up. It made me old watching her go. And Sir John—he aged ten years in two.''

She sat there a long moment, brooding upon the events she had described—and perhaps upon her own fate, too.

Then she rose unsteadily to her feet, managing it only upon a second attempt.

"Though it be early, I'm up to bed," said she. "After that grand meal on quite the best stew that ever I cooked, I feel a bit drowsy, I do. You mean to sit here and read, do you?"

"Yes, ma'am."

"Well, mind what I told you and take care of your eyes—not *too* much reading. *Bad* for the eyes and *wasteful* of candles, as I've told you in the past." A little of the old fire burned in her still.

"I've something to communicate to Sir John," said I. "I had thought to wait up for him."

"Well, you may indeed have quite a wait. I wish you a good night, Jeremy Proctor."

With that, she limped off, favoring her right leg, as she was lately wont to do, and then made her way up the stairs.

For my part, I settled in, prepared to remain at my post until Sir John arrived and I might tell him of what I had seen in the Raker's ghastly barn. I was of two minds about this. Sir John had told me plain that I was not to wait up for him. Yet surely he would want to know of poor Moll Caulfield's death, the when and where of it, the condition of her body, and so on. Surely he would commend me for telling him all at the earliest opportunity. At least, I hoped he would.

And so I settled down to read. In truth, I cannot remember the name of the book, for it did not interest me greatly. This one, like so many others I had read in the past months, was taken from the great stack that had been stored in the room at the top of all the rest which had become my own. It was, as Sir John had informed me, all that was left of his brother Henry's library. The rest had been sold off to the benefit of Henry Fielding's widow and children. These leavings contained not much to engage a boy of my age and craving for literary adventure. Still, they did me good, for reading through them diligently as I did (since they were the reading matter nearest at hand) helped instill in me the habit of study that has benefited me greatly in my career in the law. And I'm sure, too, that in the end it added greatly to my store of general knowledge, for I read through works on subjects as various as the North American colonies, the silk trade in China, and the geography of Asian Russia.

Just how completely a boy of such inexperience would have understood such matters, I can today only guess. I do know, however, that it was often necessary for me to reread whole pages and more to get the sense from them. And so, reader, you will understand if I tell you that on that particular night, in spite of my intention to stay awake reading as I waited for Sir John, my interest in the book before me flagged utterly. I found myself blinking and rubbing my eyes. Without knowing how or when it happened, I fell fast asleep right where I sat.

I know not the hour when I awoke, though it seemed to be quite late. The candle had burned down to less than a thumb's width, and the room had fallen cold. As I look back on the events that thereafter transpired, I calculate it must have been just on midnight, or shortly past.

It could not be that Sir John had arrived and, oblivious of me, gone on to his bed. Though he may not have seen me with his blind eyes, he would have sensed my presence. The man had an almost preternatural awareness of others around him—not only their proximity, but also exact location, disposition, and general description. His was quite an amazing faculty. No, Sir John had not passed by me in the kitchen.

Although awake, I was groggy and somewhat befuddled still. What might I do? Make a pot of tea for myself and return to the book that had put me to sleep? In my condition, that seemed altogether useless. Quite likely I should only fall asleep again. And so, reluctantly, I gave up my intention to meet him at the door with news of Moll Caulfield. He would hear of it from me in the morning. I picked up the candleholder with its guttering fraction of flickering light and made my way up to my garret room.

While in the act of pulling off my clothes, I happened

to glance out the window and saw a great glow in the sky. What could it be? I went closer for a better look and saw, first, that it emanated from a spot quite nearby, and second, that the glow was caused by a fire of goodly size. Flames winked up from the bottom of it. Smoke spiraled high into the night sky.

Quick as I could, I dressed myself again, grabbed my hat and coat, and ran from the room. I clattered down the stairs in a great rush, unmindful of Mrs. Gredge, who slept in the room just below mine. Through the kitchen then and down the next set of stairs, which took me to the ground floor, the area assigned to the Runners and the empty strong room. Constable Baker was there to greet me, much surprised.

"Where do you go at such an hour?"

"There is a fire!"

"Oh, indeed there is, and a big 'un."

"But where?"

I danced before him, eager to be off.

"Maiden Lane," said he. "But why must you go?"

Already I was on my way. "Sir John will be there, surely," I called over my shoulder.

"He will, but—"

Whatever caution or objection he had to offer was lost to me as I ran out the door to the street and slammed it behind me.

Out and away, I saw there was no need for me to have asked Mr. Baker for the whereabouts of the conflagration. There were people in Bow Street, and though not a great crowd, all were hurrying as one in the direction of Maiden Lane. I thought to distance them all, yet as I rounded the corner into Tavistock Street with Maiden Lane in sight, well lit by the fire, I saw there were more people still, pouring in from the Strand, carriages and coaches as well. Soon I found myself forced to a walk, darting when I could through breaks in this moving wall of humanity. Men, women, even children were there, all come out to gawk at the blaze, for such was deemed great entertainment in those days—as it is, alas, in these as well.

Yet by pushing and shoving when need be, making myself small and squeezing through when that was required,
I pressed onward through Maiden Lane until I came to a
barrier of rope that had been thrown up to hold back the
throng. There I stood, resting but a moment, catching my
breath, surveying the wild scene before me.

Less than ten rods from me was the burning building, a
structure of wood, as about half were in this area. It was
low compared to those around it—but two floors from the
street with a peaked roof that raised it somewhat and may
have also covered an attic. All this could be seen still,
though flames danced out from the windows below and
could be glimpsed through them above. The far side of the
ground floor seemed to have been near consumed. Thus the
fire burned from below to above. I could not tell, knowing
little of such things, if this was good or bad, if it meant the
structure might be saved or no. What most concerned me
at that moment was where Sir John might be.

With my eyes I searched the space confronting the burning building. There was a good deal of activity there, but
much of it seemed confused, so much running about by
men who lacked point or purpose. Not all, however. At the
far side of the house, which was where it was worst burned,
three men with hooks on long poles had engaged a thick
supporting timber above and had pulled it loose. With a
great heave they took it down, flaming, sparking like a log
from a hearth—and with it came a good-sized section of
the top-floor wall. They jumped clear, then pulled the fiery
mess back with their hooked poles into the street.

At the far side of the roped plot was a great pumping
engine of a kind I had seen only in pictures. It was manned
on both sides by a crew that kept it moving up and down,
up and down, in a seesaw action, while much nearer the
fire were two men, one on each side, directing the squirter
to the point where the flames were fiercest. The water came
from it in strong jets in the rhythm of the pump to which
it was attached by a leather hose. Impressive it was, yet
seemingly ineffectual against the burning.

Soldiers roamed at intervals along the perimeter, muskets

at the ready and bayonets fixed, holding back the crowd that strained against the rope. And far to the rear, too, there was another cluster of soldiers; one among them was unmistakably an officer and in charge. He was engaged in heated conversation with two other men, one of whom was blocked from my view. As I stared at him, the officer stamped his foot in anger and turned away from the other two, revealing to me—Sir John Fielding, looking every inch himself. Sir John slammed his stick down on the cobblestones and shouted something after the retreating officer. Well, I had my goal now; my problem was but to reach it. I attempted to catch his attention, shouting his name, yet my cry was quite lost in the tumult before me and the roaring buzz behind. I understood that this would be quite useless, and so I did what had to be done: I set my eyes on Sir John and ducked under the rope barrier.

And for my action I was rewarded with a stout clout on the back with the butt of a military musket. It sent me sprawling down to the cobblestones. Yet I caught myself with my hands and pushed up, looking left and right, trying to determine whence this great clout had come. Then I looked up and found a soldier not much older than myself glowering down at me. Very personal was he in his disapproval, as if, in crossing that line, I had declared myself his profoundest enemy.

"What say you?" asked the young soldier. "Will you move back behind the rope, or would you like to feel t'other end of this musket?"

The bayonet attached to the muzzle high above glinted sharply in the light of the fire.

"I would not, but I *must* see Sir John Fielding. He is just there," said I, half rising and pointing my finger, "and I am his assistant."

"Sure, you must be," said he. He then gave my shoulder a prod with the gun butt. "Now get back behind the rope."

Then I caught sight of one nearby who might vouch for me. "Mr. Cowley!" I cried loudly to him. "Come tell this soldier who I am."

He was behind the lad in the red coat some two rods. He seemed not to hear me.

"Mr. Cowley, *please!*"

He turned, caught sight, and gave a wave to me. Then he ambled over to us.

"Hullo, Jeremy," said he. "Wonderful big fire, ain't it?"

"Who is he, Constable?" demanded the soldier. "Claims he's the magistrate's assistant."

Constable Cowley thought about that a moment. "Well, I don't rightly know what you'd call him," said he. "He's with him all the time, he is. Does all manner of errands and jobs for the Beak, he does."

"Come on now," said the soldier. "Is he or ain't he?"

"Yes, I guess you could call him such."

Surely, I thought, he could have been more forthcoming, less reluctant. In any case, the soldier lowered his musket and turned away from me. If he could not force me back behind the rope, then he had no further interest in me. I started off at a jog trot in the direction I had seen Sir John.

"He's there," called Constable Cowley behind me. I looked back. He was pointing in the way I was headed. "That's him with the Lord Mayor and that captain of artillery."

That nearly stopped me absolutely. The Lord Mayor of London? How was I to pass the word on Moll Caulfield with Sir John in the company of one so illustrious? Yet I proceeded, for I knew I must try.

As I approached, I found the assemblage about him curiously mixed as to attitude and activity. The men of the fire brigade pumped urgently at thêir engine, and their leader shouted orders loudly at the two manning the squirter and at the three armed with pole hooks who seemed to be engaged in pulling down the house whilst still it burned. The soldiers, on the other hand, lounged about indifferently, seemingly bored, as they talked and joked amongst themselves, awaiting orders; a few of them had taken seats upon kegs that were distributed in disorder around them.

And in the midst of all stood Sir John. The evident disagreement that had raged between the three principals had reached a point where each had taken a position apart from the other two, and all maintained hostile silence. Thus had I the perfect opportunity to impart my news to Sir John. I ran direct to him and gave a tug upon his big sleeve.

"Sir John," said I. "There is something I must—"

"What?" said he, turning to me. "Who is there? Jeremy? Thank God you're here, boy. Now perhaps I can get a bit of unprejudiced information."

"Gladly will I give it, but—"

"This gentleman to my right"—he nodded in the direction of the Lord Mayor—"declares the fire to be of no consequence, says a woman could piss it out. He's all for packing up the engine and the squirter and removing them altogether."

"Now, that is *not* what I said, Sir John," bellowed the Lord Mayor. "Or it is not *all* that I said. The men on the pump are near spent. They cannot go on so all night. And besides, this appliance is most dear to use. Let the blaze burn itself out, say I. The structure cannot be saved."

"What say you to that, Jeremy? Can it be saved?"

"I could not hazard ''But then I gave it a fair look and saw, to my surprise, that I knew the house, had been inside. It was the Jewish church to which Mr. Martinez had taken us to talk with the rabbi. I recognized the strange writing above the door, now bubbling and running from the heat of the fire. "No, Sir John," said I then, "I do not see that it can be saved."

"Does it burn from the ground floor upward?"

"Yes, sir, it does."

"Would you say that—"

At that moment a great cry went up from the crowd, and in particular a sound of rejoicing and applause from one sector off to the left. I looked about, then to the burning building. There I saw a figure framed in firelight in the open doorway. It was the rabbi—Gershon was his name—and he now staggered forward, his arms hugging a sizable object wrapped in a blanket, which had sprouted little leaves of flame.

"What is it, Jeremy? What has happened?"

"It is that rabbi," said I, "the one you talked to but one night past."

"Ah, he made it back, did he? He ran back into the house minutes ago. They'd written him off for dead."

Once clear of the fire, he collapsed onto the cobblestones and beat out the bits of flame and sparks that had attached to the blanket. Even at a distance I could see his beard was badly singed. Then from the left came a whole host of bearded men, his congregation. They had broken through the barrier and, ignoring the soldiers, come forth to—what? Congratulate him upon returning with his life? No, they paid him little attention. Their concern was all for that object which was wrapped in the blanket. There was great shouting and rejoicing in that strange tongue of theirs as they removed the blanket and revealed the scroll beneath. Two or three jumped up and began dancing in the way I had seen before. I marveled at that, thinking it a queer response.

"What is it now?" said Sir John, most impatient. "What is now happening?"

I described all that above as briefly as possible. And even as I spoke to Sir John, a group of soldiers came forth to round up these Jews and convey them back behind the barrier they had breached. This I added to my tale.

"Well, then, Lord Mayor," called Sir John, "there is your relief for the pumpers. The Jews should be glad to spell them. The rabbi speaks English. Let him come forward. Rabbi!" he yelled out. "Oh, Rabbi! Over here, please."

And indeed he came. Though he bore proudly what he had saved from the fire—the scroll was near as big as he— he had himself suffered a bit for it. Not only was his beard singed, but in the barest patches the skin beneath was also burned raw. I saw, too, that his hands had suffered.

"It is a terrible disaster," offered Sir John, "what has befallen you and your congregation. I offer my sincere regrets."

"I accept them," said Rabbi Gershon, "but we are accustomed to such disasters."

"Fire and sword?"

"You make that association. Who am I to say?"

"Ah well, yes, I see. The Lord Mayor has complained to me that his pumpers need rest. Would your men, or some of them, volunteer to spell them? I would count it a great service to the city if they were to do so."

"They will do it if I ask them."

"Then by all means."

The rabbi nodded and turned to go, but Sir John called him back.

"May I also ask you to visit me tomorrow that we might further discuss this . . . disaster."

"As you wish, Sir John. Fielding. And when should that be?"

"Oh, late in the afternoon tomorrow, after my court. Let us say at five. You will need that long at least to recuperate."

"As you say."

And with that he did leave, going to his troop of bearded men, now marching solemnly back in the company of redcoated soldiers.

"Jeremy," said Sir John to me, in something of a whisper, "is that popinjay of a captain still about?"

"He is, Sir John."

"Is he within shouting distance?"

In full voice then: "Then you, Lord Mayor, must do the shouting." For he had been close and listening to every word that was said. "Inform the captain that the men of the rabbi's congregation are to do their duty for the city of London. That should satisfy you, I hope."

"It must then, mustn't it?"

"And there'll be no more talk of taking away the pump engine?"

"Not for the present."

Thus, all but ordered to do so, the Lord Mayor chose not to shout but waddled over to the captain and spoke into his ear. It must be remembered, reader, that these negotiations, such as they were, took place in the greatest din and confusion; even the fire, as it burned, made a great noise, which pervaded all the rest.

"Sir John," said I, "Jimmie Bunkins came to me, and—"

"That ass of a captain wishes to begin the destruction of this entire block of houses." This was said with a wave of his stick in the general direction of the errant officer. "He wishes to blow them up. Can you imagine such a mindless destruction of property?"

"Why no, sir, that would be—"

"Gunpowder! He brought kegs and kegs of the awful stuff over from the Tower. Says it was the only action with any effect during the Great Fire of the last century. Well, that's nonsense. Conditions differ. First of all, there is no wind, is there, boy? Lick your finger and reassure me."

I did as told. When I held up my forefinger, it remained simply wet.

"No wind at all," said I. "When I viewed the fire from my window, the smoke seemed to rise straight up."

"There—you see? And there is space between the buildings on either side, is there not?"

"Some, yes—about a rod on one side and a little more on the other."

"I've instructed the tenants to stand by with buckets and to be particularly mindful of sparks on the roof. Have they stationed themselves?"

In truth, they were quite busy, splashing, dousing, and beating out, but all to good effect. As fortune would have it, both buildings were of good English brick and would withstand much.

"They have," said I, "and so far no fire has caught."

"And on the roofs. Are they up there?"

I had noted some activity before—men looking down in dread at the flames below, water splashing over from one side of the roof on the left.

"They are, though it be difficult to see their movements. Both roofs are flat."

"They *are?* I had not been told—much easier to manage

so. You see, that is precisely the sort of information I could not get from the captain—nor, for that matter, from the Lord Mayor. I will *not* have buildings blown up to satisfy the caprice of some raw artillery captain. It's madness! The idea!''

He rumbled on a bit more, to himself rather than to me. Still I waited for the right opportunity to pass on to him what I had learned at the Raker's. I had not thus far been successful. Who knew that better than I? Perhaps this was neither the time nor the place for it. Yet if I were to make one more try . . .

"Sir John?"

"Yes, Jeremy, what is it?"

The direct route surely was best. "Moll Caulfield is—"

"Sir John! Sir John!" Constable Cowley came a-galloping up. "I have news of witnesses."

"Well, tell it me, man!"

"There were two who saw three men in black fleeing Maiden Lane just before the fire was noticed."

"Then they did not actually see the fire being set?"

"Well . . . no, sir. But they saw them right enough, moving off in all haste—and in the direction of Half Moon Passage."

"That, at least, is something. Did you get the names of the witnesses?"

"I did, sir."

"And where they might be reached?"

"Well, I have a fair address for a Mr. Goodpasture, though he was most uneasy we should use it. He prefers it not be known that he was about Covent Garden in the company of one Daisy Dillard of no fixed address. She it was who proved truly forthcoming. Said she had seen men dressed such as they a-preaching in the Garden."

"So what have we? A straying husband, not eager to be called upon, and a Covent Garden whore of no fixed address. Well, it is something. Let us do what we can with it."

Sir John then turned his head this way and that, as if

surveying the scene. Yet upon me he relied for the actual report.

"Tell me, Jeremy," said he, "how goes the fire now?"

"Somewhat weaker now," said I, in truth. "It seems to have been all but extinguished on the ground floor. Half the front of the upper floor has been pulled down by the men with their hooks. And the squirter is now aimed there above."

"Then let's be gone," said he. "We shall pay a visit to Brother Abraham and his flock of sheep."

He paused a moment to have private words with the Lord Mayor and the officer of artillery. Then, no doubt receiving the assurances he sought, he gave a nod and we set off across the roped plot in the direction of Half Moon Passage.

Constable Cowley led the way, and I behind him. Sir John held tight to my shoulder as we ducked beneath the barrier, and kept a firm grip as we pushed our way through the crowd. Cowley used his stick, holding it at shoulder height with both hands to separate the sea of men and women before us. We struggled on, and at last came to a point where we might begin to walk proper.

And so we made our way to the end of Maiden Lane where there at the corner stood our destination, all darkened and quiet—the meeting hall and hospice of the Brethren of the Spirit. When we reached that door at which we had demanded entry a day or two before, I informed Sir John; he in turn ordered Constable Cowley to beat loudly upon it.

That he did. There was silence—no answer at all.

"Beat louder," said Sir John.

And louder he did beat.

"They may be asleep," said Mr. Cowley.

"Then wake them up, Constable."

With that, Mr. Cowley thundered so loud upon the door with his oaken club that I was sure that either it must break or the door would. Yet neither came to pass. And the great racket he made did at last bring someone to the door—a modest sort of man, sad of eye and sleepy, too.

"Praise the Lord," said he, with a yawn. "How may I help you?"

Sir John stepped forward. "I am John Fielding, magistrate of the Bow Street Court, and I would see Brother Abraham."

"Ah," said the doorkeeper, "but he must be asleep. We are simple men, and we retire early."

"Nevertheless, I must see him. Wake him, if need be. If Brother Abraham has had any sleep at all on this night, then he has had more than I. Tell him that Sir John is below, and he demands his presence."

"I shall have to shut the door. You'll forgive me? The late hour."

"I understand."

The sad-eyed doorkeeper eased the door shut on us, and threw the lock. We waited. Constable Cowley and I exchanged looks, as if guessing whether or no the door would again open to us. But Sir John stood patient and waited as the minutes went by. He seemed to be deep in concentration, silent, thinking who knew what great thoughts. Would this be the time to bring up Moll Caulfield to him? No, I thought not.

At last I heard footfalls beyond the door. The lock was turned, and the door came open. Brother Abraham stood before us, making a great show of rubbing his eyes and yawning. Yet for all that, he seemed quite alert to me. I doubted he had been asleep at all.

"Sir John," said he, "to what do I owe this . . . this . . ."

"Intrusion?"

"Thou hast said it."

"Ah, quoting Scripture to me, are you?"

"All words and phrases are in the Bible," said Brother Abraham. "For one such as myself who knows it well, they come easy to the tongue."

"Well, then, perhaps you will have other such holy words in response to this. You see there is a bright glow in the night behind me? Perhaps you see flames, as well?"

"Ah yes, it would seem that a building is now burning."

"Do you hear that tumult of shouting? That buzz from

the crowd now departing? I marvel that you could have slept through such a ruction.''

"I am a sound sleeper.''

"How fortunate for you,'' said Sir John in a manner most ironic. "But since you seem to plead ignorance of the great event that has taken place quite near your doorstep, it is the synagogue on Maiden Lane that has burned—indeed, burns still. What say you to that, sir? 'Am I my brother's keeper'?''

"That I would not say, for the Jews are *not* my brothers in Christ, though I would that they were.''

"I have heard of your keen desire to make them so. You made an appearance at that same synagogue, did you not, and preached to the congregation, seeking to convert them?''

"I did, well, yes,'' said Brother Abraham, showing a degree of uncertainty for the first time. "They welcomed me, listened most attentive to what I said.''

"And in particular when you said that if preaching did not win them, fire and sword might?''

"That I did *not* say! Oh no, that is a great distortion. I told them that while the Papists offered them fire and sword, I brought them love and sweet reason. Who told you I spoke so? It must have been that misbegotten, ugly little rabbi of theirs. He is an evil man, an agent of the Devil.''

"Brother Abraham, I know naught of the Devil's agents, yet I have known a few evil men come before me as I sat on the bench, and Rabbi Gershon is certain not one.''

"As you say, you know naught of the Devil's agents.''

"If that were said to me in my court, sir, I would count it as insolence and contempt,'' said Sir John in his darkest mode. Then he added, after a moment: "However, we are not in court. We are here on your doorstep, and I wish to put before you testimony from two witnesses. Both agreed that they had seen three men dressed in black running from the synagogue moments before the fire was noted. One of the two went so far as to say that they were dressed in the style of the Brethren of the Spirit. She had seen them preaching in Covent Garden.''

"Had this witness seen faces? Could this witness identify them? I doubt it—nay, I more than doubt it, for unless these men were seen before eight o'clock, they could not have been members of our group. All were here and accounted for by eight o'clock. The members of this association would not have done such a thing, in any case. We stand for peace, justice, and understanding.''

"How admirable," said Sir John—and nothing more. He simply waited.

"And . . . and as for the mode of dress," Brother Abraham continued, altogether less assured than before, "what have you but that the three who were sighted wore black? Black, I would remind you, is a most popular color. Look about you on the streets of London, and you will see that half the men of the city wear it in some degree." He hesitated then, then proceeded, revising his statement thus: "Or perhaps *you* would not see it, but you have but to ask, and it would be confirmed to you that this is so.''

"Interesting. Black, you say. I must then ask." Simply that, and again he waited.

"The Jews! Most of them wear black. I've seen it with my own eyes. They and their fur hats and beards. I have seen them. I saw them so but the other night. They themselves could have set the fire in order that we might be blamed.''

"Their own synagogue? I think that highly unlikely.''

"They are a devious people. But put that aside. Put all talk of men donned in black aside, and let us consider how such a fire might most likely have started in such a place.''

"And how would that be, sir?''

"Why, Exodus, chapter twenty-seven, verse twenty: 'And thou shalt command the children of Israel, that they bring thee pure olive oil beaten for the light, to cause the lamp to burn always.' ''

"Meaning . . . what?" said Sir John. "I do not immediately perceive the point you wish to make.''

"But it should be plain," said Brother Abraham. "Did

you not notice the lamp burning before the Ark?''

"The Ark? I do not follow.''

"The cabinet wherein the scrolls are kept. Surely you noticed—no, I suppose you would not: your sight, of course, or lack of it. In any case, there is a lamp kept burning there always in respect to the Scriptures. Such a lamp could easily have caused the fire, been upset, or jostled, spread burning oil about. *That* is the likely cause of the fire—as indeed should be plain.''

"Is it? If I understand you aright, then the lamp would have been placed quite near the scrolls. And if that were so, the scrolls would have burned early. Yet Jeremy witnessed and described to me a heroic rescue by the rabbi—this agent of the Devil, as you called him—of those same scrolls. He brought them from the fire unburned. Commendable, to say the least. Miraculous, indeed, if they were placed so close to the origin of the fire.''

For the moment, Brother Abraham could make no response. He stood in the doorway, mute and frowning.

"But,'' said Sir John, "let us call this discussion to an end. We shall have opportunity and time to reopen it in the future. In fact, Brother Abraham, I promise you we shall.''

With that and not a word more, Sir John Fielding turned about, and extending his stick that he might find the down step, he walked out into the street and waited there for Constable Cowley and myself to catch him up. The two of us could do no more than look in surprise, each at the other, nod at Brother Abraham, and run to join Sir John. I heard the door slam after us.

"Come along, come along,'' said Sir John. "We've wasted enough time with that charlatan.''

He started back along the way we had come then, moving along at a good, swift pace. Constable Cowley and I took places on either side, fearful that he might misstep. Yet with no more than his stick to guide him he found his way sure, even as he railed every step of the way against the time wasted in the interview just past. He declared the man had messianic pretensions and should himself no doubt be confined in Bedlam.

"Yet he is clever as regards the law," said Sir John. "He knows full well that to have seen the backs of three men in black hastening from the scene would in no wise stand in court as positive identification. Well, we ruffled his feathers at least, did we not? He knows we shall give our attention to him and his band. Perhaps we can drive them from London, send them back to their New Jerusalem across the ocean. I would count that a victory, and if—"

"Uh, Sir John?"

"What is it, Cowley?"

"Just ahead the crowd grows thick again. Perhaps we should proceed as before?"

"All right, all right. Clear a path for the blind man then."

And so Constable Cowley went ahead once more and Sir John last of all, his grasp firm on my shoulder. There were not near as many gathered as before—in fact, only two or three deep at the rope and they growing restless and ready to leave. This meant, of course, that the fire was near out.

And so it was. Ducking under the rope, Constable Cowley displayed his crested baton to the soldier nearest, who took no interest but let us pass. This gave me my first fair look at the fire since we had departed it to seek out Brother Abraham. It was burned down to embers in most places. Only in one corner of the ground floor did it still flame, and the squirter was aimed square upon that spot.

This I imparted to Sir John, and told him, too, that the soldiers were now collecting the kegs of gunpowder and loading them onto the wagon.

"Well, thank God for that," said Sir John. "Constable Cowley?"

"Yessir?"

"I have for you an onerous but necessary task. The soldiers will be leaving soon. The rope barricade is to be left up, though pulled in somewhat. When the fire is fully dampened down and the engine has gone, it will be your duty to stand by what is left of the synagogue and keep all pillagers away. Let no one by—the sole exception being the Jews whose house of worship this is. If they wish to stand guard with you, let them. But advise them against entering. It will be quite dangerous inside for some time, I daresay. We will send you relief in the morning. Is this understood?''

"It is, sir, but . . ."

"But what?''

"How will I tell a Jew, sir?''

"Well . . . they wear beards, and they . . . oh, you tell him, Jeremy.''

Rather than tell, I showed, pointing out to Constable Cowley the raggle-taggle group now pushing hard at the pump.

"Those be Jews in the fur hats?''

"So they are.''

"Well, I'll not have no trouble telling them apart from the rest. All's well then, Sir John.''

"Carry on, Constable Cowley. And Jeremy? Let's to bed.''

Only minutes later, we two had made our way through the last of the fire fanatics, and thus reached Tavistock Street. We walked along at a slower pace, ambling through the night, he as well as I showing signs of the exhaustion we both felt. I knew not the hour for certain, though I thought it to be near two in the morning. Covent Garden seemed safe enough even at that late hour, for the walks were peopled with those straggling home from the night's entertainment, disappointed perhaps that the fire had not burned longer, or that no houses had been exploded.

We went in silence. I thought the time had come at last to make my report.

"Sir John,'' said I, "I must tell you of something of considerable importance.''

He sighed. "Not now, boy, I'm much too tired to give you a proper hearing.''

Then I took a deep breath and got my courage up. "I must insist you listen, sir,'' said I, with a quaking voice. "I've tried to inform you a number of times tonight, yet was always·put off or interrupted. You would not take it well if I did as you said and held it to the morning.''

"All right,'' said he, "you have me. Tell me what you will.''

And at last I did, telling my tale as a tale, from start to finish, leaving out little yet adding nothing in the way of commentary or surmise. I made it plain that Jimmie Bunkins had made the discovery of poor old Moll Caulfield's body and had taken me to witness it so that I might inform Sir John. I spoke for the Raker, saying that he had not called attention to it, for there were no marks of violence on it. Lastly, I told Sir John that on my own authority I had ordered the Raker to hold her body from burial, for someone would be by to collect it in the morning. He listened to all this without comment to the very end.

"For what purpose had you thought to hold her body from burial?" he said at last.

"Why, for an autopsy, sir. And I thought she might be given a proper church burial. She was a right pious woman."

"Well," said Sir John, "Mr. Donnelly is not here, and I trust none of the other saw-your-bones hereabouts to give an opinion. There are many ways to kill without leaving marks. Had I had this information earlier, I would have taxed Brother Abraham with it. Yet we both know that he would simply have reiterated that she left their company of her own will and under her own power. And we, of course, could not prove him wrong."

"And a church burial?" I put in.

"Of course she deserves that, poor soul. There is ample money for it from that fine I exacted from John Bilbo."

"I feel an awful guilt for this, Sir John. 'Twas I who lodged her there at Half Moon Passage."

"You thought it best at the time," said he. "You did no wrong."

We walked along in silence a good long way, taking the turn onto Charles Street, which put home in sight.

Then said Sir John by way of summing up, "You did right to tell me, Jeremy, and right to insist. There are times one must brush aside defenses, even my own."

"Thank you, sir. I, uh, trust you had a pleasant evening with Mrs. Durham before you were called away to the fire?"

"Too brief, Jeremy," said he, "far too brief."

NINE

*In which I am sent
on a mission of investigation,
and the rabbi talks to Sir John*

The next morning it was necessary for Mrs. Gredge to rouse me from bed, which she did in a manner none too gentle and most accusing. Put before you, dear reader, the possibility of being brought of a sudden to a wakeful state by a voice that shared qualities of the magpie and the screech owl. To be sure, she did not always sound so, but when she raised her voice in a scold, the Devil himself could not have bested her.

"Jeremy! Jeremy!" she squawked. "Up with you *now!* You know your first duty in the morning is to light the stove for me. Now do it ere Sir John's breakfast be late."

"Oh, Mrs. Gredge," I moaned, "could you not light it yourself? You did so for years before I came."

She shook me rudely.

"I'll have none of your sauce, you lazy boy. Get yourself out of bed this minute!"

She was right, of course. It was my duty to build and light the cook fire each morning. This required me to be the first out of bed, which usually caused me no difficulty whatever. Yet on this particular morning, having first waited for Sir John half the night, then attended him at the fire during the remainder, I found it altogether difficult to rouse myself to the task.

I pulled on my breeches as Mrs. Gredge hovered in the doorway. I knew that she would not leave until I was clear of the bed and on my feet. So with a great effort I thrust up from the bed and launched myself into a new day.

It did not take long to satisfy Mrs. Gredge. The fire flamed cheerfully. She put on a kettle for tea and brought out the bread and butter. But as she sliced at the loaf, she found new grounds for complaint.

"Now, Jeremy," said she, "I've a practiced hand at boy raising, and as it seems to me, you've a problem still, a bit of fog floating about in your head. For this I see two principal reasons. First, you ought not to have waited up late for Sir John. And second, you did not eat proper last night. Had you ate some of my stew, you would have sure been fortified against this day, ready to meet the morning, so to speak. Now, we can do naught about the first, but as for the second it is not too late to make amends. And so, Jeremy, I put it to you: Would you not have some stew for your breakfast?"

How could I refuse such an offer? I assented, and she switched pot for kettle on the fire. As it warmed, she skimmed fat from the top; that tempted me a bit more. And as it began a-bubbling, and I caught the full fragrance of it, I put behind me all thought of the sights and smells of the Raker's barn and offered my bowl to be filled. I was that hungry due to last night's fast that I ate it all, savoring the goodly chunks of meat along with the rest, and wiping my bowl clean with a thick crust of bread. By the time I had finished, I was quite willing to concur with Mrs. Gredge: I truly believed it to be the best stew that ever she had cooked.

Yet ere I had come to the end, and to that conclusion, Sir John descended the stairs and, guided by his nose, found his way to the stewpot.

"Good God, Mrs. Gredge," said he, "what sort of breakfast banquet have you prepared?"

"Nothing more than what was left over from yesterday's

dinner," said she. "Jeremy was feeling poorly, and so what he failed to eat last night, I fed him this morning."

"Is there a bit in the pot for me?" he inquired most timidly.

"There is always a plate for the master of the house," said she.

And on that she made good, heaping a bowl full from the pot and serving it forth with certain pride. Sir John ate with great relish, and having finished, let forth a mighty belch of satisfaction.

"What a treat!" said Sir John. "Lamb, was it not?"

"Young mutton—or so Jeremy said."

"And so I was told by the butcher," said I. Mr. Tolliver it was, and he had sold me the cut on Saturday at a good price.

"Well, that poor lamb forged his papers of majority, I vow, and has been eaten for his punishment. A grand stew, Mrs. Gredge—though I trust we must return to rashers and dripping tomorrow?"

"If it be your wish. Hen's eggs are ever so dear."

"It would not do to eat so well every day. We'd not give proper appreciation to the extraordinary then. Stew for breakfast—remarkable, eh, Jeremy? But what's this I hear? Feeling poorly last night? You showed no signs of that at the fire."

"I fear my appetite was quite destroyed by my visit to the Raker's," said I.

"Quite understandable," said he. "But I have investigative work for you today of a more agreeable sort."

My heart leaped within me. "And what is that, sir?"

"You are known in Grub Street, somewhat by reputation. I recall that the late Mr. Crabb invited his colleagues and competitors in to witness your skill at setting type—wanted them to know what a prodigy he had engaged as apprentice. Is that not as it was?"

Had I boasted so to him? Probably I had. "Yes, Sir John."

"Do you recall the names of those present?"

I thought a moment. "There were three he'd invited. I

have the names of two—a Mr. Trimble and a Mr. Ingold.''

"Two is better than none. Visit them, Jeremy. Make it that you seek to apprentice yourself but wish extraordinarily favorable terms. They saw what you could do as a typesetter. Claim that you are a journeyman in skill and wish a briefer period of apprenticeship than is customary. Does this sound convincing? Well, make it so. But this is just to gain entry and open discussion. Try to get them to speak of Mr. Crabb—his business practices, his enemies, et cetera. We need a fuller picture of him. For now I mean to proceed on the assumption that Mr. John Clayton is innocent of all or any of the murders, and that he gave us a full and accurate account of what he remembered. Yet he remembered so little that can truly be of help to him or to us!''

"I believed him," said I, "for what that be worth."

"Make no mistake—it is worth a good deal to me. Yet to the Lord Chief Justice in court it would be worth nothing at all." He fell silent a moment. "Oh, and there is one thing more. The two journeymen who were employed by Crabb—each has gained employment with a different printer. One of them, Isham Henry, the fellow who gave witness against Clayton, has gone to work for that same Mr. Boyer whom I want you to visit, in any case. The other journeyman—what was his name?''

"Tom Cranford—I got on quite well with him."

"Well, I know not how much help Henry will be. He seemed set against Clayton and was a strange sort, it seemed to me. Your man Cranford, however, should be sought out early. Find out what he has to say of his former employer. His present employer is a Mr. Dodsley, bookseller, printer, and publisher, also of Grub Street. Look for him there. Now, can you remember all that?''

"I can, sir."

"But it would not do to set out too early. Complete your tasks for Mrs. Gredge. Then you will be free to spend the day at it. Keep your ears open. Ingratiate yourself. Spend, if need be. You will be reimbursed.''

•   •   •

It made me feel right strange to find myself in Grub Street again. I had not been there since that terrible night on which the Raker reaped his rich harvest of bodies. Earlier, on my visits to the establishment of Ezekiel Crabb, I had grown to like the street a little. Though I liked it not that I might be separated from Sir John, I had admitted to myself somewhat grudgingly that if that must be, then I could do no better than live and work in a place in which the trade was in books and pamphlets. There was ever a minority of the gentry and the scholarly among those who crowded the street. They came to search the shops for the latest in learning, the cleverest in novel entertainments. Thus it was that despite its somewhat shabby appearance, Grub Street maintained an air of respectability—nay, more, a sense of the great world that I had hoped to find when I made my sad journey to London but months before.

There were booksellers, printers, and publishers situated on the street; often, as in the case of Mr. Crabb's enterprise, the three in one. I came upon his establishment, all boarded up it was, quite early in my visit to Grub Street, for I had traced the route to the street that I knew best, the one I had followed back and forth whilst my apprenticeship was arranged. A notice was posted upon the door to the effect that the premises had been closed until further notice by order of Sir John Fielding, magistrate of the Bow Street Court. Who would want to enter into a place where such terrible deeds had taken place? Pillagers, perhaps, or those whose warped curiosity might draw them in to gape at the places where the blood of the victims had dried dark upon the floor.

On either side of the Crabb enterprise, which was housed in a fair-looking structure, there were mean lodging houses where, I had been told, impoverished writers and printers of unsteady employment made their homes. Up and down the street were respectable eating places and taverns where such as these could eat and drink their fill for so many pence. So one might say that on this street the high and low met and mingled, and all put value on literary work and its production, if only as a means of livelihood. I knew that I could have lived and worked in such surroundings, yet actually now to be of aid to Sir John Fielding on a matter of such grave import as this investigation lent an importance to my young life I could in no wise have envisioned earlier.

We are slaves to our circumstances to a degree that I had heretofore never realized. My father, had he lived in London, might well have been as grand and successful a man as Ezekiel Crabb. In which case, I had further ruminated, he might be equally dead. Either pelted in the stocks, or hacked by a murderer's axe, what did it matter?

Albert Ingold had little to say to me. Why I should have remembered his name and not the third of that group of admirers, the one who yet remained nameless to me, I could not fathom. For there was Mr. Ingold in his office, thin and reserved as I had remembered him, allowing that yes, he remembered me and it was true that he had been much impressed by the display I had given of my ability at typesetting, but he had no place for me in any case. No, not even if I were capable of doing the work of a journeyman printer—as, no doubt, with a bit of training I could do. He would keep me in mind, however, and should he hear of one who was in need of one such as me, he would of course be happy to recommend me. Why not come by again in a fortnight, and he might have a name to offer? With that, he rose, indicating that my time with him had ended. When I tried to question him then as to who could possibly be so angry at Mr. Crabb as to wish him and his whole family dead, I received a most curious response. "Whatever punishment Ezekiel Crabb received," said Mr. Ingold, "you may be sure he brought upon himself." He took me by the arm and walked with me to the door—nay, he pushed me through it. I could think of nothing to say that might buy me permission to stay and ask more questions, and so I thanked him for his time and left.

This work of gathering information was none too easy, I concluded. When I had seen Sir John at work with witnesses, he had often come at them with the full of his force—which was considerable. When I recalled how he had made Lord Goodhope's butler squirm and sweat, how he had ultimately gotten from him what he wished to know, I could only envy him. I could only wish that I, too, had such force at my command. But I had not. I had neither the force of his personality nor the force that attached to his office as magistrate. What was it he had advised? "Keep your ears open. Ingratiate yourself." That sounded easy enough, did it not? Yet I had tried with Mr. Ingold and had nothing to show for it.

Thus I thought as I stood, somewhat bemused, outside the establishment of Albert Ingold, bookseller and publisher. Grub Street seemed a little less welcoming than before. Where was I to go now? I ambled up the street, looking for the offices and shop of Mr. Trimble, and came instead to those of Mr. Matthew Dodsley. It was Tom Cranford who worked there, and in truth I had got on well with him when I met him at Mr. Crabb's. Perhaps I might do better with him. I would try, in any case.

I entered the shop all meek and mild, with a sweet, boyish smile upon my face. The place seemed to be set out in about the same way as Mr. Crabb's. Which is to say, the bookshop was at the front of the building, occupying perhaps a third of the ground floor, or even less than that, for there was an office looking out upon it—no doubt Mr. Dodsley's. Yet when I was approached by a young man and asked, all suspicious, what business I had there, it was not for Mr. Dodsley I inquired, but rather for Tom Cranford.

"And what will you with him?" demanded the young bookseller.

"To talk to him only," said I. "I am come from the Bow Street Court, and I have information of the Crabb matter, sir." Both statements were true, yet they implied more than they said. "If you would but ask him to come forward from the print shop?"

"The Crabb matter?" Of a sudden, he was much interested. "You mean the massacre? Well, tell it me, and I shall pass it on to him."

He leaned forward, expecting me to whisper. But in that

he was disappointed, for I continued smiling and shook my head most regretfully.

"That I cannot do," said I, "for I was charged to speak only with Mr. Cranford."

"Charged? By whom?"

"Why, by Sir John Fielding, of course, who is the magistrate of the Bow Street Court."

"I know damned well who he be! Freddy?" he called to the other young man present in the ground-floor front. "Freddy, keep an eye on this fellow, will you? I must fetch someone from the back."

And so he left me. I busied myself a-browsing through the books which were there in great supply, displayed on tables and shelves of the little shop. I found that newly published third volume of *Tristram Shandy* mentioned by Dr. Johnson. I picked it up eagerly, determined to judge for myself if it be worth reading.

Freddy rushed over to me and snatched it from my hands.

"Do *not* touch the stock unless you have money to buy."

"How do you know I have not?"

"Show me then."

"I need prove nothing to you."

With a great show of pride I adjusted my coat, turned, and walked to the door. There I stood, arms folded, returning stare for stare. I did not like this Freddy, nor did I think much better of his partner who had gone to the rear to seek out Mr. Cranford. I raged bitterly within at the indignities a lad of my years was forced to endure. When, in the future, I did have the money to buy books, I promised myself I would not spend it here. No, not even to put Freddy in his place.

Just when I was warming to it and imagining disasters to call down upon Dodsley's, good old Tom Cranford appeared from the rear, wiping his hands on his apron and smiling broadly.

"Well, if it ain't young Jeremy!" said he. "Quite the fastest boy with a type stick that e'er I seen."

He offered his hand in manly style, and I shook it.

"How do you fare, Mr. Cranford?"

"Oh, far better than those I worked with but a short time ago. Nay, I cannot complain."

"I was wondering if I might talk with you at some length. Here and now may not be the best place and time, however."

"You've got that right, so you have. No doubt you'll want to be talking about employment, and that's best said confidential. Let us meet across the street at the Goose and Gander. I cannot say quite how long I shall be—yet not a great wait, I promise. Will that suit you?"

"It will. I thank you."

"I'll not be long, a short piece of work to finish is all."

With that we took our leave, and I departed, most satisfied. I gave not so much as a look to Freddy and his colleague. I suppose that in my own way I snubbed them.

The Goose and Gander, now replaced by an eating place of greater pretension, was a plain, dark tavern that would have done for workers in any trade. I entered it cautiously, not knowing what I might find, for in truth I had never visited such a place before. It seemed quiet enough. There were but a few present, men who sagged against tables placed against the wall. I sought out a table away from them and sat myself down.

When the serving maid came, I asked for coffee.

"If you wants coffee," said she, "you must go to a coffeehouse."

"What have you then?"

"Beer, ale, and gin."

Ale I knew not. Gin, from what I had seen in the streets, was pure poison. Beer, which Sir John sometimes drank, seemed safest. That was what I ordered; and when it was brought, that was what I tried my best to drink—yet could not. How could Sir John down such bad-tasting stuff? But the serving maid seemed not to care whether I sipped at it or left it untouched. Only one in that shadowy place paid me the least attention, and he it was who was furthest away, a slender man dressed most gaudy.

Tom Cranford, whom I awaited, was a man not much over thirty. He had lately married and his wife was with child. He struck me as a responsible sort, and I knew him to be most able in the printing trade. Yet for all this, there was something jolly about the man, quite boyish in his manner. He would sooner be laughed at than taken with great seriousness.

In fact, he had a wide smile on his face when he entered the Goose and Gander, still wearing his printer's apron. He stopped but a moment to dally with the serving maid and give her a good thwack upon the bottom, which she accepted with a girlish giggle; then he made off with a tankard of light ale which she offered him in reward. By the time he had reached the table where I awaited him, he was roaring with laughter. He had roused the place with his high spirits. The men who had been lolling against the wall now sat upright, watching Tom with interest, exchanging looks as if his appearance were some exciting new development in a drama they witnessed.

I had gotten to my feet. He gestured me down.

"Please, sit, Jeremy boy. I'm not the sort to rise for."

"I'm very happy to see you again, Mr. Cranford."

"It's Tom—Tom with me. And I'm sure you're very happy to be *able* to see me again. After all, one more day, and you'd have been counted among the victims."

"Ah, well I know that and count myself lucky."

"But tell me, what was it you wanted to talk about? Not about employment, was it?"

"No, in truth it was not."

"As I thought. That silly snip, Theodore, who brought me from the back shop, was all over me with questions, wanting to know the latest on the massacre, as they call it, said you had news of it. Then I recalled your apprentice papers was signed by none other than Sir John Fielding. At the time, I thought it meant no more than you was a court boy, sent to us to keep you out of mischief. But now it may be that you are a bit closer to him, eh?"

"He has taken me into his household," said I.

"Ah, lucky you are, Jeremy. Though you are well suited for the printing trade, I must tell you it is a hard one in which to rise. But I've not come to burden you with my complaints. Leave it that your prospects are now much brighter." Then, for the first time since his entrance, he grew quite serious. "Tell me then," said Tom, "have you news of what befell my fellows that terrible night?"

"Of a sort," said I, "but let it be between us only."

"I can keep a confidence," said he.

I lowered my voice to a murmur. "Well, then, it is this: Sir John now proceeds on the belief, evidence notwithstanding, that John Clayton did not himself wreak that murderous havoc."

"*I knew it!*" said Tom Cranford, with a slap at the table.

I raised a finger to my lips, pleading for silence.

He continued in a whisper: "I'd come to like that fellow Clayton. Something of a bumpkin he was, and a bit loony as all poets, but at heart a gentle soul. He had no reason to kill Ezekiel Crabb, much less all the rest in his house. His hopes was riding on that second book. He'd forced Mr. Crabb to better terms on this one and might truly have made a bit on it. It made no sense that he would murder all."

He frowned, thinking upon the matter a moment; then he added: " 'Twas me took him his clothes at Bow Street."

"I did not know that."

"Aye, and a pitiful sight he was, hair down in his eyes and in that bloody nightshirt. But he knew me. He said, 'Tom, what have they accused me of?' When I told him, he wept. I think he came along after the carnage and was put quite off his head by it."

"So he himself says. But, Tom, it was not truly to give news but to receive it that I was sent out by Sir John. I've been asking about on Grub Street if some might have any notion why such an awful, murderous deed had been done. And knowing why, then by whom."

He shook his head most solemnly. "I've no idea of it," said he, "and believe me, boy, I've given much thought to it."

"You recall, do you, that Mr. Ingold was one who was brought by Mr. Crabb to witness my skill at typesetting?"

"Oh yes—I would, Trimble, and Purvis—there was

three. He wanted them to see he was getting an apprentice with a journeyman's skills.''

"*Purvis!* Yes! I could not remember that name. But I went to Mr. Ingold pretending to seek employment but in truth to get him to talk about Ezekiel Crabb—to hazard and speculate on this question of why and who. He was not very forthcoming.''

"I ain't surprised at that. Very tight-lipped he is with all.''

"He did say, though, something that surprised me. Perhaps you can explain it. He said, 'Whatever punishment Ezekiel Crabb received you may be sure he brought upon himself.' What could he have meant by that?''

"Well, now, Jeremy, there's things you must understand about old Crabb, things you would have learned soon enough had you come to work as his apprentice. His nature was such that he was very argumentative and contentious. He liked nothing better than to get into a wrangle with another on some point of learning or philosophy. Now I myself, I had no trouble with him. I do not pretend to learning of any sort. He paid regular and, after my last threat to leave him, he paid well. We got along

"Oh, but he argued and argued well, used ridicule if need be. I recall when Isham Henry—he was the other journeyman—when Henry got religion, so to speak, there were days of disputes between them. Mr. Crabb was something of a freethinker, he was, and he cut into poor Henry most merciless, he did. He would always have the upper hand in any discussion.''

"Mr. Henry was away on those days I came. He's been proven out of town at the time of the murders.''

"Oh, he could kill no one—quite weak he was, within and without.''

"He attempted to give evidence against John Clayton. Sir John rejected it as hearsay.''

"Yes, so I heard, and he got it all from me. I told him of the great row between Crabb and Clayton on the terms of the second book. I was all for Clayton on that. He'd been properly gulled on his first book. Crabb made a small fortune on it. But Clayton brought him about. He threatened to go to Boyer for the better terms. He was not near so ignorant as some took him to be."

"Can you think of *any* with whom Mr. Crabb argued violently in the recent past?" I asked, most earnest.

"I'll give you one quite recent," said Tom. "It was just days before the terrible night, and it was another row over religion. He had been given a book to publish by a sort of preacher on the conversion of the Jews. It had been brought in by Isham Henry, who was, I believe, one of the preacher's flock."

(Did not my ears prick up at that, reader!)

"The whole thing was done up in mathematics and would have been hell to set in type and read proof on. This preacher was meaning to prove that the calculations that had been done in the last century to show that this great event would happen in 1650-something—that these previous calculations was all in error. With his own calculations, this minister or preacher or whatever he was sought to demonstrate that the conversion of the Jews would be done in this century in just a few years' time. Then after the mathematics there was all this matter from the Book of Revelation about the terrible and glorious things that would then come to pass. I know what was in the manuscript because Crabb showed it me and asked my opinion. I told him I knew naught of the content, but that, as I mentioned, setting it in type would be damned difficult. He said he was tempted to take it on, for the preacher who wrote it was willing to take on half the run, which would pay Crabb's costs.

"Yet he must have thought more upon it, for when this preacher called at the office, they got into a terrible row. We heard it all over the shop. Old Crabb was clever at argument. He did not call to question the Scripture of it. He attacked his mathematics, said his figuring was all wrong. The preacher got into a proper fury at that, called down curses upon him, and demanded that he give back the manuscript. Crabb told him then he would *not* give it back. He would offer it to a right brilliant Oxford mathematician of his acquaintance, and they would prove to him that his figuring was all wrong. In fact, he did know such a man and probably planned to do just that. He would go to such lengths to win in an argument. The preacher screamed for its return. Crabb refused, then ended all discussion with an insult to the preacher's faith—said the Jews would never be converted. They were too smart for that."

"And he kept the manuscript?"

"Oh, he kept it, all right. It must be there in his desk right this moment."

"Do you remember the preacher's name?"

"Not rightly, no—only that he had but one. Brother something, he called himself."

I leaned forward and whispered the softest I knew how, "Was it Brother Abraham?"

He frowned, then smiled. "So it was," said Tom Cranford, "so it was."

"Tom," said I, most serious, "I must ask something of you. I must ask that you repeat this story you have told me to Sir John Fielding."

"You think . . . ?" He raised his eyebrows ever so high and left it for me to finish his sentence.

Yet I said, rather: "Let Sir John do the thinking. That is what he would say. Now when can you go to him?"

"Let it be after my day's work. I reckon I've already overstayed my leave here. Tell him a bit past six."

With that, he quaffed off the last of his ale and rose to go. I, too, rose and shook his hand. There we parted, he leaving the Goose and Gander a more sober man than he had entered.

I sank back into my chair and sat for a space of time, considering the import of what I had just heard. I thought it considerable. Surely I had handled the matter rightly. Sir John would hear Tom Cranford's story from me within an hour or less, yet I knew he would insist upon hearing it from Tom Cranford himself. So, of course, I was right to request most urgently that the journeyman go to him and tell the tale as he had told it to me.

I reached out and sipped once again at my tankard of

beer. Its taste had not improved during Tom's visit. Of a sudden then, I became aware of one looming over me. I looked up and found the gaudily dressed man who had previously taken my notice smiling down upon me in a manner most ingratiating.

"How do you do?" said he. "No, I pray, do not rise. I intrude but to satisfy my curiosity. May I sit down?"

When I did not say no, he took that as assent and chose the place quite close to me that Tom had vacated.

"May I introduce myself?" said he, offering me a very soft hand which I shook out of courtesy. "I am Ormond Neville, poet and historian of the day-to-day. And you are?"

"Jeremy Proctor."

"Ah! A fine name, to be sure. Do you perchance recognize my own?"

"Your name? Why . . ." I hesitated, not wishing to offend him. What could I do but prevaricate? "Why yes," said I. "I have heard your work discussed in Grub Street—oh, and with much interest."

"But you've read none yourself? *Vulcan and Venus? Achitophel?* My great tragedy, *The Trojans?*"

"I fear not. I am a poor lad, and the purchase of books is quite beyond me, no matter what their quality."

"I understand, certainly. Perhaps I could lend them," said he. "But I came not to advertise myself, rather to question you . . . uh, politely, of course."

"Uh, yes, I see." Truly, I did not. What was this fellow getting at? He had a fluttering, self-important way which put me off a bit. Still, Sir John had instructed me to keep my ears open. Perhaps Mr. Ormond Neville might have something to tell me, in spite of himself.

"It may be," said he, "that you have read my lesser works unawares, for I do not sign them. I am, as I said, not only a poet but also a historian of the day-to-day—in short, a journalist. I am, in fact, the author of a broadsheet which received wide distribution, one entitled 'Great Massacre in Grub Street.' Did you by any chance read that?"

"Oh, I did," said I, glad to be able to tell the truth at

last. "I thought it a most complete report, remarkably so since it was got out so quick after the events it described."

"Thank you," said he. "I worked like a very demon gathering the facts and assembling them in good order. Though not a work of great inspiration, I take a certain pride in it. I used greater art in the pamphlet which I wrote on the same topic."

"You wrote that, as well?"

"Ah yes, and did you not think it well argued? It put the blame on the magistrate for shielding that fiend who was caught red-handed, axe in hand, and tucking him away in Bedlam."

I fought the impulse to argue with him at this point, to call to his attention his ignorance of questions of law and a score of other matters that he had treated right crudely in the publication's twelve pages. What I might gain in personal satisfaction, I might well lose in intelligence. It was not for me to challenge him but to keep him talking. And so, I equivocated.

"I thought it very forcefully argued," said I.

"Now that I have established myself, you may understand my purpose in approaching you thus boldly. You may have noticed that I stared at you when you came into this modest house. It is not my custom to stare. A gentleman never stares. Yet I was sure I had seen you before on an important occasion. And then at last it came to me: 'twas at that mockery of a hearing at which John Clayton was assigned to Bedlam. I sat quite nearby, and I noted that you watched the proceedings with intelligent interest.

"Then, when your friend came in, I understood that you must have some special interest in this lamentable matter, for him I recognized immediately as Tom Cranford, former journeyman in the establishment of Ezekiel Crabb. I could not help but overhear the name Crabb mentioned over and over in the conversation that ensued between you. Do not think that I eavesdropped. I would not stoop so low. A gentleman never eavesdrops. Still, I did hear the name Crabb, in particular from the lips of Mr. Cranford, did I not?"

"You did," said I, wondering as I did how much else he had heard. Yet he had sat far from us, and he would not be pumping me now had he truly overheard all that was said between Tom and me.

"How may I put this?" he asked himself. "Let me say it is not mere gossip's curiosity that prompts my interest, but rather a scholar's hunger for facts. I have it in mind to do a small book on this matter of the massacre when John Clayton is properly hanged and the thing is at an end. The fellow is not only a murderous fiend but an execrable poet—a bumpkin, a lumpkin!"

At this point he paused, realizing he had got off the track somewhat. Then reorienting himself, he proceeded: "Now, Mr. Cranford has refused to talk to me on this matter. He has his reasons, I'm sure, but will no doubt realize his debt to scholarship and open up to me eventually. However, you, young sir, are clever enough to grasp the importance of my enterprise immediately. I know you are! Now, I wonder, having heard what you've heard, and realizing your debt to the great public that awaits the book that I shall write—I wonder, Jeremy Proctor, if you would divulge to me the content of your conversation?"

What a long and devious route he had taken to get that question asked. Was this simply his manner, or did he hope to flatter me with his attention? Whether the one or the other, I had perceived his goal long before he reached it and had prepared my answer.

"Mr. Neville," said I, "what you witnessed was a conversation between survivors. As you know, Mr. Cranford was spared his life because he lived apart from the Crabb establishment. *I* was spared mine by a matter of time. I was apprenticed to Ezekiel Crabb. The papers had been signed. I was set to move into the attic room with the other apprentices the day following the massacre, as you have called it. Had I moved in but a day earlier, I would have been one of the victims."

Ormond Neville sat openmouthed in astonishment. His slender hand crept to his face till his fingers touched his chin. "But dear boy, that is *amazing!* And *frightening!*

How the fates do work in our lives! That you should be chosen to live while others would meet their ends so horribly suggests that the gods do indeed have some special design for you."

"That could be," said I. "But I only hope it is not something worse."

"What could be worse?"

I shrugged, indicating not so much indifference as resignation. "As for my talk with Mr. Cranford, we congratulated one another that we had escaped with our lives. He told me a few stories about Mr. Crabb—'old Crabb,' as he called him—and we also discussed my apprenticeship with another printer."

"Ah! I may be able to help you there."

"There was also a question I had for Mr. Cranford. I showed him and Mr. Crabb my abilities as a typesetter before my apprenticeship was arranged. They put before me a most challenging manuscript with much in mathematics and calculations of all sorts. The subject of it was the conversion of the Jews. That indeed may have been the title. It struck me as most interesting. I wondered what had become of it. Surely it was not lost when Crabb's establishment was boarded up. I would hate to think that such a scholarly work would be—"

"Say no more," Mr. Neville interrupted me. "In this I may be able to help you, as well, Jeremy. May I call you Jeremy?"

As I was nodding and smiling in a manner I thought to be ingratiating, the door to the street opened, and into the gloom walked a familiar figure, known to me not so much by his features, which I could barely discover, but by his odd dress and bearing. It was Jimmie Bunkins.

Mr. Neville, whose back was turned, continued talking as Bunkins came our way. "A manuscript of the sort you describe has appeared at my publisher's, Mr. Boyer. He discussed it with me just the other day, said he would not publish it under his own name but had agreed to print it for a price. What interest could you have in—"

Without invitation, Jimmie Bunkins plopped himself

down in the chair beside Mr. Neville. I wished that he had not. Surely, I thought, what business he had with me could wait. Yet I saw, to my surprise, that it was not my attention he sought but Mr. Neville's. Yet, clearly, Mr. Neville did not wish to give it. He attempted to continue his conversation with me, ignoring Bunkins as best he could.

"What interest," he repeated, "could you have in such a work? But no matter, we shall talk of it *later,* shall we not? Here, take my card." His hand dove into his coat pocket and pulled forth a small gentleman's calling card, which he dropped before me. He seemed to be preparing a hasty exit. What fear had he of Jimmie Bunkins?

"I live in the lodging house next to Boyer's, but can be found many hours of the day just here in this humble spot," said he, rising swiftly from the table. "I *must* hear your tale of your apprenticeship and near murder. It could make a chapter entire in the book I shall write of this most awful matter."

"Just hold for a time, chum," said Jimmie Bunkins, putting a firm hand on Mr. Neville's arm. "Don't go hopping the twig on me."

"Take your hand from my arm, you rude boy."

He attempted to shake loose, but Bunkins kept tight on him.

"I'll have me bobstick, as promised, or you know what," said Bunkins. "For here I find you layin' a trap for another unsuspecting lad, bein' up to your old tricks again. You should know better."

"You'll get no more shillings from me!" cried Neville. Then with a mighty wrench, he tore loose from the boy's grasp and jumped clear, scampering for the door. "Jeremy, believe nothing that boy tells you!"

"Don't be surprised the Beak-runners come a-calling for you!" Bunkins shouted, as Neville bolted out and into the light of day.

I sat amazed and quite baffled by the scene I had just witnessed. There could be no doubt that Jimmie Bunkins had put a great fear upon Ormond Neville—but what was the basis of it? Money was involved, a threat of some sort, but more than that I could not comprehend. What surprised me equally was the lack of interest shown by the others present in the Goose and Gander. The three men against the wall had shown more interest when Tom Cranford entered than when Mr. Neville departed. The serving maid and the innkeeper had barely turned to watch him go. I was most confused.

"What say, chum? Let's be off, shall we?"

Which was the first notice Bunkins had given me since he sat down at my table.

"What was that all?" I demanded. "Why did you drive him away?"

Bunkins stood, and failing to answer my question, he asked one of his own: "You going to drink that?" He pointed to my beer.

When I said nothing, he took that as permission granted, reached over, and seized the tankard. In three swift, great gulps he downed its contents, stood silent for a moment, then emitted a great belch.

"*Ah!*" said he in satisfaction. "Come along now. Shove your trunk."

He started away, beckoning me to follow; then at the door he beckoned again. I had no reason to remain. I knew indeed that I must get on to Bow Street to tell Sir John of what I had learned. Still, I was reluctant to leave, not wishing to put myself at his beck and call. Yet I would have regretted it had I not answered his last summons, so in the end I followed him out the door, from darkness to light, where I stood blinking in Grub Street.

We started off quickly in the direction of Covent Garden.

"What was you up to in there?" he demanded. "You ain't no nancy boy, are you? 'Cause if you are . . ."

"I was *investigating,*" said I, straining to keep up with his rapid pace, "seeking information for Sir John."

"Investigating, is it? That Tom you was talking to will investigate you right out of your kicksies if you give him half a chance." He threw me a glance of dismayed disapproval. "Jeremy, me chum, you may talk like a gentleman

and read all that's been writ, but you act like a kid sometimes, I swear.''

"What do you mean?'' I inquired, all indignant.

"I mean that if you value your arse, you will in no wise
allow yourself to be gulled up into the lodging rooms of
Mr. Ormond Neville.''

"Well, I . . . well . . .''

I had no answer for that, for in truth I had not properly
understood it. Yet since it was clearly advice given in earnest, I did not question it. And so I kept my silence even
as we rounded the corner and left Grub Street behind.

Once we had done so, Jimmie Bunkins put to me a question in great seriousness.

"Jeremy,'' said he, "you must tell me, what is the latest
on poor Moll Caulfield?''

"The latest is that she will be given a good Christian
burial, as she would have liked, out of St. Paul's tomorrow
at eleven.''

"Only that? What says the Beak? Will he send his Runners to arrest those buggers in black?''

"Jimmie,'' said I, "he cannot arrest and bind to trial
when there is not proof against them. Get him proof and
evidence and testimony of witnesses, and he will act and
act right swift.''

"To that I say what I said but a day past. Moll herself
is your proof. She passed me a note in fear, and next night
she is found dead in an alley. If that ain't proof, I know
not what it be.''

"Oh, you don't understand,'' said I, my exasperation all
too apparent.

"And I suppose you do! Well, you listen, Mr. Know-All
Proctor. I been talkin' with the flash-boys in the Garden. A
few of us was at the fire last night in Maiden Lane—right,
chum, I seen you there with the Beak—and we was plan-
nin' amongst ourselves as to wouldn't it be a great shame
if there was another such fire in Half Moon Passage. That
might take care of those buggers in black, particular if we
nailed the doors shut on them.''

He stopped of a sudden in the middle of the walk and

planted both fists on his hips. Those close by cursed him for blocking their path.

"There are others in the cellar, poor folk like Moll Caulfield," said I.

"That's their problem to work out, ain't it?" He gave me a firm nod, so firm indeed that his tricorn dropped down to his nose. He pushed it up in a defiant gesture. "We'll meet tomorrow at Moll's goodbye party, we will. We can talk about it more then."

And with that he ran away at full speed, dodging artfully through the pedestrians in the street.

I had a deal of telling to do when I reached Number 4 Bow Street, and I told it all to Sir John with the door shut to his chambers. He sat listening in that peculiar manner of his— silent, reserving comment or question, his head inclined in my direction yet without expression. I knew it as his attitude of complete attention. Others, because his eyes were hidden behind the black silk band, might have thought him dozing.

When I had finished telling him of my interview with Tom Cranford, I paused and waited that he might speak. He had no question as to the content, and no comment upon the importance of it. (I needed none.)

To me he said simply, "You did well to ask him to report this to me direct. Will he come?"

"Oh, he will. I'm sure of it. He expected to be here a bit after six."

"Very good, Jeremy, excellent."

"I have more to tell."

"Oh? Proceed then, by all means."

I took not near so long to tell of Ormond Neville. Yet I made certain Sir John knew that he was the author of the broadsheet and pamphlet on the Grub Street murders, and that Neville had attempted to persuade me to divulge the content of the conversation he had observed between myself and Mr. Cranford. Then I came to the point of it all: my question to Neville regarding the whereabouts of the manuscript on the conversion of the Jews. And his answer:

that it happened to be with his publisher, Mr. Boyer, that very minute.

"With Boyer, you say?" said Sir John, exhibiting for the first time some degree of excitement both in his tone and posture. Leaning forward he was, clasping his hands together as if to make one large fist.

"That is what was said, sir—that it would not be published by Mr. Boyer, but that he had agreed to print it for a price."

Sir John brought that double-handed fist down hard upon his desk. "By God, then there may be a way."

He sat contemplating, with his chin upraised, as if seeking inspiration from the light that came through the large window to his right. I wondered at his blindness. Could he distinguish between light and dark, or were they all one to him?

I waited; then somewhat timorously, and most reluctantly, I interrupted his thought.

"Sir John," said I, "there is one more matter that I feel I must pass on to you."

"Still more? Jeremy, you quite overwhelm me."

And so, making it that I had met Jimmie Bunkins by chance in Grub Street, for I had no wish to report on the matter between him and Ormond Neville, I told Sir John of the threat made against the Brethren of the Spirit by him. "He said," said I, "that the idea had been formed in his mind to set a fire in Half Moon Passage like the one he had watched burn in Maiden Lane to settle with 'those buggers in black.' "

"He said that, did he?"

I hesitated. "He did, Sir John. I think him a good sort. I tried to point out to him that you were gathering evidence, proof against them, but . . . well, he paid little attention to me."

"I've half a mind to let him and his fellows set their fire, and let Brother Abraham and his fellows roast in it. It would serve 'the black buggers' right. But then we should have to arrest Bunkins. You would have to give witness against him. And Lord Mansfield would have to hang him.

We cannot have that. You must tell him . . .'' He hesitated. "But very likely you can tell him nothing he would listen to. Am I right in that?''

"Indeed you are.''

"Leave it that I shall look into it. Did he suggest when you two might meet again?''

"At Moll Caulfield's funeral.''

"So be it.''

I rose, half expecting to be dismissed by Sir John, when upon the door three stout knocks sounded forth.

"See who that is, will you, Jeremy?''

I did as directed and found Constable Fuller there, just as I expected. Ignoring me, he shouted into the room.

"Sir John,'' said he, "there's a foreigner with a beard says you want to see him.''

"Would his name be Rabbi Gershon?''

"Something such.''

"Send him in.'' And to me: "You may stay, if you like, Jeremy.''

"I will,'' said I, for I thought Rabbi Gershon to be one of the most curious and singular men I had ever come across. Undoubtedly he was wise, yet in a way I had never seen before—naive, humorous, making no show of his wisdom as the preachers so often do. Withal, he was a brave man. Only one of great courage would have reentered that burning building to rescue—what? A scroll. It was no doubt of great value—still, to risk one's life for a roll of parchment seemed to me then a bad bargain.

He entered. Dressed in strange garb he was, all in black. His outer coat covered him near complete. On his feet were countryman's boots, and on his head one of those odd fur hats that seemed to be favored by the men in his congregation. His beard was not near so long and impressive as before, for much of it had been singed off by the flames he had braved. On his right cheek he wore a poultice held in place by a bandage. It covered the place I had noticed the night before that had been burned raw; I doubted that his beard would ever grow again in that spot.

Sir John stood at the rabbi's arrival and offered his hand, which the latter grasped and shook firmly.

"You are most welcome here, Rabbi Gershon. There are a few matters that I feel require discussion. Jeremy? Find a chair for him, will you?"

There was no need. Our visitor settled into the chair I had vacated, and I pulled one for myself from the corner.

"Let me first inquire as to your condition," said Sir John to him.

"Oh, I am well enough—some burns on my hands and on my face. A physician of the Jewish community gave me his attention. Mr. Martinez took me to him immediate."

I had not noticed his hands previously, covered as they were by the long sleeves of his outer coat. One was bandaged entire; the other showed the fingers only.

"You were not given a good chance of return when after you brought your family to safety, you rushed back into that inferno."

"I fear the fires of Gehenna more."

"You are lucky to survive."

"Blessed. I returned with the prize I sought."

"You must instruct me on that," said Sir John. "It must be an item of great worth for you to risk your life so."

Rabbi Gershon bobbed his head in a swift gesture. "Amen," said he. "It is indeed of *great* worth."

"An antique? Those are ancient scrolls then?"

"About thirty years old," said the rabbi. "Fifty at the most."

"Then what is written on it that makes it so worth saving?"

"The Books of Moses—the first five books of the Bible, what we call the Torah."

"And what we sometimes call the Pentateuch, the Books of the Law," said Sir John. "But you surely could have bought another. Or are those scroll editions so dear?"

"Sir John," said he, "you are right. We could have bought another. It would not have been so dear that the congregation would not have paid, for it is necessary to our worship. We read from it. We study it. We argue endlessly over its meaning. If two Jews discuss any passage of the Torah, you are sure to have three different opinions heard—at least three. We are not a people who are afraid to disagree.''

''Contentious, I have heard.''

''Indeed, that might be said. So why did I not simply say to myself, 'Gershon, it is sad that the Torah will be lost, but the congregation will buy another. The words will be the same.' In fact, something of that kind came to my mind. Then another voice spoke to me and said, 'Gershon, you *dummkopf*, these are not just anyone's words. These are the words of the Almighty. Would you not die for them?' And so back into the synagogue I went. I had no choice, you see.''

''I quite understand, Rabbi. I understand, too, your unwillingness to point a finger in accusation at those who interrupted your service some nights past. I will say, though, that men dressed in black were seen by witnesses leaving the vicinity of your place of worship only minutes before the fire was first observed.''

''I am wearing black. Many do.''

''Precisely what Brother Abraham, the man who addressed your congregation, argued when I taxed him with this bit of intelligence. No, we both knew that figures glimpsed at night with neither faces nor names to identify them would not count for much in a court of law. He is, as you yourself said, no fool. He knows, however, that I suspect him and his followers of setting the fire. Ordinarily, this would count as a distinct warning to a malefactor. Yet he seems to count himself above the law, or at any rate he seems indifferent to it.''

''There are such men,'' said the rabbi. ''Among them are counted some of history's greatest villains.''

''And some of its greatest saints,'' added Sir John. ''Yet that is neither here nor there. For I would ask you now to hark back to that evening—Friday, was it not?—when your services were interrupted by Brother Abraham and those of his sect, who term themselves the Brethren of the Spirit.''

''What would you know?''

"First, to confirm—no direct threat was made against you, your congregation, nor your synagogue?"

"No, it was as I told you before, he said in the way of an afterthought to me, that perhaps the Papists had the best way to deal with Jews—by fire and sword."

"Just that—in the manner of an observation?"

"That was as I remember it."

"And not as a direct threat?"

"A *direct* threat? No. Perhaps he was too clever for that."

"Were mathematics mentioned? Calculations?"

"Not directly, no. He cited no direct proofs. He did say, though, that it had all been worked out according to the laws of science and mathematics that this great event, the conversion of the Jews, was to take place in this century—and soon."

"This was an event that was much discussed in the last century."

"So he said. But he declared with great certainty it would take place in this one. A mistake had been made, he said, and he had made it right."

"Rabbi Gershon, may I ask you a question that may seem simpleminded, or perhaps impertinent?"

"You may ask me any question, Sir John, and I shall give it a serious answer."

"Are the Jews ever likely to be converted?"

"Ah, that is the great question," said the rabbi, "is it not? Though I promised a serious answer, it will be with a story, if you permit. Yet let me assure you that it is a serious story."

"Please proceed," said Sir John. "I like your stories."

"Once there was a great caliph of Turkey who brought into his harem the most beautiful woman in all the empire. Everyone agreed she was the most beautiful. But unknown to him, she was also the most intelligent. She knew very well that once he had tried her and enjoyed what she had to offer, she would be cast aside as so many before her had been. And so she did what no other woman before her had done. She refused him. She not only refused him, she kept his appetite whetted with tales of the indescribable joys he would eventually experience with her. She wrote poems to the glory of the love they would share, sang songs to it. He was stirred by her. His desire grew greater and greater. He demanded. He threatened. 'Of course,' said she, 'you may force me. I will yield. But what you would have from me then would be only a small fraction of the joy you will have when I surrender myself to you most willingly.' And so he did not force her. Yet she refused him still. And still he earnestly courted her. Thus years went by, and the caliph grew old. He died her suitor, and she died a virgin.

"So there you have it, Sir John. We have a part in Christian prophecy. If there are no Jews left to be converted, then the prophecy will not be fulfilled. Let them court us. Fire and sword will not do."

"Brother Abraham has not heard your story, I'm sure," said Sir John. "I wonder what his reaction to it would be."

"It is impossible to look into the mind of one like him. He has no experience of other languages or cultures. I recall I offered him but one practical objection. I pointed out to him that a great many Jews, perhaps most, live within the limits of the Turkish Empire. 'And the Holy Land itself,' I said to him, 'where the triumphant return of your Messiah will take place—that also is held by Turkey.' "

"And how did Brother Abraham respond to that?"

"I believe that was when he made his remark about fire and sword."

"I see."

"Sir John," said Rabbi Gershon, "I wonder if you might enlighten me on a point."

"I'll try, of course."

"I've heard it said in passing since we came to England that there was a great discussion of the Jewish conversion among theologians in the last century. You mentioned it yourself. When was this to come to pass?"

"Oh, there were various dates given, most of them very specific, but they all seemed to fall somewhere in the middle of the century. Conversion was to have been complete by the end of it. That was a time of great political turmoil here.''

"That is most interesting to me as a Jew, for in the middle of the last century there came from Smyrna a rabbi named Shabbatai Zevi who proclaimed himself to be the Messiah, *our* Messiah. Thousands upon thousands of Jews accepted him and followed him. He was the one we now call the False Messiah, the latest in a long line of them—but the most powerful. He eventually converted to Mohammed.

"And that, as I said, began in the middle of the last century at a time when similar delusions were discussed most seriously here. Interesting—that the Devil was busy sowing confusion in our two camps at that same time. Why do I bring this up? I'm not sure, except that when I think of this Brother Abraham I think also of Shabbatai Zevi. He seems to me a False Messiah in his own way. Do the Christians have such?'' ·

"Oh yes. They come and go, though most wear the mantle of politics. What you say is interesting, though. I had said, or at least thought, the same of our man, Brother Abraham.''

"We agree then, it is interesting.''

Sir John rose and extended his hand. "And most perplexing. I'll not detain you further, Rabbi. Let us touch hands merely. I fear I gave your burned fingers too great a squeeze earlier.''

They did as he suggested, said their goodbyes, and Rabbi Gershon made ready to leave.

"Jeremy,'' said Sir John, "see the rabbi to the street, if you would.''

I jumped to the task, escorting him through the door and down the long hall.

"Your name is Jeremy,'' said he.

"That's right, sir.''

"A good name, a Jewish name, from the prophet Jeremiah. And are you related to Sir John? A son? A nephew?''

"Oh no, sir. But I am a member of his household,'' I said proudly. "I call myself his assistant, though I am not anything so grand. I do try to help him, though."

"I'm sure you do. I want you to take good care of him, Jeremiah, for he is a good man—a good man in a bad time, as all good men have been in all past times. To help you to take care of him, I would like to say a blessing on you. Will you allow me to do that?"

"Why . . . why yes, sir. What must I do?"

We had reached the door. He paused there and gave me a smile most reassuring.

"Nothing," said he. "Just stand and be silent."

And so, as I stood by the door a bit awkwardly, he raised his bandaged hand and said some words in the strangest tongue that e'er I heard. And though he spoke not so long, the event made a great and lasting impression upon me.

When he had done, he smiled again and bade me good-bye as I held the door for him.

TEN

*In which Moll Caulfield
is laid to rest, and a
meeting is held*

When I returned, I found Sir John's door closed. Since I had no claim upon his attention, I took a seat on the bench beside it and waited. Experience had taught me that unless I was formally dismissed, it was best to remain at hand and on call. Though dinner time was not too far off, I suspicioned there might yet be duties to perform.

And I was not wrong. I had sat but a few minutes when the door opened and Mr. Marsden emerged, looking this way and that.

"Ah, there you are, Jeremy. I have written out a letter for Sir John, something in the form of a summons."

"I'm to deliver it, sir?"

"Go in and talk to him. I believe he has special instructions for you."

In I went and closed the door after me.

"Jeremy," said Sir John, "I fear I must send you back to Grub Street, boy."

The letter mentioned by Mr. Marsden lay on the desk just before him, sealed with wax, his sign of office stamped upon it. He pushed it toward me with his pointing finger.

"I would like this delivered to Mr. Boyer, the publisher, and only to him."

"I have that, sir—only to him."

Taking the letter, I held it tight and made ready to go.

"Ah, but wait. That is not all. First of all, you must make haste, for I know not when his establishment closes for the day—soon, I think. Just as important is this: You must take pains *not* to be seen by that journeyman Isham Henry, who worked before for Ezekiel Crabb and now works for Boyer."

"But he was not about during my visits to Mr. Crabb," said I. "Off visiting somewhere, I believe."

"Yet he might now know you by sight. Mind me in this, now."

"As you say, Sir John."

"Off with you then, and when you are back, wait for me, for there may be further tasks for you. Go now."

"Like the wind!"

And I ran off, letter in hand, tricorn perched atop my head, coattails flapping. Out on the street, I avoided the crowd along the way by running on the cobblestones next the curb, leaping to the walkway to avoid being trampled by oncoming horses, jumping over their leavings. I thus made my way near as swift as Jimmie Bunkins might have done. I know not the time I set out for Grub Street, but it was still a bit before six when I arrived, so I had won my race against the clock. If Tom Cranford would be let off at Dodsley's back shop at six, surely Boyer's front shop would stay open till seven, and Mr. Boyer would just as surely stay as long as there was money to be made.

On this visit I found his establishment in no time and with no difficulty. It was the largest on the street, twice the size of Number 4 Bow Street and just four doors down from the Goose and Gander. Seeing that the bookshop in front was well filled with customers still, I took a moment to stand before it and catch my breath. It looked a good place to buy and an even better one to look; there were piles of books scattered higgledy-piggledy about the place, and gentlemen nosing through them contentedly as clerks busied themselves arranging shelves and attending to other clerkly matters. I liked the permissive air about the place.

I vowed that the business I had taken from Dodsley's I would give to Boyer's.

Then into the store. I went straight to the nearest clerk and declared that I had a letter from Sir John Fielding for Mr. Boyer, and it was to be delivered only to him. I waved it in front of him that he might see the official seal that it bore. The young man promised me that he would find him, and left in a great rush.

Thinking to test them, I picked up a book from the nearest pile on the nearest table, and in full sight of another clerk began to peruse its contents. It was not ripped from my hands. I thumbed its pages. I began to read. It did not take me long to realize that quite by chance I had taken up a copy of *Vulcan and Venus, a Romance in Verse,* by Ormond Neville. Since I had that very day met the author of the book, I took more than casual interest in it.

So it was that the book was before my face and my back turned when I was jostled most rudely by one who seemed to give me no notice at all. I looked up, indignant, and saw a figure in black making swiftly for the door. When he turned slightly in opening it, I saw that he was none other than Isham Henry, whom Sir John had said I must avoid at all cost. Well, strictly speaking, I had not avoided him, for he had near knocked me over. Yet had he actually *seen* me? I thought not. I hoped not. And would he have recognized me had he looked upon my face? Probably not. I was satisfied that I had satisfied the spirit, if not the letter, of Sir John's instructions.

"All right, all right, let's have it, boy."

The man who looked at me most impatient was well over sixty, with a pouchy, florid face. He seemed the sort one would not dare to trifle with. Still, I told myself, I must be sure of his identity. I had seen him but once before, pointed out to me at Bow Street.

"Are you Mr. Boyer?"

"Of course I am. Give me the letter."

I fumbled so in handing it to him that I nearly dropped it. Yet he grabbed it from the air and seemed to rip it open in the same motion. His eyes moved quick over the single page.

"Is it urgent as all this?" he demanded.

Knowing not what else to say, I declared, "It is just as Sir John has stated in the letter."

"Oh, bother!" He looked about and found the clerk who had fetched him. "Philip, run into the street and wave down a hackney for me, like a good fella. I must get my hat and stick."

Thus Philip made for the door, and Mr. Boyer disappeared, then reappeared but a moment or two later properly attired for the street. He bustled past me, paying me as little attention as had Isham Henry but a short time before. I followed him through the door and outside. Philip had done his work. A hackney waited at the curb.

"Now, Philip," said Mr. Boyer, "if Mr. Nicholson has not returned, you must clear the front shop and close up. I may be back in time, then again I may not."

With that he ascended into the coach without a look in my direction, and shut the door tight. The hackney drove off. I had hoped to be offered a ride back to Bow Street.

Left there on the walkway, deserted by the clerk, I sighed deep and began trudging back the way I had come. I soon picked up my pace, moving along with the crowd. This was also a time I liked well in London—that space between dusk and dark, when the streets were full and safe and people had begun hastening from their places of employment to the places they claimed as home. There was a sense of relief and freedom in the air of this great city. The streets seemed to hum with possibility as men and women talked and laughed together. This was London as I had pictured it in my childish dreams as I labored in my father's print shop.

So, in truth, I felt not so much put upon by Mr. Boyer's discourtesy as disappointed by it. The evening was fair and warm and good for walking. Something of spring still lingered. And I was much cheered indeed when halfway home, I glimpsed ahead of me the figure of Tom Cranford.

I hopped to catch him up. He walked along, head down, looking somewhat troubled.

When I touched his arm to notify him of my presence, he started a bit, then smiled to see me there. Yet he seemed not near so jolly as he had in the past.

"Ah so, Jeremy. It's you again, is it?"

"It is," said I. "May I walk with you to Bow Street?"

"My pleasure," said he, though he seemed little pleasured by the prospect. We went along in silence for a space until he spoke up, revealing what troubled him: "Our last conversation brought me a bit of woe."

"I'm very sorry, Tom. How was that?"

"I was upbraided proper by Mr. Dodsley when I returned to the shop. I told him, first, that I had gone at a slack time, and second, that the meeting had to do with the Crabb matter. Then he demanded to know what was discussed, and I refused to tell him, for I knew Sir John Fielding would not have me bladdering about what I had told you—then didn't old Dodsley get himself into a fit! He would not hear of secrets from an employer, said he. 'But sir,' said I, 'this is a matter of the law.' He said he cared naught for the law, that my first loyalty and duty was to him, and I was to remember that always in the future."

"Then he did not discharge you?"

"No, he did not. But he gave me a stern warning, and I must heed that warning, for I've a wife and a child on the way. Ah, Jeremy, 'tis bad to work under such rule. I may have given you the wrong picture of Mr. Crabb. Contentious and a bit tight with a shilling he may have been, but he allowed a man to work at a reasonable pace, and if work was slack he thought it not a crime to pop out for an ale. Things is different now, for fair."

"You must tell Sir John of this," said I.

" 'Twill do no good," said he, "and may do much harm."

So saying, he lapsed into silence, and I, not knowing what I might say to give him heart, said nothing. Thus we came at last to Bow Street. I showed Tom Cranford inside to the magistrate's chambers. Yet the door was shut, and I heard Sir John's voice rumbling beyond it. We were obliged to wait on the bench for some minutes until the door opened.

Out stepped Mr. Boyer. His face, which I had noted had a meaty, reddish hue, had paled so that it now seemed quite ashen. He took no notice of either Tom Cranford or me, yet staggered away as one who bore a heavy burden.

Tom and I exchanged looks of surprise and puzzled surmise. Then from within my name was called. I went to the door.

"Yes, Sir John."

"Is your friend Tom Cranford here?"

"He is, sir."

"Show him in, by all means; then take yourself up to dinner. I'll not be needing you further. I'm to dine tonight with Mrs. Durham again. Please God I'll not be called away to another fire tonight."

It was a small party which saw Moll Caulfield from St. Paul's into the churchyard the next morning. There were six of us bearing her body in the plain oaken casket. Before me was Constable Cowley and behind, Constable Baker. Jimmie Bunkins, who was as surprised as I to be pressed into service as a pallbearer, was directly across from the casket from me to my right. Ahead of him was none other than Black Jack Bilbo, who had insisted to me before the service he had come merely to see how his money was spent. Behind Bunkins was Benjamin Bailey, captain of the Bow Street Runners.

Following us, dressed in ritual array, his prayer book open, was the young vicar who had conducted the brief service within the church. And behind him, in no particular order, came Katherine Durham, Moll's chum Dotty, and a few other old dames from the Garden. It must have been the humblest funeral cortege to pass through the portals of St. Paul's in many a year.

A place had been dug for old Moll in the far corner of the churchyard. The grave, which I had inspected before the service, was a bit shallow, only about four feet deep, so I suspicioned there would be another beneath her to keep her company, perhaps a nun from the ancient, long-destroyed convent that had given the Garden its name. It was Moll, however, who would get the tombstone. Mr. Bilbo had promised it.

The six of us moved together at a slow, solemn pace proper to the occasion. Constable Cowley and Black Jack steered a true course through the paths that crisscrossed the graves, while behind us the vicar intoned his prayers, no doubt from memory. I heard no pages rustle behind me.

"The Lord is my shepherd," declared the vicar. "I shall not want." And on he went through that familiar psalm, known well even to my doubting father. But then he came to these words: "Yea, though I walk through the valley of the shadow of death, I will fear no evil: for Thou art with me." And I knew that poor Moll had feared the evil she perceived about her, for she had sent a note to Sir John asking to be taken from the Brethren of the Spirit. By the time we had received her plea, the poor woman was dead. I felt the burden of her death hard upon me. I had not told Bunkins it was I who had put her in the hands of Brother Abraham—nor would I ever. Of that I felt deeply ashamed.

At last we had come to the grave site. The hole was prepared with two stout boards across it whereon the casket would be balanced. It was laid thereon by us six, who then stepped back right smart, three on one side and three on the other. Thus we stood as the mourners circled round. There we listened again to the vicar. How different it had seemed inside St. Paul's that morning from my earlier occasion there. The big nave of the church was near filled to overflowing at the funeral of Lady Fielding. All of Covent Garden and more had come to pay their last respects to her and express their continuing respect for Sir John. Yet here at graveside it was not much different for Moll Caulfield than it had been for Lady Fielding. The day was better. There was little likelihood of rain. But the same final prayer was said.

"Dust thou art, and unto dust shalt thou return," de-

clared the vicar, and continued on in a strong voice until
at last it was all said and done.

He then gave a nod to us pallbearers, and we set about
our work in the manner we'd been told to do. The four men
lifted the casket as high as need be off the boards that held
it above the grave, whilst Jimmie Bunkins and I each seized
a board and pulled it clear. Then came the slow release of
the ropes in time together as the casket was lowered into
the grave.

When it touched bottom, the vicar invited all present to
toss a bit of earth upon the casket in remembrance of Moll
Caulfield. I held back, as did Bunkins. He had been near
silent through it all, only saying to me before the service
that he would speak to me later of "re-venge," for it was
only proper that something be done in the name of poor
Moll. I looked forward to that conversation with him with
the greatest foreboding, for I feared there was nothing I
could say that would dissuade him. But now he stood across
the grave, then bent down of a sudden and pitched in a
handful of dirt. Giving me a hard look then, he silently
mouthed a word to me: "Rev-enge."

As one by one, we mourners repeated that same grim
gesture, Mr. Bailey on one side and Mr. Cowley on the
other hauled up the ropes with which the casket had been
lowered.

Katherine Durham, who had come perhaps to represent
Sir John at the funeral, tossed in a bit of earth and took me
aside.

"Jeremy," said she in a whisper.. "You must not be
shocked at what happens. It has all been arranged by Sir
John."

"But what has—"

"Soft," said she, "and make ready to leave swiftly."

Then she gave a nod to Benjamin Bailey, and he to Black
Jack Bilbo.

Giving no other sign, these two powerful men fell upon
Jimmie Bunkins.

Their intent was not to do him harm, but rather to bind
him with the stout rope Mr. Bailey had pulled from the

grave. How Jimmie Bunkins fought against them! He kicked with his feet and pounded with his fists—and well I remembered their stinging power from my first encounter with him! Yet he was no match for. them. They wrapped him top and bottom with the rope and bound his hands, as well.

What was remarkable was that he barely uttered a sound through this brief struggle, except for grunts and gasps that he delivered with the blows and kicks he rained upon them. But now, trussed up like some wild animal, he began bellowing and screaming for help, more in frustration than in true expectation, surely. Yet Mr. Bilbo would have none of that. He pulled a silk handkerchief from his pocket and jammed it into Bunkins's wide-open mouth.

Indeed, who would help him? The vicar, who had apparently been forewarned, clapped shut his prayer book and made swiftly for the church. Dotty and the old dames gaped in surprise, then timidly shrank back. Mr. Baker and Mr. Cowley clapped their hats upon their heads and made ready to leave. And as Mr. Bailey tossed Jimmie Bunkins over his shoulder like a sack of turnips, Mrs. Durham gave me a tug upon my sleeve.

"Come now, Jeremy, we must go."

"No, I want to tell him that . . ." And then, realizing that the information I had given Sir John regarding Bunkins's plans had put the lad in his present predicament, I saw that there was little I could tell him.

And so I did no more than nod my assent and follow Mrs. Durham along the pathway toward the church. About halfway to the door whence we had exited, I turned and looked to see what had become of Bunkins. Riding atop Mr. Bailey's shoulder, he was about to leave the churchyard by way of the gate to the piazza. Mr. Bilbo and the two other çonstables trailed close behind.

"Where are they taking him?" I asked Mrs. Durham. "To Bow Street? Will they put him in the strong room?"

"No, Jeremy," said she, "he's done nothing *yet*. It's to prevent him that they've taken him away. They mean only to talk sense to him."

• • • •

Sir John Fielding had called the meeting for half past six, not long before the hour that the Bow Street Runners customarily assembled to make their nightly rounds, or to organize raids upon nests of known malefactors. For although the Runners maintained a reassuring presence on the streets, they were best known then, as today, for their swift attacks and counterattacks upon the criminal element. Thus had the first Bow Street magistrate, Henry Fielding, conceived the dual mission of this band of worthies; and thus had Sir John Fielding maintained them.

While I rightly supposed that the meeting planned by Sir John might be one such council, I had no notion of the size and extent of the strategy he meant to put in operation. This would eventually go down in the annals of Bow Street as the grandest maneuver ever attempted by the Runners. Yet how was I to guess that when, while seeing the day go calmly following the burial of Moll Caulfield and the disappearance of Jimmie Bunkins, I was sent to Johnson Court with an invitation to the Great Cham that he might come by for a visit about half past six? There was so little urgency in Sir John's manner that I thought he intended perhaps to go out and dine with Dr. Johnson. In fact, Sir John had been notably relaxed and cheerful all afternoon following his court session, humming to himself, wandering about, exchanging jibes with Mr. Marsden. I marveled at his ability to put the burden of office from him. For my part, I was still much troubled by Bunkins's abduction and the role in it I had played. Though I knew I had done right in informing Sir John of Bunkins's incendiary intentions, the memory I kept of him helpless in his bonds and riding on Mr. Bailey's broad shoulder plagued me all through the day. Truth to tell, I found it a relief from those confused pangs of conscience to be sent off on the errand to the home of Dr. Samuel Johnson.

The first hint that something quite exceptional was planned came in Dr. Johnson's response to the invitation. He had come at once to meet me and seemed in an agitated state.

"Have you a letter for me, boy?"

"No letter, sir," said I, "but an invitation. Sir John wishes you to come by to his chambers at half past six."

"Oh, I will," said he. "Tell him I shall be there, that I would not think of missing an opportunity to see the end of this dreadful matter."

Though puzzled, I thanked him and turned away to go.

"Tell him also," said Dr. Johnson, "that I had been quite prepared by Mr. Boyer and that I acted my part well during the expected visit."

If I had been puzzled but a moment before, I was now confused and curious. How had Mr. Boyer prepared him? Who was the expected visitor?

Yet knowing my place and asking no questions, I took leave and hurried back to Bow Street, hopeful that I would receive some explanation from Sir John.

Vain hope it was. He took the news of Dr. Johnson's acceptance of the invitation without comment, and when I added the lexicographer's postscript, he simply nodded, smiling, and began once more to hum the ditty he had kept going through most of the afternoon. I had never known him in quite such a state.

"Have you anything to do?" he asked me then, surprising me with the generality of his question. "Any tasks for Mrs. Gredge?"

"None that I know of, sir."

"Then I advise you to go up to your bed and have a nap," said he. "You'll have a late night of it tonight, and I mean for you to be alert. Should Mrs. Gredge object, tell her that you go under my command. But be sure that you, too, are here at half past six. Inform Mrs. Gredge of that. Tell her to wake you in time." He then made a quick, dismissive motion with his hand. "Now, do as I say—go."

I left as bidden, thinking that it had all become even more difficult to understand. Not only had I the questions that Dr. Johnson had raised to puzzle over, I must now also wonder at Sir John's purpose in wishing me present at his meeting with the lexicographer. Was John Clayton also to

be present? Was I to read his face again? Why should that
be the cause of a late and strenuous night?

Thus baffled, I went to my attic room, having instructed
Mrs. Gredge to wake me when the clock struck six. I
looked out the window, dubious that I should be able to
sleep in the daylight hours. Yet looking, I saw that the sky
was changing, darkening, as a wall of dark clouds scudded
in from the east. A wind had blown up of a sudden. But I
laid me down upon my bed and took up the book that had
put me to sleep a couple of nights past. What could it have
been? I recall that about that time in my young life I had
attempted without success to read Burton's *The Anatomy
of Melancholy,* and so perhaps that was it. Yet whatever
the book, it worked upon me better than a sleeping potion.
After a mere couple of pages, I drowsed. My eyes drooped,
and soon I slept.

There was a dream, and a great confusion of a dream it
was. There was in it a whole host of men in black. There
was fire and before the fire the men in black danced—not
for joy, as the Jews had done, but in a wild and uncon-
trolled manner, as I then supposed that Red Indians danced.
There was the face of one who threatened me, who threatened us all, for I was in the company of others. It was the
face of Brother Abraham, and he mouthed words which
seemed biblical but were all a jumble of threats and promises. Then were there great explosions in the dream, yet
this seemed quite reasonable in the logic of the dream, for
if there was a fire, then it would be necessary to blow up
surrounding structures with gunpowder, as the captain of
artillery had proposed. Yet the explosions grew louder and
more frequent, and the loudest of all waked me, for it was
thunder, and rain beat hard against my attic window.

I rose from my bed, listening to the storm outside, noting
how the wind rattled the window; then I pulled on my shoes
and coat and, remembering my hat, left the safety of my
room to descend the stairs. The clock struck six as I entered
the kitchen, where Mrs. Gredge bustled about the table.

"Ah, there you be," said she. "I was just on my way
to fetch you down. I've made you a pot of tea to wake you

up proper. But a moment or two more, and it should be well steeped.''

I thanked her and took a seat. She pushed a plate at me with a great slice of bread and a chunk of cold beef upon it.

"Eat that," said she, pouring my tea. "You'll need it. Myself, I think it not right to bring a boy out on a night such as this. But it's plain you'll need something inside of you."

Even Mrs. Gredge seemed to know more about the plans for the coming night than I did. Yet I asked her no questions, but fell to the job of eating I had before me. I had not known until I began how hungry I was; nor until I drank the tea, how sorely I needed it to wake me. I ate in silence, and having finished, got up to do the little washing up there was to do.

"No," said Mrs. Gredge, "I'll attend to that. Get yourself down the stairs and join the crowd of them that's there already."

Saying a goodnight to her, I then made my way down the stairs and found most of the Runners already present, either in their rain gear, having just arrived, or pulling it off. They talked but little, but those who did so spoke in loud tones. There was indeed something in the air that night, and it was more than the rain that fell.

Seeing Mr. Baker, second in command of the Runners, standing somewhat apart from the rest, I presented myself to him and asked after Sir John.

"He's in his chambers," said Mr. Baker, "where us all will gather. My understanding is he wants you there right quick."

Though not a large room, it was made smaller by the addition of a number of chairs set left to right before his desk. Behind that desk, Sir John paced in slow, deliberate steps. Yet I had not done more than enter when he stopped and turned in my direction.

"Who is there? Is it you, Jeremy?"

"It is, Sir John."

"Ah, good. I want you to serve as my butler."

"Sir?" I could not suppose he wanted me in livery, to puff and prance about as I had seen it done at the Goodhope residence.

"You need not worry yourself over it. Our guests will be arriving by hackney carriage and coach on such a night as this. Be at the door. Meet them as they arrive and convey them through that rowdy bunch in the hall to me here. Understood?"

"Very well, sir."

"Well rested, are you? Had a bite to eat?"

"Yes, sir."

"Then get on with it, for they should begin arriving at any minute now."

First to come was Dr. Samuel Johnson—or so I discovered when I leaped from the shelter of the entrance and threw open the door to his hackney. He extricated himself with some difficulty, but once on the cobblestones he moved easily enough—through the door and into the hall. He followed as I called my way through the Runners, and I deposited him at the open door to Sir John's chambers.

Next came Mr. William Boyer, arriving this time not in a public conveyance but in a coach drawn by a team of two horses. When I moved to open the door to it, I was pushed aside by the single footman who had leaped down to the street. He had under his arm a package of no great size, wrapped in cloth. Mr. Boyer appeared quite timorous at my first sighting of him. He looked left and right and then at me.

"Are all here?" he asked of me. "Are the Runners here in force?"

"Oh, they are, sir. Right this way."

I led him through the milling mass. There could not have been more than twenty of them there that night in the long hall, though to me they seemed a great throng. Their presence seemed to reassure Mr. Boyer, as well. A short man, not much above my own height, he seemed to take heart in the very largeness of the Runners. When at one point I turned to assure myself he followed close, I saw him staring in wonder at the top of Mr. Bailey, who stood near six and a half feet above the ground. Yet he hastened along then, and I soon deposited him at Sir John's open door. I noted, as I did so, that two more chairs were left to be filled.

Then back to the entrance of Number 4, where I stood long and waited, half sheltered from the rain, for the next arrival. The wind was greater than the rain, however. It had me backed up against the door. When on a couple of occasions I heard hoof beats and looked out left and right, I had to lean out against the wind, to fight it as one might struggle against a physical, carnal presence.

At last I heard a steady clop-clop-clop that made sure announcement of a vehicle approaching, a hackney from the sound of it. I waited, knowing not who might make an appearance. Yet in no wise could I have supposed who would first emerge from that carriage when I jumped to open the door.

He was a boy of about my age, well scrubbed, in clothing of good quality, who leaped nimbly to the cobblestones. It was not until he was down at my level, his face near mine, that I recognized this young and unexpected visitor for who he was—Jimmie Bunkins. He turned to me, most bold and assured, and gave me a broad wink.

Then came Black Jack Bilbo from the hackney. He tossed the driver two silver coins and dodged into the open doorway where Bunkins and I awaited him.

"Sorry to be late, young Jeremy," said Mr. Bilbo. "There was matters at my establishment demanding my attention. Has the proceedings begun?"

"No, sir," said I. "I believe Sir John awaited you." Then, remembering there were two empty chairs, I added, "And your companion. This way, please."

Mr. Bilbo's companion seemed somewhat intimidated by the assemblage of constables. "Crikey," said he behind me, "I never seen so many hornies of a darkey in one place in me life!"

Yet we made our way through them, the Runners taking greater notice of Mr. Bilbo and Bunkins than they had the other two I had moved through their midst. Both were known to them—though by diverse means.

At the door to his chambers, Sir John interrupted his conversation with Dr. Johnson and Mr. Boyer, aware of our presence.

"Mr. Bilbo, is it you?"

"It is, Sir John, and I come offering regrets for my tardiness."

"That's of no matter. We shall have a bit of a wait ahead of us in any case. You have the young man with you, as well?"

"He is here."

"Then sit you down, both of you, in the two remaining chairs. And Jeremy?"

"Yes, sir?"

"Go now and tell Mr. Bailey to bring the Runners in. 'Twill be a bit crowded, but they must all be present to hear."

Crowded it was. Once the constables had trooped in, they seemed to take up every bit of space in that room of modest size. They were lined up against three walls and in each corner. Room was given to Sir John to move about, though he chose not to. He sat down in his chair and tucked himself under his desk. From my place in the corner beside Mr. Bailey, I saw him only from the side. Yet when he spoke to the silent, waiting room, his voice quite filled it.

"Mr. Boyer," said he, "will you stand and exhibit the contents of that package you brought with you tonight?"

He did as Sir John asked, holding up before him a great sheaf of papers, near two inches thick, which were held together, horizontal and vertical, by lengths of stout twine.

"And what is that, Mr. Boyer?"

"It is a manuscript," said he. "I am a publisher, and many such come into my possession."

"How came this one in your possession?" asked Sir John.

"It was brought to me by one Isham Henry, a journeyman printer whom I had just hired. There was some question if I might publish it. In the end I declined to do so: I did not wish to put it out under my imprint. But it was agreed, through Mr. Henry, that we would take it on as a job of printing and binding. I would not put my name upon it, but for a price—and a good one—we would deliver five hundred books, printed and bound, and moreover, we would store the plates for two years, should it be necessary to print more copies.''

"I take it," said Sir John, "that this sort of arrangement is common in your trade.''

"It is common, yes, though we have not engaged in the practice much lately. Still, as I said, the agreed-upon price was a good one.''

"I have some questions for you, sir. First, why did you decline to publish the book under the name of your firm?''

"Well, it was not badly written, though it relied much on mathematics and calculations to make its point.''

"Were the mathematics accurate?''

"I have no way of knowing. I am, God knows, no hand in such matters. Had I taken it on to publish, I should have shown it to one competent.''

"And what was the point of the book? What was its content?''

"That, for me, was the greatest problem," said Mr. Boyer. "Its subject was not one to appeal to many readers. It was on the supposed coming of the conversion of the Jews. In my opinion, a run of five hundred copies greatly overestimated its appeal. This was a topic much discussed by theologians many years ago as a precondition of the second coming—it's all in the Bible—but even then it was of interest only to theologians. The predicted time came and passed in the last century. The author's intent was to prove that earlier calculations were wrong, that it would all come to pass in this century.''

"And who was the author?''

"Though the book was to be set forth anonymously, he was in fact a man named Abraham Watt, the leader of a sect which calls itself the Brethren of the Spirit.''

"And finally, this man Isham Henry, who brought the manuscript to you, how came he to be hired by you?''

"He was formerly in the employ of Ezekiel Crabb, who along with his family and apprentices was murdered in what is commonly called the Grub Street massacre. Because Mr. Henry is a journeyman, he lived away from the premises and escaped their fate.''

"Did you know him to be a member of that sect?"

"I did not, though I strongly suspect it now."

"That will be all, Mr. Boyer. But before you sit down, hold the manuscript up once again."

He did so, raising it high above his head and turning in a wide circle that everyone in the room might see. Then he took his seat.

"There," said Sir John, "you have the cause and purpose of the six murders on Grub Street. That same manuscript was to be published by Ezekiel Crabb, until— But two witnesses have given testimony as to what happened then. Perhaps they should be here to tell you what they heard, but that would have been difficult for one witness and impossible for the other. However, their examiners are here, and they are known by person or reputation to most of you. Jeremy Proctor, will you tell us what you heard from Tom Cranford, a second journeyman in the employ of Mr. Crabb?"

I stepped forward, and in fewer words than Mr. Boyer had used, repeated what I had been told by Tom Cranford of the quarrel that had erupted between Ezekiel Crabb and Brother Abraham when Crabb had had the temerity to challenge his calculations and retain the manuscript. Mr. Crabb became insulting and ridiculed Brother Abraham to the point that the latter called down curses upon him. And I added, finally, that Mr. Crabb had told him that the Jews would never be converted, for they were too smart for that. At the end, when I quoted Mr. Crabb on the Jews, a ripple of embarrassed laughter passed around the room.

"Thank you, Jeremy," said Sir John. "That was well delivered. And I can vouch for its authenticity, for Mr. Cranford told me of hearing the same conversation between his former employer and Brother Abraham. Mr. Cranford unfortunately could not be with us tonight, since his present employer insisted that he perform added labors, that he might be compensated for the time spent in telling the tale to Jeremy. In effect, it would seem, he has been kept after school.

"Yet, having heard it myself, I was more than interested when Dr. Samuel Johnson came to me with a story from a separate source this morning which matched it right well. Since John Clayton was moved from the Hospital of St. Mary of Bethlehem to the Fleet Prison, Dr. Johnson has visited him every day, encouraging him to remember more details of that dreadful night. What I heard from him this morning seems quite significant in the light of what Tom Cranford had to tell us. Dr. Johnson, will you repeat it?"

The great bear of a man rose firmly to his feet and spoke as follows: "I will and I shall, Sir John. As you say, I have visited Mr. Clayton often, for I am convinced of his innocence in this matter. And while we two went through his memories of that night repeatedly, because of his . . . condition at the time, there was little more to be learned from him than Sir John had heard in his interrogation in these chambers, at which I was present.

"Yesterday afternoon, however, or perhaps better said, early in the evening, he told me something that I considered of potential importance. It was not a memory of the night in question, but of the day previous to it. While conferring with Mr. Crabb on the production of Mr. Clayton's second book of poems, Mr. Clayton was told by his publisher that he had had a nasty encounter a day or two before with an author when he, Crabb, had called to question the content and conclusions of the book in question. The author had been so vexed that he called down heaven's judgment upon Crabb. 'He consigned me quite to hell,' said Crabb to Clayton. When Clayton asked Crabb if he regretted what he had said, the latter said that he did, though not because he thought himself in the wrong, but rather because of the unpredictable nature of the author. 'There is no telling what such a fellow would do,' said Mr. Crabb. 'He is a raw preacher and such are not always restrained by ordinary laws of human conduct.' When Mr. Clayton asked the subject of the book, he was told that it was the conversion of the Jews, and that same was also the title."

With that, Dr. Johnson gave a great, certain nod of his large head. "That, sir," said he to the magistrate, "is as accurate a summary of what I heard as I am capable of giving."

"Then I thank you, sir, and please sit down." And to the room at large said he: "Now, you may not give great weight to what Mr. Clayton had to say, for he, of course, was discovered on that night whereof we speak with an axe in his hand, the weapon by which at least one of the victims had been dispatched. But a moment on that. What do we know of that axe, Mr. Bailey? You borrowed it that you might study it and remember better something of its origin. What have you to say of it, sir?"

"Not so much as I would like, Sir John," said Benjamin Bailey, stepping forward from his place beside me. "Yet I can say with fair certainty that it is of colonial manufacture. I saw such often during the late war with the French."

He suddenly produced it. And though he did not surprise me or the Runners, for we knew he carried it with him that night, he gave Dr. Johnson a start, who sat nearest him. Its handle was perhaps a bit shorter than one might see on an axe of regular manufacture, and it was also bent to suggest that it had been cut direct from a tree branch. Yet it was not the handle to which he wished to call our attention.

"This particular head is of a sort they favor in such parts as Pennsylvania and New York. You see here on this side it's a proper axe blade, but on the back it's sharp and pointed, as an awl is—axe in front, awl behind. I'm told by Constable Cowley that some of the wounds, particular to the heads, must have been delivered with awl end out—deep gouges, they was."

"Is this true, Constable Cowley?"

"True, Sir John," said the young constable.

"Well, you should have written it in your report—or told me of it, at least."

"My error, sir."

"Go on, Mr. Bailey. You have something to add, I believe."

"Right, Sir John. In western Pennsylvania—but off in a

corner, it was, quite removed from the fighting around Fort Pitt, there was an odd sort of bunch of settlers had a community—all religious, they was said to be. They say—I was not witness to it, I heard this only—but they say that at the fall of Fort Pitt and the massacre that followed, these so-called religious folks thought to teach the Indians a lesson, and so they went out to the village that was nearest at hand one night, and they murdered them all—to the last man, woman, and child. Only these Indians was friendly, more or less, neutral was more like it. Anyway, it was done as a warning, you might say, to all the rest. And so far as that went, it worked. They was left alone.''

''And who were the people that did this deed?''

''All I remember, sir, is they called themselves the Brethren.''

''And so, if indeed this group, who admit that they came here from that part of the colony, may have committed this act in Grub Street, in revenge, at what they thought to be an insult to their leader, or for whatever strange motive, then it would not have been the first time?''

''Not to my way of thinking, sir. I believe it's the same bunch.''

''Thank you, Mr. Bailey.''

The captain of the constables nodded smartly and retired a step or two to his place beside me.

''Do not think,'' said Sir John, ''that these men who called themselves the Brethren, or perhaps as they would have it, the Brethren of the Spirit—do not think that they were content to make theories upon converting the Jews. Mr. Bilbo, will you tell us your experience with two of their number when you happened to attract their attention?''

''I will, Sir John,'' said Black Jack Bilbo, rising from his chair, wherewith he told the tale he had told in court— of how he had been accosted, taken for a Jew because of his beard, preached to, and finally had his beard pulled by one of them. He told it with less restraint than he had earlier, however, and even dropped a curse word in now and again for purposes of emphasis, so that by the time he had done, the room was filled with laughter. Black Jack told a good story, after all, and he delivered this one with a rolling of the eyes, a wild pitch of his head, and so on, so that his audience was quite won over to his performance. There was laughter. There were cheers. There was applause.

It seemed a less solemn occasion of a sudden, and Sir John hammered loud on his desk with the palm of his hand, calling the Bow Street Runners to order, as he might have done with some unruly court crowd.

"Stop, gentlemen—let us have order, please! I will *not* have this inquest turned into an occasion for laughter. Mr. Bilbo, sit down."

"Sorry, Sir John," said he, most meekly, and sank back to his chair.

"No, this is no matter for laughter," insisted the magistrate, as the room quietened down, "for these black-clad, hymn-singing colonials, at the very least, seemed bent upon disturbing the fragile peace we maintain here. Directly after the insult upon Mr. Bilbo, for which they paid dearly, as you heard, members of the Brethren of the Spirit held prisoner the congregation of Jews during their Sabbath services, forcing them to listen as this Brother Abraham preached conversion to them—this same Brother Abraham who authored the manuscript that Mr. Boyer described to you and displayed.

"When the preaching failed to have the desired effect, the church of the Jews—their synagogue, as it were—in Maiden Lane was burned. You all know of the fire. It was only because there was no wind on that night that we escaped the horror of a general conflagration. Constable Cowley, you discovered two witnesses. What did they tell you?"

Constable Cowley stepped forward smartly.

"They told me, sir, that they seen three men leaving those parts just before the fire flared. The three men was in a great hurry, so they said."

"And did not one of the witnesses say they were dressed as the men who preached in Covent Garden?"

"Yes, sir, she did."

"Yet could not identify them?"

"No, sir, they was seen only from the back."

"When we presented this to Brother Abraham, he saw it for the flimsy and useless testimony that it was and sent us on our way. That will be all, Constable Cowley.

"Now, there remains one more crime which I attribute to these Brethren, so-called," continued Sir John, "and that is the death of Moll Caulfield, pushcart woman of Covent Garden, known to nearly all here. She was given to the care of the Brethren when we knew naught of their villainy, only that they housed and fed a number of the destitute. She had been rendered homeless and with no means of support in the collapse of the building wherein she made her domicile in St. Martin's Lane. A few days later, she made an attempt to communicate with us. Master Jimmie Bunkins, will you stand and tell us of that?"

Bunkins hesitated, turning to Mr. Bilbo for counsel. All he received from him was an emphatic nod of the head. He rose then uncertainly, and though at first unable to find his voice, he managed after some hesitation to begin to mumble.

"Speak up, boy," said Sir John. "They cannot hear you. I can barely hear you myself. Please begin again."

"I said," repeated Bunkins in a louder voice, though still uncertain, "that I knowed this old blowen—old woman— Moll a good long time, and she helped me full many time, giving me food and such. I heard she lost her lumber, like, in the big wind and had been put up by these preachers. So I was not agog when I seen her amongst them. I was, though, when she catches my eye, and passes me a letter which was meant for the Beak—uh, for Sir John. Well, I'd managed not to meet the gent, but I seen Jeremy once with him, so I come to him and told him I had a letter for his cove."

"A point to be made, Master Bunkins," said the magistrate, interrupting. "Moll Caulfield was seen, was she not, in passing the note to you? And you were chased?"

"Oh, right you are, guv. But I scampered swift and got away."

"And you came to me with Jeremy and delivered the

note. In it, Moll said things were not right with the Brethren of the Spirit, and she would tell me more if we removed her from their care. It seemed to me she was being held against her will. And so we went next day to collect her and were told again, by Brother Abraham, that she was in no wise kept prisoner, that she had in fact departed their midst the night before of her own volition. I could not prove otherwise, and so I sent out a message to you all to be watchful for her. Jeremy, too, went a-searching. And you, Master Bunkins, also looked, did you not?''

"Aye."

"And you found her?''

"Aye. I found her amongst the dead at the Raker's by the river. She was due for a place where they bury them three or four deep in the hole.''

"And do not mark the graves.''

"I fetched Jeremy and showed him she was dead, and the Raker was all afeared he'd done wrong. He told us she'd been taken up from an alley, and since there was no marks on her, and Moll was an old blowen, he figured she'd just given out. He made no call to the Beak-runners.''

"It is, I'm told, true that there were no marks upon her," said Sir John. "She was given a superficial examination by a Mrs. Katherine Durham, who confirmed it. Yet Moll Caulfield could have been poisoned. She could have been smothered. I lay her death, in any case, upon those preachers in black. Perhaps she learned in some way of their culpability in the awful murders in the Crabb household. Perhaps they, with their suspicions and guilty consciences, thought her a spy for me. Who can say why they thought it necessary to do away with a poor old creature like Moll?

"Yet none of this can be proven. There were no witnesses, no confessions, no incriminating evidence. That can also be said of that great slaughter in Grub Street. The fact that the murder weapon, or one of them, was very likely of North American manufacture and that Mr. Bailey can recall a story from the war in which he took part of a massacre similar to the one of which we are now so well acquainted—none of this would count at all in Old Bailey.

Nor would Mr. Cranford's memory of the heated, angry disagreement between Mr. Crabb and Brother Abraham, nor would Mr. Crabb's fears of what he might expect from said Brother following such a disagreement. None of this would count for much in a court of law. Finally, the ill done direct to the Jews. The rabbi of the congregation on Maiden Lane would not make a complaint, so I was unable to charge the Brethren with so much as disturbing the peace. As for the fire which burned down the synagogue, to say that three men in black were seen leaving the area is much like saying three men were seen leaving the area—no identification, no proof, no evidence of any sort that might be accepted in a court of law.

"This is my problem throughout," said he. "They are a disruptive force. They are capable of murder and arson, and who knows what else? Yet none of this can be proven! What can we do? Simply sit by and wait for more murders to be committed? More arsons? And thus, being patient, simply hope that they might make a mistake?

"No, gentlemen, no. There is one thing only we can do to deal with the Brethren of the Spirit, and now we have done it. Gentlemen, we have set a trap for them."

ELEVEN

*In which the trap is sprung
and the great wind blows*

Hours later we sat together at a table in the Goose and Gander. There were five of us there—Mr. Boyer, Dr. Johnson, Mr. Bilbo, Sir John, and I. We had all crowded into Mr. Boyer's coach and driven over together. I counted myself lucky to have been included in their number. I thought myself to be in quite distinguished company. With the possible exception of Mr. Bilbo, all would have been welcome at any dinner table or in any drawing room in London. Yet more, to be one of them surely meant that I should play a part in the plan when the time came, though as yet my role was not near so well defined as Jimmie Bunkins's.

The Goose and Gander had been cleared of its clientele about an hour before. This had been done, I understood, without so much as a by-your-leave. Two constables had arrived—I knew not which—and turned the few in the place out into the storm, telling them that it would be closed until further notice. They had sent the serving maid home. The innkeeper had most indignantly demanded to know why he had been shut down, and one of the constables had said that it was by order of Sir John Fielding, Magistrate of the Bow Street Court, and that he might discuss it with him when he arrived. Discuss it he did, at great length and most contentiously, when we arrived.

"This is a matter of the law," Sir John had told him. "We shall require the use of this place but one night only. It will serve as my command post."

"Truly so?" asked the innkeeper, most impressed. "Then I believe it only fair that I remain to be sure no harm is done, no glasses broke, nor goods drank without my permission."

"Oh, stay if you must," Sir John had said. "I suppose that only fair, but keep silent and understand that you may neither complain nor take sudden leave at the sound of gunfire."

"Gunfire?"

"That is what I said, and having heard what I said, you must certainly now remain. Make yourself scarce like a good fellow."

That he had done by hiding behind the bar with a bottle of gin to fortify his courage, should shooting actually begin. So in addition to the five of us at the table, there was another in the Goose and Gander, one who would raise his head above the bar from time to time to ask if there was anything the gentlemen required. As it happened, Dr. Johnson drank a considerable quantity of beer during the hour we sat that night; Mr. Bilbo contented himself with a single glass of gin; the rest of us had nothing at all.

Though the rain had diminished somewhat, the wind persisted. If anything, that great blow from the east now blew greater. We sat near the door, which seemed to rattle incessantly. All the table candles had been extinguished, so as to present a darkened, and presumably deserted, interior to any passerby who might peer inside and wonder at the early closure. The only illumination within came from the oil lamp that hung above the bar, which the innkeeper said customarily burned all through the night. It cast a dim and eerie light over the place in which shadows seemed to move and what was deeper dark seemed darker still. In such surroundings, little talk passed among those at the table. We sat listening to the wind growling angrily outside the door, heard the drops of rain thrown against the windows. There would be few or none out on Grub Street this night and that suited Sir John well. He asked the time twice as we sat; at the second inquiry Mr. Bilbo pulled out his pocket watch, held it to the light, and gave the hour as five minutes to midnight.

"It should not be long now," said Sir John.

Perhaps the reason so little was said in that last hour was that so much had been said during the hours before. The plan, as it pertained to the participation of the Bow Street Runners, had been swiftly outlined to them by Sir John in his chambers. Each knew the role he would play, and more important, each knew the schedule according to which the operation would proceed. They were gone from the room, into their rain gear, and out into the night in no time at all, or so it seemed.

But immediately they had left, Mr. Boyer and Dr. Johnson fell to argument between each other, and both with Sir John, regarding details of the plan. Surely it could proceed more swiftly! How would the Runners know where to station themselves? Could Mr. Nicholson be counted upon? Why was he not here? Et cetera.

In order to put an end to such wrangling, Sir John demanded a full report from each of the two on his separate act in the unfolding drama. It was then, listening to them with Mr. Bilbo and Jimmie Bunkins (who had also remained), I came to understand the earlier machinations of Sir John's design. In short, I saw how the trap had been baited. This is what I learned from their reports and what I later heard from Sir John:

When the magistrate had summoned Mr. Boyer on the evening before and told him that the manuscript he had contracted to print, regarding the conversion of the Jews, had been the cause and motive in the Grub Street massacre, Mr. Boyer was quite understandably much disturbed. When Sir John suggested to him that he summon the author and tell him that having read the manuscript carefully, he now had doubts about even printing the book, Mr. Boyer was even more disturbed.

"But . . ." Mr. Boyer had said, "he may react just as he did when Mr. Crabb refused to publish the damned thing! He may send his men to massacre us all!"

And to that Sir John had said, "Exactly!" Then he gave to him a preliminary sketch of his plan.

The next morning it was done as Sir John had suggested, with a few refinements worked out between them and one or two improvised on the spot by Mr. Boyer. Brother Abraham was summoned. The complaint was made on the basis of theological inaccuracies, suggestions of heresy. Brother Abraham reminded Mr. Boyer that a contract had been signed. Yet Mr. Boyer said he would honor the contract— *if possible*—but he had the Church of England to fear, which was his most considerable customer. When Brother Abraham then demanded the return of the manuscript, Mr. Boyer had told him that because he truly did wish to fulfill the contract, he had sent it on to another, far wiser man than he for an opinion in the matter. He had sent it, he told him, to Dr. Samuel Johnson.

Now, as I reflect upon it even today, reader, this was the detail that made it possible for the plan to work. Sir John had himself gone to Dr. Johnson, described the matter to him, and asked him to play a part in it. Dr. Johnson, who but the day before had heard from John Clayton of the fears expressed by Ezekiel Crabb of him who had written of the conversion of the Jews, was most willing to participate in the charade. He would meet with Brother Abraham, should the same come to his door, and he would give him an opinion of this manuscript, which he had not read and probably never would read. Still, an opinion from Dr. Johnson on any manuscript carried such weight that its author could not think it specious—could not think it part of a plot to hoodwink him, to anger him, to drive him for a second time to violent action and an attempt at retribution. Without Dr. Johnson's cooperation, the entire maneuver—Mr. Boyer's sudden reluctance even to print Brother Abraham's book—might well have seemed to one as intelligent as this raw colonial genius (for in his own perverse way, he was that) a transparent repetition of the earlier circumstances—

and therefore a crude attempt to bait a trap. Yet if none other than Dr. Samuel Johnson was involved, this must be an altogether authentic repetition of a nightmarish sort, of the earlier conditions. Thus framing Brother Abraham's probable reaction, had Sir John persuaded Dr. Johnson to lend his reputation to the enterprise, giving to it a sense of the bona fide and real.

As expected, Brother Abraham had left Mr. Boyer's on Grub Street and gone straight to Johnson Court, where he informed him that he was the author of the manuscript which Mr. Boyer had sent to him. Brother Abraham was somewhat intimidated to be in the presence of so august a literary personage. He asked him, as any neophyte scribbler might, what opinion Dr. Johnson had of the work.

"It held my interest," admitted Dr. Johnson, in his severe mode. "Parts of it I thought to be quite well written."

Brother Abraham, quite overjoyed to hear this, asked which parts he thought to be best written.

"Why, the parts about the Jews, of course. They are a fascinating people."

"But, Dr. Johnson," said Brother Abraham, "they are all about the Jews."

"Sir, of course they are. Yet I thought you did best in writing of their history. The mathematics, however, were quite beyond me."

"But they are important," insisted Brother Abraham.

"No doubt, no doubt," said Dr. Johnson in a dismissive manner. "But Mr. Boyer gave me no brief to comment upon the mathematics, for which I am grateful, nor did he solicit any opinion on the literary qualities of your manuscript, though I did comment upon them favorably. He asked me, rather, to keep an eye out for heresy and what might be actionable. To be frank with you, I know little of heresy. I am a confessor and a communicant, and I leave it go at that. The theologians and the bishops argue about the greater matters. I, frankly, have little interest in them. I do, however, know something of the law, and though I am no lawyer, certain things troubled me in your manuscript."

"What were they?"

"Why, sir, you have written things at which the Jews may take offense."

"Let them!" cried Brother Abraham. "They murdered our Savior!"

"Strictly speaking, sir, it was the Romans did that."

"But Pontius Pilate simply bowed to the demands of the Jews."

"To certain *specific* Jews who are now many centuries dead."

"God put a curse on the entire people for the hardness of heart shown by those specific Jews. It is in the Holy Writ, Dr. Johnson—stated by Paul, implied by our Lord."

"While that authority is not open to disputation in the ordinary way, I admit, there are nevertheless possibilities of interpretation—as scholars and theologians have proved throughout the ages. If the possibility for theological interpretation exists, then there is also an opportunity for legal interpretation, though perhaps a narrower one, I allow."

"It has never been done!"

"That is not to say it *could* never be done. In my opinion, sir, it would make a most interesting lawsuit. If found against, you would have to pay damages, of course, though to whom and how many I could not hazard. But so might Mr. Boyer, for as printer he bears some responsibility, though not so great as he might as publisher. And of course, too, the coming conversion of the Jews, which you argue for so powerfully, would be rendered thereby moot."

Brother Abraham, exhausted and frustrated by this short debate with one of the great minds of our age, sagged visibly (according to Johnson) at this point and in a quiet voice simply asked for the return of his manuscript.

"Unfortunately, I cannot grant your request."

"But—but—why not?" asked the preacher, now truly in confusion.

"Because, sir, only minutes before your arrival I sent my man to Mr. Boyer with said manuscript and a letter from me in which I made some of the very points I have in this discussion with you. Which, by the by, I have enjoyed immensely and found stimulating but must, unfortunately, conclude. I daresay your manuscript is in Mr. Boyer's hands by now. I thank you again for the opportunity to meet you, sir, and now I wish you good day.''

With that, Dr. Johnson strode from the room, leaving Brother Abraham to be shown to the door by the maid.

Quite in frustration and in growing anger, the preacher then marched back to Grub Street, stormed into the office of Mr. Boyer, and without further ado, demanded the return of his manuscript.

Mr. Boyer tut-tutted, hemmed and hawed, and finally said straightaway that he preferred not to do that.

"And *why* is *that*, sir?" asked Brother Abraham, making some attempt to regain his former composure and take command of the situation.

"Because on the advice of Dr. Johnson I must show your manuscript to my solicitor. Then, since my doubts continue as to its theological soundness, I shall present it to a bishop of my acquaintance and ask his opinion of it."

"Why do you not simply relieve yourself of that burden and hand over my work to me?" said Brother Abraham.

"You reminded me previously," said Mr. Boyer, "that we have a contract between us. Now I remind you, as well."

"I would willingly release you from the contract—if I may have my manuscript."

"I choose *not* to be released until your manuscript be examined by my solicitor and by Bishop Baxley. If at all possible, I wish to fulfill the contract and earn the money it will bring us. Yet I will not do it at the risk of lawsuit, nor of censure by the Church. Remember, Mr. Watt—which is your name, I believe—it takes the consent of both parties to abrogate a contract if all its terms are met."

"That is your final word then?"

"No, sir, my final word comes after I have heard from the bishop and my solicitor."

"Then I cannot be responsible."

"Pardon, sir?"

"Whatever woe comes upon you now, you have brought

upon yourself. 'Vengeance is mine, saith the Lord.' "

"Are you threatening me?"

Mr. Boyer told Sir John he got no answer to that, for by the time the question was fully out of his mouth, Brother Abraham had left the office and was near out the door to Grub Street.

Each of the two men, Dr. Johnson and Mr. Boyer, had told his story to Sir John with a certain zest and style. The lexicographer, an accomplished literary stylist and dinner table conversationalist, had no doubt given the better recital. Still, the dramatic flourish at the end of the publisher's account—"Are you threatening me?"—struck a sort of chord within us, his listeners, which made it certain, without poll, that the enterprise designed by Sir John Fielding—which he had termed "a trap"—would indeed attract those rats in black, who were the objects of the hunt.

And Sir John, who would surely qualify as the Pied Piper of London Town, sat forward with a smile of anticipation fixed upon his face, tapping his fingers together as one who had naught to fear and naught to doubt.

Yet the two who had just reported insisted on discussing the matter further and yet further, each offering critiques of the other's conduct, each with a question to Sir John as to some detail of that part of the plan which remained yet to be executed. Mr. Bilbo, too, joined in with a few questions of his own. Thus it continued until Sir John threw his hands up in exasperation and suggested that, the storm notwithstanding, all adjourn to the modest but respectable eating house, Shakespeare's Head, which was nearby. The rule being, however, that the plan, which was now under way, could not be discussed once they left the premises of Number 4 Bow Street. All agreed, and so together they left.

The general invitation that was issued, however, did not extend to Jimmie Bunkins and myself. Perhaps Sir John felt that, while respectable by the standards of these men of the town, Shakespeare's Head, popular with the Covent Garden crowd, was in no wise suitable for boys of our years. In my case, he would indeed have been correct. With regard to Bunkins, however, he had greatly underestimated the degree of experience of the wrong sort the latter had crowded into his thirteen or fourteen years (he was ever unsure of his true age).

In any case, as they made for the door, Sir John took me aside and whispered to me that I was to take my young friend up to our kitchen and feed him.

I was glad to have the chance to talk to him alone, as I was most curious to know what had transpired during those hours after he had disappeared, trussed up like a live pig on Mr. Bailey's shoulder.

So I brought him along up the stairs into the kitchen, happy to find it empty. A candle burned on the table still, so Mrs. Gredge could not be long gone. Finding bread and beef, I cut him a slice of each. I found the teapot had still a cup of cold tea in it. As I poured it for Bunkins, he looked upon it somewhat disdainfully.

"No beer?" he asked.

"No," said I. "Sir John will drink a bottle after court. It is brought to him each day." I then added priggishly: "Besides, it will do you no good to drink such stuff."

"Black Jack gave me beer. He's a grand fellow, is Black Jack."

Jimmie Bunkins said nothing more for a minute or two as he tore away in canine fashion at the bread and beef. He washed it down a bit reluctantly with a swallow of the tea I had put before him. Then he gave me what he meant to be a hard look.

"You turned snitch on me," said he accusingly.

"What did you expect?" I asked, most indignant. "You boasted that you would set a fire, said you cared not if innocents were burned in it, so long as you had your revenge. Of *course* I told Sir John of it, and would do so again if the circumstances were the same. He is my master. I owe him my first loyalty and always shall."

He listened to this, chewing on, and ruminated further once I had stopped, as if giving the matter weighty consideration.

"That's as Black Jack put it to me," said he at last. Then

he winked reassuringly. "All's good between us. You done right."

"Mr. Bilbo seems to have given you wise counsel."

"He said *my* trouble"—pointing at himself—"was that I had no cove to tell me what to do, to make me toe the line. He said if I kept on the knuckle I'd wind up in Duncan Campbell's Floating Academy, or more likely at Tuck 'em Fair. Which is what I myself knowed but always made not to."

(The first reference here in his curious flash-boy talk was to the hulk which was permanently moored in the Thames and served as a prison for long-term convicts; and "Tuck 'em Fair" was Tyburn Hill, where public hangings took place.)

"The last I saw, you were riding on Mr. Bailey's shoulder. What was it happened?"

And so Bunkins began the tale of his redemption, or its beginning, at the hands of one who was said to have been formerly a pirate. Mr. Bailey and Mr. Bilbo had come to a parting just beyond the churchyard gate. The load, which was Jimmie Bunkins, was transferred from one strong set of shoulders to another. Mr. Bilbo conveyed him by means of hackney carriage to his recently acquired residence on St. James Street. (I knew it well; it had been the home of Lord Richard Goodhope.) He had just taken possession, and the place was quite bare but for a few pieces of furniture Black Jack had filched from his gaming establishment. He dumped Bunkins in a chair, untied him, and took the handkerchief from his mouth. Then he began to lecture him.

The fact that the only piece of furniture in the room was the one in which Bunkins sat allowed Mr. Bilbo to roam free around him and, incidentally, to bar his avenue of escape. Yet it soon was apparent that Bunkins had no intention of "scampering," as he put it, for he was in awe of the man, his reputation, and the fact that the lecture that was delivered was given in no small part in "flash." Mr. Bilbo knew the cant which was Bunkins's native tongue. Bunkins may well have heard the content from others (including, briefly, from Sir John himself), yet he had never heard the sermon preached to him in the language of Covent Garden. Besides, was this not one who was rumored to have made his stake at thieving on the high seas? Did he not show a fierce, even frightening presence as he rolled about the empty room on his short, strong legs? Did he not command attention when he thrust his dark, bearded face close to Bunkins's own and predicted the boy's future, rotting in prison or jerking at the end of a rope on the gallows tree?

"Yet," Black Jack Bilbo told him, "there is hope for you. You've a talent for survival. I'll give you that, for to have lived even to your young years, you've shown considerable enterprise. You know naught of the world beyond Covent Garden, I'll wager, but that can be remedied. I was your age myself before I learned to read and do sums. I'll take a chance on you, Jimmie Bunkins. I'll offer you a job right here and in my gaming establishment. What say you to that?"

Bunkins had never in his life been offered a job before. What he had seen of the world of work did not much attract him. Yet to work for such a man as this . . .

"What shall I do in this job?" he asked.

"Do? You will do whatever I tell you to do. I'll be your master, your cove. If I tell you to give up thievin', as I certainly shall, then you will give it up—no more on the scamp! If I tell you to deliver a hundred guineas to a gentleman, you will do so and not short him by one. If I tell you to learn to read, by God, you will learn to read. I'll be a damn good cove to you, and if I ain't, you may tell me so, and I shall listen. Your pay will be what I think you're worth. Bed and board will be included. So what say you? Yea or nay?"

Jimmie Bunkins said yea. He took the big hand that was offered him and shook it awkwardly. A bath came later and a plain suit of clothes and a proper hat that was brought to him afterwards by Nancy Plummer, one of the hostesses from the gaming club. He'd done wipe prigging with her in the old days in the Garden and was quite happy to hear her good report on the cove. Truth to tell, he was happier than he had ever been in his thirteen or fourteen years.

And this he admitted to me in our kitchen when he had finished the beef and bread I had given him and sipped the last of the cold tea. At my suggestion then, we descended the stairs to await the return of Sir John and his party. And as we waited, we watched in fascination as the Bow Street Runners returned dripping wet, singly and in pairs, from their first round of the night on the streets. Thus the evening would begin as any other. Yet upon their return to Bow Street each was armed by Mr. Baker—a brace of pistols, a packet of powder and ball, and a cutlass. Then they departed, singly and in pairs, for Grub Street. They would take the back streets and avoid, insofar as possible, being seen by whatever souls were out on such a night, braving the storm. In this way, the Boyer establishment would be fortified most inconspicuously.

Sir John then returned with the others, grumbling mightily that he could not keep Mr. Boyer and Dr. Johnson from bladdering on in the eating house about the coming maneuver. Yet he seemed pleased to learn that all else was going according to plan.

"Has the Raker been notified?" he asked Mr. Baker.

"He has, sir."

"How many have come through and gone off to Grub Street?"

"Ten, sir. They should all be on their way in a few minutes' time."

"Jeremy?"

"Yes, sir?"

"You will be going with us in Mr. Boyer's coach. And Master Bunkins?"

"Yes, guv—uh, yes, sir?"

"I have a special duty in mind for you. I understand that you are specially known for your fleetness of foot."

And so we sat in the Goose and Gander, waiting for Jimmie Bunkins to appear. He had been placed at the junction of Maiden Lane and Half Moon Passage in a doorway, where he had a proper view of the house of the Brethren of the

Spirit. It was his duty to keep a sharp eye on its entrance. Should they move out in number, or even in twos and threes, he was to take an estimate of their strength, pull away undetected, and then run as fast as he could, using his knowledge of the back streets and byways, and inform those waiting in Grub Street that the black-suited Brethren were on their way.

This, Sir John reasoned, would give the Runners who had hidden themselves at various points throughout the Boyer establishment a few minutes' notice—yet an important few minutes they would be. The Runners would settle down in an attitude of silent waiting; and by the time their quarry arrived, the ambuscade would be set, and the trap would be sprung.

And still we waited.

I, who was youngest, believed I had the sharpest ears, and so I shut my eyes and concentrated on the manifold sounds of that stormy night—the rain, the wind, the rattling of the door, the measured breathing of those of us at the table.

Then said Sir John of a sudden: "I hear the boy now. He is coming."

And but a moment later I heard him myself—a steady beating upon the cobblestones. It was Jimmie Bunkins— indeed it had to be—running at full speed.

I jumped up and made for the door. The others were on their feet.

There was a great bar of wood across the frame of it. I tugged at it hard. It would not at first budge, and I was about to call for help when at last it gave and slid from its housing. The door came open.

I leaped out into the street and saw Jimmie Bunkins, now not three rods away, coming directly at me. Not daring to cry out, I waved him inside the Goose and Gander. He seemed not to see me, so intent was he on pumping his legs to the limit of his strength. I put out both arms that he might see me better and braced myself for a collision. Then I was seen. He did what he could to slow himself, yet like a launched projectile he had no control. The collision came, though it was not so great as it might have been. I leaned forward to take the impact, threw my arms about him, and staggered back with him a full five steps. I was immediately aware of his breathing, which struck me as most unnatural. It came in great, heaving sobs. I had not heard such tortured inhale and exhale since my mother breathed her last with typhus.

Mr. Bilbo was there. He separated us and carried Bunkins inside, whispering to him how well he'd done, how proud he was of him. I followed them inside quickly, pushing the door shut after me. Bunkins was on the floor, vomiting up the beef and bread I'd given him. Sir John reproached himself, saying he'd asked too much of the boy. Dr. Johnson and Mr. Boyer stood in the dim light of the bar lamp, looking on with great concern. Mr. Bilbo had a hand on the boy's chest.

"He'll be right soon," said he. "His heart is beginning to slow a bit."

"But we must—" began Sir John.

Then he stopped, for Bunkins was attempting to speak. What he said came out in a near inaudible whisper. But Mr. Bilbo's ear was close. He listened, nodding, waiting for the next whispered phrase, then touched the boy's lips lightly with his fingers to silence him.

"He says there were many, yet they left in twos, so he had to wait to get a fair count, which was over ten. They were still coming when he left."

"Jeremy—" said Sir John, yet again he was interrupted.

The unbolted door of the Goose and Gander flew open quite without warning. I looked up in terror, half expecting to see one of the Brethren there, his axe poised above his head. Yet it was not.

The figure in the doorway took a few uncertain steps forward. And as he came, he shouted loud and belligerently.

"Innkeeper! Where are you? I am drunk and wish to get drunker!"

To my astonishment, I recognized the uninvited guest as Ormond Neville, poet and historian of the day-to-day.

"Why is it so fucking dark? And who are these men? *Innkeeper!*" He roared out the last so strong I feared he would be heard all the way to Bow Street.

"Silence him!" Sir John hissed it in an urgent whisper.

Dr. Johnson grabbed the unfortunate poet and grappled with him, which only brought forth more loud shouts. Then Black Jack Bilbo rose up from his place with Bunkins and put an end to the noise with a clout on Mr. Neville's jaw which knocked him senseless.

"Pray God," said Sir John, "that the Brethren were not so close that they heard. Now, Jeremy, you must go and tell the Runners they are on their way in force and could arrive at any minute. Go, boy, now!"

I slipped from the Goose and Gander, looking up and down the street to be certain there were none of the men in black at either end. Then, moving close along the buildings between, I made swiftly for Boyer's. The rain had all but stopped—yet how the wind blew! Surely it would have covered over Mr. Neville's cries.

I had not been told whether I should go to the back or front. I know not why, but when I came to the walkway which ran the length of the publisher's building, I ducked down it, moving to the rear. As I came close to the end of the structure, a noise caught my ear, then another and another. I heard the clank of metal, the slip of a foot, a grunt. These were not noises from inside the house, but from just ahead of me—perhaps in the mews behind it, or in the plot at the rear. The Brethren were already here!

I had come soft, and I left softer, hastening on tiptoes to the front door. I tapped quiet but insistent upon the window, caught movement through it, and a moment later the door to Boyer's came open a bit and a firm hand dragged me inside. I recognized the man as Mr. Nicholson, Mr. Boyer's young partner, as he had been pointed out to me at the court appearance of John Clayton. Mr. Bailey stood behind him.

"They are here!" I whispered. "In the rear, perhaps yet in the mews."

Without a word, Mr. Bailey turned and gestured to others

invisible to me. Then he himself faded away, all six and a half feet of him, and I was left alone with Mr. Nicholson.

"Come," said he in a whisper, "we must disappear."

He led me swiftly to an alcove in the back of the book-shop, which was all but filled by a good-sized desk. He put us behind it in a squat, then eased the bottom drawer open and from it took two dueling pistols of a small caliber. Handing me one, he put his pointing finger to his lips, urging me quite unnecessarily to silence.

We waited. We listened.

There had been some brief discussion at Bow Street as to the placement of the Runners within the Boyer house. Mr. Bailey had favored challenging the Brethren upon the ground floor, the moment they were all inside. Yet Sir John insisted that they allow them to the upper floors that they might prove their murderous intent. "You'll have them trapped upon the stairs," he had said. "That way, if there must be a fight, it will be waged under better circumstances."

Quite naturally, Sir John prevailed. And Mr. Nicholson had seen to the stationing of the Runners in the vacated bedrooms—the entire household had been moved to a lodging house some distance away for the night. There was a large common room, which also served for dining, as well as a kitchen, on the floor directly above. And above that were the bedrooms of the Boyer family—Mr. and Mrs. and the two unmarried daughters. And at the very top were the quarters kept for the apprentices and the Boyers' two female servants. (Mr. Nicholson, as well as a master printer and three journeymen, lived off the premises.) The plan called for the largest parts of the force to be placed at the top and bottom of the stairs, thereby forcing the Brethren downward, and at the same time denying them the possibility of escape.

There were six Runners sequestered around us at various points on the ground floor, including Mr. Bailey. All were so well hid I had no idea of their whereabouts.

It did not take long before we were aware of the Brethren inside. The wind made a cold sweep through the premises as the door in the back remained open long enough for a considerable party to file in. Then it must have closed, for the draft ceased, and I was aware of the slightest footfalls approaching. They moved as silent as ever grown men in boots could move. There must have been a dozen who ascended the stairs. One, if I was not mistaken, remained here below. They seemed to know the design of the house well, for they moved quickly beyond the floor directly above to the bedroom floors. Isham Henry had done his traitorous work well. Not only had he provided a key to the rear door, he had also acquainted his fellows with the exact positioning of their putative victims.

Moving slowly and silently as they did—there were but a few creaks upon the stairs—it seemed to take an eternity for them to reach their assigned locations. Then it seemed that for an equally long time, there was nothing but the purest, most absolute silence, broken only by the rattling of the door by the wind. I could bare hear my own self breathe. Then the silence was broken, not by the sound of doors banging open, nor shouts, nor shots, but rather, the steady voice of Benjamin Bailey.

"You have the chance to surrender," called he in a tone of command that resounded through the house. "Resist and no quarter will be given."

But drowning out Mr. Bailey's last few words, another voice: *"We have been betrayed!"*

I popped up from my hiding place behind the desk just in time to see in the dim light that one of the Brethren had raised his axe to Mr. Bailey and was advancing upon him. The constable shot him dead. The man in black fell not ten feet from where I watched.

Then, as if by that signal, shots rang throughout the house—from high above and not so high above. There were thuds. There was scrambling on the stairs. Now there were shouts aplenty above us.

I felt myself being pulled down by Mr. Nicholson.

"Get *down,* boy! Do you wish to be killed by a stray ball?"

Then there was a great stampede above our heads, and

a call for help from one of the Runners: "They're makin' a stand in the big room!"

"Come along, lads!" shouted Mr. Bailey. "Up we go!"

And he led the way up the stairs, every inch the sergeant major·he once was, and his constables followed, pistols drawn, brandishing cutlasses.

All this I witnessed, peeking above the desk. Yet seeing them go, I realized something was amiss. The way of escape was no longer barred. I squeezed out from behind the desk.

"Where *are* you going?" shouted Mr. Nicholson, right petulant.

"To protect the door," said I.

Yet at the moment I pulled back the hammer of that pistol in my hand, hoping it was loaded, hoping I would not have to try it to find out, that very door I sought to defend was thrown open wide and Black Jack Bilbo came rushing in.

"Where is the fight?" he yelled at me.

The commotion above answered him. He looked up wild-eyed, quite frightening in appearance.

"I must have a weapon!"

I pointed to the fallen Brother on the floor. His axe lay half beneath him. Black Jack grabbed it up and turned to the stairs. But at that moment two figures of even more frightening aspect crashed down them—black clothing torn, blood dripping from face and hands. Somehow they had got through. One carried an axe, and one did not.

Black Jack went for the armed man, who threw his axe about him so strong and with such skill that he near tore the weapon from the hands of the former pirate when first they clashed.

The unarmed man gave them a wide berth, which brought him in my direction.

"Stop!" I yelled. "I'll shoot!"

Yet he was past me before I had the pistol up and aimed proper. Just as he pulled open the door, I saw my shot and took it. Smoke billowed so from the barrel when I fired that my target was for a moment quite invisible to me. When the smoke cleared but a moment later, I saw that he was gone. I had missed.

"You hit him, young man, you did!" crowed Mr. Nicholson with great enthusiasm, standing to his full height behind the desk where we had hid. "I saw him stagger and clutch at his shoulder. Well *done,* young sir!"

"Yet still he escaped," said I, disheartened. "Sir, may I borrow your pistol?"

"Indeed you may—and I shall load the one you have just discharged. Here—"

We exchanged pistols, and I went to find Mr. Bilbo. He, it seemed, had proved an apt pupil at axe-dueling, for far in the rear of the print shop I found the two of them; the man in black was disarmed and cowering.

Then came Mr. Bailey down the stairs, announcing a great victory.

Sir John, as it proved out, was not so sure of that. One had got away. He would go straight to Half Moon Passage, and warn the others, he said.

"But Jeremy put a wound in him," said Mr. Bailey, "or so says Mr. Nicholson. The fellow may not have made it back home."

"Then again," said Sir John, "he may have. Let us quickly be on our way."

In short order, Mr. Boyer's coach was brought round. In effect, Sir John commandeered it, for he persuaded the publisher to remain and survey the damage done to his establishment, while giving to them the use of the coach. It was given hard use indeed, for into and onto that vehicle of modest size was crammed and piled a whole squad of constables, as well as Sir John, Dr. Johnson, Mr. Bilbo, Jimmie Bunkins, and myself. The horses could barely pull the load when we started out.

It was lightened somewhat when, along the way, we chanced upon a hackney carriage for hire, surely the only one in London at this late hour on this stormy night. Sir John banged on the roof of the coach and ordered the driver to stop. Then, quite peremptorily, he ordered Dr. Johnson,

Mr. Bilbo, and Bunkins out and into the hackney.

Dr. Johnson offered no objection, saying with a sigh that he had heard enough gunfire and seen enough dead men to last him a lifetime. He wanted no more of it. He climbed down.

Mr. Bilbo, however, objected mightily, on the grounds that they were not near enough along to take the Brethren by storm, which would be necessary if they had lost the advantage of surprise.

"You need me, Sir John," said he. "I have experience along these lines."

"Whatever your former qualifications, Mr. Bilbo, you are now one of the populace and are to be protected by such as us. You angered me greatly when you rushed into Boyer's to do battle. You are impetuous, sir."

"It is my nature."

"Furthermore," added the magistrate, "we need only block the departure of the Brethren and wait for the full of our force. Go now. The boy is still half ill from the task I gave him. Look to your responsibilities, and I shall see to mine."

And having thus spoken, Sir John turned from him, indicating there was no more to be said.

Reluctantly, Mr. Bilbo then climbed down, took Jimmie Bunkins in his arms, and over the latter's protestations, carried him to the waiting hackney.

Sir John then struck the roof with his stick and bade the driver move on.

"Is that the plan, sir," asked Benjamin Bailey beside me, "to hold them inside until the lads come to help?"

"It will do as well as any."

And that was the last that was said until the end of the journey. Still the wind blew, in tones that ranged wide from the guttural to a high scream. It was as if some passage to hell had been opened and we were made to hear a great chorus of the damned. As we passed a burning streetlamp, I caught the eye of Constable Rumford, like Mr. Bailey a veteran of the French war. He gave me a nod which I'm sure he meant to be reassuring, though the expression of concern on his face made it less so than it might have been.

I, too, was apprehensive of what lay ahead, though not quite fearful. I took heart that I had behaved well in the fray just past. What had moved me to take part I cannot say—necessity, the excitement of the moment, the wish to behave as a man, probably all three. I had shot at a fellow human being with no more thought than to stop him. And though I had not stopped him, I was greatly glad I had not killed him. That would have been more than my young conscience could bear.

Near all the prisoners were wounded—all but one. He had thrown down his axe and thrown up his hands at first command. When he was pointed out to me, I recognized him as the small, sad-eyed fellow who had answered the door at our last nocturnal visit to the Brethren of the Spirit. Sir John, acting on some intuition, had instructed that he be kept apart from the five other prisoners.

They had suffered six dead, and we, two wounded. The wounds given by those sharp axes, however, were so fierce that they required the immediate attention of a surgeon who lived not far distant. It seemed likely that Constable Perkins might lose his arm at the elbow.

And so, with our wounded, one who accompanied them to the surgeon, another who would remain behind to help the Raker reap his harvest, and the three who would march the prisoners to Bow Street, it was evident that even when reinforcements arrived, we would not be reinforced by many—hence, Constable Rumford's concern and my apprehension.

On Maiden Lane right near the burned-out synagogue, Sir John spoke up: "We must be close."

Mr. Bailey instructed him as to our location.

At which Sir John banged a final time upon the roof of the coach and called for the driver to stop.

"We shall go the rest of the way on foot."

In no more than a few moments, our little troop was assembled on the cobblestones, as the coach drove off into the night. Sir John was forced to talk loud over the wind as he gave instructions: "Two to the rear, two to the front.

Don't hesitate to shoot any who seek exit, though you must shout a warning first. Pistols loaded?''

There was a general affirmative.

"Then let us proceed. Mr. Bailey, set me in the right direction.''

He seemed to have quite forgotten about me. Though I had said not a word and had sat apart from him in the coach, I was sure he had been aware of my presence. Could he smell me? Did my breathing come in a different rhythm from others'? In any case, I did nothing to call attention to myself as we made our way to Half Moon Passage. I trailed the rest.

We came in short order to the hostel of the Brethren of the Spirit. There I spied what surprised and confused me no little. The front door of the place stood open. It seemed a bad sign. When he was informed by Mr. Bailey, Sir John thought it so, too. We gathered around him before the entrance.

"I like not the look of this," said he, attempting to talk quiet. "Divide back and front as I directed, but I fear Mr. Bailey and I must enter to determine whether anyone is left inside.''

And so they proceeded. Sir John and Mr. Bailey delayed until such time as the two men sent to the rear might have taken up their places; then they went forward. I followed on tiptoe. Having not been told, specifically, to remain behind, I had chosen to accompany them, if somewhat surreptitiously. When I saw Mr. Bailey draw his pistol, I reached into my pocket and grasped the butt of mine—or Mr. Nicholson's, which remained loaded and in my possession.

I stepped past the doorstep and was immediately aware of things not right. There was, first of all, a strange smell pervading the place. Secondly, I was aware of an awful creaking and cracking within the building as it was jostled and pounded by the wind. It reminded me ominously of the sounds that issued from Moll Caulfield's ancient court building in St. Martin's Lane just before its collapse. Finally, I saw a most peculiar sight illuminated by a candle, as if to call attention to it. A pair of legs swung from above, the shoed feet near touching Sir John's shoulder as he turned this way and that in confusion. The rest of the body was invisible to me. But I approached cautiously in morbid curiosity, never before having seen a hanged man.

"No, sir, I don't know him," Mr. Bailey was saying. "I don't know any of them, except for their black clothes."

I stepped up beside Mr. Bailey and gazed up at the corpse. The face was hideous—quite distorted, with a darkened tongue drooping from the mouth. Yet I recognized him.

"Who is there?" demanded Sir John. "Is it you, Jeremy?"

"It is, yes," said I. "But the hanged man, he is Isham Henry."

"Ah, the printer. They must have hung him for a traitor—Brother Abraham thinking it easier to believe he had a Judas in his midst than that he himself might have been deceived." Sir John turned in my direction, giving me his full attention. "Thank you, Jeremy. You were most helpful. Now leave."

"But Sir John—"

"Leave."

"This building—"

Before I could warn him, and before he could direct me once more out the door, another voice sounded a distance away that won our immediate attention.

"Sir John Fielding! Come forward!" It was the voice of Brother Abraham, I was sure.

Without a further word to me, Sir John began moving forward in the direction indicated by the sound of that voice. Mr. Bailey and I looked at each other—he in curiosity and I in alarm.

"What is that smell here?" I whispered.

"Lamp oil," said Mr. Bailey. "Now go. You heard Sir John."

Then he, like the loyal soldier he was, hied after his chief, who was just then turning left through an open door. It led, I was sure, into the hall of worship which had been converted from the large dining room of the place that previously occupied these premises.

These premises indeed! I was sure they would not last the night from the terrifying sounds I heard above me and all around me. As the wind buffeted, the house responded with groans and shrieks. Last the night? It seemed to me that the place might collapse on us at any minute. Could they not tell? Was Mr. Bailey deaf? I knew Sir John was not. Or perhaps it was that unless one had been in an earlier, like situation, then it would seem quite impossible that such a catastrophe might actually take place. How could one believe that the very roof was quite ready to cave in? Or the walls about to collapse? Ah, but that was the message I received from this poor house. I felt it incumbent upon me to transmit that message to Sir John.

He had told me that it was sometimes necessary to batter down even his defenses. I would batter them down. I went—still ever so quiet—to that door wherein Sir John and now Benjamin Bailey had disappeared. I stood quite uncertain at the entrance, flattened against the wall, wondering how I might convince the two of them to leave.

They had stopped at a point about halfway to the end of this long room. At its end, behind the pulpit, stood Brother Abraham, a burning torch in his hand.

"Come closer," he called to them.

"No," said Sir John, "this is quite close enough."

"You do not trust me! A pity, yet the distrust is mutual. Tell your man to put away those pistols he has in his hands, or I shall plunge this torch down where I stand and set us all on fire. It is in my power. Revelation thirteen, thirteen: 'And he doeth great wonders, so that he maketh fire come down from heaven on the earth in the sight of men.' "

At a sign from Sir John, Mr. Bailey tucked away his pistols.

"If I remember aright, the 'he' in that which you have just quoted is one of those great beasts which crowd the pages of that confusing book. Surely you do not cast yourself in such a role?"

"The great beasts play an important part in the prophecy.

It is not a confusing book if you have the key, as I do."

"Oh, no doubt you do. Yet I have not come to argue Scripture with you. I have come to persuade you to surrender."

"To you? You old blind fool, the very boards on which you stand are soaked with . . ."

Brother Abraham's last words were blotted by a great thumping from well above, the sound of scraping and falling. Perhaps part of the roof had given way, or perhaps a chimney had collapsed. Yet from the smell that rose all around, and from its identification by Mr. Bailey, I well knew with what the boards had been soaked.

"And where are the rest of the Brethren? They must also surrender."

"Did you not understand? You are a dead man, as is your constable—as dead as your spy that we hanged but minutes before you arrived. He betrayed us, as the old woman also tried to do. All who oppose me will die and suffer eternal damnation. It is writ in the book so. I—and only I—have the key."

"Neither of the two you named were my spies. You were not betrayed by Isham Henry, rather by your own self-conceit. You, sir, were the greater fool."

"But . . . But think of the great havoc a conflagration will wreak on a night of great wind such as this!"

"If I am, as you say, a dead man, then there is nothing I can do to prevent it. I can but appeal to you one last time to surrender."

"And I, one last time, reject your appeal, and I call down a curse from heaven upon you."

"Mr. Bailey," said Sir John in a tone of steady authority, "take out your pistol and shoot that man dead."

Brother Abraham, who could scarce believe his ears, pitched down his torch, and a weak, steady flame began—hardly the inferno he seemed to have anticipated.

At the same time, there began a great ripping from above. I ran down the aisle to Sir John and Mr. Bailey. All manner of plaster and other debris rained down upon me. I grabbed at both of them, just as Mr. Bailey fired his pistol at Brother

Abraham, who ran in panic for a door behind the pulpit to the right. The shot went awry.

"Come away, *now!*" I shouted. "The ceiling is collapsing!"

Brooking no argument, I took Sir John by the arm as all that was above began to fall in great chunks; the very walls trembled and then shook mightily. I dragged him bodily for the door. Mr. Bailey caught us up and grasped his other arm. Sir John's legs pumped stoutly; he required only direction from us.

Then we were out of the big room, running past the corpse of Isham Henry, which swung wildly from its length of rope. His feet kicked at me as I passed; I pushed them away.

Thus we three emerged and ran well out into the street. Constables Kelly and Sheedy fell upon us, thumping us and pummeling us as they shouted their congratulations upon our escape.

With a great final roar then, the walls collapsed. They fell inward for the most part, though the one nearest us, with the weight of the others upon it, seemed almost to disintegrate before our eyes, spewing wood and glass well out into the street so that we were all forced to fall back even further to the opposite curb.

Then came what seemed a silence—though it was not, for the wind still blew. Yet there was nothing of the building left to fall. It was but a great heap of wooden rubble. Then I became aware of a most peculiar sound. It was the sound of laughter. I looked to my right and found Sir John quite shaking with laughter. I feared that perhaps the poor man, overcome by the experience, had of a sudden become hysterical.

"What is it, sir?" I asked. "Are you well?"

"Oh, quite well," said he, still chuckling most heartily. "I was thinking upon Brother Abraham."

"He has escaped."

"Oh, perhaps, though I doubt it. No, what struck me was that though the fellow may know his Scripture well, he is certainly no chemist. His expectations of lamp oil astound me."

"It would not burn?"

"Oh, it would burn indeed. I take it you were there to see it light up."

"Uh, yes, sir."

"But it burns slow and steady. That is its advantage. It burns all night. The poor fool did not know that. He had probably never been to a city before London that had street-lamps on its every corner and along each way. He must have looked upon them with wonder and said to himself, 'I can make a great fire with this.' Well, he might have done so tonight had it been given time enough to catch. Now the house has collapsed upon it and snuffed out its beginning. You see no smoke, do you?"

"No, sir—dust but no smoke."

"Even so, we must wake the Lord Mayor and tell him to send the pumpers in case it should flare up." He paused, frowning. "But am I deceived, or is the wind not dying down?"

So it was indeed. What had roared now whispered. We now spoke in our normal voices where but minutes before it had been necessary to shout.

"Oh, Jeremy, Jeremy," said Sir John, with a great shake of his head, "God save us from the evil deeds of such bumpkin preachers as Brother Abraham."

Having said so, he lapsed for a moment into silence. Then he burst out laughing once more. At last, he managed to gain control of himself.

"Come to think upon it, he has."

TWELVE

*In which justice is done
and an agreement is made
with the Lord Chief Justice*

The end of Abraham Watt, otherwise known as Brother Abraham, proved to be somewhat anticlimactic. Having rushed out of Benjamin Bailey's sight for fear that a shot from the constable's second pistol might prove more accurate than the first, he ran to join a small party of his followers who stood near the rear entrance, praying in fear at the noise and shaking of the house in collapse. They sensed—nay, they saw—that the ceiling was coming down on top of them, yet they remained, as Brother Abraham had instructed them to do. For though their faith was in God, they knew Brother Abraham to be his prophet and obeyed his commands without question.

Seeing him appear even more fearful than they, the remaining Brethren were thrown into confusion. He did not stop to exhort them. He did not even pause to instruct them to follow him to safety. He simply flew into them, pushing aside any who stood between him and the door. And when he reached it, he threw it open and fled. This inspired panic in them, as well, and they pushed, and squirmed, and fought to follow him out the door.

Constable Rumford, faced by this sudden exodus, counseled young Constable Cowley to hold fast, then shouted to the first from the collapsing house to stop and surrender. Yet Brother Abraham did not stop. Constable Rumford raised his pistol and shot. He, being a former soldier, knew only to shoot to kill, and kill him he did. It was a clean shot at close range, direct through the heart.

The effect upon the Brethren was immediate, and to Constable Rumford somewhat puzzling. Oh, indeed they stopped. Yet as he reloaded the pistol, he saw them milling aimlessly about their fallen leader. He had once, in battle, seen a cannonball decapitate a soldier where he stood; whereupon, the dead man's trunk had wandered a few steps before it collapsed. Just so, said he, did they seem as they silently moved about without purpose.

All this was reported by Constable Rumford to Sir John when he and Constable Cowley marched their prisoners around to the front of the collapsed house. Yet by then, with the wind down and the wakened neighbors out gawking at the ruin, Sir John was faced with a new problem. Cries for help had been reported from deep inside the fallen structure. The poor and dispossessed had been locked inside their cellar quarters, presumably to burn or suffocate in the great fire that Brother Abraham had planned. The prisoners were put to work at digging them out. Only one was exempted from that work, and he because of the gunshot wound in his right shoulder—the man I had shot. Having been told what to do, they worked with great industry and released the poor folk in no time at all.

The pumping unit came with their great engine after an hour's delay. They took it ill that they had been summoned with no fire in evidence. Sir John's explanation did not much mollify their chief, yet he agreed that they should remain awhile and inspect for incipient fire danger. They did not stay long, however, and left in a dark temper.

We, too, eventually left this site of so much misery and deceit. Sir John left a single constable on guard—Mr. Jaggers, who had marched over with the few from Grub Street—and warned all those who had come to watch back into their houses. So it was that we came at last back to Bow Street and the end of this long night.

I know not how late he stayed up, nor how early he rose. I learned, however, that he had taken his place upon the bench that day and heard evidence against those of the Brethren who had survived the battle at Boyer's—including, of course, him I had wounded.

The sad-eyed Brother Elijah, who had immediately surrendered, gave witness against his fellows in the matter of the murderous expedition against the Crabb household. He admitted having been there himself and allowed that he had struck a blow, yet was so sickened by what he had done and by the dying cries of the victims that he had vomited and thrown down his axe. Which, of course, explained how John Clayton had had it in his hand when he was apprehended. Brother Elijah had been severely punished for this and had been sent out with the murder gang to Boyer's in order to prove himself. Tom Cranford gave testimony, as well as Mr. Boyer himself. And the prime mover in these horrible crimes—to which were added the murders of Moll Caulfield and Isham Henry—was named by Sir John as Abraham Watt, now deceased. All the prisoners were bound over for trial at Old Bailey and sent to Newgate—save for Brother Elijah, who was sent to the Fleet Prison.

All this I heard about, rather than witnessed, for by Sir John's strict orders I was allowed to sleep the day through. When I stumbled down the stairs it was near dinnertime, and I was obliged by Mrs. Gredge to wait till then to be fed. Sir John appeared at dinner and gave me the events of his busy court session. Yet he seemed somewhat dissatisfied with matters as they stood. There was the problem of those who were taken prisoner by Constable Rumford as the house collapsed.

"Now, one of them we know took part in the action at Boyer's," said Sir John to me, "for you wounded him there. By the by, I would much rather you have nothing to do with firearms, Jeremy. I allowed you to brandish a pistol some time ago, which was a mistake. You still have in your possession the pistol passed to you by Mr. Nicholson, do you not? Please return it tomorrow."

"Yes, sir," said I.

"But as for the remaining five, one or two at least must have taken part in the hanging of Isham Henry. That fellow, Brother Elijah, was quite explicit that none of the five had been involved in the earlier assault on the Crabb household. I know not how to separate the guilty from the bystanders in that matter, for none will give evidence against the rest. I have not charged any, but leave them in the strong room to reflect—either on trial for murder, or giving evidence and going free. That is what I offer them."

"I see the problem, Sir John," said I. "Could you talk to them and convince them that it is foolish to hold back?"

"I have tried," said he. "Yet they all talk the same and seek to confuse me in the same way. I fear that Brother Abraham lives still through them."

"Could you put them with Brother Elijah? Perhaps he might persuade them."

"Perhaps they might hang him."

Thus we talked in the kitchen that evening, long past the time when Mrs. Gredge had bade us goodnight and charged me not to forget my after-dinner duties.

At last he came to the matter that may have induced him to begin this conversation with me.

"We have something between us," said he.

"Yes, sir."

"You disobeyed me."

"It's true, sir."

"I specifically told you to leave after you were kind enough to identify Isham Henry for me. Yet you did not leave, did you?"

"No, sir."

"You did not depart the building and then reenter?"

"No, sir."

"So in no way did you follow my instructions. Your first impulse was to disobey me, and you followed that impulse through to the end. Were you merely curious? What have you to say for yourself?"

In truth, I had no prepared answer for him, though I well knew this occasion would arise between us. Now that it had, all I could do was speak from my heart.

"Sir," said I, "though I was curious and am always so in your handling of matters of the law, it was not that which prevented my leaving. When I helped Moll Caulfield from the collapse of that building which left her without a home, it was quite the most fearful experience of my life. I knew that I would always remember the groans and shrieks of the timbers that preceded their final coming apart. That night, last night, I heard those same dreadful sounds in that house of the Brethren of the Spirit. I tried to warn you that it would soon collapse, but I'm sure your mind was on what lay ahead. I felt that in this case only, I knew the danger better than you. And so I remained. I told myself that I would know when the final fall was near, and when that came I would run forward and pull you out, no matter how you resisted. And, Sir John, that is what I did. I did not interrupt you to plead you out of there. I did not intentionally listen—though I admit I heard all. I did but wait until I could wait no longer." I paused, then added, "I was told—"

"Do you think you can—" Then he paused. "No, proceed. I would have you say all you have to say."

"I was told by that rabbi that I was to look after you, and he said a blessing on me to help me do that."

He slammed the table with the palm of his hand. "I will *not* be looked after by a thirteen-year-old boy, *nor* a rabbi. You did insult not only to me but to Mr. Bailey, as well. I can look after myself, and in those instances when I cannot, Mr. Bailey will protect me."

"Yes, sir."

He sat silent longer than I liked, his face quite inscrutable.

"You must not overreach yourself, Jeremy," said he at last. "Remember your age. Respect it. Enjoy it—insofar as is possible. It is not proper for a boy of your years to join in the fray and discharge firearms, any more than it is that you decide which of my instructions are to be obeyed and which are not. Though you did not think it so, both Mr. Bailey and I were aware of the danger signaled by the loud creaking and groaning of the rotten timbers in that old house. I have, as you know, very keen hearing. Yet we proceeded. It was my decision that we do so. Mr. Bailey did not challenge it, though he could have. We took that risk together. It is our lot at times by the nature of our work to take such risks—Mr. Bailey, bless him, more often than I.

"However, since in both instances, the firing of the pistol and the disobedience of my instructions, your actions were well intended and had not bad results, I would be less than just if I did not overlook them."

"Thank you, sir," said I, most gratefully.

"In the future, for many years to come, remember my words, if you will: Do not overreach yourself. Make no rush into manhood."

Then, having had his say, he clapped together his hands, signaling an end to it, and rose from the table.

"Remember your after-dinner duties for Mrs. Gredge, and do all else she has charged you to do. But I, Jeremy, will now go to bed, and I hope to sleep sound for many more hours than is usual with me. I am quite exhausted."

Next day, late in the morning and following my release by Mrs. Gredge, I returned to Boyer's in Grub Street to seek out Mr. Nicholson and return to him his dueling pistol. It is an awkward thing to go through the streets of London in daylight with a pistol in your hand, and so I tucked it deep into my coat pocket and over it put a linen handkerchief supplied to me by Mrs. Gredge in order to disguise the true contents of my pocket. Even so, I kept my hand thrust inside on the walk to Grub Street as a safeguard against "wipe-priggers" (one of a number of new terms I had picked up from Jimmie Bunkins).

I found Boyer's establishment quite crowded with the curious. Word had circulated far and wide of the events of two nights past. There was even a broadsheet sold on the streets—"GRUB STREET KILLERS CAUGHT IN AMBUSCADE"—which had no doubt been dashed off by Ormond Neville and published quickly by Mr. Boyer. It had brought in their regular clients to exclaim and question, as well as many who had never before been in their shop. Many books were bought, a few stolen, but the increase in trade would more than compensate for the damage done in subduing the Brethren of the Spirit.

I squeezed through the many at the door, and seeing that Mr. Nicholson was not at the alcove desk behind which we had hid, found that same clerk who had brought Mr. Boyer to me. I asked for Nicholson.

"He is back in the print shop. What business have you with him?"

"I must return his pistol."

"His *pistol?* Ho, I know you. You're the one had that letter from Sir John Fielding started this entire affair. Now you wish to return Mr. Nicholson's pistol. You must have been present during the great battle."

"I was, yes," said I most modestly.

"Tell me true, did he really shoot and wound one of those black-suited devils?"

I fought the impulse to set him right with a boast. "Oh yes," said I, "it was just as he said."

"Well, I'm damned," said he. "Imagine! Our Mr. Nicholson!" He shook his head, quite overcome. "Well, you may go back and find him yourself. I'm sure he'll be glad to see you—comrades in arms, so to speak."

I thanked the fellow and passed through the door to the print shop and bindery. Boyer's was near twice the size of the modest workshop at Crabb's, and it hummed with industry and purpose. I found Mr. Nicholson inspecting a title page proof and greeted him in friendly manner. He, however, seemed somewhat embarrassed by my coming. He muttered his thanks, inquired after my health, and excused himself, complaining of the burden of work that had been heaped upon him. Perhaps he feared I might expose him if I remained longer than the moment he had allowed me.

A lesson, thought I, in human frailty. As I glanced back at him on my way out, I noted that he had tucked the pistol in his belt like some buccaneer from the Caribe. He would cut quite a figure so.

"Jeremy! Jeremy, boy!"

Hearing myself hailed, I turned and found an aproned Tom Cranford approaching. These were for him strange surroundings. I wondered at his presence here. He grabbed my hand and gave it a great squeeze. All his high spirits were returned.

"Come through the great battle well enough, did you?"

"Oh, well enough indeed." Then, not wishing to seem intrusive, yet quite curious, I asked, "But Tom, may I inquire, what are you doing here at Boyer's?"

"Why, I work here," said he. "My first day it is. Mr. Boyer and I both gave testimony at Sir John's court yesterday. And afterwards, I put it to him, I said, 'Mr. Boyer, you're down a journeyman, for that traitorous fellow Isham Henry has now gone on to his just deserts. I should like to apply for his position, for I am twice the man at setting type he ever was.' "

"And what did he say to that?"

"He says to me, 'I like your manner, young man. I remember you applied at the same time as Henry, when Crabb's was murdered out of business. I chose Henry because he was your senior—made journeyman five years before you, as I recall. Besides, you gave good testimony today.' So Mr. Boyer tells me then to report to his master printer, Mr. Rees, in the morning—which is today."

"So it was goodbye to Mr. Dodsley?"

"And up your arse, says I. This will work out well for me," said he. "Mr. Rees informs me they allow regular recess! Makes the fellows work better. But this ain't it for me, so I'd best get on with my job. I could not let you go without greeting you."

"You'll do well here."

"I know it. Give my best to Sir John. He's a grand man, he is."

The man whom most had forgot in all the commotion of the great ambuscade at Boyer's was none but John Clayton. He languished still in the Fleet Prison. Yet Sir John had not forgot. On the morning I visited Boyer's to surrender the pistol, he took a hackney to Bloomsbury Square and visited William Murray, Earl of Mansfield, the Lord Chief Justice. From him he sought the papers necessary for Mr. Clayton's release. In point of fact, Sir John had it in his power to make the release; he sought the Lord Chief Justice's signature merely as a matter of courtesy, since he it was who had been so eager to try him. Yet that was many arrests and a broadsheet ago. The Lord Chief Justice would surely be most cooperative—and he was, to a point. He did, however, make one request: that upon Mr. Clayton's release from the Fleet, he be brought to him for a brief interview.

While that seemed a modest enough request, Sir John thought it an opportunity to make a point regarding Mr. Clayton. And so he arranged that upon Mr. Clayton's release the next morning, he would be met by Dr. Samuel Johnson at Lord Mansfield's, and that I myself would convey Mr. Clayton from the prison to the residence. We would all be present at said interview.

"In this way," said Sir John, "you shall demonstrate with Dr. Johnson's presence the poet's high standing in literary circles. This was Johnson's idea, for he means to give Clayton a helping hand. He has offered him his hospitality until matters are settled for him."

"And what will my presence demonstrate?" I asked, all innocent.

"That this former inmate of Bedlam, this accused murderer, may without fear be entrusted to the care of a boy of your tender years. . . . You *are* without fear in this matter, I take it?"

And so it came to pass as he had planned it. Entrusted with money to pay for the hackney carriage, reminded to tip the driver, I set off alone quite early next morning for the Fleet Prison. When the carriage arrived, I instructed the driver to wait, and presented myself first to the gatekeeper and then to the governor of the prison. I offered the papers for John Clayton's release and was told he would be brought presently.

"Who is to accompany him?" asked the governor of the prison.

"I am, sir."

"Hmmmm," said he—and no more than that.

I waited in the governor's office a moderate length of time until Mr. Clayton was brought forth. He looked no worse than he had when last I had seen him in Sir John's chambers—actually a bit better. Clean-shaven he was and properly washed. He would indeed have looked fit to present to any, were it not for his filthy clothing. They smelled a bit unpleasantly, too.

I could not help but note that he seemed slightly disappointed to see me, and only me, awaiting him.

"I had thought that Dr. Johnson might be here," said he.

"We are to meet him at the residence of the Lord Chief Justice."

I could not resist a look at the governor. He took careful note of our destination, and as I bowed my thanks to him, he quite amazed me by standing and offering Mr. Clayton his hand. Mr. Clayton was also amazed, yet he shook it.

"Well," said the governor, "I trust your stay with us was not too unpleasant, Mr., uh, Clayton."

"Nevertheless, I am glad to leave."

"Oh, no doubt, no doubt." He forced a laugh. "I can have the gatekeeper send a man to fetch you a hackney."

"We have one waiting," said I.

"Oh, so you do, so you do."

"Mr. Clayton?"

I gestured to the door, and together we left.

Once in the hackney and on our way, Mr. Clayton seemed most uneasy. He folded and unfolded his large hands, then spread them out and grasped his knees tightly. I feared he was in some sense slipping from me. I did not wish to see Eusebius make an appearance, much less Petrus.

"Is the Lord Chief Justice responsible for my release?" he asked of a sudden.

"Oh no, sir. It was Sir John Fielding did it all. The Lord Chief Justice merely accommodated him."

"He seemed unfriendly to me when I met him. On what condition am I released?"

"On no condition at all. You are quite free. Did you not hear the news?"

"Why, no," said he. "Dr. Johnson, who was my source, was unable to come visit yesterday. What have you to tell?"

A great deal had I to tell to him, and I spun the tale out so that it lasted the entire distance to Bloomsbury Square. I told how his information on Mr. Crabb and the surly preacher was well confirmed by the testimony of Tom Cranford. I gave him the trap set by Sir John at Boyer's. I described the great battle, and even (though it would have displeased Sir John) my modest part in it. Then, reminding him of the great wind that blew three nights before, I told Mr. Clayton how the very house of the Brethren of the Spirit had fallen near upon them, and how their leader had been shot in a blind attempt to escape.

I flatter myself that I told it well. If I were to judge from Mr. Clayton's response, then I told it as a master. Once it was begun, he seemed to hold tight to every word and was quite transported from his anxieties. When I finished, he heaved a great sigh, which had naught of misery in it, but a great relief.

"Then," said he, "these were the men who murdered all those in the Crabb household? Them it was I heard when I hid? Was it so?"

"Indeed it was."

"And they have been arrested for those terrible murders?"

"Yes, sir, and bound over for trial."

"Then hallelujah, and three great huzzahs for Sir John Fielding. He was on my side, after all."

"You may be sure of it," said I.

Then, looking through the window of the hackney, I saw that we had come quite near to Bloomsbury. In fact, as we drew to a halt before that grand palazzo, I spied Dr. Johnson at its front, pacing impatiently.

"I have but one question," said Mr. Clayton to me. "If

I am free without condition, why must I now meet with the Lord Chief Justice?''

"That I cannot say, sir. He wished it so, and Sir John thought it best to honor his wishes.''

I paid the driver what he asked, then tipped him a full shilling, as Sir John had instructed me, for waiting at the Fleet. As I attended to this, Mr. Clayton rushed over to Dr. Johnson, who greeted him cordially, and confirmed (as I overheard) that all that I had told him was true.

I went confidently to the door while the two men continued to discuss passionately the events of the past three days and nights. I had dressed carefully in my best clothes, and in my own eyes at least, looked quite the figure of the young man of the town. Well I remembered having been refused entry by the butler because of my ragged appearance. He would not turn me away this day.

I knocked loudly upon the door, and the butler arrived promptly. He was not impressed.

"Yes, boy, what is it?''

"Mr. John Clayton, Dr. Samuel Johnson, and Master Jeremy Proctor are here to call on the Lord Chief Justice at his invitation,'' said I.

"I thought *only* Mr. Clayton, but''—he sighed—"come ahead.''

And so we entered, I last of all, in good position to note the butler's disdain at poor Mr. Clayton's attire, which was more ragged and dirty than mine at my worst; he raised his eyes to heaven and wrinkled his nose at the smell. Yet he remained ever proper.

"This way, please.''

He led us to the library and bowed us inside. The Lord Chief Justice rose from his desk and offered his hand all around, yet remained on his feet, signaling that we were to do so, too. This was to be indeed a brief interview.

"Well, Mr. Clayton,'' said he, "out now, are you? A free man.''

"So I was given to understand by this young man who presented the papers for my release and accompanied me here.''

Pointing to me, he said in surprise, *"He* was your escort here?"

"Yes, sir, I was," said I, unbidden.

"Well," said he to me, "you may tell Sir John he has made his point." Then to Dr. Johnson: "And what brings you here? I had thought you had better things to do than appear at such occasions as this."

"My Lord," said Dr. Johnson, "I am come to vouch for this man, John Clayton, if that be necessary, to assure you of his poetic talent, and of his ability to earn with it. He has told me he has fair copies of all the works which were to comprise his second volume of verse. A reputable publisher has agreed to bring it out at terms favorable to him. It is likely to sell better than his first book, which was a considerable financial success . . . to the publisher, the late Mr. Crabb."

"I see. Tell me, Mr. Clayton, where is this fair copy of your manuscript?"

"Why, sir, it is back in Somerset."

"Then do me a great favor and post it to the publisher. In other words, Mr. Clayton, go there and stay there. We have quite enough on our hands trying those who, like most of us, can claim but a single nature. For those, such as you—and I accept your account in this—who are cursed with more than one, the law is not prepared to deal. I want no such difficulties ever put before me or my other judges. Am I clear in this?"

What was most clear was that Mr. Clayton found it hard to accept this provision. He hesitated. "Well . . . I . . ."

Dr. Johnson stepped forward. "My Lord," said he, "while what you propose may be difficult for Mr. Clayton, it may be the best medicine for him as a poet. I have counseled him myself to remain in the country, where he derives his inspiration and lives more comfortably on less. 'Leave London to the hacks,' said I to him. However, even for a country poet, it may be necessary to make trips to London in order to see his works through the press and handle incidental matters regarding their publication."

"I understand and accept that, Dr. Johnson, just so long

as Mr. Clayton continues to reside well outside London and his visits to the city are simply that—visits."

Then to Mr. Clayton: "In order to ease this burden I put on you, I offer you this, sir—" And from his large coat pocket he brought a small pouch which clinked of silver when he dropped it on the table. "With the amount inside, I hope to compensate you in small measure for the time you spent in Bedlam and the Fleet Prison. There is sufficient to buy you a new suit of clothes, which you badly need, and to pay your coach fare back home. I ask you to sign no paper agreeing to the condition I have set forth, for no such paper would be valid; I only urge you to take this amount, for in doing so you will be giving your assurance to remain in residence away from this city. Is it agreed?"

John Clayton nodded. He stepped forth and took the pouch from its place on the desk.

"You give your word as a gentleman, Mr. Clayton?"

"I do, my Lord."

"Let me have your hand on it."

They shook hands solemnly. The door opened as if by magic, and the butler appeared to show us out.

And there on the street, John Clayton said aloud to himself, rather than to us, his listeners: "That is the first time ever in my life I was called a gentleman—and then it came from the Lord Chief Justice himself."

The Brethren of the Spirit were dealt with far more harshly by the Lord Chief Justice. Those captured at Boyer's, as well as the wounded man apprehended at the house in Half Moon Passage, were condemned to hang; the single exception was made for Elijah Biggle, also known as Brother Elijah, who gave testimony against the rest, and for it was given twenty years' transportation to the colony of Virginia. A similar sentence of transportation was handed down for the five in connection with the hanging death of Isham Henry. They were sent on the same ship with Brother Elijah, who, midway on the journey, was said to have hanged himself in remorse for his betrayal of his fellow Brethren.

John Clayton kept his word and remained at home in

Somerset. His second volume of verse was a great success when it was brought out by Boyer and Nicholson, due in part to the unwelcome celebrity that was thrust upon him by his arrest, hospitalization, and imprisonment in what would be known ever after as the Grub Street massacre. He earned sufficient on that book alone to marry and buy a cottage, where he continued to write. The fact that his succeeding books were not near so popular—nor, according to Dr. Johnson, as good—led him to drink. Petrus reappeared on a few occasions, which led to further stays in the local mad hospital, not all of them as short as the first one. Yet he continued to write, whether in or out of it, and he assured Dr. Johnson (by letter) that the work at which he was then engaged would be his greatest.

Sir John Fielding and Katherine Durham were married in a quiet ceremony at a chapel in St. Paul's Covent Garden in the month of September. Tongues wagged at the short space of time that had elapsed since his first wife's death. Yet Sir John cared nothing for the wagging of tongues; and after a brief wedding trip to Bath, the two, now man and wife, set to work on a charity that would occupy them for years to come, the Magdalene Home for Penitent Prostitutes.